The Water Lily Pond

*A Village Girl's Journey
in Maoist China*

Han Z. Li

Wilfrid Laurier University Press

WLU

We acknowledge the support of the Canada Council for the Arts for our publishing program. We acknowledge the financial support of the Government of Canada through the Book Publishing Industry Development Program for our publishing activities. We acknowledge the Government of Ontario through the Ontario Media Development Corporation's Ontario Book Initiative. We acknowledge a publication grant from the University of Northern British Columbia.

National Library of Canada Cataloguing in Publication

Li, Han Z. (Han Zao), 1956-

The water lily pond : a village girl's journey in Maoist China/Han Z. Li.

(Life writing series)
ISBN 0-88920-431-4

1. China—History—1949-1986—Fiction. I.Title. II. Series

PS8573.I15W38 2004   C813'.6   C2003-907133-2

© 2004 Wilfrid Laurier University Press
Waterloo, Ontario, Canada N2L 3C5
www.wlupress.wlu.ca

Cover design by Leslie Macredie using a photograph by Fang Nai-ping. Text design by P.J. Woodland. Chinese calligraphy by Liu Guan-you.

Printed in Canada

This is a work of metafiction. The events are based on facts but the characters and institutions are fictitious with the exception of known historical figures whose actual names are herein used. Therefore, any resemblance of characters and institutions to real-life counterparts is coincidental.

This book is dedicated to the memory of my paternal grandmother, Wei Ju-xiang (chrysanthemum), whose teachings have shaped who I am today.

The spirit of water lily

by Zhou Dunyi, a Song Dynasty poet and mandarin

Peony is dazzling with large globular red flower.
Chrysanthemum is charming with alluring blossom.
I love water lily more.
It stands above the water though in touch with it.
It is pure and clean though it grows out of mud.
Its petals are pinkish white, soft, yet durable.
Thunderstorms cannot destroy it.
Raindrops only make it fresher and more adorable.

ONCE UPON A TIME, there was a land called Red China. Everything in it must be Red, from people's thought to deed. Anything less Red is reformed; anything White or Black is denounced until red blood trickles out.

This is a tale of an observant village girl, growing up by a water lily pond, interpreting and coping with this tremendous Red world.

The Water Lily Pond

ONE SOOTHING JULY EVENING while I was humming a tune to congratulate myself for being born into a Poor Class family, my grandma ushered me to her room and told me the following story.

"We should thank your great-grandpa for picking up the habit of smoking opium." She took a match and lit the small oil lamp on her old, still-elegant dressing table. "Selling his land. Paying for his habit. Otherwise we would be in the Landlord Class."

She sat on the bedside and signalled me to sit on a wooden chair opposite her. Unlike other village women, her bed was always neatly made—with her quilt folded in a ready-to-sleep fashion. The inside cover was a home-made white cotton sheet, and the outside a faded dark blue with many lively sparrows standing in twos on small tree branches.

I had learned in our history class that in the 1800s, Britain and France sent a great deal of opium to China in exchange for gold bullion. The Chinese fought two Opium Wars, first with Great Britain between 1839 and 1842, then with Britain and France from 1856 to 1860. Defeat of the Chinese resulted in the ceding of Hong Kong to Britain and the opening of five treaty ports to foreign traders. I had not known that our family benefited from opium.

After sipping some tea, my grandma continued, with a serene composure.

"Your great-grandpa was a respectable schoolteacher who owned a large amount of farm land, about three hundred mu. My father was also a schoolteacher, and they were good friends. When your grandpa was three and I was six, we were engaged. A few years later, your great-grandpa started to smoke opium and became addicted to it. He could not carry on with his teaching job and sold most of his land. Your great-grandma complained and wept constantly. In one of their bitter arguments, he broke two of her front teeth. Feeling greatly humiliated, she drowned herself in a pond. Your great-grandma was from the Song Clan, the biggest and wealthiest in the Song Village across the Han River. Her brothers were indignant. They gave your great-grandpa a good beating and burned his house. Deep in debt and poor in health, your great-grandfather sent your grandpa, who was barely nine, to work as a cowboy for a rich villager.

"When he was sixteen and I was nineteen, we were married. Although your grandpa was poor and my family was much better off, an engagement was an engagement."

She sighed, a complex expression in her luminous dark eyes. Lament? Submission to fate? I couldn't tell. Framed by night, illuminated by the oil lamp, her tender, lined face was unfathomable. Sitting with her creased hands folded neatly in her lap, her whole being was a statue of time elapsed, of legend relayed.

"By 1949, we had about ten mu of farmland and a small house. Naturally we belonged to the Poor Class. Thanks to opium, your uncle had the option of going to university and working in the army. Your father joined the Party. Now you may have the opportunity to go to senior high school."

I was a fortunate girl. At the age of fourteen, I could be one of the seven, among fifty-six junior high school graduates in our class, to be chosen by the best senior high school of Mian Yang County. In 1970, eligibility to attend a senior high school depended upon grades as well as one's family background. Fifteen of us passed the exams, but there were only seven spaces. Among the seven, at least two must be girls. I knew that my chances were good because my math was the best of all the girls and my Chinese was the second best. I also had a third advantage: my family belonged to the Poor Class.

In 1949, Mao Ze-dong classified every household: the Landlord, the Middle Class, and the Poor. The landlords were the exploiting class and were the target of the proletarian revolution—they needed to be reformed into labouring people. The Middle Class were the friends of the revolution, while the Poor Class were the revolutionaries. In terms of promotion and school opportunities, the Poor Class was the priority.

2

Our village, Qiong-li-he, or Riverside, was right at the centre of the Jianghan plain, an agricultural zone stretching miles and miles through the middle of Hubei Province. The high land grew cotton, wheat, and beans, whereas the low land produced two seasons of rice.

The thirty-six households in our village were either in the Poor Class or Middle Class as none was a big landowner. To provide a target for the frequent class struggle meetings, the commune leaders moved a Landlord Class family from a neighbouring brigade to our village. The Jans were arranged to live next to our house because nobody else wanted them as a neighbour. My father volunteered to have them as he was then the Party secretary of the production brigade, which was made up of ten teams or villages.

The Jans had four daughters and a son. The eldest daughter, Da-ju, had married into another Landlord family miles away from our village. In the early 1950s, the Communists shot her father-in-law because he was the biggest landowner in the region and had exploited many poor people. Their land was distributed among the poor and later confiscated by the state. Her husband kept a diary of the events and was found out when their house was ransacked in 1964 during the Four Cleansing Socialist Education Movement. Fearing the harsh treatment from the Communists, he and his brother hanged themselves. Da-ju followed them a few days later.

Their second daughter, Er-Ju, was married to a man who was paralyzed from the waist down. Their parents were hesitant but Er-Ju was willing. Since the man was injured while making bricks for the collective, his injury was a "glorious one." He could protect Er-ju politically.

Lan-ann, the Jans' youngest daughter, was four years my senior and became one of my three best friends in my early childhood. Although she was from a Landlord Class family, I liked her the most. She was honest, tolerant, and generous.

Lan's mother had a great sense of humour. One rainy afternoon, I had broken an expensive thermometer and my mother smacked me. With tears in my eyes, I went to see Lan. Her mother offered me a snack and teased me, "May-ping, what's the matter with you? Raindrops in your eyes?" Amused, I forgot my sorrow immediately. Drying my tears with my handkerchief, I observed that Lan's mother carried her thick hair in a rather elegant fashion—a sickle-shaped green jade pin fastened the round bun.

To strengthen the will of the Poor Class revolutionaries, it was necessary to have class struggle denunciation meetings. Lan's parents were the target at such meetings, being the only Landlord Class family in our village.

In the early 1960s, I saw Lan's parents criticized several times but none was as devastating as the one in 1964, when I was eight years old. One moonlit evening in June, all the villagers, except the elderly and children, were summoned to the large threshing ground of the production team. A reddish ray from a small oil lamp hanging on the pole of a water pump crane signified a bad omen to me. Usually we just used the moonlight for a normal production team meeting.

I squeezed through the many legs of adults to the front. Lan's parents were kneeling down on the small earth stage. Her father's face was anguished, her mother's submissive.

A young man named Bere jumped up in front of Lan's parents and shouted loudly, his right arm waving in the air, "Jan Shi-yi and Yun Jiu-xian, I denounce you. Listen, why did you name your youngest daughter 'Lan-Ann'? What was your motive? 'Lan' means 'to stop,' and 'Ann' means 'entering.' Do you mean to stop the Communists from entering mainland China? Do you dream of the return of the Kuomintang from Taiwan? You miss your lost paradise under the Kuomintang, don't you?"

Bere's thunderous performance upset me. Pushing my way out, I looked for Lan. She was hiding at the back of the crowd. "Let's go home," I said gently to her. She shook her head, not looking at.

I started to resent Bere. I had some faint idea that Bere was seeking some personal gain by being so active because we all knew that he had only one eye, the other being a false one from a dog. We also knew that he was having a hard time finding a girlfriend—several times the go-between's efforts had failed because no girl wanted to marry a One Eye. By being politically progressive, he hoped to attract the attention of a girl.

A few more people denounced Lan's parents but with milder remarks. Next the crowd shouted some slogans: "Down with dishonest landlords!" "Consolidate our proletarian dictatorship!"

Then the crowd started to sing:

Thinking of the old days under the landlords,
ahr, ahr, ahr (rising tone),

Tears rolling down my cheeks, ahr, ahr, ahr (falling tone),
The landlords wearing silk and jade and no work, ai ha yo,
They had rice piling up like mountains, ai ha yo,
We worked in the fields all year long, ai ha yo,
All we harvested went to the man-eating landlords, ai ha yo.
Suddenly, thunder shook the sky, hai hai hai,
Here come the Communists and Chairman Mao, hai hai hai,
We were liberated, we became master of the land, hai hai hai.

"Um, um, um," Comrade Liu, a cadre sent by the county organization, purposefully cleared his throat. "Who would like to speak of the bitterness under the Kuomintang, the bandits who ruled China before our great saviour Mao came in 1949?" Quickly sweeping the crowd, he smiled awkwardly, as there were no volunteers.

Liu turned to my grandpa, who was comfortably sitting on a bamboo chair, smoking his home-rolled cigarette, apparently unaffected by the emotion of the crowd.

With an even voice, my grandpa talked about his miserable childhood working for a rich villager after he lost his mother. He spoke of the hard times from 1958 to 1960 when we only had vegetables and sweet potatoes to eat, as we had to support the new China with our grains.

My brother was standing beside him. He pulled the back of my grandpa's cotton shirt signaling him to stop, but he didn't. Comrade Liu smiled awkwardly, overlooking my grandpa's misplaced "bitterness," an error from old age and poor memory.

"The Communists were leading from 1958 to 1960, not the Kuomintang," my brother reminded him afterwards. Grandpa chuckled. We never found out whether he could distinguish between Communists and Kuomintang or confused them on purpose.

I ran home while the crowd was singing:

To sail, a ship depends on a helmsman,
To grow, crops need the sun,
To carry out a revolution, we need Chairman Mao.

When I got back my grandma was still up talking with a few grannies. Though as anxious as an ant in a hot frying pan, I held my breath. I stood beside her, waiting for the first possible break in their gossip-conversation, which was usually as long as the wrapping cloth for their bound feet.

"Her door was locked in the front for a long time after lunch. I saw her walking to her back door through her yard. Then I heard the back door bolted. What do you think she was doing? Ai ha, it's as clear as daylight. She is stealing a man," a square woman named Yan in her fifties was sharing her scholarly analysis with the group.

I became intensely interested. I stared at her loose-muscled face, yearning for more details. I knew she was referring to Lu, a woman in her forties, who carried her long dark hair in a bun fastened by a butterfly-shaped silver pin. She had large breasts and a big bottom, which the village men considered sexy and attractive.

Rumour had it that besides a loving, thick-headed husband she had three lovers in the village: Team Leader Yin, Accountant Zhang, and my grandpa. For this reason, Lu was all flattery with Grandma on the rare occasions when they ran into each other.

Lu lived two doors from our house. Only the night before, while dozing off on our bamboo chair outside, I overheard Lu talking with my mother, cursing Yan, "May her tongue rot from gossiping; her private parts mildew from long-time-no-use." Then they started to talk in whispers. I strained my ears but couldn't make out what they were saying. In a minute, Lu started to hum an underground song, "Eighteen Touches," by which a man engaged a woman prior to the act. Her soft voice came:

> Your long, dark hair feels like silk,
> Your forehead broad and smooth,
> Your eyebrows a willow-branch,
> Your eye lashes thick as a bush, in which I am lost,
> Your eyes luminous, inviting as autumn water…

I didn't understand the meaning of the lines and soon I fell asleep. I had forgotten all about it until now.

"An elf, that's what she is!" Yan's condemnation sounded more jealous than contemptuous. Her husband died of starvation in 1959 and no man had been attracted to her for the past five years.

"A fox elf!" a short, skinny woman named Mar echoed.

"Um, she even uses two mirrors, one in the front, one in back, to do her hair!" Yan seemed exasperated now. My eyes moved from

Mar's to Yan's face and rested there. Her three-layered chin was like a loosely stitched oil-cloth bag, opening and closing as she stretched her head to emphasize a point.

"Don't stare at me like that, child. Go and play!" She suddenly became aware of my intensely curious eyes.

I shuddered and drew my eyes to moonlit ground, where my shadow was tiny compared to her massive bulk. Embarrassed, I pinched Grandma's thin shoulder, a signal that I wanted her undivided attention.

"Ai-ya-ya, my precious granddaughter wants some cold tea," my grandma said affectionately while slowly getting up from her homemade willow chair, holding my eager hand.

"Grandma, is it true that Lan's father exploited the poor peasants before Liberation?" I asked as soon as we were alone.

"Not really. I knew Lan's grandpa. He was a man of learning and Lan's father was just a spoilt young man. Lan's mother has worked hard to serve her parents-in-law and her husband. Poor thing! She doesn't deserve this harsh treatment. Lan's grandpa hired a dozen people to help in the fields but he treated them well." My grandma was tall so I had to stretch my neck all the way back to see her expression. Her thin face looked meditative and earnest.

I believed my grandma's words and trusted her judgment. I started to doubt what we learned in school, that all landlords were bad people, but I kept my thoughts to myself.

That night I had a frightful dream. My grandma, dressed in an elegant, traditional blue silk Qi Pao and gold earrings, the way she looked in an old photo, was being denounced. "Wei Ju-xiang, why did your father name you chrysanthemum? Bourgeoisie! Your father was a well-off genteel intellectual, wasn't he?" The voice was Bere's, but I couldn't see his face. "Ha ha, gold earrings?" He tore the earrings off my grandma's ears. Blood trickled down her silk dress. "Oh, Grandma!" As I ran to her, I awoke.

After the denunciation meeting, Lan played alone. I tried to talk to her several times but she pretended not to hear me. One starry evening I asked her to jump elastic ropes with me.

"My name is no longer 'Lan-ann' but 'Ju-ying,'" she told me in a flat tone. She appeared to be very serious when she talked; her childhood playfulness was gone.

"I don't like the sound Ju-ying. Can I still call you Lan?" Two drops of tears, as big as soybeans, were glistening in her large black eyes, one drop in each eye. I did not know what to do when a big girl like Lan cried. Taking out my red-green dotted handkerchief, hesitating for a moment, I put it in her hand. It was a sacrifice for me because I did not share my handkerchief with anybody, not even my sister.

Taking the folded handkerchief, she dried her tender tears.

"Yes, you can call me Lan, but don't let my father hear it," she whispered.

I nodded, understanding. I knew Lan was afraid of her father. So was I. I never saw him smile or laugh even once. He was assigned to do the dirtiest and heaviest work in the production team.

A few days later, another "mass meeting" was held on the same spot.

"Silence, silence," Comrade Liu declared importantly, "Today, we are going to denounce Yin, who has abused his power."

Silence. The silence was immediate and solemn.

The villagers could hardly believe their ears. Yin was the team leader who had had great power over their lives for several years.

Yin walked slowly to the front of the crowd, his usual majestic air disappeared. In a repentant voice, he started his confession, "I have committed a crime, an unforgivable one. In the past three years, I have stolen at least one thousand jin of grain from the production team. My trick was quite simple: after midnight when the village was quiet, I would open the storage bin, put about a hundred jin of grain in my large bags, and carry the bags home with a shoulder pole." He lowered his head as if feeling ashamed of his conduct.

"Ai-ya! My Heaven! Who would have thought of that!" Many villagers were shocked.

"Son of a turtle egg!"

"Man's face, wolf's heart!" Others were angry.

They felt betrayed. After all, Yin was a Communist Party member and a symbol of Mao's revolutionary line.

About a month before, I heard that a villager going to the outdoor toilet in the middle of the night had seen Yin carrying grain home, but did not dare to report it for fear of Yin's retaliation. The night before, Comrade Liu, the county cadre, who was living in our village to help carry out the "Four Cleansing Movement," happened to come back late from a district meeting and ran into Yin with two bags of grain. Yin was so scared that he wet his pants. He knew then that his future was cast with dark clouds, and so were his children's.

About two months after Yin's denunciation meeting, while I was eating a late lunch after school, my grandma casually remarked, "Lan-ann's family and Yin's are voluntarily moving to Sha-hu. The government has given them each a thousand yuan, enough to build a new house in Sha-hu."

I had heard about Sha-hu. It's in our neighbouring county, Hong-hu. An area where farm hands were needed to open new land, it is known as a place of rampant schistosomiasis. The disease is caused by a parasite that crawls into a person's body through blood vessels. Village men who went to work in Sha-hu often came back with bloated stomachs and swollen legs.

"I tried to persuade Lan's mother not to go but she isn't the one who makes the decision. It's Lan's father. He has set his mind to go." After putting some cotton stalks into the stove, Grandma stirred the long beans in the wok.

"I'm used to this place and don't want to go anywhere."

Placing the bowl of cooked beans in front of me, she murmured, "Gold nest, silver nest, not as good as the old nest."

At this moment, I heard noises in the direction of the pond beyond our front yard.

"What's the noise about?" I asked Grandma.

"Oh, it's Tan, Team Leader Yin's wife. She is pretending to drown herself in the pond." My grandma spoke as a matter of fact. After a sigh, she went on, "Well, Yin wants to go to Sha-hu but she doesn't. Now the decision is made and she wants to have it reversed. She has been begging the Party secretary for days but he wouldn't change it."

Frowning at my half-finished bowl of rice and stealing a look at Grandma, I complained, "Mn-hmm, you have put too much rice in my bowl. Now I can't finish it."

She knuckled my head affectionately and said, "That's a bad excuse. Now run along. Monkey. I know you want to see Tan and the crowd." I was born in the year of monkey and was thin and quick like a monkey.

I ran to the pond in one breath. Who wouldn't want to see a show like this? A dozen kids were already there when I arrived. Among them was my classmate, Rong, who lived at the lower end of the village.

She took my hand and we sat down on a dead tree trunk. It was a cloudy day so we didn't have to worry about the sun scorching our faces. We carefully watched Tan's every movement as if she were a circus performer.

Tan was sitting at the edge of the pond patting the water and howling loudly, "My good neighbours, save us! Please save us! I don't want to be parted from you. I am one of you, alive or dead." Tan was petite, wrapped with energy. She was in her early thirties and had borne three sons and a daughter for Yin. Her dark hair was loose on her shoulders; her suntanned face was determination incarnate; there was not a drop of tears in her round dark eyes.

Behind her were many vigorous lily pads, some sleeping on the water, others standing above it. A light current of air was rocking the standing pads back and forth as if improvising a back stage dance for Tan. Rong whispered to me that Tan had been there since morning. She was waiting for the Party secretary to come and relent.

As Tan chanted the same words again and again, I lost interest in her. Instead, I examined Rong. My friend was three years older than me, taller and fuller. She had stunning black eyes and a round chubby face matched with cherry red lips. Unlike me, Rong's interest was not in books but boys. At the age of eleven, she received love notes at least once a month.

"Look, more people are coming." Rong pulled my thoughts back to Tan.

Three village women came to the edge of the pond to pull Tan out of the water. But Tan would not go. Her wailing was louder than ever.

I heard the women say, "Come on, you don't have to go. There must be some way to change the decision."

"Why? Yin didn't consult you when he made the request to go?"

"No. He was so ashamed for what he did that he felt he had to leave."

"No, no, no. A thousand no. He doesn't have to. We have known him since he was a boy. He didn't mean to steal the grain from us. It was an honest mistake."

"Everyone makes mistakes."

"We are ready to forgive him."

After these sweet and useless words, the three women left, for it was near dinnertime.

Tan slid into the water again and started another round of howling.

Darkness fell; the Party secretary still did not show up. Finally Tan got up and went home.

There was much excitement in the village in the following week. Lu's second daughter Qing's engagement to Yin's second son was called off since Yin was no longer the team leader. Lu sent words that she was willing to engage her daughter to Dan, Rong's brother, for Dan, being intelligent and articulate, would have a bright future. Rong confided to me that Lu paid an evening visit to her mother; Dan and Qing were to be engaged as soon as Yin's family left. For the sake of formality, they needed a matchmaker, which would not be a problem as several women in our village specialized in matchmaking.

A month later, Yin's family was gone, and so was Lan's. Before they left, Lan's father had their house torn down and sold the wooden frame.

The night before Lan's departure, she revealed to me her biggest secret. She liked Dan very much. Lan said that Dan had integrity, a quality she most appreciated.

"Oh?" I was dying to know more details but I sounded as if I was *barely* interested.

"Dan rescued me from an embarrassment. Last Wednesday afternoon between classes, two girls were bullying me and calling me names. Dan came over and stopped them with a severe look." She was completely self-absorbed and happy.

"Oh, he is so good. I've never had a chance to thank him." Lan's face lit up with love, the most divine feeling in the world.

"Do you want to say goodbye to Dan before you leave?" I was more curious than wanting to help, for I had never seen with my own eyes how lovers express their feelings for each other.

"No. He doesn't even know I exist. He is so grown-up and I must look insignificant to him. Besides, who wants to marry a daughter from a landlord family? I don't want to drag him down. I am telling you this only because I am leaving and perhaps will never see him again."

I had read somewhere that true love was about making sacrifices. Now I was witnessing it. How exciting! Lan and I were going to talk more, but her mother called her to sleep; they had a long journey walking to Sha-hu the following day.

The first few weeks of Lan's absence were unbearable. Every time I passed by the spot where her house had been, I ran fast before tears came out.

When I missed Lan, I would sit by myself or ask my grandma to tell me a story from her "old days." She was my caretaker and first teacher, the best I had ever had.

I was born at dawn on a fine May day so I was named May-ping. Although there was a small clinic a mile away, nobody bothered to go to the clinic for childbirth. Instead, my father sent for a trained nurse. My mother was twenty and she could barely take care of herself, to say nothing of me—a skinny baby—about five jin. My grandma wrapped me and took me over to her warm blanket.

I remember this rainy afternoon when I was three years old. My mother was embroidering a new pillowcase for me. I said that I loved her the best. Later when my grandma asked me if I loved her the most, I said yes. At dinnertime, everybody was present—Grandpa, Grandma, Father, and Mother. I was sitting on the lap of my grandma when she suddenly asked, "May-ping, among all the people in the world, whom do you love the best?"

I looked at my mother who was nervously watching me, and I said loudly, "Both Grandma and Ma!" Everybody laughed.

According to my grandma, I should become a schoolteacher when I grew up. I started to talk when I was barely two. Furthermore, I had a sharp tongue. She compared my tongue with that of a dozen other kids in the village, and mine was the sharpest—with an almost pointed end and slim all the way through. She would brag how I defeated a well-educated provincial cadre who was in our village for three months to assist with the Great Leap Forward. Comrade Ai, the cadre, was arranged to live in our house because my grandma was noted for her open-mindedness toward new things.

China had a hard year in 1959. Rice was scarce because we had to "sell" most of it to the state to support the socialist construction in cities. Our great leader Chairman Mao said, "Workers and peasants are one family, and it is the Big Socialist Family." Therefore it was our duty to supply the workers in the city with cotton and grain.

In springtime when we ran out of grain, we ate carrots, sweet potatoes and vegetables. Some villagers complained, but my father never did. "It's a necessary sacrifice since our socialist republic is very young," he would say.

Grandma usually prepared my meals and fed me before the adults came back for lunch. One day, Comrade Ai returned earlier than usual. He appeared to be very surprised: "Aha-aha, May-ping, I got you. You little brat! How come we don't have egg fried rice, yet you can have it?" His eyebrows puckered.

I pretended that I did not hear him, pursing up my lips. As soon as his back was turned, I said proudly, tilting my head and stealing a look at my all-smiling grandma, "I'm not eating yours. It's my grandma's!"

He put on a serious face and looked into my naughty eyes: "I am going to report you."

"I am not afraid of you. Our family is in the Poor Class!" I knew that only Landlord Class people were criticized in our village.

But I was still worried that he would report me. I had some faint idea that to have more than others was disapproved even if you belonged to the Poor Class. It seemed that everybody in the village should be poor together—that's why we needed a revolution.

2

On August 16, 1970, I finally received the news of my acceptance to MianYang Senior High School. Holding my excitement, I observed my grandma as she said, "Now we have to figure out the expenses. If your father can't afford it, would you learn to be a peasant?"

"No way!"

"We will see." She looked serious!

Now I started to worry. I knew that our money situation was becoming tighter as the number of my siblings increased. I behaved myself very well the whole afternoon: I helped take care of my younger sister, Nan-ping, who had just turned three. I swept the living room and my grandma's room with extra care. And in between, I studied my grandma's face. But her expressions were unreadable.

At dinnertime, my father came home on a nice bicycle owned by his working unit, a privilege enjoyed by state employees. He had been promoted to be the director of the People's Bank in our district. Tall, thin, with alert brown eyes and stern facial features, he was in a white cotton shirt, light grey pants and a pair of soil-brown rubber sandals. No sooner had he put down his broad-brimmed straw hat than my grandma signalled him to the kitchen where my fate was to be decided. I held my breath.

A few minutes later, they came out. I saw a little worry in their eyes.

"Your father said that he is going to send you to senior high school no matter what," Grandma informed me with a gladness only I could detect. She did not normally express her feelings explicitly, a virtue cultivated by her learned father who agreed with Confucius that feelings are to be stored in one's heart, not shown on one's face.

The following afternoon, Uncle Xin happened to come home for a short visit from Beijing. He was the only one in the family with a university education. My father and mother had sold their wool blanket, a wedding gift, to help him through university. Upon graduation, he was assigned to work in the army as an electrical engineer, a high-ranking position with a good salary. He was thirty years old, still single. He had thoughtful brown eyes, a bookish face, and a medium build. Unlike my father, who liked to give orders, my uncle talked softly. I felt connected with him right away! In no time, he bought me a new basin, towels, pens, and toothpaste and gave me thirty yuan for other expenses. My uncle also promised to send me ten yuan every month, which made me well off.

After dinner, Uncle Xin lit up an oil lamp in the living room and read us children a fable, "The Song of Tomorrow." It started with the shivering voice of a bird: "Oh, oh, oh, the cold wind freezes me. I'll make my nest tomorrow." By the third day, the bird died in the cold with its nest unmade.

"What's the moral of this fable?" Uncle Xin quizzed us.

"It's important to have a warm house in the winter." Came my twelve-year-old brother Nian's showy voice.

"Wen-ping, what do you think?" Wen-ping was eight, with shimmering dark eyes. Her peach-shaped face was blushing crimson with so many eyes on her.

"Do things today. Don't wait till tomorrow." Quickly uttering her answer, she buried her head under my grandma's apron.

We cheered her intelligent reply.

While we were laughing, my grandpa put his favourite suitcase in front of me. Mother gave me a silver lock for it. Father handed me a red-covered diary with a bird standing on the branch of a tall tree bathing in the morning sun. I understood the implication. He wanted me to be like a bird: flying high and successful.

Soon the big day arrived, and the seven of us, four boys and three girls, marched to our dreamland: Mian Yang County First Senior High. I carried my suitcase and cotton quilt with a bamboo shoulder pole. My uncle walked me as far as the main road and asked if I needed anything else. I shook my head and joined my comrades.

We were talking and laughing excitedly as we walked along the Han River. Beyond the riverbank were waves of rice and cotton fields. It was September, harvest time. I was humming a folk song:

Accompanied by wild ducklings and water lily flowers,
I am harvesting the golden rice and snowy white cotton.
People say that heaven is the best.
How could it be better than my hometown?

It seemed that somebody called my name from a distance. I stood still for a moment to make sure that I was not imagining it. I turned my head. There was my grandpa, panting, a red-and-black-oiled-paper umbrella in his right hand.

"May-ping, wait, I thought it might rain." He pointed at the massive clouds looming over the other side of the river.

"Our side is fine, Grandpa." I did not want to be the only one of the seven carrying an umbrella.

To further persuade him, I quoted a proverb he once taught me, "Summer rain, dividing line, buffalo spine."

"When going on a journey, one should always take an umbrella. There is no telling about the weather," he threw back an old saying.

I felt his expectant gaze and accepted the umbrella. Grandpa grinned as he headed home. When I turned to look at him again, his vigorous figure became a small dot. While my companions were ardently arguing about whether Chu-yuan, one of the most beloved ancient poets, was murdered by the emperor or committed suicide, I was lost in my thoughts.

My grandpa's face looked like a bronze statue, wrinkled and dignified. He was sixty years old and as strong as a buffalo. He was a man of few words. Although he could not read, he wanted us to get a good education. He would sacrifice the money for his cigarettes to buy me exercise books when I ran out. I made up my mind that I would repay his kindness when I could make money of my own someday.

In about an hour and a half, we reached our destination. The school was fenced with a high wall. At the door, we each filled out a three-page form, asking about our family class, our parents' names, and their political stand (whether they were Party members), as well as close relatives and their political stand.

We were then guided to our classroom on the second floor of an old brick building; the stairs were faded, red-painted wood. From the window, I could see a long stretch of the riverbank and the county town. It was my first time in a building with a second floor. *Maybe I can see the stars better in the evening since I am standing at a higher spot!* I heard my name called. It was our teacher.

"Welcome to Class Two. My name is Peng." Peng was his last name. Superiors never revealed their first names.

With a timid voice and a flush on my face, I quickly said, "Teacher Peng." After the introduction we returned to the registrar's office to pick up our luggage and our bedroom key.

I was assigned to live with nine other girls in a large classroom-converted bedroom. I chose an upper bunk as it offered a little more privacy.

There were forty-five students, eighteen girls and twenty-seven boys in our class. The eldest was nineteen, and the youngest fourteen. All the girls, except me, had well-developed figures. I was the youngest, thinnest, and shortest. On the surface, I did not care, since I was going to catch up someday anyway. But I did admire their mature figures and many times I wished I were taller and fuller. Sometimes the big boys and girls flirted right in front of me, without acknowledging my presence, as if I were a desk or a chair.

In order to check on our teachers' work, an inspection team would walk into classrooms unexpectedly—a way to tell the teachers that they should do their jobs well at all times. One normal Thursday morning, we were about to begin our math class when we heard noises at the back door: the inspection team had arrived! The teacher's face changed colour, drops of sweat glowed on his forehead. After offering a brief summary of the previous chapter, he explained the major formula of the new chapter step by step on the blackboard. He then asked a question to see if we understood him.

No sooner had he finished than I put up my hand. A little nervous, I talked fast, but I answered his question, and to the point. He nodded at me with appreciation and a little surprise. Maybe he never expected that the little quiet girl in the corner could rescue him in times of difficulties. The secret was that I never missed one class in my whole career as a student and I always previewed one chapter ahead of schedule. In the preview, I could understand ninety percent of the content. Marking the places that I could not figure out for myself, I paid special attention in class. When the teacher finished his lecture, I could usually answer any hard question instantly. In one mid-term exam, I got a hundred and ten in math—ten bonus points.

The older girls started to talk to me more after that and called me "little genius." But the two girls who came from my junior high were jealous. One afternoon while I was napping in my bedroom with my mosquito net down, the two thought that they were alone. "I don't know why that little daughter of a dog mother always gets good marks. Tar-Ma-De!" One complained, the other echoed.

I slowly opened my mosquito net and walked straight out of the bedroom without even looking at them. *The highest contempt to pettiness is to ignore it entirely.* I observed my motto.

Lingering in the garden, I realized that I had assigned them a new challenge. In the past, they had been nice to me although they hated me.

Now what side of their face are they going to display, I wondered, *false kindness or true hatred?*

By the end of the second semester, I was taller than three girls in our class though still thin. One early morning before class as I was jogging along the track field, a physical education teacher approached me and asked if I would like to join their gymnastic training class. I had a ready answer for him, which was "No." To join the gymnastic team meant missing many classes. One of my roommates was on the Beijing opera team and her grades had gone downhill. I did not know exactly what I wanted to do in the future, but my cherished wish from childhood had always been to excel in school.

In each of my grandma's many stories, there was always a learned woman, who would surpass all men in any challenges arising under the circumstance, and win respect of all in the end.

My mother had taught me about the importance of education through her own life story. According to her, education was the only way a woman could gain independence. "Because I have no education I can't find a job. I have to depend upon your father for money, and he is not very generous."

While I was growing up, I saw her pregnant every two or three years. She had to work in the fields until a few days before she gave birth to a baby. When the baby was a girl, nobody was happy with her. My mother often said to me, "May-ping-ah, I don't want you to live a life like mine. I want you to do well in school and get a high-salary job so I can depend on you when I am in old age. I can't count on your father. His heart is made of stone." Every time when she said that to me I kept silent because I was not sure if my grades would be good enough to go to a university.

During my childhood, I only saw my father once or twice a month because he stayed in town for his work. When he was home, I would call him "Pa," and run away swiftly. Sometimes he would ask to see my report card. I would stand in front of him nervously while waiting for his reactions. It seemed that all my value to him was in my grades.

At the end of my first year in senior high, I took home a good report card. I received an average of ninety-two percent for all the subjects. My father nodded at the report while helping me unload my school bag. He then opened up a can of my favourite pears. For the first time, I was not afraid of him! Although he wrapped himself with a stern face, I started to feel his care for me.

Next, he asked me questions about my courses, my teachers, and my classmates. I told him what my English teacher, Shao, had said in class.

"In a few years, our county town, Mian Yang, will become a city open to foreigners and you will have a chance to use your English."

I then showed my father the two volumes of classic poems I had borrowed from my classmates. I was obsessed with poetry during that period. He looked at my excited face with a slight hint of a smile. Encouraged, I told him about the movies we had recently seen and asked him if he had seen any of them. He shook his head.

"You haven't lived if you don't see those movies!" I declared. He looked at me and smiled again without a word, indicating that I was just making a naive remark.

From that time on, I liked to talk with my father. He was no longer the fearsome figure of my early childhood. I rarely saw him lose his temper with any of his children. When he had a bad day, he would air his frustration to my mother, since she was the one destined to share his life.

One suffocating July dusk I was teaching my sisters a new song in our front yard. Grandma called from the window and gestured me to her room. With a serious face, she whispered that Lan had drowned herself.

"What for?" Tears streaked down my cheeks.

"She didn't want to marry the man her parents chose for her." My grandma sighed a long sigh.

Lan's brother could not find a wife because he was from a Landlord Class family. Lan's parents had decided to marry Lan to another landlord's son so that his sister would agree to marry Lan's brother.

That was called a marriage exchange. Lan said that she did not love that man.

"Besides, he has pock marks from measles," Lan argued.

"But how can you bear to see your only brother single all his life?" her mother begged her.

Lan's father reasoned, "Our family line needs to be continued. Your brother must marry. Do you understand?"

According to Confucius, a daughter should unconditionally obey her parents. Defying parental arrangements was considered nonfilial, a crime by itself. Punishment was severe. Stories were told of parents who, to maintain dignity, had rolled their rebellious daughter in a straw mat, tied the mat up, and threw it into a lake. The parents would not be punished for drowning the daughter. Instead, they would be admired for their strong moral principles.

For thousands of years, Confucius was taught in schools. In 1949, Mao banned his books, but the deep influence remained. Lan's father was a close follower of Confucius and had threatened to drown Lan if she dared to defy his arrangement.

In despair, Lan took her own life.

That night, I did not sleep. Lan's tragic death had cast dark clouds on the beauty of our socialist class struggle theory. If it were not for Mao's Class classification, Lan's brother would not have had difficulty finding a wife and Lan's parents would not have tortured her to death.

3

THE SECOND YEAR OF MY SENIOR HIGH SCHOOL was more interesting. I found myself talking a lot with the two boys who were the best in math. One was Rong's brother, Dan. He was four years older than me, observant and analytical. His seat was in front of mine and I still remember how I hurt his feelings. We were having a history class that morning when our teacher sketched the head of an ape on the blackboard. It looked very much like Dan's. Elbowing the girl next to me, I pointed at Dan's head with my index finger. We both chuckled—very gently. Dan moved his head a little and tilted it to the right, pretending not to have heard us.

Dan's attraction lay in his impenetrable dark eyes which seemed perpetually thinking. About what, I could not figure out. At the age of nineteen, he carried five horizontal brush stroke-like wrinkles on his square and darkish brown forehead. Constant dripping erodes a rock. There was little doubt that the continuous use of his brain formed deep furrows on his forehead. Dan had big ears, erect and floppy like a palm leaf fan. He was short even by southern Chinese standards for men, and average looking in anyone's eye but his mother's.

There was whispering in our village that Dan was illegitimate. His mother took two lovers to help clothe and feed her children, for her husband was a good-for-nothing, even in bed.

The villagers believed that *that* explained why Dan was exceptionally intelligent. Illegitimate children were the results of passion, whereas legitimate ones were the products of duty. In arranged marriages, husbands and wives did not make love, they made children.

According to this line of reasoning, Dan was doubly intelligent, for his father was also suspected to be illegitimate. Dan's grandmother had a long-time affair with a single man in our village. She was a rare beauty with harmonious facial features, smooth complexion and three-inch bound feet—as delicate as a lotus. At first, the villagers pointed fingers at her when she was seen with her lover. After a while people's curiosity died out as the three of them, husband, wife, and lover, had meals together and got along quite well. Lush women need two men, just as men of power and money had several women.

Nevertheless, Dan's grandfather, the legitimate one, was not respected in our village. He was a turtle, a man who willingly shared his wife.

The other boy I liked was Fang, who was tall and muscular but had too many bumps on his square face. He did not walk with his back straight either. He was good at both Chinese and math, a rare combination. In order to send him the message that I liked him, I made fun of him—mostly by sarcastic words. One day, we had a fight, a real fight. I threw his books on the floor and he threw mine. I threw more of his books and he grabbed me. He was not punished because I did not make a case. I was sure he never knew I liked him. He probably thought the opposite. So much the better; he was too dumb for me anyway.

In those days it was taboo to like a boy. So we developed a unique way to express our feelings. To argue. To insult. To torture and to fist fight. In this way, other classmates would not become suspicious and we could spend some time together without fear of being reported.

Another way to escape punishment was to fall in love with somebody outside our school, and that was what I did.

When the second year of my high school was over, I returned to my village for the summer vacation. We students were required to work in the fields during summer holidays.

Rong and I were carrying a big pail of manure to the rice fields on a fine August morning. Barefooted, we walked on narrow ridges between the patches to reach our destination. No sooner had someone warned us to be careful than we slipped and the manure spilled all over our legs and feet. The next thing I heard was loud laughter from all over the fields—about three-dozen peasants and students were giggling! For some reason, we were not embarrassed. Rather we found it very funny. After washing ourselves in a nearby pond, we were excused to go home and change. When I walked to my shoulder pole and pail, a good-looking young man, whom I had never met before, was helping us clean the mess. I thanked him and left for home.

After the cotton was picked in the fields, it needed five suns to dry out before it could be stored or sold to the state. The following morning, when we were spreading cotton on the sunny ground, I saw him again. "I have heard many good things about you. Now I know who you are. My name is Sun-bin, by the way." He had sensitive dark eyes.

"Are you here for your re-education?" I spoke to him like a hostess because I grew up there.

According to our great leader Mao's 5.7 directive, every high school graduate from towns and cities should go to the countryside to receive re-education from the peasants.

Sun-bin's father was a member of Mao's army and followed Mao across the Yangtze River in 1948. He was a senior cadre in Mian Yang County and earned a high salary, though without much power due to his poor health.

Since my senior high was close to his home, many of my schoolmates had been in the same junior high as Sun-bin. We chatted about our school, our teachers, and updated each other on the latest news of our common acquaintances. That morning seemed a minute.

Near the end of the day, he asked if I would like to go to a movie in a nearby village that evening. "We are not going alone," he added as an afterthought. "Several people are going; Rong and Dan are among them."

"Sure," I answered gladly.

The gigantic movie screen was on a huge open ground crowded with villagers from near and far. Since we did not bring any chairs, we stood through the two-hour movie. It was a black-and-white movie about Mao's army, using self-made explosives, fighting the Japanese in a northern Chinese village.

Most of the movies in the 1960s and early 1970s were either about Mao's heroic army or the eight exemplary Beijing operas endorsed by Mao's wife, Jiang Qing.

During *Fighting Japanese in Underground Tunnels*, Sun-bin was standing on my right-hand side and tried to move a little closer from time to time. He explained to me the process of making the film and playing the tapes. I did not quite understand his profound theories, but his learning impressed me immensely. It was about nine-thirty when the crowd started to disperse and we realized that the movie was over.

The nine of us walked back in the moonlight. No one showed any sign of fatigue. Finally the hot air started to cool and I felt the gentle night breeze touching my face. On one side of the country road were the exuberant cotton plants. On the other side stood the young rice seedlings half soaked in water.

Approaching our village, we saw empty bamboo beds in the large front yards of every household. The villagers cooled themselves on those beds after a day's work under the hot sun. Now they had gone into their houses to sleep inside the mosquito nets.

Passing Zong's front yard, we heard movements, giggling and moaning from a large closed mosquito net. We understood: the newlywed couple were wrestling vigorously inside the mosquito net. The boys winked at each other wickedly and we girls bashfully said good night.

Early next morning as I was washing clothes in a wooden basin beside the lily pond by our front yard, a love tune played on a two-string violin floated to my eager ear. Sun-bin was the only one who played musical instruments in our village. He lived in a room beside the hall of the production team, about two hundred feet from our house. The cheerful tune penetrated the liquid morning air and my youthful heart. I was too excited to sit still—I felt that he was playing the love tune for my ear, and mine alone.

My happiness overflowed to the lily buds which were tossing in the morning breeze. At the age of sixteen I was, like the budding lily flower, eager to unfold my life in this sunny world, totally unaware of the insidious dark clouds and malicious rainstorms.

The big bell rang, and it was time for the villagers to begin work in the fields. Most of the villagers had started their day long before the bell rang: they had to wash their clothes and cook their meals for the day. That morning, our task was to pick worms cloaked in the cotton leaves.

Passing by Sun-bin's place, we saw him hanging things on the front bars of his new bicycle, the only new bicycle in the whole village. He was admired in every way: he had a rich and powerful father, he was articulate and had good manners.

"Sun-bin, where are you going?" someone asked and everyone looked and listened.

"I'm taking today off to pick up a few things from home," he answered, a sweet smile on his face.

By mid-August, I started on my homework with my classmate Xian, who lived at the other end of the village. As Sun-bin lived in the middle of the village, I passed his place four times a day. This particular afternoon, he happened to come out to fetch some water in the brook when I walked by. He asked me if I had Rainbow brand blue ink for his fountain pen, since his had run out. On my way back, I brought him some ink and ten ripe peaches from my grandma's large peach tree. I naughtily threw the peaches to his straw-mat bed one by one and took my leave. He handed me a four-page letter written in pencil.

"Please don't read it till later." His smile was shy.

I did not open the letter until I reached a trail between the grown cotton plants. His handwriting was beautiful! Although I did not fully understand his sophisticated expressions, the main idea was clear. The letter started: "My dear [in English!] May-ping." My blood started to swirl!

> *I have been in love with you for some time without my knowing it…Do you think we are too young to fall in love? No. Karl Marx and Yian Ni fell in love when Marx was only fifteen and she was nineteen. Now I am nineteen and you are sixteen. It's definitely time. It's arranged by God and we can't escape our fate…I am anxiously waiting for your reply. Even one word is precious for me. Hold your hands tightly, Yours, Sun-bin.*

Most of the novels with any description of falling in love or being in love were banned when the Cultural Revolution started in 1966. I had read a few love stories in secret and imagined being in love with some nice, handsome guy. I had never thought it could *actually* happen to me. It came too soon and I was not prepared for this thunderstorm in my quiet, sunny life.

"I must admit that I really like him," I said aloud. "Do I have to give him a reply? God, what should I do?"

It was taboo to even talk about love. How could it be possible to tell anyone and get advice? If my father knew, he would kill me.

By the time I reached Xian's home, I finished reading the letter. I put it in my pocket as if nothing had happened. But I was afraid it might fall out of my pocket if I didn't get rid of it immediately.

"I am not feeling well, Xian. You know what? I have a migraine headache, the disease I have inherited from my father," I said, conjuring a miserable look.

25

"I'll make you some tea." She was about to run to the kitchen.

"May I take a walk in your backyard?" My eyes beseeching.

"Of course," she said, watching me walk unsteadily out of the back door, with one hand on my forehead.

I went to the outdoor toilet, threw the letter in and stirred it in with a long stick. Now nobody could have any evidence to persecute me. I felt relieved.

My headache continued till dusk fell. Luckily I knew the English word "dear." It was in the first lesson of my English textbook: "Long live our great leader Chairman Mao! Long live our great, glorious and correct Chinese Communist Party! Long live our heroic and dear people!"

I ate only a small bowl of rice porridge and a little vegetable for dinner. My grandmother was puzzled, for ordinarily I ate three times as much.

"What's the matter with you, dear?" She examined my brown eyes and pale face.

"I hope I don't have jaundice hepatitis. My eyes don't look yellow, do they?" I had to make up something; otherwise she would force me to eat two more bowls of porridge.

As it was sunset, an amberish light reflected on my face through the leaves of the peach tree in our front yard. My eyes may actually have looked a little yellow.

"They seem to be a little yellow." She looked closely. "Did you drink unboiled water in Xian's home today?" She always made sure that we drank boiled water as "unboiled water bears many bacteria." According to her, "The cause of all diseases is attributable to what you eat and drink." Since I did not eat anything in Xian's place, I must have drunk something unhygienic.

"Xian's mother never reserves boiled water in her kitchen. I know she doesn't have the habit." Grandma had complained about Xian's mother before.

"I must have drunk a little unboiled water. Can't remember," I stammered.

"You don't remember? Didn't I tell you never, never to drink unboiled water?" She became very serious.

She made me lie down and put a cold towel on my forehead. In her comforting presence I soon dozed off. When I opened my eyes, a sparkling starry sky greeted me.

"May-ping, are you feeling better?" My grandma examined my eyes again in the moonlight.

"Much better." I said that I wanted to take a walk down the path by the village. She looked hesitant.

"A little walk after a meal, you will live to ninety-nine years," I quoted her.

She went in and got a light jacket for me.

"Take this with you. Be back soon." I walked very slowly as I knew she was watching me.

I stopped by a brook and put lots of cold water on my face. Lifting my head, I saw the Silver River among the stars, which reminded me of a fairy tale:

Long long ago, a poor, kind-hearted cowboy was herding his cows at the top of a mountain when he heard a message from a magpie: "Seven fairies are bathing in the river at the foot of the mountain. Pick up a pink dress and walk slowly back to the top of the mountain."

The cowboy did as the magpie suggested. About half way to the top, a beautiful girl of eighteen ran to him naked asking for her dress back. With a big flush on his face, the cowboy handed her the dress. She put on the dress and smiled at him. She liked his good-looking eyes and honest face. He smiled back at her. They fell in love at first sight! The fairy girl stayed with the cowboy and they had two lovely children in the following three years.

The fairy was a weaving girl working for the empress in the sky. On the seventh of July of the third year, the empress came down to take the weaving girl back. When the cowboy came home from work in the sunset, he found his beloved wife gone. She had left him a silk scarf. Carrying his two children with the magic scarf, he flew to the sky looking for his wife. Seeing that the cowboy was almost catching up, the empress took a silver pin from her hair and drew a line behind her. The line became the Silver River, wide and full, with current. The cowboy could not cross it. The two lovers were only allowed to see each other once a year on July 7th, the day they were parted.

What a tragic love story! A sad smile fleeted my face. I gazed at the Silver River for a long time. Now I seemed to have an answer to my predicament. I defied all conventions! For thousands of years, the Chinese had never had the right to love at will. Now it was time to shake off the yoke of arranged marriages!

I got up at daybreak the next morning. Unfolding a small table and a stool in our backyard, pretending to do my homework, I started:

> *Sun-bin, I think I love you too. Do you believe it? Here is the evidence: when I am with you, time flies; when I hear your violin, my heart jumps out of my chest. When your name is mentioned, I become alert. I want to know more about you, every detail.*

Although I liked my eloquence I was not satisfied with my handwriting. It took me five drafts to finish the letter. I carefully folded it in a butterfly shape and swiftly pressed it to his hand when I saw him in a crowd that afternoon.

When my sisters and I were soaking and playing in the lily pond in the dusk, I heard the sound of a flute from Sun-bin's room. It was my favourite song: The Beautiful Lake by Our Hometown. The flute sounded so clear in the serene village air that we could not help humming the tune. Somewhere in the distance was the singing of frogs—what a symphony!

Dressed in my sleeveless blouse and a light skirt, I walked in the opposite direction from where Sun-bin lived. Through a big circle I reached his place. He opened the door and greeted me with his shimmering eyes. I observed his small room: in the middle was a double bed framed by a white mosquito net; a small, unpainted wooden desk stood by the small window, which afforded a view of our lily pond (ha!). An old chair of faded blue paint was placed at the desk. Close to the door was a washing stand with a bird-patterned towel and a colour-glazed basin, at the bottom of which were two painted fish happily tangling.

"Have a seat," he said, with an endearing shyness. Not knowing where to place his hands or his being, he poured me a cup of boiled water from a bamboo shelled thermos flask. Although he was trying to hide his feelings by not looking me in the eye, I could tell from his trembling voice that he was very happy to see me.

It seemed too much a hardship to cross the narrow space to reach the chair; I remained standing. He took a thick book from under a new pillowcase, and showed me the cover: *The Bitter Flower*. I jumped with joy!

"Where did you get this?" *The Bitter Flower* was one of the forbidden novels.

"That is a s-e-c-r-e-t." He smiled mysteriously. His eyes were not very big, but glistened like a profound sea of knowledge.

"Have you read it?" He was trying to tempt me, and I was dying to read all forbidden novels.

"No. May I borrow it for two days, please?" I was afraid that the book might disappear under his arms.

"It all depends. Can you promise not to show it to anyone else?" he said half seriously, with a dry but affectionate laugh.

"No, I won't. I promise." I was very earnest.

"Okay, you may have it for three days," he said slowly to make sure I heard "three days" clearly.

"Sure." We smiled.

I turned the pages and found that many were nearly worn out.

I put the book on the desk and had a good look at the cover: a sketch of a spellbinding young man gazing at the delicate face of a young woman, who was bashfully looking down at a flower with tiny yellow petals.

Sun-bin pulled the chair out and I sat down, my eyes still fixed on the book. I wanted to know every word on each and every one of the pages. Sun-bin smiled at me and sat on the edge of the bed facing me. We talked about the book for a while, and then he suddenly became silent. I could feel his eyes touching every part of my body. I looked down because I did not have the courage to meet his burning eyes. Neither of us moved.

The silence was broken by the sudden opening of his door. A fellow villager came in to ask for a light for his cigarette. I quickly stood up, took the book and hid the cover under my arm.

"Thanks for the book. I will finish it as soon as possible," I said normally, intending to create the impression that I was there only to borrow an ordinary book. I left the room before the villager had a chance to react.

Four days later, school started. We could see each other only when I went back for my monthly visit to my family. One evening right after our evening study session, I was reading in bed. A roommate called me that I was wanted at the door. It was Sun-bin! What a surprise! With a shy smile on his naughty face, he said, "Your mother has asked me to bring you these."

I opened the parcel. There were some snacks and a wool sweater.

"Your mother sends word that you should put on the sweater in the morning and evening." A warm feeling flew through my whole body like an electric current. I could not tell whether it was from his love or my mother's.

"Thank you." Our eyes met.

I folded the sweater and felt something else in it, but did not dare to open it in case my roommates saw it. I said goodbye in a low voice. He refused to leave. It was a moonless night with a few flickering stars in the deep blue sky. Watching my face and feeling my presence, his lips trembled. I shook my head quickly, signalling him not to talk. I was afraid my roommates might come out and overhear him. I could be criticized in public if my teachers knew I was dating.

He nodded understandingly. Gracefully sliding onto his new bike, he disappeared into the darkness. I could not walk him to the campus gate; it would arouse suspicion to walk with a man in the dark.

I returned to my bed and pulled down my mosquito net, a screen providing some privacy. I opened the sweater and saw a red diary with two branches of a green bamboo shoot on the cover. Inside was a picture of Sun-bin, smiling at me with his usual naughty expression. On the first page was Sun-bin's handwriting: "For you—my darling May-ping. Wish you the best for the new semester. Hold your hands tightly, Sun-bin."

I put the diary on my heart and fell asleep. That night I dreamed of being with Sun-bin. We were sitting by a lily pond with our feet in the water and hands touching.

In the evenings we had a two-hour self-study session. One could chat or study or hum tunes. From time to time I would walk toward the window, stare at the starry sky, and look for the Silver River and wonder,

What is he doing at this moment? Is he thinking of me as well?

The first month of the semester was like a year. When I finally went home for a visit, Sun-bin was away, summoned by the district Party secretary to write criticism articles about Lin Biao, the chosen successor of Chairman Mao. Lin Biao had just died in a plane crash while fleeing to the Soviet Union after his plot to murder Mao failed.

The second time I was home, all the male peasants were called to build a new dam for the district. The worksite was many miles away. Due to his father's influence, Sun-bin worked as a telephone operator on the worksite and was in charge of broadcasting the exemplary deeds of some to encourage the rest. That was called "learning from each other, helping each other and encouraging each other." According to Mao, efficiency came from motivation and motivation came from revolutionizing people's brains. Besides praising articles, the worksite loudspeaker broadcast the items from the central government people's radio station or the provincial radio station. There were no other stations.

There were loudspeakers in every village as well and they were on from sunrise to sunset. I learned the eight Beijing operas by heart, every tune and every word from the loudspeaker.

Sun-bin's good performance and his father's influence got him a Party membership. He was promoted to work in the commune office. I did not hear from him until the following July upon my graduation from high school.

He came to our house one afternoon under the pretense of looking for his lost sweater. My mother told him that she had picked it up in the fields and passed it to the team leader. When my mother turned her back, he swiftly pressed a note into my hand.

I met him later in the woods at the river bank. We each sat on a small rock, as there were no big rocks for two people. He told me that he wanted to go to university the following year and I told him that I also wanted to go when my re-education was complete. Later, we walked along a dried river bank flooded by a full moon. It was so bright that it felt like daylight. Walking on the cool sand path barefoot was like walking on clouds. Happiness filled my heart.

We reached an old dam sided by dense, tall poplars. The trail between the trees became too narrow for two people to walk side by side without touching each other. I said that he should either walk in front of me or behind me, not beside me. Gazing at my face for a second with a flicker of annoyance, he shrugged and followed my wishes.

I was indoctrinated with the revolutionary idea that the noblest love should be platonic. It never occurred to me that we should have any physical contact.

When we came to a small brook, he offered to carry me over. I told him that I could jump over by myself, and I did.

4

My father arranged a teaching job for me in Temple Primary School as part of my re-education in the countryside. Temple Primary obtained its unusual name because the main building was a Buddhist Temple before the Communists took over in 1949. By the time I arrived in 1973, it had developed into a full-sized primary school with six brick classrooms.

I was assigned to teach Chinese for Grade Three and music for Grades Two and Five. For the first class, I wrote the title of lesson one on the blackboard "I am a little commune member," then some new words. I asked the whole class, forty-five boys and girls between the ages of nine and twelve, to read the new words aloud after me. Big boys and girls from Grades Five and Six rushed to my classroom windows to watch the "little teacher." I was seventeen, tall, thin, and inexperienced.

On Wednesday afternoons we had a staff meeting, at which we usually studied editorials in the *People's Daily* or exchanged teaching methods. One afternoon, I sensed a tense air in the meeting room. The school director said, "We are going to expose Teacher Wu's deceptive behaviour. He took a pair of army shoes from Teacher Liu under the condition that Wu would give Liu fifteen yuan. But Wu ate his words after Liu gave him the new shoes." I glanced over at Wu: his head down, pallid face expressionless, a thin, short person shrinking at the corner desk. He must be wishing a hole would crack open in the office floor so he could dodge the sharp words and mean looks of the director. In his late forties, Wu was the most talented Chinese teacher in our school.

We knew that a pair of army shoes was worth one-third of our monthly wage and that Wu had been identified as "a rightist" in

1957. Many intelligentsia were crucified as rightists because they did not like the way Mao ran the country. In order to trap them, the Party leaders encouraged them to comment on the Party's policy at various meetings. Those who criticized Mao's policy became rightists and needed to be reformed. Some did so in jails; some through hard labour in the fields, and others in their working units. Teacher Wu belonged to the last category.

In order to purify the Chinese, Mao launched one political campaign after another: one in 1953, called the "Three and Five Againsts"; in 1957, "Against the Rightist"; in 1964, the "Four Cleansing"; and the biggest one in 1966, the "Cultural Revolution." Mao was a master of mob psychology. In each political campaign, he superbly manipulated the process so that some people were provocateurs and others targets, leaving him the righteous judge. Bloodshed was common and necessary, Mao said, because revolution meant violence.

Being the only "rightist" in our school, Teacher Wu was closely watched for any error in his daily activities, and was eligible to be criticized whenever necessary because the Party needed to strengthen its proletarian dictatorship. That afternoon, Wu was condemned for two hours, first by our director and then by two "red" teachers.

I was so scared that I did not fall asleep as I usually did at those meetings.

While we were playing basketball after the meeting, the mailman arrived. "A letter for you, May-ping," he shouted, waving the letter in the air. It was from Sun-bin. "My dearest, please forget and forgive me…" He did not give any reason for his breaking up with me. Instead he praised me excessively. I ran to my bedroom and cried for an hour, as if the sky had fallen on me. My soul was broken into a hundred pieces and my heart was stabbed and bleeding heavily.

The hurtful wounds and humiliation woke me during the night. It was not considered proper for a girl of seventeen to fall in love and our relationship was a total secret. I could not talk to a friend or consult my grandma. During the day I acted normal: taught my classes, marked the exercise books, and prepared my lectures. During the evenings I attended gatherings of young people in our village where I hoped to hear his name mentioned.

The front yard of Dan and Rong's parents' house was a popular gathering place. The guys were there because of Rong's attraction and most of the girls were there to be with Dan.

In the past year, Dan seemed to have grown a few inches. His skin was still dark brown but his shoulders were broad with muscles.

Dan and Sun-bin were friends. Although I suspected that Dan had guessed what was going on between Sun-bin and me, I doubted that he knew much. After Sun-bin broke up with me, I found myself talking to Dan more and more, mainly looking for traces of Sun-bin. As he got to know me, I noticed that he actually approved of my unconventional ways.

Although I was a schoolteacher, I was required to work in the fields on Sundays. The tasks for me and other frail girls were usually minor, weeding between the cotton plants or carrying dried organic fertilizers to the fields. One crisp October morning, I was walking barefoot with an empty wooden pail, humming a tune, when Dan appeared from the direction of the production brigade.

Watching my light steps, Dan called me a skylark—agile and full of happy songs. Reluctant to interrupt my tune, I only nodded at him and started another trip. I was pleased to have his approval of my deviant ways. The local custom disapproved of giggling and singing in teenage girls because it was considered too "wild." However, I could not help it. I liked to sing and laugh loudly, and nobody could stop me.

I sang loudly at home, too. My father, mother and grandparents would watch me, listen to me and smile at each other. Sometimes my grandma would say that as a girl, I was not supposed to show my teeth when I laughed.

"How can you laugh without showing your teeth?"

"You smile. You don't laugh." She showed me how to smile without exposing any teeth and made me practise three times.

At that time, Dan was working as an accountant for the production team, and was the second most powerful person in the village. Due to his fresh ideas, he constantly conflicted with the team leader. However, he was not afraid, for truth was on his side, he said.

The evening gatherings in Dan's front yard sometimes lasted till the small hours of the morning. We sang songs; we argued and explored philosophical issues such as the meaning or meaninglessness of peasant life.

As we had few books to read and few movies to watch, we used our lively minds to generate entertainment.

It seemed that no one knew very much about Sun-bin's where-abouts. Perhaps they had a conspiracy of not letting me know. One night I woke up at four in the morning and made a decision: "I will do well in life and make him regret losing me." The following day, I began to study for the university entrance examination.

 August was the time for university enrolment. From 1966 to 1971, universities stopped enrolling new students and most of the teachers were classified as bourgeoisie and sent to the countryside to labour in the fields. Beginning in 1972, a few universities enrolled a small number of new students after a token examination. University curriculum was changed from four to three years. Young people whose parents were high-ranking officials usually went to the good universities. In 1974, the token examination was cancelled. Sun-bin went to a famous university in Beijing and his new girlfriend, Yang-yang, went to one in Shanghai.

Fang, my high school study mate, told me that Yang-yang was Sun-bin's high school classmate. He had been interested in her in high school, but she hadn't paid any attention to him. The year before, Yang-yang suddenly changed her mind. Now she went to a good university as Sun-bin's father had "back doors." This news did not surprise me; I had guessed something of that sort.

About two months later, Fang told me that Sun-bin's father had gone to Beijing to see Sun-bin who was in a psychiatric hospital. After using his father's influence to enter a good university, Yang-yang wrote to Sun-bin that she did not love him any more. Sun-bin attempted suicide but was discovered and rescued by a roommate.

Dan also went to university. He was to study Chinese literature at a third-rate university—Wuhan First Normal University, because he did not have big "back doors."

On a rainy afternoon as I passed by Fang's house after picking up a cotton blouse at the tailor's in Moon Crescent Village, Fang signalled me to stop by. He seemed to have a mission so I went in.

Fang lived with his mother and younger sister in an old but spacious white lime-washed brick house; the front and back yards were swept clean. His mother lined up all their shoes on a rack along one wall of the living room, making the place look old-fashioned but tidy.

His mother was about fifty and had poor eyesight. She passed me a cup of hot water and went back to the kitchen. Fang ushered me to his little study and confided that Dan wanted to break his engagement to Qing. Before mailing the letter to Qing, Dan sent a draft to Fang for comments. Fang showed me the letter. It was very tactful but to the point. After praising Qing to the sky and beating around the bush for two pages, he finally revealed his intention. Apparently Dan was worried about hurting Qing's feelings.

I laughed. "That's quite unnecessary. Qing has wanted to break the engagement for quite a while. She told me so herself. She hasn't done so because her mother wouldn't let her. Qing likes Wang-fu in Willow Village. Wang-fu is handsome and intends to join the army. He is crazy about Qing." Sipping some hot water, I continued, "I think Qing is almost as pretty as Rong. Don't you think?"

"Well, they are different. Rong is a traditional beauty but Qing is a wild swan. I wouldn't want Qing myself."

"I don't mind Qing. She has spirit in her, a fine spirit, untamed by convention. She is a bit vain perhaps, but who isn't?" After a slight pause, I went on, "Although Wang-fu doesn't have much of a brain, Qing is not exactly the intellectual type either. They will make a good couple!"

"Ai-ya! That's great news for Dan. I will write him this evening." Fang clapped his hands and shouted excitedly.

"I wonder why Dan agreed to the engagement in the first place. He was about twelve then." I was perpetually analytical.

"Dan didn't really want it but his mother said that all he had to do was to drop some gifts to Qing's family twice a year and he could cancel the engagement any time." Obviously Fang had more information than I did.

Glancing at Dan's draft, I asked, "Do you think Dan's decision has anything to do with Di-Di's reputation?"

Di-Di was Qing's elder sister who had been working as the director of women's affairs at the headquarters of Evergreen Commune, which oversaw a population of twenty thousand. It was said that our former Team Leader Yin secured the job for her when she was eighteen years old. Di-Di was shrewd, articulate, and blessed with attractive facial and body features. A few months after she started her job, she slept with Commune Party Secretary Hu Zhong. Two years later, when Hu Zhong was sentenced to an eight-year jail term because he slept with an army man's wife and seven other peasant women, Di-Di was transferred to another commune twenty miles away. Last year we heard that she slept with the Party secretary in that commune as well. Now her mother was trying to marry her to a retired army man in Yichang, a city two hundred miles west of our village. It was thought that the retired army man did not know a thing about Di-Di's past and had found her a job in Yichang where a huge dam was to be built on the Yangtze River in the hope of supplying electricity to a large part of China.

"I wouldn't say it's unrelated. But the mere mention of Di-Di sickens me." Fang shook his head with disgust.

"Di-Di's mother says that Di-Di did that to keep her job."

"Nonsense! Di-Di is rotten." Fang protested.

"If you think Di-Di just likes men in general, why didn't she sleep with *every man* at the headquarters, not just the Party secretary, the most powerful man?" I glanced at his indignant face and went on, "Has it ever occurred to you that the Party secretaries are taking advantage of her?"

"If she were firm, they wouldn't have succeeded."

"Now tell me how many directors of women's affairs at the brigade, commune, and district levels have not slept with their Party secretaries?"

I felt that Fang was starting to see my view. Hammering the iron while it was still hot, I continued, "I am not saying that all Party secretaries are philanderers. Once they become the most powerful person in their little kingdoms, they forget themselves. Power erodes the human mind like a virus. A good human can become a devil when he has ultimate power, and some humans are not good to start with."

"My dear philosopher, I couldn't agree with you more. Women are at the bottom of society. We need to rescue them this minute." Fang took a fishing net from the closet and dashed to the door. He stopped at the door and laughed sarcastically.

Hearing his laugh, his mother asked if we needed more boiled water. I thanked her and said that we were fine. She then went back to the kitchen. She was gentle and loving but a bit worn out. Her hardened face and gnarled hands were records of her hardships over the years. Fang's father died when Fang was barely eight and she raised her two children single-handedly.

I knew Fang got my point of view but was too proud to admit it. I did not say a thing, a way to let him save face.

Winking at me with a mysterious and broad smile, he whispered, "By the way, I called my engagement off last year."

"I didn't know you were engaged." I was amused but not surprised. Most rural boys and girls of my age were engaged.

"I was engaged when I was five years old to my little cousin who lives on the other side of the Han River. She has never been to school, you know. I told my mother that won't do."

"Is she pretty?" I decided to be naughty.

"Yes. She is quite pretty. But I need someone to talk to, not just sleep with." His broad face grinned and he changed the topic to me. "Were you ever engaged?"

"No. My grandma learns fast. She doesn't believe in arranged marriages any more." I walked toward the window and watched the raindrops beating the smooth ground. I always liked warm rain — refreshing without being harsh. Half-heartedly I continued, "You know she never nags me about learning to do needlework or cook. She encourages me to do my own thinking and excel in school."

"You are dangerous," he said decidedly.

"Oh?" I turned my attention from the rain to him.

"A smart woman is hard to control," he said jokingly.

"Isn't marriage about loving and equal partnership?"

"That's only for say, not for do."

"You think so?"

"A household needs a head and the man is by default the leader."

I confess I knew little about Fang's views on love and marriage. He took me by surprise but my face did not show it. I yawned, said that I was tired, and took my leave.

About two weeks later, Qing's mother, Lu, spread word in the village that Dan was a heartless young man who forgot his roots as soon as he went to town. To save face, Lu declared Qing's engagement to Wang-fu the following week. To show to the whole village that her daughter could catch a man in no time, Lu had Wang-fu send five candies to every household. Engagement candies were unprecedented in Riverside, though wedding candies were common.

Life finally quieted down and went on as usual in the village. In the fall semester, I was promoted to be an assistant director of the school. I taught one Chinese class, three music classes, and was in charge of the school finances. Without my signature, no receipt could be reimbursed.

When Teacher Zhai bought five yuan's worth of kerosene on the school account and took it home for his personal use, I refused to sign his receipt. We argued for four hours at an evening meeting in the presence of the other six teachers and an assistant Party secretary from the production brigade. No one offered any definite suggestion because Zhai was the cousin of the brigade Party secretary.

It was close to midnight when I walked home alone, accompanied by the bright moon and singing my favourite Beijing opera:

> *Whenever I am in difficulties,*
> *I look at the brightest star in the North,*
> *And think of Mao's teachings,*
> *Which enlighten my soul;*
> *Give me courage, strength and direction.*

The heroine in the opera was in a far more difficult situation than I was. It was war time, her platoon was running out of food and ammunition, and they were surrounded by the Japanese who were armed to the teeth. *What excuse do I have for not going on with my fight against that hoodlum?* I imagined I was the heroine in the opera and sang all the way home.

I knew that Zhai was capable of any threat. A few months ago he had fought with his wife and threatened to kill himself. He made a small cut in his penis to show he was serious. Frightened, his wife gave in and begged him not to die. Many villagers, including me, saw him walking to the clinic holding his bleeding penis. Anyway, a true revolutionary should not be afraid of threat or death. I was prepared for any consequences.

My heroic deed reached the ear of a provincial leader who had been recently assigned to work in our district. He wanted to promote me to be the assistant director of a large tractor factory. Knowing that if I worked there, they would never let me go to university,

I tried to disqualify myself from the job. I said to him, "I am a little near-sighted which will create inconveniences in operating a tractor." In those days, spectacles were rarely seen in rural China. Three of the villagers were very nearsighted and had never owned glasses.

"Comrade May-ping, you won't need to operate a tractor. Your job is to organize political studies," he declared.

"How can I be convincing if I cannot even operate a tractor?" I made my argument based on Mao's teaching: "Our revolutionary cadres must work with the people and get to know the people."

He thought for a minute and said, "How about the assistant director of the local women's health centre? And would you like to join the Party? Hand in an application to the Party secretary within the next few days." Joining the Party was the wish of everyone who wanted to get anywhere in their career. I was delighted.

When I broke the news to my father, he smiled. I knew I had his approval.

My new job would start immediately after the Chinese New Year.

5

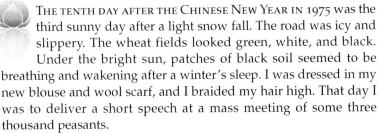 THE TENTH DAY AFTER THE CHINESE NEW YEAR IN 1975 was the third sunny day after a light snow fall. The road was icy and slippery. The wheat fields looked green, white, and black. Under the bright sun, patches of black soil seemed to be breathing and wakening after a winter's sleep. I was dressed in my new blouse and wool scarf, and I braided my hair high. That day I was to deliver a short speech at a mass meeting of some three thousand peasants.

When the introduction was done, I first read a notice from the central government on new directions for the women's health centre in the coming year. I then explained the content to the peasants. In the end, as I became comfortable with the large crowd, I talked briefly about my tentative plan for the new job. My mother was in the crowd. She told me later that my voice was very clear in the loudspeaker and she heard many words of praise.

My task was to help deliver preventive medicine to the villagers and to ensure that all married women practised birth control. As birth control was a new idea with the Chinese, it was very difficult to implement. In the early 1950s, Mao encouraged Chinese women to have many children, "The more, the better." Women who had three or more children were presented with red flowers and were called "Glorious Mothers." Mao based his population policy on his wartime experiences, when more children meant more soldiers, and more soldiers meant victory.

In the late 1950s and 1960s, birth control was advocated but never implemented due to the interruptions of one political movement after another. By 1970, Mao decided that our population was too large. Birth control became a priority issue nationwide (the one-child policy was not introduced till 1978, two years after Mao's death).

Director Wang, an experienced woman cadre in the health centre, was put in charge of this work. In principle, each couple was allowed two children. If a couple had two girls, they were allowed one more, but it had to be included in the quota. Each year, our production brigade was allocated a quota of fifteen births, on the basis that our population growth should not exceed five per thousand.

It was decided that married women who did not "have a quota" that year were required to use intrauterine devices. To prevent unplanned pregnancy, they were sent to the county hospital for a free check-up every three months. As Director Wang was illiterate, I organized the trips and did the paper work.

If a woman was pregnant because her intrauterine device moved or fell out, she was expected to have an abortion. If the woman resisted, a group of militia men and women would go to her house in the middle of the night and take her to a clinic to have the abortion. Sterilization, though not mandatory, was recommended for women who were not eligible for any more children.

One early morning in March, the loudspeakers woke every member of Hobar Production Brigade, "Attention! Everybody! Mei-xian and her husband from Riverside village have disappeared! Ten days ago, Mei-xian told their neighbours that they were going to visit Mei-xian's sister for a few days in Cang Yang County, but they didn't return after a week. Feeling suspicious, I went to Mei-xian's sister's place three days ago but they were not there. Yesterday we, together with Mei-xian's father, searched three of their relatives' places, but Mei-xian was nowhere to be found." Taking a breath, Gong-hong, the militia leader, continued, "If anyone knows Mei-xian's whereabouts, please report to me immediately."

The couple had three "useless" daughters and no son. They had begged the Party secretary to give them another quota but were denied. There was a strong possibility that Mei-xian's intrauterine device failed and she got pregnant illegally.

Mei-xian's father was taken to the production brigade to "reform through studying Chairman Mao's quotations." He was shut in a small room with a hard bed, a bench and a desk, on which were Mao's Red Book, paper and a pen. He was allowed visitors twice a day and was responsible to arrange for a relative to send him meals.

By the seventh day of his imprisonment, the militia leader asked me to write a report of this "serious case" for the local newspaper. When the militia leader interrogated Mei-xian's father that afternoon, I made notes.

"Are you going to confess or not?" Gang-hong shouted. Sitting down on the only chair in the small room, he placed both his legs on the frail desk. He then took out a package of New China Brand and lit a cigarette. He sucked the cigarette hard, blowing a thick ring of smoke in the stale air of the tiny room.

"I really don't know where they are." Came the weak voice of Mei-xian's father, wincing on the earth floor in a corner. He was about sixty-five years old, tall and thin, with white hair.

"Of course you know. You are the one who encouraged them to have another baby," Gang-hong blackmailed his victim. He jumped from the squeaking chair, fiercely throwing the cigarette end in the little rusty tin garbage can. Red veins bulged in his round eyes, the horizontal muscles on his fat face twitched.

"I am sorry ... I don't ... know," Mei-xian's father stammered.

"Confess! You cunning old fox!" Gang-hong waved his fist in the air and yelled at Mei-xian's father in a thunderous voice. He was a tall man in his early thirties with strong arms and legs but a void brain. He believed that terror was the best weapon to conquer a person's will.

"If you play tricks with me, I'll have your retirement salary frozen." Mei-xian's father was a retired state employee.

"I ... I ..." Mei-xian's father was terrified by Gang-hong's loud yelling and perhaps the prospect of losing his salary. During the interrogation, he coughed a few times and breathed with difficulty. Seeing his face turning very pale, I signalled Gang-hong to take a break. I called the barefoot doctor and he suggested that Gang-hong let Mei-xian's father go home.

"He is very ill. If you don't want him to die here, you'd better take him home," the barefoot doctor said gravely.

But Mei-xian's father was not sent home; he was to remain there "for a while." The second day, his condition became worse and Gang-hong reluctantly agreed to send him to the county hospital.

That evening, the birth control committee had an emergency meeting and passed a motion to freeze Mei-xian's father's pension until Mei-xian was found. A report was drafted there and then.

"We must send the report to the county Party organization as soon as possible. We shall not allow any one to sabotage the birth control policy," the Party secretary said emphatically.

Gang-hong and his assistant sent the report to the county birth control committee and received a "hundred percent support." Then Gang-hong went to Mei-xian's house and put a white poster on the door: "No entrance without permission from the militia leader."

After six months in hiding, Mei-xian and her husband came home with a chubby baby boy. There was nothing the militia leader could do after the baby was born. The birth control committee decided to fine the couple five thousand yuan which meant ten years of payments. Their baby boy could not be registered as his existence was illegal.

When the baby was a month old, Mei-xian and her husband hosted a lavish party at which I saw Mei-xian's father holding the boy in his arms and gently rocking him back and forth. He was watching the baby's lovely face intensely and smiling contently. "It's worth it; it's worth it," I heard him muttering to the baby.

The strange thing about many Chinese: they would walk through a knife mountain and a fire sea to have a male heir.

I unexpectedly received a thick letter and a package from Dan. He sent me the newest Beijing opera, a nicely bound music book and revolutionary songs from Wuhan. Between the pages, he had put some dried lily petals. When I opened the book in the post office, they fell out. A naughty friend of Dan's picked them up and blackmailed him, asking him to "confess" when he came back for the summer vacation. When Dan asked me if I had seen the petals in the book, I said no. That "no" sent chills to his spine.

In his long letters, he commented on urban snobbery, the decadence of Communist leaders and thought spies among university students. I wrote him long letters too, because once I started discussing life in general, I could not stop. Life was unfolding new horizons for me every day. At the age of eighteen I had numerous responsibilities in the health centre and Youth League. I started to go to various meetings with the cadres at the brigade and the commune levels and learned a great deal about how the system worked. I was amazed to learn how comfortable the cadres' lives were in comparison with those of the peasants. When the lily nuts were first in season, we, all fifteen cadres from the production brigade, had a feast. There were ten production teams in Hobar Production Brigade. Our Party secretary would ask one team leader to prepare a "casual" meal for us one day and another team leader some "snacks" the next day.

I also found that none of the cadres actually worked in the fields although they carried a shovel or a hoe at all times. They walked around the fields to "check things out" with the team leader. I felt uneasy not working when the peasants were labouring ten hours a day. So I asked to have a small plot of cotton field. In the summer, the cotton plants grew shoulder high with brawny branches and leaves. The soil underneath was shady, cool and soft. One hot afternoon, I was pruning "lazy branches" when the Party secretary walked by and asked me to join them for a meeting. Looking at the branches I had clipped, he winced a little. A few days later, a few cadres made fun of me, "You can't even distinguish a fruit from a fruitless branch!" Although their jokes did not carry any menace, I felt inadequate in spite of my efforts. To look like a true peasant, I wore old clothes, walked barefoot on the rough roads, and worked in the fields whenever I could.

When I excitedly shared my new discoveries as well as frustrations with Dan, he seemed unimpressed. He said that he knew all the secrets of the cadres because he had worked with them. He also said that the socialist system was decaying; China needed a new system. I wrote him that he should be careful about what he said. If his ideas became known, he could be arrested as a counter-revolutionary, which meant a jail term.

Besides writing to Dan, I also consulted Fang, who had been a team leader for a year when I started my job at the health centre. He had grown taller and more muscular, with a shiny sun-tanned complexion. He informed me of each cadre's background and their major characteristics. Every now and then, we discussed our new discoveries and had a good laugh together. Sometimes we talked about other things, like literature and poetry; other times we exchanged our observations and analyses of rural life in general. Once we got into a huge argument when I disclosed to him that I found most peasants boring to talk to.

His face was stern, smouldering with silent anger. "What do you know about peasants? On the contrary, I find them very interesting."

"Give me an example," I was ready to stand by my statement.

"When I was eight years old, my next door neighbour, Tie, told me that he caught eighteen sparrows with a buffalo whip when he was ploughing in the rice paddies. What do you think of his story?" With a sarcastic smirk, Fang sat down and waited for my reaction.

I searched my brain quickly, but did not come up with a smart answer as I would have expected of myself.

I could feel Fang's arrogant air floating all over me. Dumbfounded, I opened my mouth, but no sound came out. What a loss of face! I could kill myself.

He continued, "It recently dawned on me that this story can't be true because when you hit one sparrow, the rest would fly away. Tie is a humorous and wise man who is full of jokes and stories. Although he is illiterate, he practises the Taoist philosophy 'to learn to be content with what you have.' His wife adores him and his children admire him."

From this argument, I learned the importance of not jumping hastily to a conclusion or generalization. I was humbled.

At the end of March, Mao issued five new quotations and everyone in the whole country was expected to memorize and practise them. Fang and I were assigned to check a group of women from Willow Village.

About thirty women dressed in colourful spring garments were hoeing weeds between the cotton plants, talking and laughing loudly. We chatted with them for a while before we asked volunteers to recite some new quotations from Mao. One bright young woman recited five; a few did three and others did one or two. We then walked toward a few women who had not participated. Pretending not to have seen us, they busied themselves with their farm work. We got the message: they did not know any quotations of Mao. We decided to let them go.

At the summary meeting, Fang entrusted me to do the reporting. It was my first time to speak in front of the commune leaders, and I started with a big blush. Nevertheless, I decided to lie, "Of the twenty-nine women we checked, four recited five quotations of Mao; five did four; ten recited three; five did two and the rest recited one. They were fluent and impressive."

My face was feverish but I felt determined to protect the village women who were mostly illiterate and did not give a damn about Mao's quotations. The commune leader praised my report as superb.

After the meeting, Fang and I ran to a nearby pond to wash our sweaty faces and hands before lunch. Bursting into loud laughter, we agreed that it was silly to take the orders of the commune leaders seriously. Fang said that my improvised report was heroic and extraordinary.

As we stood up, Fang moved closer and gently encircled one arm around me. I quickly extricated myself and ran back to the pond. Squatting down, I put both my hands into the cool water, waiting for his reaction. Five seconds, ten seconds...one whole minute must have elapsed; I still did not hear him move. All was quiet except the occasional *deng deng dengs* produced by an energetic woodpecker on a nearby birch tree.

Fang was not a frivolous man, though a little whimsical sometimes. I enjoyed talking with him but I did not love him. I cherished his friendship and did not want to hurt his feelings.

At least three minutes must have passed; he was still standing there like a deeply rooted tree.

"Lunch must be ready. I am famished," my voice was calm.

No response. He seemed to be in a trance, his big black eyes fixed at the distance, his broad face tender and feverish.

Alone, I walked back to the meeting hall where delicious and free food was waiting. Unaware of Fang's misery, the woodpecker was still joyfully pecking, *deng deng deng...*

Twenty minutes later, I noticed Fang at a corner table eating his lunch by himself. After that, he no longer sought my company alone. Our friendship was no longer the same.

 About five weeks after I declined him by the pond, a radiant Fang walked toward me and handed me a letter.

"Give this to Rong. She is right there." He pointed to the most attractive girl in the crowd.

"Sure. That's what friends are for," I hid my surprise that he should dare to be interested in Rong, Dan's sister, who was surrounded by four dashing young men.

Rong was a lush beauty, with a round, radiant face and a well-developed figure. She wore her long, thick, dark hair in two braids, each tied with a red ribbon folded in a butterfly-shape. When she walked, her braids swirled on her round bum and the red butterflies bounced with the rhythm of her youthful steps. When she smiled, there were two distinct dimples on her charming face. She was not successful at schoolwork but she was popular. An old Chinese saying had it that a man's virtue lay in his talents, a woman's in her looks. A woman without learning was virtuous—like a tamed horse—obedient and pleasurable to ride.

In early May, the central government issued No. 44 document, calling for "killing any capitalist-road tendencies in the cradle." Each household was allowed to keep only five chickens since they were hard to control: they could walk to the fields and eat the crops. The collective took half the vegetable patches from every household. The peasants were told that vegetables grown in their yards were for their own use only. Selling extra vegetables on the market for cash was "walking the capitalist road." We all knew that the biggest capitalist-road walker was Liu Shao-qi, the former state chairman who had been expelled from the Party and died in a prison cell.

At a brigade council meeting, our Party secretary assigned me a glorious task: to organize a class-struggle exhibition. I had several Youth League members paint cartoon characters of peasants attempting to grow economic crops such as soy beans in their back yards.

Rong had a beautiful voice, so I invited her to be the receptionist. In order to make the hall look solemn, we borrowed the enormous white sculpture of Mao from Temple Primary. I had carried the bulky sculpture from the school to the hallway. Observing my difficult steps, Rong unloaded the sculpture from my stiff arms.

"Be careful! Hold it tight," I stretched my tired arms.

"Ai-yar!" Came a crash and a frightful scream.

"Oh, gosh, I can't believe this!" Rong's gaze was transfixed on the floor, where many white plaster pieces lay smashed.

I rushed into the hall and quickly shut and latched the door from inside.

"I was just about to put it on the ping-pong table, and I...I...my arms suddenly became a little weak...and I...bumped it on...on...the wall."

She was pale with fright. Beads of sweat, as big as grapes, were hanging on her forehead.

Breaking Chairman Mao's sculpture was no small matter!

About six months earlier, a man in a neighbouring village had been condemned to eight years in prison after he dropped a red badge of Mao's portrait and accidentally stepped on it. His teenage son, who was a Red Guard and had sworn to defend Mao's glorious image, had seen and reported him.

If reported, Rong would be done for.

"We must find a bag to put the pieces in," I murmured.

I searched every corner of the hall for a bag, any bag. But there was no bag to be found. In a panic, Rong and I removed our sweaters and tied the collars and sleeves with strings from our braids. We promptly threw all the pieces into the two "bags." We designated a corner for the "bags" and dragged a pile of large cartoon signs over them. We checked several times to make sure no trace of the "bags" could be detected with any shrewd eyes.

"Now what should we do?" While I anxiously walked up and down in the hall, Rong half-collapsed on the floor, her body shaking, her teeth chattering.

It was a damp and suffocating afternoon. Rong's long black hair was dishevelled, mine was in no better condition. We were sweating and thirsty. But who would have time to care about such trivia just then?

"Don't do anything or say anything to anybody till I get back." I shook Rong by the shoulders to make sure she heard me.

Tying my hair back with a handkerchief, I went to the school and found the director. I told him that an accident had happened to the sculpture and the production brigade would be willing to buy a new one. Not wanting to hurt the close relationship between the school and the production brigade, the director said that we did not need to bother. I decided not to report the accident to the Party secretary for the time being.

I ran back to Rong and told her not to worry, although deep down I was scared to death. In an attempt to dispel her shivering fear, she kept pacing up and down the hall, continuously braiding her long thick hair.

I strode steadily to the brigade kitchen to get some cold tea, and spotted a large plastic bag near a heap of turnips and cabbage.

"May I borrow this bag for a day please?" I asked as casually as I could.

"Oh, sure. It's yours. I have no use for them." The generous chef lifted his wrinkled eyes and answered absent-mindedly. He was busy chopping red turnips.

I picked up the bag in slow motion; folded it and returned to the hall with a calm face and steady steps. Rong and I lingered in and around the hall the whole afternoon to make sure that no one moved anything in "that" corner. We took turns for meals and the washroom. Luckily not a soul visited the hall that afternoon.

Darkness finally descended. There was no moon, only a few stars flickering indifferently in the cloudy sky. "Oh, you hateful stars, go into the clouds!" I heard Rong rumbling. As if the stars had ears, they vanished the next minute. "Oh, Heavenly Father is kind to me," grumbled Rong.

We swiftly shifted the plaster pieces into the plastic bag, which Rong decided to take home. "I'll hide it in my suitcase, lock it and keep the key with me at all times, even when I go to sleep. I won't tell a soul about it, not even my mother," she disclosed her well-composed plan as we parted.

A month passed, no questions were asked about the sculpture.

Rong finally felt relieved. Her large black eyes resumed a charming glow; the spunky Rong had come back. She thanked me immensely for covering up her "mistake" at the risk of my own future. "A true friend is hard to find these days," she contemplated. "I don't know what would have happened to me if...oh, I dare not to imagine," she kept murmuring.

I wanted to tell her that she had not done anything wrong in the first place, but did not say it. I was extremely discreet about such an important matter as I had heard of too many similar cases in which the kind protector was betrayed by the protected.

She then began to trust me with her secrets. She told me that Fang had sent her two more love letters besides the one I delivered. And they had been seeing each other.

About four months after I became the assistant director of the women's health centre, I was awarded a conference attendance. One woman representative was required to attend an "Iron Women" conference at our county town. Being the only literate one of the three women cadres at our production brigade, I was chosen. For thousands of years, women's position had been so low that Mao decided to raise them up. The women delegates, called "Iron Women," stayed for free in the county hotel with free meals and free movies in the cinema every evening. Iron Women were those whose bodies were as strong as iron. They could work continuously without a rest. Chairman Mao keenly endorsed the Iron Women spirit because it was an essential component in building our young socialist republic.

At the beginning of the meeting, each of us Iron Women was asked to provide some basic statistics such as the kind of cotton we were growing and the number of jin produced for each mu in the last three years. I was lost: *What in the world do I know about cotton?* I whispered to the girl next to me. She showed me her form. I wrote down exactly what she did, and handed in the form. The last half day of the conference was devoted to entertainment: each of us was asked to sing a song on the stage. I walked to the big stage and was about to start when I felt that my belt was loose. I held my skirt with my right hand, pretending that I was making a pose before singing. I finished the song; my skirt did not fall down, and I walked off the stage calmly. "Ha! Some Iron Woman, eh?" I chuckled to myself.

6

DIRECTOR WANG'S HUSBAND, ZHENG, who worked in the county electronic factory, had died unexpectedly. I was to be the representative from Hobar Production Brigade to assist the factory leaders with the funeral. The cause of Zheng's death was controversial. The factory leaders said that Zheng had died of heart failure, but his relatives thought that was impossible since he had never suffered heart problems before.

On the day of the funeral, a group of Zheng's relatives, mostly illiterate peasants, launched a plot: they were going to carry the dead body to Zheng's home village to have a parade. The temperature was 36° Celsius that day; the corpse would decay under the hot sun. The factory leaders were very worried. They heard of the plan but were apprehensive to stop it since the relatives suspected that the factory leaders had poisoned Zheng.

The factory leaders came to me for help. The leaders trailing, I marched to the room where the relatives were staying, and told them the following: "You think you are helping your cousin by carrying the body to the village? You are not. She is not herself right now because she is overwhelmed with grief. Anything you say, she would agree to. But let me tell you, on behalf of the Party organization of Hobar Production Brigade, that we don't support you. If you want to carry the body to the village, go ahead. You, and you alone are solely responsible for the consequences of what you do. I have no more to say." I left the room, followed by the factory leaders.

My next task was to write a memorial speech for the Party secretary of our production brigade. As I knew very little of the deceased, I manufactured several fine qualities shared by all revolutionaries, such as serving the people heart and soul and devoting all of himself to the Cause—he had worked until he dropped. I decorated these fine qualities with beautiful adjectives and adverbs. I felt safe to use my imagination as the deceased would not protest the inaccuracy and the living would not mind the exaggeration. In fact people usually became very generous with words toward the deceased because there was no danger of a threat.

The funeral proceeded normally. Zheng's relatives did not carry the dead body to the village. Afterwards, the factory leaders asked me if I would accept an offer to be the women's director in the factory. I shook my head.

I did not consider it necessary to tell my father about the job offer. However, he soon got the news. It was late at night when my father came home and woke me to talk about it. Putting an oil lamp on my desk, he sat down on a new wooden armchair and asked me to tell him the whole story. I was only half awake but I knew what I was talking about. I told him that I was not interested in any job because my mind was set for university.

"If it were not for the Cultural Revolution, I would be in university now, probably a good one," I said peevishly, partly because he woke me up in the middle of my dreams.

He smiled and said that it was fine with him whatever I decided about my future. He just wanted to know.

"Go back to sleep," he got up and yawned himself.

Now I was wide awake. Bouncing up, I opened the thin cloth curtains. The midnight moon was high and bright. The old peach tree in the front yard projected its mysterious shadow onto the white wall and the unpainted wooden window rails of my room. The air was serene. I let my bare arms rest on the window sill and indulged myself in recalling the details of my high school graduation day.

Huang cheerfully walked into our classroom. She was the teacher-in-charge, a tall woman in her mid-thirties with stunning facial features and a slim figure of a movie star. She spoke standard Mandarin with a voice of a singer. She was a survivor too, taking care of her two young children and managing a full teaching load. We all liked her for her fairness and good lectures. Indeed, she had a way with students; even the naughtiest of the students opened their hearts to her.

We also heard that her husband was a math professor at a University in Wuhan. They fell in love when they were studying in the same class. Occasionally we saw her husband visiting. Once a person was assigned a working unit upon graduation, it was usually for a lifetime unless one had big "back doors." It was common for couples to live their lives hundreds, even thousands of miles apart.

Teacher Huang announced the five people who received the highest grades for the final examinations of each subject. To my surprise, I received one hundred and twenty in Chinese, twenty bonus points, the highest among the one hundred and thirty graduates.

At lunch time, my classmates congratulated me. I gave them only a faint smile: "What's the use of high marks? Universities have been closed for several years and I have no idea when they will be open again. With the unpredictable political situation, who knows what fate will bestow on me?"

Now my re-education in the countryside was drawing to an end and I finally saw some hope of going to university. I felt like embracing the dawn I had waited for in the endless nights of darkness. I returned to sleep, but left the curtains open, letting the silver moonbeams into my room and my dreams.

On July 2, 1975, I informed my leaders that I wished to go to university. The Party secretary was reluctant because he had trained me for so long and wanted me to stay. He showed me a document that gave me another promotion. However, my mind was made up.

Behind my back, my brother suggested that I stay in the production brigade to be an important cadre, so he and my sisters could benefit in future. My father shook his head: "She will hate me the rest of her life if I ask her to do that."

It was a sunny day after lunch when my father asked me to fetch the Party secretary. When he arrived, my father said to him, "If Mayping doesn't go to university this year, she would want to go the next year anyway. Since there is only one quota for each production brigade, your younger brother would not be able to go next year because my daughter should be considered first, whether on the basis of her performance in the past two years or the fact that she started her re-education a year before your brother." He was succinct and to the point.

After some cost-benefit analysis, the Party secretary agreed to let me go.

I admired my father for his profound understanding of the human mind, his comprehensive analysis of critical situations, and most of all, his vision. He knew by heart the strategies of the military men in the Chinese history books *The Arts of War*, by Sunzi, and *The Three Kingdoms*, by Luo Guanzhong. To my father, life was like a battle and leadership demanded vision. A good leader should be able to anticipate what was going to happen in the near and far future and be prepared for it.

Compared with his illiterate colleagues, my father was privileged: he received twelve years' solid education from his grandpa on his mother's side. In the early 1950s, educated people from the Poor Class were in high demand. My father was entrusted to do most of the writing for the commune Party secretary. Later he was in charge of training hundreds of accountants for the district and was appointed director of the People's Bank.

To send me to university, my father cut down a tall willow tree in our backyard and sold the log for thirty yuan, about half his monthly salary. It was a hot day; my father started early in the morning and finished late in the afternoon. Although he was sweating and tired, he smiled when he handed me the money. My mother offered me the red pinewood suitcase, one of the best pieces in her dowry. And my grandparents spent a whole day preparing a delicious meal for our family. There were ten dishes in all: steamed fish, steamed pork, steamed lily roots and vegetables, baby chicken soup with vine melon.

7

I SPENT THE NIGHT BEFORE MY JOURNEY to university in my grandma's house on the large bamboo bed where I had slept in her arms until I was six. There was no preschool in the village and children were not supposed to start school until they were seven. When I was four, my grandma began to teach me Chinese characters and arithmetic. By the age of five, I could write over a hundred Chinese characters, count over a hundred, do some adding and subtracting, and recite several poems from the Tang Dynasty.

My father was a friend of the school director, who agreed to take me two years earlier if I could pass the tests. After I passed the Chinese and arithmetic, I recited three poems by Li Bai. I was in!

We had no clock in the house and every morning my grandma woke me for school. While I got dressed, my grandma would ask me to count from one to one hundred, and recite the Chinese text I learned the previous day. According to her, the mind was the freshest in the morning: "The prime time of the day is the morning and the prime time of the year is spring. What you sow in spring is what you get in autumn."

In wintertime, we had no indoor heat. December and January were the coldest months with the shortest daylight. The Chinese New Year was usually around the end of January and the winter semester was not over until fifteen days before the Chinese New Year. School started at daybreak and I had to get up when it was still pitch-dark. Most of the winter days were rainy, windy, or snowy. For me, the hardest moment was getting out of the large warm cotton blanket and into my cold cotton-padded jacket. If, after calling me three times at five-minute intervals, I was still in bed, my grandma would whisper in my ear, "May-ping, remember, those who can bear the most hardships will succeed in life and those who can't will be nobody." Other times she would quote Confucius: *Those who work with their minds rule and those who work with their hands are ruled.* I knew if I did not go to school that morning, I would become a bad pupil and end up being a peasant—working with my hands and being ruled.

I knew how hard a peasant's life was: to get up at daybreak and come home in the dark all year round. They still could not earn enough money to buy new clothes or bicycles for their children. They had to sell their chicken eggs to buy salt and vegetable oil. No young person wanted to stay and become a peasant. I knew I never wanted to be one.

Sometimes my grandpa would get up and walk me part of the way to school. He taught me how to walk on the frozen and slippery road and how to hold my umbrella in the driving rain. He also told me to throw myself under my school desk if there was a hurricane because my classroom was very old and shaky.

One stormy afternoon in the early part of June, the classroom was so dark that we could hardly see the blackboard. The teacher said, "Read the text by yourselves," and left for tea at his office.

We watched the heavy rain outside and sang the text which was a riddle of rain: "A thousand lines and a million lines, drop to the sea and lose their way." A strong wind was howling outside as if competing with our singing. Suddenly a thunderstorm struck and lightning lit up our classroom. The next thing I knew I was being carried to our teachers' big office. I was shivering all over: my red-and-white-striped silk shirt and skirt were soaked. Three boys and a girl in our class had broken arms and legs. I felt my head, eyes, arms, and legs: I was intact. My grandpa was very glad that he had taught me the emergency skills. He said that I must have thrown myself under the desk when the classroom collapsed after being struck by lightning.

Soon after we had a new classroom and I was assigned to sit with a boy who never studied. His arms were usually on my side of the desk and he enjoyed throwing my exercise books to the dirt floor, which was sometimes muddy because raindrops came in through the glassless windows. He threatened to beat me if I reported his behaviour to the teacher. I wished I had an elder brother who could beat him up. My brother was two years younger than me and was beaten himself most of the time by bigger boys. One Thursday afternoon I came home with tears in my eyes after the boy took my fountain pen and put several drops of blue ink on my new red-dotted white silk blouse. The following day, my grandpa waited for him on the road and taught him a lesson. I was safe after that.

While I was in primary school, I had four arguments with my grandma. One was after she washed my brother's small red flag—a badge for the Young Pioneer League.

"Grandma, those red flags are dyed with the blood of our revolutionary martyrs who sacrificed their lives for our happy life today. How can you wash their blood away?"

When I was in Grade Three and my brother in Grade One, we joined the Young Pioneer League. It was June 1, Children's day, sunny and hot. All the children were sitting on the sports ground under a big, red flag with a sickle and a hammer surrounded by five stars. "To join the Young Pioneer League is your greatest glory," our school director solemnly started. "In a minute, you will be given a small red flag, a corner of the big flag. You should wear it every day and cherish it as you would cherish your eyes. From this moment on, you are chosen as the successors of the revolutionary Cause left to you by our heroic martyrs. On your shoulders is the Cause of our revolution and you are the future of China!"

I felt that I was rising to an unknown height—body and soul. The burning rays of the sun were piercing my hair and skin. My throat was dry. But who would pay attention to trifles like discomfort and thirst? I was ready to devote all of myself to the Cause. I happily glanced around. Not a leaf of the poplars was stirring. Not even a single cloud was floating in the unusually high and blue sky. All was still and solemn.

Accompanied by the inspiring music of "The International," twenty of us marched to the stage. Holding our little hands into fists and lifting them in front of our foreheads, we swore to be loyal to our great leader Chairman Mao, to our glorious Party, and to our dear people.

When I got home that day, I showed my red flag to my grandma and told her not to touch it without washing her hands very clean. I also told her not to wash it because I did not want to lose one drop of our revolutionary martyrs' precious blood. But I forgot to tell her not to wash my brother's red flag as well.

I warned my grandma that if she ever washed our precious red flags again, I would report her to our school director. She said that she was not afraid of my school director because she was not a student. I did not speak to her for three days.

Another time she forgot to wash my short-sleeved cotton shirt. I told her that I just wanted to wear that particular shirt that day to school. "How can you forget, Grandma, I only have two short-sleeved shirts and I cannot wear the same one for two days because it smells. I cannot wear a long-sleeved shirt on such a hot day." I cried and stamped my feet in our front yard, threatening not to go to school that afternoon. Grandpa smiled and offered to buy me a big candy with a stick in the middle and wrapped with beautiful green paper. That was the only time that I ever wore the same shirt two days in a row.

The third time I argued with my grandma was after I peed in my cotton-padded pants on a snowy winter day. When I was in Grade Five, the Great Cultural Revolution started. Our teachers were criticized and dismissed. Classes stopped. Students from Grades Seven and Eight became Red Guards, and some went to Beijing to see Chairman Mao. They got free rides on the trains and free meals and hotel rooms because they were Mao's Red Guards.

We younger ones became little Red Guards. Our task was to stand on the main road for two hours a day to stop passersby and ask them to recite a quotation of Chairman Mao. Whenever we saw somebody coming up, we would wave the big red flag and say, "Comrade, please recite a quotation of Chairman Mao." Sometimes they did not know any and it was our duty to teach them one.

This cold winter afternoon, I had stood on the road for a long time and the next girl had not shown up. I badly wanted to pee, but I could not leave my station and flag unguarded. Finally the girl came and I ran to the nearest bathroom. For some reason I could not open my pants in time.

When I got home, there were tears in my eyes. It was a shame to wet my pants when I was in Grade Five. I angrily told Grandma that the pants she made for me had very tight openings for the buttons. She smiled, "You little fool. It's because your hands were frozen."

She washed me and brought me some hot soup. While I was warming up in her large blanket, she washed my pants and put them to dry over a big hot clay pot filled with embers. She murmured that she lived all her life without knowing any quotation of Mao and she was fine. I warned her that she talked like a counter-revolutionary but it seemed that she did not care.

In the cities, everybody participated in the Cultural Revolution: factories and schools stopped for several years. In the countryside, however, one hardly felt its impact. Peasants worked as hard as before and school resumed a year later.

In our Chinese classes, we mostly studied Chairman Mao's quotations from his little *Red Book*. Sometimes we studied his many poems, which were "as lofty as a thousand magnificent rainbows spanning in the blue sky." Every morning we had a one-hour session devoted to memorizing Mao's three essays: "Serve the People," "In Memory of Norman Bethune," and "An Old Man Moves a Mountain." After school, we would go to the fields to sing revolutionary songs to the peasants so that they could learn about Chairman Mao's ideas.

During the afternoon breaks, the peasants were supposed to learn how to sing and dance—to show their loyalty to Mao. Some peasants participated, but some stubborn ones never did. Before every meal, the whole family were supposed to pray: "Wish our great leader Chairman Mao to live for one hundred thousand years and Lin Biao Vice-Chairman ten thousand years." My grandpa prayed once before our lunch. We kids joined him, but my grandma started to eat without saying a word. I looked hard into her eyes, a way to tell her that I was angry with her, but she ignored me entirely. We never prayed again before meals.

From Grades Seven to Twelve, students were required to work in the fields during summer vacations. The rice fields were timed for two seasons every year. The first crop was planted at the end of April and harvested in the middle of June. All the seedlings for the second season needed to be planted in the last week of July to guarantee a forty-five day growth before the first chilly wind of September. As there were no machines, we hand planted the seedlings.

The big bell woke us right after the cock crowed the first time, about three o'clock in the morning. The team leader cried out, "All up, up! To the fields!" Sometimes there was moonlight to guide our sleepy steps. Other times we walked in the pitch dark, often slipping off the muddy ridges of rice paddies. Sitting on a wooden stool, we pulled the seedlings out and bound them into small bundles. To prevent any slacking, our team leader monitored our speed. At dawn, we loaded seedlings into bamboo baskets and carried them to their new homes. By noon the shallow water in the rice paddies was boiling hot; we kept planting. Toward the end of the day, our hands became swollen with red peeled spots from holding the wet, fertilized seedlings and our feet itched from standing in the rich soil for too long.

When the day finally ended, my grandma would wash my hands and oil them. She then fed me with a spoon while my grandpa put willow leaf juice on my toes to ease the itchy, burning feeling. Sometimes I would fall asleep before finishing my meal.

 It was a sleepless night full of remembrances of times past, of a childhood nurtured and guided, little knowing that millions of other childhoods in the cities were lost when their parents were tortured or jailed.

I was dozing off when I heard knocking at the door. "Time to get up, my dear," it was my grandma's familiar voice.

"Getting up, Grandma," I got up before she called me a second time, to show her that I could take care of myself so she wouldn't worry about me when I went to university.

I walked toward the lily pond by our front yard: it was greenish blue and very clear. I splashed some cool water on my face to wake up. The sun was rising, reddish-golden rays slanting to the crystal drops of water inside the big lily leaves. A group of mature mackerel jumped to catch a dragonfly that was happily skimming the surface of the clear water.

It was illegal to catch fish in the pond, but my brother and I had found a way. At the far end of our front yard, a narrow but long brook connected the pond with a lake. During the day, my brother would build dams with a small opening at both ends of a section of the brook. He then scattered chaff in the segregated section to attract fish. As soon as darkness fell, we closed the openings and drained out the water using a basin and a pail. My grandma encouraged us with food, drink, and fruits. It sometimes took us three or four hours to drain the little section of the brook, but it was worth the work: we could usually pick up several jin of carp and eel.

8

I walked to my small garden: the gardenia plant was growing bigger and bigger every day. I had watered it often in the summer and fertilized it with leftover soup. When the white flowers blossomed yearly in May and June, I could not wait to see how they were coming out each morning. I sometimes put a flower in my braids and a few in my pocket so I could feel and smell them in class. Whenever my brother had a fight with me, he would threaten to destroy my beloved gardenia plant. I hated him for understanding me so well and winning fights by playing dirty.

I watered my gardenia plant for the last time before my journey. Everyone walked me to the bus station half a mile away, except Grandma. She had bound feet and could not walk any distance. She had told me that in her time, bound feet was a virtue for girls. "When I was six years old, my mother began binding my feet with a six-foot long cloth. It was so hurtful that I could not walk or sleep. With tears in her eyes, my mother told me to hold my cries. 'My dear, it is unfortunate to be a girl and a woman. It's for your good. You will understand it when you grow up. A girl with big feet will not be able to marry a decent man.'"

My grandma told me that I was very, very lucky not to have bound feet, and that I could go anywhere. I told her that that was exactly what I wanted: To go anywhere I like!

Though she was smiling, I could see tears in her eyes. I took her wrinkled hand and pressed it on my cheeks. I whispered to her that I would be back in four months for the Chinese New Year.

It was my first time to go to the provincial capital city, Wuhan, and I was very excited. As the bus passed miles and miles of white cotton fields and golden rice paddies, I felt like a bird flying far and high. I congratulated myself: Thank God, I won't have to work in the fields for twelve hours a day anymore.

In about two hours, I started to see tall buildings and crowds of people. Our driver announced that we were now entering Wuhan, a city of four million people. Wuhan was made up of three cities: Hankou, Hanyang, and Wuchang. Hankou was the commercial centre, Hanyang the industrial area, and Wuchang the cultural centre where Sun Yat-sen rose to power in 1911. The three cities were separated by the Yangtze River and connected by the Yangtze Bridge. Miles away from the city proper, I saw heavy smoke in the direction of Wuhan Steel and Iron factory, one of the five major steel manufacturers of the country. Ai Hui, my high school friend worked there, and she had told me that their factory was nicknamed "The Ten-mile Red Steel City" because the sky looked reddish dark for ten square miles.

Every university had student volunteers meet new students at the bus and train stations. When I saw the sign "Wuhan First Normal University," my heart started to beat fast. I was soon in a school van with other new students driving to the campus in the suburb of Wuchang District. We were told that it took half a day to walk around the well-known Osmanthus Mountain and that our campus was situated within its layers of hilltops. As the van reached the mountain summit, we saw many old trees. Among them were Osmanthus trees in full blossom, the sweet scent filling the autumn air. We were told that ours was among the oldest and most beautiful campuses in the country and that before the Cultural Revolution it enrolled fifteen thousand students, though now we only had three thousand students. The Foreign Languages Department had the newest teaching buildings and modern teaching equipment because it used to hire several foreign language experts from Britain.

I was guided to a three-storey building with faded-red-painted wood floors and black tile roofs. The first and second floors were for the boys and the third for the girls. Each room had four low-high bunk beds, a long desk with many drawers, and seven chairs. In one corner was a basin stand which could hold fourteen wash basins. Evidently, the room was for seven girls. Outside the window was a square wooden frame for hanging wet clothes. Each floor had a communal washing room where we could take a shower and handwash our clothes. The pipes supplied only cold water. To take a shower, we would need to carry hot water from another building and mix it with cold water in a bucket. From time to time, the water supply would stop altogether.

While I was unpacking, someone called loudly in the corridor that I was wanted outside. It was Dan, grinning like a little boy, showing a tiny cigarette stain on his front tooth. It was so nice to see a familiar face in a new place.

"Welcome!" He was beaming. "What's your impression of the campus? How do you like your dorm?" He showered me with questions. I was dazzled with the new environment.

"I like it very much." I pointed out the window. "Our room is on the third floor; the third room from the left. Where is your dorm?"

"Right there, next to your building. Ours is on the second floor."

"It's a pity that we don't eat in the same kitchen. Our Chinese Language Department shares a kitchen with the Political Science Department. The guys in our department would rather eat in the same hall with girls from your Foreign Languages Department. There are a lot more girls in your department and the girls are lively and stylish."

"Who says?"

"Near the red, you become red; near the black, you become black; learn foreign languages, you become Westernized."

"Westernized? I don't think I will ever be."

"Not too fast. In a year or two. I hope you will still talk to me now that you are going to know many guys from all over the country."

"Of course, I will. We grew up in the same village."

"Behind your dorm are the Political Science and History Departments. Math, physics, and chemistry are on the south side of the campus. They have old teaching buildings and we call them country bumpkins."

A group of girls passed by, chattering and laughing loudly. Each carried a white-glazed bowl of eggplant on rice; the smell of hot food filled the evening air. Apparently they were the returning students of our department.

"Have you got your meal tickets yet?" Dan inquired.

"Not yet. I will get them tomorrow."

"Do you need anything? I have some spare soap."

"No. My father bought me two bars. He also got me some white sugar. Do you want some?" Soap was rationed, one bar per family per month. Sugar was also rationed, one jin per family per month.

"No. I am fine. You will need it, reading English from morning till night. Ginger and sugar tea is good for dry throat."

"Right. I ran into your Ma the other day. She sends word that you should quit smoking."

"Yes, yes, I will try. I promise I'll be a saint soon." Scratching his head awkwardly, he added, "How is she?"

"She is fine except for worrying about you." I looked him right in the eye, making him a bit uneasy.

"Ha, I am not three years old." He gave me a mischievous grin.

Searching for news from the village, I said, "You know Fang and your sister Rong are going out?"

"Yes, I saw signs last time I was home. Fang was hanging around Rong every day."

"It's good that Fang helps with the household chores while you are away."

"Yes, but my parents need Rong. I don't want her to get married so soon. You know Fang is a sly one. He may get Rong pregnant and then she will have to marry. She is naive and impulsive."

Actually there were murmurs in the village that Fang and Rong had been seen together late at night coming out of the cotton fields. Not wanting to upset Dan, I changed the subject. "How is your play coming along?" Dan had told me during his last winter vacation that he was writing a screenplay based on characters in our village.

"The first draft is almost done. I need another summer vacation to do some rewriting and polishing. I promise, you will be the first to read it when it's done."

"Am I in your play?"

"You will see when it's done. I want it to be a surprise."

"Okay. No more questions." I made a face.

"Your handkerchief." My little cotton handkerchief had fallen from my braids and Dan picked it up for me. While I was tying up my dishevelled hair, Dan said gently, "You must be tired. I'd better get going." He lingered for a second, then disappeared in the unfolding dusk. The last thatch of sunrays was dancing happily on the treetops and hilly grounds; I observed the huge campus expectantly, "Oh, university! Cradle of high learning! I am finally here!"

The following evening, all the new students, eighty-six English and fourteen Russian majors, met in a large lecture hall in the Foreign

Languages Department building. Our political instructor introduced himself and then divided us into six classes.

I was in Class Four and was appointed the monitor. Soon after, we went to our classroom to get to know each other. There were seventeen of us: ten girls and seven boys. Half the girls were from Wuhan, two from a county town, two from poor mountain areas, and one from a dreamy village—that was me. Three of the seven boys were from poor mountain areas, and four from county towns. The girls from Wuhan were better dressed, more sophisticated, and spoke Wuhan dialect, the most popular one. Those from the mountain areas spoke dialects that I could hardly understand. Since my grandma had taught me never to be afraid of new situations, I had no fear. I spoke calmly to our class, "From now on, we are one big family. We should help each other and care for each other."

We started with the English alphabet and political slogans like "We study hard for the revolution and the people." After the first class, our teacher informed me that she was having a very hard time with the boys and girls from the mountain areas. It seemed that their strong accent prevented them from pronouncing the English alphabet correctly. Once a person's major was decided, there was no way to change it. The people in charge of university enrolment had determined our major months before we came to campus. To be a teacher, especially a primary and middle school teacher, was a thankless job due to the disrespectful treatment teachers received during the Cultural Revolution. Only young people who did not have much "back door" were enrolled in a normal school. I was chosen to study English because I had "a good voice, could speak Mandarin, and learned some English in high school." I tried to argue that I liked math better, but in vain. A decision by the Party was final, no argument, period.

Besides studying, we were to work on the university farm for one day a week. Every Thursday morning, we lined up in six columns and walked the two miles to the farm. We cut sweet potato canes and dug sweet potatoes. They were huge and looked lovely.

"We need one person to help cook the sweet potatoes for lunch," our political instructor noted. I volunteered since I was the monitor and expected to do the dirtiest and heaviest work before everyone else.

The clay stove in the kitchen was three times larger than my grandma's. I tried to light the stove but the rice stalks were too damp. No matter how hard I tried, the fire would not start. Seeing my awkwardness, the chef passed me some old newspaper, and it worked. While I was feeding pieces of wood into the stove, the chef asked, "May-ping, have you ever cooked by yourself before?" He looked about fifty years old, a kind smile on his square face.

"My grandma would not let me because she didn't trust me."

I did not tell him what my grandma had said to me when I was nine years old.

The large stove in our home kitchen was made of dried mud. It was first moulded in wet mud and then dried out for a few days. The fuel for the stove was cotton and wheat stalks, so it was vital to keep the kitchen clean after cooking. Any stalks left near the stove could catch fire since the ashes were still "alive" long after the stalks stopped burning. To be on the safe side, my grandma sprayed cold water on the ashes before we went to bed every night.

One afternoon after school, I was starved, but my meal was not ready. While Grandma was stirring the vegetables in the wok, I fed some cotton stalks into the stove.

"Stop it!" she shouted.

"Can't you see I am helping you?" I shouted back.

"Sit on the bench and wait for your lunch." She passed me a cup of boiled water.

While I was drinking the water, she told me a terrifying story.

It happened many years ago when my grandma was thirteen years old. A friend of hers was home alone and craved fried dumplings. Not waiting for her mother to come home from working in the fields, she started the fire in the stove and fried a few dumplings. When she was about done, she heard footsteps outside the kitchen. In a panic, she pulled the half-burned cotton stalks out of the stove and threw them back to the fuel bin where many bundles of stalks were stored. Smoke and fire quickly spread through the kitchen. Only with the help of their neighbours did they manage to save the house.

"What happened to her?" I was scared.

"She was denied food for a week."

"Did she die of hunger?"

"No. But she became as thin as a cotton stalk and very ugly."

I remembered this story and constantly cleaned the kitchen from that day on.

"Is your grandma still alive?" the chef asked curiously.

"Yes."

"Does she allow you to cook now?" The chef laughed.

"No. She still doesn't trust me." I shook my head and smiled.

In addition to our weekly farm work, we devoted a week each term to digging air-raid tunnels. Should the Russians invade us from the air, we were prepared. First, the workers blasted the holes. We then carried the earth out of the tunnel so the workers could blast more the next day. I was not good at anything. The shovels were not sharp enough to cut the chunks of earth into smaller pieces and it took a tremendous amount of energy to lift the earth from the ground to the cart. I could not wheel the heavy cart either. Every time I got out of the damp and chilly tunnel, I felt lucky that I was still alive.

Only a week before my arrival at the site, a student from the Math Department was buried when the tunnel collapsed. His department held a grand funeral for him. First, his political instructor read quotations from Mao: "Our goal in life is to serve the people. Therefore, we are not afraid to die for the people. Death is a common occurrence in daily life. As long as we die for the people, our death is weightier than Mount Tai." Then, the political instructor enumerated the martyr's many good qualities, one of which was to work extra hours in the tunnel when one of his classmates was ill. "On the day of his death, he had worked for ten hours in a row. Although he has left us, his spirit will encourage us forever."

Despite all the glory showered on the boy, I did not want to be a martyr. Whenever possible, I would get out of the tunnel and work outside. By the end of the day, I was doggedly tired, aching all over as if my body were breaking to pieces.

To prepare the Chinese for possible Soviet invasion, university students were also required to learn to shoot. In October, we packed our luggage and took a train to an army camp three hundred miles northeast of Wuhan.

Our first lesson was to learn to stand still for an hour. Our eyes were looking to the front; hands down the midline of the pants; chests raised; abdomen stretched; legs in two straight lines, and feet in a triangle. By the end of the hour, I felt dizzy and stiff, walking back to our dorm like a piece of wood.

During the night, we could be randomly summoned by a whistle and had to get ready in five minutes for a sudden trip, like real soldiers in wartime. One night, we were woken by a piercing whistle. Quickly putting my clothes on, I packed my luggage and ran to the front of our dorm to line up. I got myself ready on time, but forgot to take my glasses. Next we ran to the bushes across a large field full of barricades to hide as if the enemy was coming. I almost stepped into a deep trench as we frantically ran across the fields. Probably the bright moon helped me, though I did not have time to look at it.

The late autumn days were sunny but chilly. From dawn till dusk, our task was to lie on the grass to practise shooting and throwing hand grenades.

One morning our army teacher observed that my eyes were very red and swollen. The doctor at the clinic told me to stay in bed for a week, but I still went for the final shooting test in the snow. I was told that I received good scores, but I could not have cared less.

Returning from the army camp in early November, I learned that my grandma had come to live with my uncle Xin, who had just moved from Beijing to Wuhan. Civilians were not allowed to move around, but army men were shuffled frequently to prevent the formation of strong regional forces that could threaten Mao's centralistic power. My uncle and his family lived in the provincial army headquarters, about a mile from our university.

As we had classes six days a week, I had to wait till Sunday, and Sunday finally came. I got up early, practised my English pronunciation for an hour at the hilltop in front of our dorm, and had my usual breakfast in the dining hall—two small wheat buns and a bowl of rice porridge with pickled cabbage. I was on my way to see Grandma!

The early November sun was deceptive: it looked warm but felt cold. To keep myself warm, I walked fast, reaching the high-fenced gate of the army headquarters in twenty minutes. The entrance was guarded by two young soldiers with long guns hanging on their right shoulders.

"Comrade, please show your identification," said a young soldier as he stepped out of the sentry box. Looking at his earnest face, I took out my student card, which did not seem to make him believe that I would do no harm to the headquarters. I was required to fill out a two-page form that asked at least fifty questions about me, my father, and my uncle. When the soldier looked at the title of my uncle, he became all smiling and polite.

I walked in at a leisurely pace. Along the main road were tall poplars and green lawns with flowerbeds here and there, amid which, was a magnificent three-storey stone building. Two majestic stone-carved lions were sitting in front of the main door.

A cobbled path led to the residential area behind the office buildings. From a distance, patches of green vegetable gardens could be seen. After asking several people, I finally found my uncle's apartment. Knocking loudly at the door, I called, "Grandma, open the door. It's me, May-ping."

"Coming, coming." Oh, how good it was to hear my grandma's voice!

Grandma was home alone. My uncle, his wife, and children were out shopping.

"Now, let me look at my university student granddaughter." She examined me from head to toe as if she had not seen me for centuries.

"Um, you are thinner." She then showered me with questions. "Do you have to study very hard? Are you getting enough sleep? Are your classmates nice to you? What kind of food does your university kitchen provide? And most of all, do you have boiled water to drink?"

"I am fine, Grandma." I did not know which question to answer.

"So, how do you like university?" Her eyes were still on my thin face. "Tell me some details, dear."

I told her about our fancy English record players and sang an English song for her. "Twinkle twinkle little star, how I wonder what you are. Up above the world so high, like a diamond in the sky…" I then translated the words into Chinese for her. She was quite amused.

"You know what, Grandma, our university has a three-storey library, and it has many novels in it. And many foreign novels too, some are translated into Chinese and some in English. I want to read them all, every one of them." I was thrilled, as I had never seen a library before.

Then she asked about my training in the army.

"I don't like it at all. It's a waste of time. Life in the army camp is very boring. The soldiers are obsessed with sex. They joke about each other's fiancées or wives all the time."

I also told her that I never want any of my sisters or my brother to join the army although it seemed fashionable and practical at the time, the benefit being a job offer after three years' service.

I did not dare to tell any of my classmates about my true feelings; I told her.

While sipping hot tea, I observed my uncle's three-bedroom apartment. The floor was shiny, red-painted wood, the bathroom modern, the kitchen spacious. They also had coal gas for fuel, whereas civilians used coal.

My grandma told me that the army headquarters had its own shopping centre with goods which were not available in other stores and a kitchen that provided delicious and inexpensive food.

My uncle's wife was a gynaecologist at a small clinic downtown. They had two children, the boy three, in preschool, and the girl, two, in daycare. My grandma's job was to cook dinner and look after the children when they came home.

In spite of all the privileges and materials, my grandma was not happy. She said that she missed the village very much.

In mid-January, a day before my winter vacation, I went to see her again. She was sitting in the sun warming herself and I touched her shoulders from behind. Helping her get up, we walked inside. As she was talking, I observed her. The tranquillity on her face seemed to have left. Her eyesight was failing. When she spoke, she was unsure of herself.

"I am useless; I am getting old," she said repeatedly.

"*She*, you know who, likes to talk, and everything she says is right. When she is home, I am a mute." I saw twinges of pain on my grandma's used-to-be calm face.

"*She* thinks my ideas are out of date. Even the children talk back when I ask them to put a sweater on."

It hurt me to know that my grandma was not treated with respect. My uncle was a bookish and kind man who had never learned how to argue or fight for his stand. He expected everyone to be reasonable and nice. His wife took care of the money and my uncle had no access to it when he wanted to buy things for my grandma.

"Would you like to go back to the village, Grandma?" I proposed gently.

"I wish I could." She sat down and continued. "*She* said that it's unfair for a mother to look after the children of the elder son but not the younger son. Here I am, ruled by my daughter-in-law. Oh, times have changed!"

In her time, it was just the opposite: mothers-in-law dominated daughters-in-law.

I boiled some warm water, washed my grandma's thin white hair and cut it for her. How I wished I could help her out of this predicament!

The next morning, my uncle took me to the bus station in Hanyang district across Yangtze Bridge. He bought me a bus ticket which cost two yuan and fifty fin. He told me not to let *her* know that he bought me the ticket, otherwise *she* would make a scene. I felt very sorry for my uncle and never again let him buy anything for me.

9

I WAS VERY HAPPY TO RETURN HOME after a four-month absence. As I had no money to buy gifts, I borrowed a pile of storybooks from our library for my sisters and brother. That evening I read to my sisters *The Snow Queen*, *The Little Match Girl*, and *The Ugly Duckling* by the Danish author Hans Christian Andersen. I also told them that Andersen was the son of a shoemaker. His family was very poor and he almost starved. Through hard work and persistence, he eventually became a novelist.

The following morning, Nan-ping, my second sister, told me that she knew why I read that story. The ugly duckling was her—the other girls in our family were slim and tall, but she was a little chubby. The other girls resembled our father and mother, but she resembled our grandma on my mother's side, who was considered plain.

"Like the ugly duckling in the story, I can change my station in life. I am going to study hard and get good marks. Then I can go to a good university; then I will get a good job; then I'll make big money; and then I'll give ten yuan to Mother every month. Isn't that grand?"

Nan-ping was only nine years old but talked like an adult. Looking at her dark shining eyes and determined face, I nodded approvingly.

Nan-ping told me that Chinese literature was her favourite class. During the two-hour lunch break, her teacher usually wrote down on the blackboard episodes from a novel for them to enjoy. Though it was not mandatory, Nan-ping copied them into a special notebook and read them after class.

"You are the only person to share my secret," she looked at me with trust. I could tell how much she was hurt by the neglect she received from our family members. The first three children received more attention and love than the last two. I was the eldest, then my brother, followed by my first sister Wen-ping who had a mild temperament and was considered exceptionally good-looking. When my brother tried to take my share of food or bully me, I would definitely fight back, though I knew I could not win most of the time. He was strong and good at fighting. Wen-ping never fought with him. Perhaps she figured that she did not have a chance to win anyway. The last two sisters were not well accepted because my parents were expecting sons. When my youngest sister was born, my father was so discouraged that he decided "that was it." From a very young age, the two youngest learned that they were not wanted.

After dinner, all the girls, four of us, were gathered together to read more stories when my brother ordered Nan-ping to make him some tea. When she did not move after the second order, my brother slapped her hard on the head. I started to argue with him; all my sisters were on my side. They said that my brother was a tyrant in the house. He could criticize or punch any of them for any or no reason at all. Even my mother was afraid of him. My mother worked all day in the fields and then cooked and cleaned at home. Sometimes she burned the food when she tried to do the washing while she was cooking. My brother would complain about the food and threaten to show it to our neighbours, which would be a loss of face for my mother. "None of us can get very far because father favours him," Wen-ping said angrily.

I remembered an incident when I was ten years old and my brother was eight. We were playing hide and seek when he bumped his head on the wood latch of our back door. He burst into loud crying; my father came over and slapped me hard on the head without asking a question. When my brother was sick, a doctor was fetched immediately no matter how late it was. When any of the girls was sick, there was no hurry. Sometimes, my father would not even bother to ask what was wrong. It was my mother who cared for the girls and gave us as much love as she could afford. She would have liked to give more, but she lacked both money and energy. Luckily, all of the girls were healthy, as tough as the small grass on the sidewalks of the village road.

About five days before the Chinese New Year, we began a general cleaning in the house. I spent a whole morning handwashing the four mosquito nets and then hung them to dry in the front yard.

The cotton nets were very heavy when wet. I washed them in warm water in a large wooden basin, then rinsed them in the icy cold pond. By the time I finished, my hands were frozen. My father, who had been sitting on a couch smoking for a couple of hours, saw a stain on one of the nets. He asked me to wash it again and I did. The stain would not completely go away. My father took a basin of warm water and some soap, and washed it himself. Sure enough, the stain was gone. I felt inadequate all day.

As a matter of fact, my father first noticed my inefficiency at housework when I was twelve. One summer afternoon, he asked me to cook some sweet potato soup as my grandma was visiting her brother's family on the other side of the Han River. Watching me chop the potatoes, he commented, "You don't look like you can do the job. Whatever your brother does in the fields or at home, he does it well." I tried hard to cut the potato the way my grandma did, but my arm was not strong enough for the heavy kitchen knife.

The Chinese New Year required special preparation of many foods. We needed to grind sweet rice flour on the stone grinder for cakes, grind soy beans for tofu, and prepare dozens of dish ingredients.

As cooking was women's work, my father and brother would join us when the food was ready. Their role was to sample our cooking and comment on our labours. If my father's remarks were favourable, my mother would feel very pleased. I told my brother that if he did not like the food, too bad. The earth would still turn in spite of him.

The feast came at the eve of the New Year. All our family members sat around a huge table and devoured fifteen or more delicacies. Before and after eating, we bowed three times to our ancestry altar, which was placed in the most important spot of our living room. In the midst of the burning incense, I heard my grandpa whispering, "Please, safe and sound for your filial offspring, all year round."

After the lavish meal, the children played while the adults chatted or played mah-jong till the small hours of New Year's Day. Early the next morning we were awakened by the loud noises of firecrackers. The villagers competed to see whose firecrackers were the loudest and lasted the longest. In the splendour of the firecrackers, the villagers solemnly saw the old year off and welcomed the New Year with high hopes of a bumper crop.

I arose early to make tea and prepare warm water for the family. This had been my mother's job for years, and before that it was my grandma's.

After tea and breakfast we were on our way to visit our grandparents on my mother's side. They lived about five miles away on the other side of the Han River. On the ferry, my father asked us to guess how we got our names.

Jing-ping responded quickly, "Because I am going to build a Jing Dynasty, right?" She moved to the middle of the boat and gestured us to kneel on the deck as if she were the emperor and we were the ministers. While Jing-ping was saluting back to her subjects, my brother squeezed her aside and took her emperor's seat. That was his old trick. He had taken our share of things since he was five, from good food to new cups. He would say, "Look, what's there?" When we looked in the direction he was pointing, he would snatch our share of food and run. By the time we caught up with him, he would have eaten it.

Gazing at Wen-ping's eager face, my father said, "You were only a month old when your mother and I carried you to your maternal grandparents' place for the first time. It's called 'getting the baby out of the cradle.' While crossing the Han River, we suddenly realized that we had not decided on your name. Watching the morning sun rising over the river, we named you Wen-ping, which means warmth and tranquillity." My father looked at Wen-ping thoughtfully. I did not know that my father could be so poetic.

"What's the meaning of Nian-Cai?"

"Your brother was born on the tenth day after the Chinese New Year. Anything good that happens at the beginning of the year is supposed to bring wealth. So we named him Nian-Cai, meaning that wealth will come every year." My mother looked at her only son with such pride as if he were the *meaning* of her existence.

None of us girls liked my brother's name because we did not think that material wealth was the most important thing on earth. We liked names with imagination and a poetic touch. All the children except my brother seemed to rebel against the old values.

My attention was distracted by the graceful movements of the ferryman. His weather-beaten face looked relaxed as his strong arms and large hands rhythmically moved the oars. The water was calm and the little ferry advanced fast. Suddenly a cargo ship full of coal came up.

"Please don't move while the ship is passing us. No matter how high the waves are, we will be fine if we stay still." The ferryman glanced at the ship and oared as usual. The passengers were quiet while the huge waves rocked our little ferry up and down. We took a deep breath when the waves finally receded.

The ferryman's calm face and wise words deeply imprinted in my mind. *No matter how dangerous the situation may be, if one remains calm, observes and thinks first before acting, one will survive*, I thought.

As the boat slowly landed, we saw our maternal grandparents at the dock waving to us. We called them Jia-Dia and Jia-Po meaning outside-grandpa and outside-grandma because we did not share their last name. Since Jia-Dia and Jia-Po had no son, they were afraid that they would have no one to look after them when they were in old age. Therefore, they gave half of their large house to the eldest son of my mother's uncle.

Their adopted son, Hong, had eight children, five sons and three daughters. The boys had a few years of education, the girls did not. Chickens and ducks shared their house and sometimes their pig would walk in the living room. When we passed their place, Hong asked us to come in and have tea. To be polite, we stepped in for a few minutes, then excused ourselves to Jia-Dia and Jia-Po's place. Their home was clean and warm. My mother's parents grew silk worms and made silk, which they sold in the market.

After a delicious meal, Jia-Dia told us that he had intended to send my mother to school when she was seven but Jia-Po would not have it. She did not want my mother to be out of her sight for fear that something harmful might happen to her only daughter. While speaking, he stole a teasing look at Jia-Po who rolled her dark eyes and assumed her usual contentious role with him. She had a kind heart but a slow mind. Over the forty years of their married life, Jia-Dia had learned both to accept and to ignore her argumentative ways.

I could not imagine how my mother had looked when she was seven, but I remembered how she looked when she was in her mid-twenties. She was tall, slim, and fair skinned. Her cheeks were a natural rose matched with cherry lips and white teeth. When she walked, her two black braids bounced on her waist like the two wings of a butterfly. She often wore a pair of gold earrings and a satin jacket.

"Oh, how she has aged!" I glanced at my mother who had several wrinkles on the corners of her dark eyes. She now wore her hair short. Her gold earrings were taken away in 1964 when the Four Cleansing Movement started in our village.

Looking at each of us lovingly with his glistening dark eyes, Jia-Dia continued that my mother never worked in the fields when she grew up. That was why he hesitated to marry her to my father. But the go-between was an eloquent woman and he was persuaded at last.

"Here you are," he gently rocked Jing-ping, my youngest sister, who was perched on his lap. "If I had not agreed to let your mother marry your father, none of you would be born." He was tall and strong, and had a great sense of humour.

"I might be better off to be born in another family," Jing-ping retorted with her silver-bell voice.

"Okay, all my grandchildren will receive a five-yuan gift but you. What do you think of this idea, Jing-ping?" Jia-Dia laughed. When he laughed, his face was as happy as a child's. They wanted us to visit often, but the distance was a hardship to walk as there were no buses.

When I was ten, my mother sent me to visit Jia-Dia and Jia-Po by myself. I knew the way on our side of the river, but not after I crossed on the ferry. I finally found their place after asking many people along the way. Right after dinner, I became homesick.

"I want to go home, Jia-Dia!" I announced.

"May-ping, dear. It's too late to go home now. The hungry tiger in the woods will eat you up if you walk in the dark," Jia-Dia teased me.

Hearing that I could not go home that evening, I started to cry.

"I want to go home, I want to go now!" I stamped my feet in their front yard.

"I will send you home as soon as the day breaks tomorrow morning," Jia-Dia coaxed.

"I haven't brought any clean clothes with me. I didn't know I couldn't go back on the same day." I temporarily stopped crying.

Jia-Po said that she could borrow some clean clothes from the girl next door. I said that I did not want to wear anyone else's clothes because they smelled.

By dusk, several friends and cousins of my mother's came to see me and they brought their children with them. I was fascinated by the small bird eggs offered by the twin sisters, Da-ma and Shao-ma. They were about my age but taller and stronger than me. I had known them since I was five when my mother took me to see their mother during Chinese New Year. While our mothers were busy playing mah-jong, we ran around and played hide-and-seek in a small cave where sweet potatoes were stored.

Da-ma had her thick, dark hair in two braids, whereas Shao-ma and I had our fine, brown hair cut to shoulder length. To show our admiration for Da-ma's long braids, we would tie them to the arms of the chair she was sitting on. Of course we would each receive three fists in return for our misplaced admiration.

It was hardly daybreak when Da-ma and Shao-ma came to wake me the next morning. We ran to the woods hand in hand and climbed to the top of the old willow trees looking for nests. Near noon, we captured several nests with baby birds just coming out of the eggs. We put them in a cage and fed them millet.

Resting on the riverbank, we watched cargo ships coming and going on the broad Han River. The water was sandy yellow and full of fast swirls.

"Can you cross the river from here?" I squinted at them.

"Only in the mornings and evenings," Shao-ma replied absent-mindedly.

"Don't take the ferry from here. They are bewitched." Da-ma looked serious.

"How so?"

"You see, Yan-xin's father, our next door neighbour, was drowned here last month." Shao-ma shook her head while narrating the sad news. "He was not even on duty that morning. Someone couldn't make it so he was called to work. When his ferry was near shore, a sudden gust of wind made several high swirls around his boat. He lost control and his boat capsized. There were twelve people on the boat and they all swam to shore except him. You see, they built their house last spring and the front door was facing the west, bad *feng sui*!"

"Because of the unfortunate *feng sui*, Yan-xin lost his eye-sight last fall."

"How?"

"Yan-xin and my brother were filtering the grains on the threshing ground of our production team when a huge surge of wind made a dust swirl around them." Da-ma and Shao-ma talked in turn and with such a fast pace that I could hardly keep up. "For a moment, they felt like they were lifted to the air and thrown to the ground. The wind was gone in a few seconds but Yan-xin's eyes were swollen and red. He couldn't open his eyes for the whole afternoon and when he finally opened them, he couldn't see a thing. My brother was right there and he was fine."

Just then, a sudden wind stirred the sand and dry leaves. We heard a dull whistle in the woods. Getting up, we ran like crazy. When we ran past the old house of Peng-Po, we were stopped.

"What are you up to?" She looked at us with stern eyes and questioning eyebrows. Peng-Po was about sixty years old, with disarrayed long white hair. When she spoke, her mouth was a black pit except for two yellowish front teeth.

"Ha, this is Ying-Di's daughter." Her red-veined eyes fell on my face and she smiled, which frightened me a little. Coming down the stone stairs from her front door, she took me by the hand. She sat down, put me in front of her, and examined me from head to toe.

"Um, you don't look like your mother. You are a copy of your father. You know I'm the one who made the happy match for them." She looked like a witch; I took my hand away from her. "Of all the matches I have made, your parents are the happiest couple. Now come and thank me." She laughed loudly with self-indulgent satisfaction while grasping my hand again.

I wanted to say, *You have ruined my mother.* Instead I looked at her with a question mark in the form of a big frown, as big as I could make. She seemed puzzled.

My father loses his temper at my mother all the time, I shouted at her with my inner voice. Breaking her grip, I ran away with Da-ma and Shao-ma.

When we were at a safe distance, Da-ma and Shao-ma whispered to me that Peng-po had Guan-ying, the female Buddhist shrine, inside her. Anyone wanting to talk to a dead relative could get through by way of Peng-Po's abdomen.

"You see her bulged belly? That's it. That's where Guan-ying is hiding."

"The visitor sits on a chair in Peng-Po's room while Peng-Po sits inside her mosquito net in a lotus posture murmuring requests for the dead relative to come." Da-ma had quite a mysterious look about her.

"You have to be very patient because it takes a while for Peng-Po to find your dead relative and another while for the dead to cross the border of the *ying* and *yang* worlds. Sometimes one has to bribe the border guards just like in our *yang* world," Da-ma continued.

Shao-ma finally got some words in edgewise. "Last week my mother got to talk to her mother who died last year. Grandmother said that she needed money so my mother bought a pile of rough yellow paper with punched holes and burned it to my grandmother."

I thought of what my grandmother once said about sending *ying* money to the dead: "You have to burn the 'money' after midnight because that's when ghosts come out. The difference between the living and the dead is very small. The dead sleep through the night and day whereas the living wake up in the morning."

My grandma also said that she wished to sleep through and never wake up so she would not have to bear my grandpa's bursts of temper. Whenever my grandpa lost his temper at her, I would follow her around fearing she might kill herself like my great grandmother did. Sometimes my grandma called me a dear and other times a nuisance. But she said the latter in such an affectionate tone that I knew she would rather like to have me as a nuisance.

I was still deep in thought when we reached Da-ma and Shao-ma's house. Da-ma took out a honeydew melon and *Cha!* Her fist split the melon into three pieces and we each had one. Their house was spacious with tall willows in the front and back yards. We sat on the stone stairs eating melon and waiting for the sun to enter the door—that was the time when adults came home for lunch.

In the next few days I visited several households, some big and clean, and others small and messy.

It seemed that the villagers did not care much about the collective. Many worked on their own; some profited by making nice silk, and others made fishing nets and sold them in other villages. Their pace of life was slow and relaxed. And they were even friends with the landlord family in the village.

One day I was very shocked to hear them cursing Mao for his bad leadership, saying that they were better off before he came to power in 1949. It seemed that they were not at all worried about being reported. They said it very loudly on the big dam where many other villagers were also present. Puzzled, I started to observe them more carefully.

As time went by, I discovered that the Peng clan was the largest in that area, and my mother was a Peng. *No wonder they treat me so well.*

For the first time in my life I felt I belonged. In my village, the Zhao clan only had seven families, and we were often ostracized by the Yians who comprised twenty-five of the thirty-six households.

I started to like the people and the woods, which pleased Jia-Da and Jia-Po immensely. Every day they cooked different dishes for me. When Jia-Da went to sell his silk in the market, he would buy water lily seeds or preserved duck eggs for me. He believed that the summer heat could get into my system and that the preserved eggs would cancel the heat out.

From that summer on, I often visited Jia-Da and Jia-Po and spent part of my summer and winter vacations with them.

On the second day of the Chinese New Year, my Auntie Mei's sons and daughter came to visit us. On the third day, my father's friends came to play cards. My mother cooked many dishes for them and we girls worked as waitresses. On the fourth day, the villagers, dressed in their new clothes, invited each other for tea or dinner. They wished each other best wishes—happiness and wealth, ideally coming hand in hand.

Those few days were the only holidays for the peasants. Unlike city dwellers, they had no Sundays off.

10

WHEN I RETURNED TO WUHAN, I took my grandma her favourite snack: fried sweet rice chips. She confided to me that she missed chatting with her village friends.

"Here I am like a prisoner. I know only one person and have no one to talk to. The girl next door who is taking care of her brother's children comes from Zhao Yang County. I don't understand her dialect and she does not understand mine. We can only nod and smile at each other." There were tears in her eyes. My grandma was a strong woman and I seldom saw her weep. I held her hands for a long time and left for school.

After the first semester, I declined the position of monitor. But I had to take some position as a Party member. My new job was to collect the monthly fee for the Youth League organization for the six classes, a high position with little responsibility, and I liked the idea.

I soon found myself lonely in the crowd. Although I was with my classmates every day, I dreamed of home every night. My classmates from the cities were very different from me. They treated others with guardedness, whereas I treated people with trust and kindness; I was brought up that way and did not know any other.

One cheerful Monday during lunch hour we were chatting about fashion in our dorm. I commented that apple green would look good on Zhang-fen, a tall girl standing beside me. Our new monitor warned me immediately, "Comrade Zhao May-ping, you are a Party member. Be careful about what you say." I instantly shut up and nodded at my monitor to indicate my gratitude for her warning.

In those days, colourful clothes were not encouraged. Mao said that Chinese youth should not love good clothing, but rather good weapons to protect our country. From 1966 through the 1970s, the army uniform was the most popular dress among young people, and army green was the most revolutionary colour. Seldom did girls or women wear bright colours or skirts. In our English Department, a few brave girls wore skirts, but only in black.

Sunday evenings, all six classes met in the departmental lecture hall. Our political instructor summarized our performances over the past week. He would praise some students; criticize others, and warn a few.

Tuesday afternoons were designated for political activities, including a thorough study of all five volumes of Mao's articles. I found his war articles very boring so I would put both hands on my cheeks and daydream to pass the time. In order to show that I seriously studied Mao's articles, I wrote down some paragraphs from here and there. When I was asked to write political essays, I quoted those paragraphs with specified page numbers and article names, which greatly impressed our political instructor. He asked me to become a member of the political essay writing team and told me, "You have talent writing political essays. Your articles are to the point and succinct. What is more, you can write an article in an hour, a speed needed for our revolutionary cause."

I was embarrassed by the compliment and accepted the job with no hesitation. In fact, I would not dare to decline. Now I had to sacrifice another evening writing political essays. A glorious task!

On Thursday mornings, we had political economics classes, in which we studied Marx's *Communist Manifesto* and *Das Kapital*. We also studied Hegel and Lenin. We were taught that the communist system was the ideal in which everyone was truly equal: "People work because they enjoy working and goods are allocated according to the needs of the individual. There is no exploitation and oppression of the poor."

Our instructor was in his forties, with short hair, a style considered out of fashion. He wore a pair of old cotton patched shoes that slipped off from time to time as he walked back and forth on the lecturing stage.

Thinking about his communist ideal and looking at his shoes, I could not help chuckling. He noticed me and asked, "Do you have something to say?"

"No, No. I enjoy your lecture enormously." I made a face.

He looked around and no one expressed any desire to talk, so he continued his lecture. I could tell that he was dying to have a dialogue instead of a monologue. However, most of the students either dozed off or did homework for other classes. I felt genuinely sorry for the instructor.

I loved our weekly physical education class. We learned gymnastics; played basketball or volleyball. Though I was not very strong, I was fast and agile. During one of the sessions, our teacher asked me if I ever tried gymnastics or ballet when I was young.

"No. I never thought I could make a living out of it." He seemed to be a nice person so I told him the truth. He said that it seemed a waste of such a good figure. I shrugged, did a three-step throwing-in, and the ball went into the basket.

Friday evenings we had thought cleansing sessions. Everyone was supposed to criticize oneself or somebody else. These criticism meetings made students very careful about what they said and did. Nobody trusted anybody. When I went to bed each evening, I recollected my day's behaviour, making sure that I did not say or do anything wrong. The three faults for which I was mainly criticized were: (1) reading books at our Tuesday afternoon mass meetings, (2) forgetting to wash my own bowl after meals, and (3) folding my blanket not in a nice square but in a rectangle.

At one session, Lin Bo, the "backward" student in our class, raised a criticism against the Party leader Kang-hua, who was from the army and very popular with the political instructor. Lin Bo said that Kang-hua seemed to like one particular girl more than others in the class. A Party leader was not supposed to show favouritism.

Kang-hua stood up in his esteemed green army uniform; his thin face twitched, narrow eyes flaming and judicious voice quivering with agitation: "Comrade Lin Bo, you must be more specific about what you are saying. To like a girl is no trivial thing. You must specify what kind of relationship I have with her and offer your evidence to prove it."

"I did not say that you and Du-hong have any mysterious relationship. I only feel that something seems to be going on between you two. I know that she bought you some sugar once and some fruit another time. Why didn't she buy me any? Because you have power and she wants to join the Party. And you like her, too. Isn't that true? Do you still remember Chairman Mao's teaching? He says that we should always accept criticisms with modesty. If we are in the wrong, we correct our mistakes; if we are not wrong, we learn to avoid them. You are a Party member, and I am sure you know Mao's teaching better than I do."

Lin Bo's discourse was flawless from any and every revolutionary perspective. An almost discernible scornful grin crept over his distinct pale face as he slowly sat down.

Lin Bo's dramatics were utterly satisfying. I held in my gladness and discreetly observed my classmates. The whole classroom seemed engulfed with excitement; some were rapturous in secret because they detested Kang-hua and Du-hong's foul play, and a few were rigorously shaking their heads to demonstrate their unshakable loyalty to the Party.

Our political instructor's guideline was to make every class a united collective. Lin Bo and Kang-hua each made some self criticisms and were told to forgive each other. On the surface, the incident was settled but I knew that Kang-hua would avenge Lin Bo someday.

Some Tuesday afternoons we would gather in the university auditorium to have criticism meetings. For the first three months of the year, the target was a vice-president of the university named Tong. A few months later, the target changed to the man who had criticized Tong, and Tong chaired the meeting. We all knew that Tong was a follower of Vice-Premier Deng Xiao-ping and that his opponent was on the side of Jiang Qing, Mao's wife. The campus was full of political slogans hanging over the main roads, a reflection of the fierce power struggle in the central government during the days when Mao was very ill.

In January 1976, Premier Chou En-lai died of cancer. We were summoned to the sports ground where many loudspeakers were located. After the sad music and the news, we started to weep. Some cried loudly; others sobbed sorrowfully. I shed some tears, but that was all I had for someone I had never met or read about. Fearing that not having enough tears might get me into trouble, I tried to think of the saddest part in a novel such as the time when Tess was parting with Angel after he told Tess that he was leaving for Brazil without her. Tears ran down my cheeks because I sympathized with Tess. She loved Angel more than herself and in the end he treated her so badly. Poor Tess was left to do hard work on a farm, digging turnips in the biting cold in order to make some money for her poor parents and younger siblings. Thomas Hardy was a magician and he helped me out.

By the end of my first year in university, I had developed a habit of hiding from my classmates. In the mornings, I usually went to the top of the hill in front of our dorm to practise my English pronunciation and intonation. In the afternoons, I liked to go to the garden to read Charles Dickens, Jane Austen, and William Thackeray in simplified English versions. If somebody passed by, I would take out my textbook. To be different from others could bring me trouble.

Another good place to hide was the tiny English tape recording room, where I listened to stories or daydreamed. I did not understand why I could not make myself belong. I tried shopping with other girls a few times, but found it not rewarding at all. The time waiting for each other was usually longer than the time to buy the few things I needed. I did not mind doing things with others, but I did not want to waste time. Ever since I was three, my grandma had taught me the value of time: "An inch of time is worth an inch of gold, but an inch of gold can't buy an inch of time."

Besides wasting time, to be with a group had another potential danger: being reported. In order to join the Party, some students would do anything: flirt with the Party secretary, report others on false grounds, or criticize others to show how "red" they were.

I also disliked the many meetings, especially when I had to listen to the same central government document three times. The first time, the party members listened; the second time, the student cadres listened, and the third time, all students listened. Unfortunately, I had membership in all three.

In order to save some of my time, I developed a habit of dozing off at meetings. With one hand on the arm of the chair, one hand covering my eyes in the direction of the speaker, I could take a good nap. They could not criticize me because no one could be sure whether I was asleep or listening with my eyes closed.

11

SUMMER VACATION FINALLY CAME. I was back to the embrace of my lily pond for comfort and inspiration.

Lying on the deck under the puzzling stars, I asked, "Do you think I should change? To become popular with the Party and live without a soul?"

Silence, silence, and silence.

I gazed at the lilies under the soft moonlight; they were gracious, aloof, and resilient.

I found my answer in the powerful silence of the water, in the serene strength of the lilies.

Gradually, the clear, green water soothed my wounded soul and nurtured my spirit back. I started to read in a leisurely fashion.

I read a Russian fable of a Tile Wok and a Steel Wok. Before the two started a long journey together, they decided that neither should desert the other no matter what. After half a day's journey, the Tile Wok grew very tired and could not continue. The Steel Wok waited and waited until his food and energy ran out. They died together. The lesson was that two incompatible people could never make a journey together through to the end.

Fables had long been my friends. I remembered the story of a bookish man and a wolf. Mr Dong-guo was on his way home from a trip when a wolf approached him: "Mr Dong-guo, please save my life. The hunter is after me." Mr Dong-guo took his books out of his bag, let the wolf into the bag and put it on the back of his donkey. When the hunter came by and asked if he had seen a wolf, Mr Dong-guo shook his head.

In no time, the wolf started to shout, "Let me out! I can't breathe here." Mr Dong-Guo let him out accordingly. The wolf stretched his neck and asked if Mr Dong-Guo could save his life another time.

"How?" Mr Dong-Guo was puzzled.

"Let me eat you and your donkey." Now Mr Dong-guo started to regret: "I should never have saved the life of a wolf."

Fables are allegories of life. To be acquainted with them, we hope to gain insight and reduce the number of mistakes we make in life. However, my book wisdom seemed to have its limits in dealing with wolf-like humans in real life.

I read during the day and visited old friends in the evenings. The first person I visited was Rong. She had recently written me that Fang had proposed and they were getting married soon.

A few months earlier, Fang had written me a poem in which he described himself as a weed and me as a flower.

"Although the fate of a weed and flower may differ, they nevertheless grow in the same soil and share the same spring." I knew how bitter he felt about his fate: to be a peasant for life. According to Mao's classification, his family belonged to the upper middle class, which automatically disqualified him from going to university. Although he did not dislike being a peasant, he wanted to try his talents in other things. In my reply, I said that I understood his ambition as well as his disappointment. For some reason, I never mailed the letter; it still lay in my desk drawer. Maybe it did not sound convincing to myself.

During the first few weeks at university, I constantly missed the frank discussions with Fang. Sometimes on campus, when I saw someone who looked like him, I wished he were among us.

Rong and I met at the entrance of a newly built bridge over the Han River. Though the steaming heat of the day had subsided, the concrete surface of the bridge was still panting with warm breath. The cool breeze from the river was comforting—it carried the smell of the tranquil land. Somewhere a water buffalo cried happily and lazily, perhaps flirting with a cow and wrestling in the cool muddy water of a brook. The loud chattering of the villagers, like a flock of sparrows, could be heard a mile away. Except for the moon, the stars, and the bouncing river, we were all alone—the villagers did not take sentimental walks. Oh, it was so nice to be home!

"Rong, tell me what to do." I looked at her oval face and poured out my dilemma.

"Should I give up my innocence which nature has bestowed upon me?" I looked at her. She was processing my sentences as fast as she could.

"Okay, how do you think I should appear to be: pretentious or truthful?" I was ready to argue with her should she take either stand.

She shook her head after some serious thinking. "I don't know. I do not like hypocrites but society requires us to be hypocritical." She put her right hand on her head and looked up to the pale sky as if searching for an answer there.

"The problem is that I can't be like that: always say things correctly; do things without a flaw, and sell my soul to please our political instructor and my classmates. I don't know how I can ever do that." I lifted my face and gazed at the silent moon.

Legend has it that there is a pagoda tree in the moon, under which the fairy Sang-er sits in a lotus posture. In her dainty hands is a six-colour glazed pottery bowl filled with osmanthus-flower wine. If you look at fairy Sang-er with a sincere heart, she will bestow a drop of her age-old wine on you. After you drink her wine, all your distresses will disperse into the clouds.

Oh, fairy Sang-er, please bestow upon me a drop of your wise wine!

"Some people can." Rong pulled me back to reality. "Sun-bin's girlfriend Yang-yang exchanged her body for a place in a good university. After achieving her goal, she ditched Sun-bin."

"Umm." I hardly knew what to say.

"Sun-bin put big posters in front of the brick factory where Yang-yang's father is the director. Sun-bin said that Yang-yang's father has taught his daughter to deceive Sun-bin's feelings by writing him love letters and poems. As soon as she got what she wanted, she threw him away like a wet rag."

I kept nodding while Rong told me the gossip. I did not tell her what had happened between Sun-bin and me. It was not necessary.

She paused for a while then continued, "Nowadays, people will do anything to get out of the countryside. Ding-yi is engaged to Sun-bin's brother who is an imbecile and works in the Wuhan Iron and Steel Factory. There is no doubt that Ding-yi will go back to Wuhan this year. A good move, eh? Marry some idiot."

I could not believe my ears. I despised Sun-bin. He used his father's power to get a girlfriend for his brother?

"Do you still remember Fong-yi?" I nodded. "She has adopted the brother of our Party secretary to be her sugar daddy. Who knows what kind of relationship they have? I heard that her sugar daddy has slept with most of the women in his village. Fong-yi got a job in town, you know."

Rong looked down as if feeling ashamed of these ugly behaviours among the people we knew. She seemed in a trance.

 Walking back home on the country road, I was at a loss. I felt out of place in Wuhan, the city. I had come back to find my childhood dreams, but they were gone. Reality was so cruel that we were not sure if we could keep our faith and soul any more.

When I said goodnight to Rong in front of her house, she pointed to the lights in Dan's window. "My brother is still up. Would you like to say hello to him?"

I knocked at his window pane.

"Hi, May-ping, come in." He craned his head behind the window.

Although we were at the same campus, we seldom saw each other. The conduct code for university students specified no dating. If we were seen together, we would be suspected of dating and punished severely.

I saw a notebook on his desk. Apparently he was writing something.

"You were deep in thought?" I teased him.

"Actually, I was." His expression intense.

After a pause, he said, "Socialism is not working well in China, although it is a beautiful idea. Everyone is equal and goods are allocated based on needs. But some people have more needs than others and some are more equal than others."

He passed me some tea and poured himself a cup.

"You see, the problem is that this theory does not agree with human nature. Human beings are greedy. A person has power, money; he always wants more, more! Do you know anyone who wants to share power?" He looked me in the eye.

"Me. I don't want power. When a person does not know how to handle power, it becomes a headache." I talked from my experience of being a director of the women's health centre when I was barely eighteen years old.

"Ha, you are an exception." Gently he pinched my nose and smiled. His smile seemed to say, "You have made a good argument and I like that."

"But exceptions don't overthrow my theory," he defended his ego.

"Be careful. Don't let anyone know your profound theory. It could get you into jail." He nodded gravely.

When he walked me home, the moon was high and half "eaten" by clouds. The village was asleep but the fields were wide awake. Frogs were chirping vigorously. Roots of the cotton plants were stretching deeper into the moist soil. New leaves were opening to fresh dew. The night air was chilly but I was wrapped with warmth—the warm feeling of Dan's shoulder touching mine from time to time as we strolled side by side.

Approaching the empty lot where Lan-ann's house used to be, I suddenly remembered something.

"Dan, do you know that Lan had a crush on you when you were in Grade Four?" I recalled what Lan had told me the evening before she left for Sha-hu a few years back. Now that she was dead, I felt an obligation to relay her message.

"No. No idea. Lan was shy and quiet. I hardly ever talked to her." He was lost in thought.

Scratching his head, he continued, "Her life was such a tragedy. The girls bullied her all the time. I rarely saw her laugh the four years we were in the same class."

"A society that takes laughter away from innocent children is ailing." I caught myself talking like Dan and that took me by surprise. *That's dangerous! Remember never talk like that with anyone else*, I heard my inner voice warning.

"Not just her laughter. It took her life." Dan was agitated. "Injustice and cruelty," he sighed.

Suddenly he seemed to remember something and said emphatically, "Mao once said that old China had tumours, so he launched a revolution to make it healthy. Now our new China has developed tumours as well. Only they are a different kind. It's up to us young people to do something about it." His eyes were glazed and his whole being charged with patriotism and youthful idealism.

At this moment, we heard a cough from a distance. Without looking I knew it was my grandpa. He was a chain-smoker and had a specific hoarse cough. He was coming home from his evening card game in the village meeting room.

Dan hurriedly said goodbye to me with a meaningful look and sauntered home.

That night I slept fitfully. In my dream I saw Lan running to me, in her twelve-year-old form and sky-blue cotton shirt. She was laughing and shouting excitingly, "Our family is in the Poor Class! My grandfather smoked opium and sold all our land just before the revolution." She held both my arms and we jumped up and down with joy!

My body quivered and I woke up. In reality, the opium story was our family story, narrated to me when I was fourteen years old, waiting for the good news of being accepted to Mian Yang First Senior High.

Oh, fate! I was favoured while Lan was cast away! How fate had exerted a cruel hand on Lan! The image of the two characters made up of the word fate, *ming yun*, kept hovering over my mind. *Ming yun* takes in the sum of chances, negative and positive, *ying* and *yang*, at any given time before and after a person is born.

12

IN THE GRIM AFTERNOON OF SEPTEMBER 9, 1976, every student and staff member was summoned to the university auditorium. The loudspeaker started with very sad music; I realized that another high-ranking official had died. The stage was vacant except for a gigantic portrait of Chairman Mao flanked by two red flags. A male broadcaster's deep, low voice solemnly announced, "Our great leader Chairman Mao has passed away at the age of eighty-three."

"Wra…" After a few seconds of stunned shock, the mass burst into loud cries and sobs as if the sky had collapsed. Waves of sorrow, genuine and fake, engulfed the auditorium. I buried my face in my arms and wept for a few minutes.

Mao brought independence to China. He also raised the social status of women.

Rapid thoughts were fleeting through my mind. His blunders: the Great Leap Forward, the Cultural Revolution, and the persecution of millions of innocent people.

These reflections put an abrupt stop to my tears. Stealthily I looked up and saw that everyone else was still vigorously sobbing and weeping. I quickly buried my face in my arms again, this time, to pretend crying. I twitched my head intermittently for a dozen times while waiting for the hall to quiet down. But the wailing did not stop. On the contrary, it became louder as if the whole place was bewitched.

About half an hour later, the crowd started to disperse in an orderly fashion. Some people were still sobbing uncontrollably. They must be either very naive or very Red. The Reds had a great deal to grieve for. Without Mao, they would never have made it to university, as they had never passed their grade school exams. Thanks to Mao's continuous political movements, the Reds were always in fashion. Now their brilliant careers were in shambles because these people had learned absolutely nothing in school other than how to denounce others.

While we were walking dejectedly to our dorm, a girl from the next class whispered to me that she had heard people say, "You lose some and you win some." I was very shocked at her bold comments, and hushed her to stop.

That night we were up till midnight making white paper flowers to show our loyalty and condolence.

In the following month, many important changes occurred in the central government. First the Gang of Four, headed by Mao's wife, Jiang Qing, were exposed and arrested. A minor actress in Shanghai, Jiang Qing had found her way to Yian-an, where Mao and his army headquarters resided in the 1930s. She attracted Mao's attention, and soon became Mao's third wife. Mao arranged to send his second wife for psychiatric treatment to a Moscow hospital, his first wife being killed by the Kuomintang a few years earlier.

During the Cultural Revolution when Mao ousted the state chairman, Liu Shao-qi, Jiang Qing seized her opportunity to gain control over the whole country. Using Mao's influence, she monopolized the Ministry of Culture. From 1966 to 1976, the only plays allowed in theatres throughout the country were her eight exemplary Beijing operas. She and her three close followers came to be known as the "Gang of Four."

Three months after Mao's death, Deng Xiao-ping, a close follower of the late State Chairman Liu Shao-qi, obtained power. The situation changed rapidly: the strict university entrance examination was to be resumed; university curriculum was changed back to four years; efficiency became the slogan in factories, and each peasant family was allowed a plot of land, still owned by the state, to till and to look after.

I no longer needed to hide the novels I borrowed from the library. I could study without being criticized for "being white," not "red." Now we were encouraged to be both "red" and "expert" in our major. To be "red," we still had our Sunday evening summary, Tuesday evening Party member meeting, Wednesday afternoon three-speak out, and Friday evening thought-cleansing session. To become "expert," we studied during the minutes and seconds when we were meeting-free.

Although Mao was dead, his thoughts still lit the way for the Chinese for several more years. According to Mao, intelligentsia who only cared about their studies were "white," and should take time to learn about what was going on politically—to be "red." No "red" was too red, but being "white" would be criticized.

Several "rightist" professors were now allowed to return to campus after years of working on our university farm. At a departmental meeting, our political instructor introduced a rightist to us. The rightist was asked to stand at the back of the meeting room so we could all see him. His name was Hufeng and he looked about fifty-five years old. He had studied English literature at Stanford University in the 1940s and returned to China after the new republic was formed in 1949 with the hope of contributing to his home country. He was labeled rightist in 1956 because he cared only about his teaching, not the political progress of the Party. Mao said that he would rather have revolutionary illiterates than counter-revolutionary intelligentsia. Hufeng was sent to raise pigs on the university farm. Now, twenty-six years later, he had come back to work as a researcher. Our political instructor advised us to watch him closely and not to talk to him so that his bourgeois ideas would not poison our healthy minds.

Human minds have a natural tendency to try the forbidden. A few bold students secretly visited his lab. He told them about his life in the United States and lent them a novel, *Gone with the Wind*, which was banned because of its description of sex and love. Only Mao's wife Jiang Qing and officials in the central and provincial government had access to these kinds of movies and novels, as they were not as susceptible as the ordinary people. We all read *Gone with the Wind* in secret.

Lin Bo had the most contact with Hufeng. It seemed that Lin Bo was not afraid of our political instructor either.

One Tuesday morning, just as we were finishing the second class, our political instructor came to our classroom to talk about some serious matter. "This morning," he started, "something very bad happened." We held our breath.

"Someone in your class broke the glass door of my room and dumped a pile of garbage on the floor. It's everywhere: my bed, my desk, and even my bookshelf. I know it is a person from your class, because there is a piece of paper in the garbage with Class Four on it. I believe I know who the person is, but I would rather that you confess to me first." He left the classroom with his injured pride.

That evening, we were not surprised to learn that Lin Bo had done it. He was not going to be punished severely, for our political instructor "never punishes anyone for personal reasons."

Two months later, Lin Bo was severely criticized for another scandal: he took two shares of a feast meal by cheating the chef. As university students, we enjoyed free tuition and meals. At the beginning of every month, we received our meal tickets: a calendar book with three stamps for each day. Upon each stamp, it was printed: breakfast, lunch, or dinner. Ordinarily we had wheat buns and rice porridge for breakfast and a vegetable or tofu dish over rice for lunch and dinner. At the end of the month, we usually had a special meal with two to three fish or pork dishes. No matter what day and what meal the feast happened to be, each student could only get one share. This was guaranteed by the tickets issued.

In order to get two feast meals, Lin Bo first put his lunch ticket on the board of the small window so that the chef saw it. When the chef turned to pass him the fried meatballs, fish, and steamed pork, he swiftly put his bowl on the ticket. The rice on the bottom of his bowl stuck to the ticket so that the chef could not see it. The chef thought that she had already put the ticket in the box.

Lin Bo went back to another window to get another share when he finished his first one. Of course, he could not eat the two shares at once. He took some of the food back to his room and put it on the shelf for later. When his roommates saw the food, they wondered, *We saw him eating his food in the dining hall. How come he still has so much left?* They soon figured it out and reported him.

This clever trick of Lin Bo's provided a good opportunity for our political instructor's premeditated revenge. Our political instructor analyzed Lin Bo's behaviour with Mao's standards for revolutionary young people, and pointed out that Lin Bo was the most undeserving youth.

That evening, our political instructor also criticized the "improper behaviour" of two other students, a male and a female. They were seen sitting very close to each other in the woods behind the teaching building. The young man was stripped of his titles in the Party. The girl was criticized but not named in order to protect her "privacy."

97

She now walked on campus with a lowered head as if she had committed a crime. Her grave expression often reminded me of the scenes in Hawthorne's novel, *The Scarlet Letter*. Communist dogma and Christian virtues both have great power over people's thinking and conduct.

To punish the two lovers, our political instructor would purposely assign them to work in two middle schools several hundred miles away from each other.

13

FOR MY SECOND SUMMER VACATION, I took home Chinese and English versions of *The Dream of the Red Chamber*, the most famous Chinese novel. The book was written in old Chinese which was difficult for me to comprehend. The simplified English version helped me to decipher the Chinese verses. I shared the realization of the heroine, Dai-yu, about the cruelty of life. She compared cold winter wind to knives, and autumn frost to arrows. And she felt that these knives and arrows seemed to be aiming at her at any moment and from all directions.

I felt the same way about my existence. Although I was home on holiday, I could not completely relax. The watchful eyes and mean looks of my classmates haunted me. In order to dispel these ghostly mental images, I sometimes played with my younger sisters, and I played hard as if I were a child. Other times I would lie on a bamboo couch in the shade of a large willow tree by the lily pond reading *The Dream of the Red Chamber* or watching the clear greenish water. Oh, how I loved the tranquility of the country!

One evening my father and I had a scholarly discussion on Karl Marx.

"You know what, Pa? The reason…" I imitated our teacher's tone. "The reason you don't like to visit Grand-aunt Suo is because the relationship is not equal, therefore, not enjoyable for you. Grand-aunt Suo lives in Wuhan and you live in a village; her husband makes one hundred and twenty yuan a month and you only make fifty-four," I paused to draw his attention further. "According to Marx, all human relationships are built upon money, and society is operated by economy as a car by gasoline."

My father's eyes were shining. I could tell he was intrigued. As he had never been to university, this must be his first time hearing about the impressive theory of Karl Marx.

Then he said, "When you go back to school, write me a letter every week." He went on to say that the first half page of my letters was usually readable, but the characters were flying in the last part.

I said, "Chinese is such an inefficient language, and I don't have much patience to write the characters slowly. Some day we should change it into alphabets. What do you think?" I looked at him for an answer.

My father smiled. He seldom offered advice or opinions when he was not sure.

The summer vacation was forty-five days. I spent half this time visiting my auntie Mei, my father's younger sister. She had recently moved to our county town with her husband and their three children from Jing Meng County where her husband was an army officer. Before she went to Jing Meng, she had worked as a seamstress in an army coat-manufacturing factory in Long-Short District.

When I was in Grade Four, I started to feel dissatisfied with the old-fashioned blouses my grandma made for me. Auntie Mei offered to help. She asked me to pick them up on a certain day, but my blouses were never ready on time. Whenever I visited her, she would give me fifteen fin to buy a bowl of wonton soup in a nearby restaurant.

"You must be hungry after an hour's walk." Holding my hand, she would apologize. "I'll make your blouse soon. I promise they'll be ready before the Children's Day, June the first."

I would nod and say that I could visit again the following Sunday. With the money she gave me, I would go to the bookstore and buy a picture book for myself. To make it believable that I had a bowl of wonton soup, I would spend some time reading more picture books at a stand where books were rented for one fin each.

Hiding the new picture book in my school bag, I would then go back to watch Auntie Mei sew until it was time to go home. My auntie had plenty of fine freckles on her round face, which I found very good-looking. The colours and patterns of her outfits were simple but elegant. From then on, I visited her frequently on Sundays and we enjoyed each other's company.

She was now working as a shop assistant in a farm tool store in town. As all the shops and department stores were owned by the state, she made the same amount of money whether business was good or not. When business was bad, she and her colleagues would chat or read newspapers. I liked to sit around the shop and discuss fashion with her. We would buy pieces of cloth, then design and make our own clothes together on her days off. We were about the same height and size. It was great fun to try on new clothes in front of her large mirror. My auntie was in her mid-thirties, tall and slim with short dark hair. In the mirror, we looked like sisters.

As it was too hot to sleep inside the building before midnight, Auntie and I would talk for hours sitting or lying on the large bamboo bed in the yard. I told her about the unfolding love between Dan and me and she told me about her miserable marriage. Her husband, Tie, was apparently the wrong match for her. She was intelligent, sensitive, kind, and caring. Her husband was street smart, practical, and callous. It seemed that he was always trying to prove himself in some way. I once heard Tie say to his eight-year-old daughter, "As a girl, you need to learn to be obedient and do housework." Those were probably the exact words his mother had said to his sisters years before.

Once, my auntie talked to a male colleague while walking home after work. Her husband saw it and started a quarrel with her that evening. Later, my auntie's legs were black and blue and his right thumb was bleeding. My auntie said a divorce would be bad for the children, so she had decided to sacrifice herself. When I asked her how she could live a life without love, she would look at the stars in the sky and smile sadly, "Other people live a day; I live a day too." Her tragic smile imprinted in my mind.

I thought of Anna Karenina in Tolstoy's novel. It seemed that women all over the world and throughout time shared the same fate: victims of callous men. I told my auntie that Tolstoy said that men were selfish animals. She pondered for a moment and said, "He is right." Like my grandma, Auntie Mei was open-minded and had an enormous intuitive understanding of things.

Although my auntie only had a Grade Four education, she picked up a great deal later on. She told me that she had enjoyed the letters I wrote her from university. I told her that when I talked with her, I felt like I was talking with a friend, not just an auntie. She seemed to be amused and quizzed me about the difference between a friend and a relative.

"A relative is imposed on you while a friend comes into your life by choice." I made the statement based on my own experiences with bad relatives such as my brother and good friends such as Rong.

She smiled and said that she wished she had not left school at Grade Four.

"I was engaged to Tie when we were in Grade Three. My school-mates made fun of us all the time. I couldn't stand it so I gave up school." She shook her head with regret.

"Why didn't you ask grandpa to break the engagement so you could continue your studies?" I inquired curiously.

"Oh, that's impossible. Breaking an engagement would be a big loss of face for Tie's and my parents, and they were good friends," she said.

I shrugged and felt sorry for all women born before my generation.

Sometimes Auntie Mei would say that her husband had found her a good job. He also helped with cooking and other household chores. I knew she was trying to justify her marriage and did not say, *Those are not the reasons for you to stay with him*, though I wanted to say it badly. I loved her too much to hurt her. In my mind, she was the "steel wok" and her husband a "tile wok," they were made of different materials. They would either die together or survive separately. But I could not tell Auntie my insightful analysis either. Sometimes, when truth is too revealing and hurtful, we choose to be silent.

One afternoon while I was napping on her bamboo bed, Auntie woke me and handed me a letter. From the familiar handwriting, I knew it was from Dan, my secret boyfriend at university. Auntie smiled mysteriously and asked me to read it aloud. As she never experienced love in her life, she wanted to know how love letters were written. I said, "Sure."

But as soon as I opened the letter, I forgot my auntie. With one breath, I finished reading the four-page letter. Things were not going well with him in school. Dan was a Chinese literature major and had written several satires to release his pent-up anger. He had been the target for the "Three-Speaking Out" movement in his class for several months. If he agreed that his satires were purposely attacking the Communist Party, they would let him graduate, but he would have admitted a crime. If he refused to confess his motives, he might not be able to graduate, and he did not know what they would do to him. He had decided to "confess" so that they would let him go.

In the past four months, Dan and I had tasted the forbidden pleasure of falling in love. One Saturday evening near the end of April, I went to his dorm to return his four-hundred-page manuscript, a screenplay based on his experiences in the countryside. The plot was interesting and the handwriting impressive. All characters were neatly written in small brush. He asked if I would take a walk in the woods with him. I shrugged and went. As we reached the top of a hill, he suddenly stopped. "I will regret the rest of my life if I don't tell you now that I love you." Gazing at my face in the dark, he continued with a trembling voice, "I have loved you as long as I can remember." It was drizzling; he threw away the black umbrella in my hand and kissed me.

I then mischievously asked him why he loved me. "I can't quite define it. You have something special. Maybe it's your quick mind; the combination of intelligence, truthfulness, and simplicity." He was very excited.

"Tell me what you like about me the most." He touched my eyes and face with his gentle look. Although it was dark, I could still see the glow in his eyes and the glistening beads of sweat on his broad forehead. He had dense dark hair, an exceptionally intelligent face and tanned skin like a peasant's. I put my hands on his shoulders and we hugged another time. I could feel his breath on my face and I liked it. He put his strong hands on my waist and fixed his eyes on my face for a long time. He was about five inches taller than me and much stronger.

I whispered, "I like your poems. I appreciate the changes you made for my poems. You made the changes as if you knew exactly what was in my mind. I also like to hear you singing songs." Dan had a voice of a tenor and often performed at the university auditorium. His dorm was fifty feet away from ours and I heard him practising on the balcony from time to time.

We stood in the light rain for a long time holding each other.

"What time is it?" I asked.

He looked at his watch: "It is almost ten."

I picked up the umbrella and we ran back. Before we parted on our separate routes, he kissed me on the forehead, "God bless you."

"Thank you." I knew I would need it. The four girls from Wuhan had gone home for the weekend and the other two girls, one from Xing-jiang, the other from a mountain area, were not very vigilant.

That evening the electricity was out all over campus and they had gone to bed early. I gently opened the door and went to bed as quiet as a mouse. About five minutes passed and nobody asked a question. I took a deep breath and made a gentle turn. I started to recall every scene, every touch and every syllable I exchanged with Dan. This was the first time that I ever touched the lip, forehead, and face of a man. It was such a wonderful sensation.

The following Sunday afternoon, Dan ran out of his dorm when I passed by. He asked me if I would like to take a walk to the South Lake with him. We started from different paths and met at the bank of the large dark blue lake. He brought with him some poems by the famous Russian poet Alexander Pushkin. I brought William Wordsworth and read my favourite poem to him:

> *I wandered lonely as a cloud*
> *That floats on high o'er vales and hills,*
> *When all at once I saw a crowd,*
> *A host, of golden daffodils;*
> *Beside the lake, beneath the trees,*
> *Fluttering and dancing in the breeze.*

As I finished reading, a soft breeze turned the page over. We looked at each other and smiled.

"Our life is a poem, isn't it?" I said dreamily. He did not say anything; he only nodded. I could tell that he did not agree with me but did not want to spoil my happy feelings.

"Your whole being is a poem, a remarkable one," he uttered softly, gazing at my dreamy eyes.

I looked at the big lake: no waves, no boat, not even a single bird flying on the surface. The sky was unusually blue with strips of white clouds here and there. There were no daffodils, only grasses and nameless wild flowers of all kinds dancing in the spring breeze. It was early May, the best season in Wuhan, the cold winter was gone and the hot summer had not yet arrived. I was wearing a dark-red shirt with chequered patterns and black slacks. He was wearing a grey shirt and black pants with matching grey sports shoes.

"Is grey your favourite colour?" I tried to break the awkward silence.

"Yes. My days have been grey since I came to university." He was quite cynical.

"Why?" I asked.

"Because the tallest tree in the woods will be the first to be destroyed by the wind. An individual who is better or different from the others will be spotted out and attacked. Under such circumstances, he has two options: one is to change into one of them and the other is to be destroyed." He sounded fatalistic.

"Have you ever thought of a third route?" I explored his topic.

"What's that?" He looked at me with surprise.

"Disguise yourself to be one of them and hide your true self," I said matter-of-factly.

"How?" He looked at me curiously.

"Most of the time, I pretend to be stupid. When they tell me that I did not fold my blanket in a nice square, but a rectangle, I either pretend not to have heard them or say, 'Sorry, I guarantee I will do better next time,' and smile innocently. What can they do to me? Put me in jail? I have developed a system to filter them out and concentrate on my studies. What do you think of my technique?" I smiled triumphantly.

"You smart devil." He kissed me on the cheek.

I took out the food I had brought for both of us and started to eat. He took a wheat bun and an apple.

After lunch, he went to take a pee in the woods and I enjoyed the scenery by myself. The serenity of the country always gave me genuine happiness. I lay down on the grass and fell asleep. When I woke up, he was sitting beside me writing something. He smiled and told me that he had watched me sleeping for quite a while.

"You belong to nature, not the busy city, my dear," he concluded.

"You are right. I hate political studies and those criticism and self-criticism meetings. Why does one human being have to criticize another in order to prove one is good?" I looked at him for an answer.

"Do you know why there was a Cultural Revolution to start with?" he asked me and I shook my head.

"It was because Mao wanted to keep the power all to himself. In 1957 he rid himself of Defence Minister Peng, the marshal whose expertise was essential for Mao to win the war against Japan, the civil war against Chiang Kai-shek and the Korean War against the Americans. Marshal Peng was an outspoken man, a real man. In the late 1950s, three million Chinese died of starvation largely due to Mao's unrealistic economic policies. Nobody in the whole country dared to tell Mao the truth. Marshal Peng wrote Mao a long letter and told him the truth. Mao was outraged and purged Peng immediately.

"When the intelligentsia aired their differences, Mao silenced them by throwing them a 'rightist' hat and sending them to the countryside to work in the fields. From 1962 to 1966, state Chairman Liu Shao-qi and Vice-Premier Deng Xiao-ping greatly improved the country's economy. Mao felt threatened and decided to launch a Cultural Revolution to expunge Liu Shao-qi and Deng Xiao-ping. Mao used the Red Guards. Who are the Red Guards? Mao's running dogs, barking and biting his political rivals. I am ashamed to say that I was a Red Guard, but I did not beat or kill anybody.

"Liu Shao-qi was badly beaten by the Red Guards and died in a cold jail cell. Deng Xiao-ping was sent to a remote village to work in the fields for eight years. Marshal Ho Long, from our neighbouring county, Honghu, died of diabetes in a jail cell. Sad, very sad.

"Lin Biao was a clever man. He published a *Red Book* of Mao's quotations and instantly became Mao's trusted successor. Lin couldn't wait for Mao to die and wanted to murder Mao when he was on a trip to Southern China. Lin failed and not surprisingly 'died in a plane crash' in 1972 on his way to the Soviet Union. Mao's wife, Jiang Qing wanted to be the empress. Now she is in jail."

I passed him the canteen. He gulped some water and went on, "Do you know why everything has been rationed for ten years, from cigarettes to sugar? The factories have stopped producing anything. In my cousin's factory, they sold their machines to pay the workers' wages. In Sichuan province, millions of peasants have starved to death since the 1950s. If you tell me that a million people in Helan or Anhui province died of starvation, I wouldn't feel this bad. But Sichuan! Sichuan is a blessed place with fertile soil and ideal climate for farming."

He lit up a cigarette, put it between his pale lips, which were trembling with anger, then continued, "Where did the food go? To Beijing and the army headquarters. Whom do you think the Communists are serving? Themselves. Their children go to the best universities without passing any exams. They live in spacious houses while ordinary people live in slums. My cousin has been a lecturer in Wuhan

University for five years. He has been married for two years now and still hasn't got a room of his own. His roommate, a sympathetic young man, offered my cousin and his wife the room. My cousin is criticized for occupying a room which is not allocated to him. For this offence, my brother is fined eighteen *yuan* a month, a third of his salary. Do you think there is justice? Where is it?" He looked at the sky as if asking for an explanation.

"How come I have not read anything like this in the *People's Daily*?" I looked at him puzzled.

"You won't. The *People's Daily* is the tongue of the Party, not a window for the people. Do you know what is going on in other parts of the world? They have advanced to the next century. Look at the tools our peasants use today. They are not very different from those our great-grandfathers used. Where is the way out for China? Why is it so backward and poor? The Chinese are an intelligent and diligent nation. They don't deserve poverty."

He was walking up and down the bank of the lake as if the water was a large audience. I looked around: there was not a soul in sight. I nodded at him to indicate that he could go on.

"Look at the burden we have now: a thousand million people, a quarter of the world's population! In the 1950s, Ma Yin-chu, the population specialist, advised Mao to encourage birth control. Mao ignored him. The Soviet Union was the model for China at that time. Stalin encouraged Soviet women to have more children. Mao echoed: the more, the better. Unlike European women, Chinese women want to have more children to start with.

"Mao did not realize until the early 1970s that a large population could become a hindrance to the economic development of a nation. Why should a military man pretend that he knows about economy? He committed a crime history will never, never forget." He was indignant.

Although I had heard pieces of the stories here and there, I had never put them together. His analyses and summary enlightened me immensely.

We walked back to campus in silence. The sun was setting. A fierce-looking hawk darted in front of us, made three circles, then fluttered to the blood-tinted sky, leaving behind a ring of sinister and coarse sound: *wra wra wra*. I shuddered with a cold shiver; a black hawk was a bad omen. Dan's approach to politics worried me.

107

At dinnertime, I asked my friend Su-wen to go to the dining hall with me. As it was dangerous to have friends in the same class as me, I made a few friends in other classes. Su-wen was a year ahead of me and we had different political instructors. She came from the same county as I, though from a different commune. I liked her the first time we met. She was four years my senior, caring and trust-worthy, qualities also owned by my late friend, Lan. In the past year, we had often spent time together trying to figure out our daily happenings. I had told her about Dan.

That weekend, Dan, Su-wen, and I went to Red Mount Park to take some photos. Dan met us at the foot of a statue near the entrance of the park. I had told Dan the day before that I was going to bring a friend with me, and he did not seem to mind. Now he seemed uneasy to have Su-wen around. We took a few pictures and walked along the main road of the park. Su-wen whispered to me that she wanted to go to the bathroom and I went with her. On the way, she said that Dan seemed displeased to have her around.

"Maybe I should find an excuse to leave you two alone." Having a little scar on her left eyelid and tiny gaps between her upper front teeth, Su-wen was generally considered plain looking and was not confident with young men.

"Never mind about him." I tried to disperse her misgivings.

We walked fast to catch up with Dan, but after about twenty minutes, we still could not see him. I looked around and walked to a thick bush where a path led to a small pond. Here he was! Sitting beside the pond, staring at a few ducks wading in the muddy water, he was wearing one of his "thousand-mile" stares. He was not looking at the ducks; he was not looking at anything.

The afternoon was getting hot, and I suggested that we call it a day. It took two weeks for the black-and-white photos to be developed. I showed them to Su-wen; she liked one and I liked none. Dan seemed to have forgotten about those pictures.

Soon it was summer vacation. The day before I left for home, Dan asked me to wait for him on the road to the South Lake at one in the afternoon. He finally showed up an hour later. He said that he could not get away because they were having their pre-graduation party.

"I am sorry to be late." He forged a smile.

I sensed something very grave in his mind, but could not define it.

He passed me a leather notebook and a dark red fountain pen.

"May-ping, these are the things I have used every day at university. I want them to accompany you," he said those words slowly and emphatically as if he were never going to see me again.

I had bought him a new leather notebook and a fountain pen as well. I had put one of his pictures in the notebook. When he asked for a picture of mine, I said that I would mail him one later. I observed the motto "never give your photo to a man unless you are absolutely sure of his feelings." I gave him my auntie's address in case he wanted to write during my vacation.

I told part of the story to my auntie and asked her not to tell my father. The second day I went back to my parents' place. It was a Sunday, my father's off day and I had promised him I would come. My father had brought a pail of live fish of various kinds: eel, carp, and bream. I smiled at him—that was my way of saying thanks. He smiled back; that was his way of saying, "Your note of thanks is acknowledged."

Resting his loving eyes on my face, he observed, "You are thinner." Not knowing what to say, I went to the kitchen to get some food, a way to show him that I was healthy and had a good appetite. I knew he did not want me to be any thinner as I only weighed about ninety-five jin. The ideal young girl should be a little chubby. When I grew up, the villagers teased me, "Does your grandma ever feed you?"

That summer, I borrowed several foreign novels in simplified English versions from our university library. When it was too dark to read, I would tell the stories to my sisters and ask them each to retell the stories with their own imagination.

One evening my brother Nian was eating his dinner while we were telling the stories. After finishing two bowls of porridge, Nian asked if there was any more in the kitchen. My youngest sister Jing-ping said, in a comical tone, "This boy has asked for more." We all giggled at Nian, who was completely puzzled.

Jing-ping explained to Nian that this exclamation was from Charles Dickens's novel *Oliver Twist*. Nan-ping offered a brief summary of the story.

Slowly getting up from his seat, Nian knocked both Nan-ping and Jing-ping on the head with his chopsticks.

"Oh, I want you to educate me! You forget yourself!" he shouted half jokingly, feeling quite a loss of face to be outwitted by his little sisters.

A week passed. I was daydreaming on a bamboo couch, under a tall willow tree by the lily pond, when Jing-ping came to wake me. "May-ping, Su-wen is here."

I opened my eyes. "Here you are!" I was overjoyed to see her.

Before graduation, Su-wen had three days off and she had come back to visit her family who lived about eleven miles from our village.

It was a hot afternoon and she was sweating profusely. I picked up a small basin, fetched some cold water in the pond. "This will cool you off fast!" I splashed some on her face.

She took off her sandals and sat on the shady deck, dangling her feet in the cool water. "Oh, this is great." She said. "I like this lily pond." Glancing over the pinkish-white water lilies and green lily pads, she was enchanted. Then she slipped into the pond with a splash. I followed her. As local custom discouraged girls from swimming, we never learned.

After soaking in the cool pond for a few minutes, we got up and sat on the wooden deck chatting.

"Oh, I like the shady deck," she said as she wrung her long braids still dripping with water.

"You know, I almost drowned in this pond."

"Where?" She was bewildered.

"Over there." I pointed to a dam in a far corner where a thatch of green reeds stood still in the windless heat.

"When?" She winked as if I was telling a fib.

"I was nine years old and we were looking for clams along the edge of the pond. Lots of children, almost every child in the village was there. It was a very hot summer afternoon; I remember it distinctly."

"Then…"

"I waded into a deep hole which was created the previous day when a huge water pumping machine was placed there."

"You didn't see the machine?"

"The machine had been removed."

"Who saved you?"

"Guess who?"

"Who?"

"Dan."

"Ha! I knew it! You two seem to be made for each other," she said good-naturedly.

"Yes and no." I stretched my eyebrow.

"Um?"

"I feel near and far from him at once, like Dai-yu feels about Bao-yu in *The Dream of the Red Chamber*, I said analytically. "He understands me better than I understand myself and I understand him most of the time. But one part of him, I can't fathom." I sighed. "His ideals."

"Oh."

"Have you read *The Thorn Birds*, an Australian novel?"

She shook her head.

"I bought a copy in the foreign languages bookstore in Hankou. The Chinese translation has just come out. Here it is. I've just finished it." I picked it up from the footstool and passed it to her.

"It's an agonizing love story of Ralph and Meggie. Although Ralph loves Meggie dearly, he loves his ambition more. That is, to be a priest, then to become a cardinal." I narrated very slowly, more to sort out my thoughts than to make a presentation to Su-wen.

"Men!" she exclaimed.

"Dan is like Ralph; he loves me but he loves his ideals more, which will lead him to trouble."

"Is he aware that he is heading for disaster?" Su-wen looked worried.

"Yes. But I have a feeling that nothing can stop him, not even me."

I walked up and down the little lawn and gazed into the distance.

"Su-wen, a man is not a man if he dies only for love. A man must have something bigger to strive for—an ideal, a cause," I said bitterly.

"Where is he assigned to work?"

"I don't know. Neither does he. Somehow I fear he may end up in a labour camp." I wrung the corner of my skirt hard; tears filled my eyes. Not wanting Su-wen to see me sad, I skipped to the pond and washed my face.

"So, do you know where you are assigned to work?" I changed the topic.

She told me that she wanted to devote her life to teaching rural children. "Whenever I pass the fields and see peasants working under the burning sun, I feel extremely guilty to have the privilege of going to university and being so comfortable," she said heartily; her eyes glazed as if experiencing the beautiful feeling of realizing an ideal.

I said that I admired her ideal but I did not share it.

"In a rural high school, you would be the only one who knows English. You would be teaching English to all eight classes. When your teaching load becomes too heavy, it would be difficult to keep the quality. Nowadays, every school emphasizes the number of students passing the university entrance examination, so quality teaching is of vital importance. However, your teaching load would make it impossible for you to devote the time needed for the students. The system has been set up in such a paradoxical way that you can't do a good job even if you work to death." I waited for her reaction.

"Where do you want to work in the future?" Su-wen looked at me.

"I don't know yet. I don't want to teach in middle schools. I'm not very good at disciplining children, especially teenagers. I want to spend the forty-five minutes transmitting knowledge instead of stopping them from fighting," I spoke from my trying experience teaching grade school. Apparently Su-wen had not thought of the difficulties teaching in middle schools since she had never been a teacher before.

"I would like to teach in a college or university where students are motivated to learn," I continued.

Observing Su-wen's earnest face, I knew I could not change her mind. So I encouraged her. "Maybe you have a way with teenagers. You seem to be firm and patient."

"Maybe." She seemed to be unsure now.

"Well, good luck. Let's go in and make you some lunch." I was hungry myself.

By this time, our thin skirts were dry. We went to the kitchen and boiled seven eggs. It was our custom to offer either five or seven eggs to a distinguished guest. Odd numbers brought good luck and even numbers bad luck. Six was especially bad because the sound *liu* was close to the sound *luo*, which meant to stop eating forever. "Therefore, you should either eat seven, or five, or three, or one."

How we giggled!

14

WHEN I RETURNED TO SCHOOL IN SEPTEMBER, Su-wen was gone, assigned to work in a high school in Mian Yang County. Dan had also left, and I had no idea where he was.

September was unusually gloomy. It rained constantly and blew often. The leaves on the tall poplars in front of our dorm soon turned colour. I started to resent autumn: the beginning of the end of beautiful things. Before long the six large poplars were completely bare. I could not do my morning readings there. Instead, I visited the small hill where Dan first kissed me on that rainy spring evening. When I read there, I felt that he was listening to me and encouraging me: "Be brave and hold on till the day of graduation."

Students became more vigilant about each other's movements as the dark cloud of graduation job assignment day approached. I made absolutely sure that I was not one minute late for any collective activities and I dared not read any books at our weekly mass criticism meetings. I washed my bowl the minute I finished my meals and mopped the floor with extra effort when it was my turn to clean the dorm.

At the end of October I finally received a letter from Dan. He had been assigned to teach in a middle school in Yun Yang County, a remote and barren mountain area of Hubei province. As no train went there, it took eighteen hours by ship, then six hours by bus.

"As the ship moved on the Yangtze River, the waves in my heart were as big as those on the river. This ship will take me away from you, the only thing in the city I miss. My fate in the new place is as unknown as that of a ship on the rippling river." I read his poetic lines several times to make sure that I did not miss anything. I could tell between the lines that he liked me but he did not renew his love for me. He did not explain why he had taken so long to write, nor was there a return address.

After some painful contemplation, I concluded that he did not love me enough to write me immediately and did not respect me enough to offer an explanation for his delay. Maybe I never meant much to him. All he cared for was his ambition. I felt deeply hurt and decided to erase him from my memory.

In my last year of university, grades became very important. Deng Xiao-ping had just started his ambitious plan to modernize science and technology, industry, agriculture, and national defence. Education became valued again.

By this time, we had six required courses for every semester. One Monday morning in May, as our intensive English class was about to start, our political instructor told us that some Australian schoolteachers were coming to sit in on our class the following morning. We must prepare for the event. Our teacher, Mr Cheng, divided us into several groups and then assigned each group different tasks. Whenever Professor Cheng asked a question, all of us should raise our hands, but only the people who were prepared for the specific task would be called up.

The next morning, the Australian teachers arrived on time. One slim lady in her fifties walked into our classroom. She was introduced as a middle-school teacher from Melbourne. Professor Cheng's dark brown eyes were radiant and he was dressed with extra care. He was in his mid-thirties with curly, silky dark hair which was rare in Chinese men. He carried his well-built figure with the shy expression of a scholar. Although he disliked the idea of performing instead of having a normal class, he did it anyway. Except he forgot who was assigned to which task. He ended up calling me three times which made other classmates jealous. The third time, my conversation partner, a girl sitting next to me, and I were called up to the front of the class to talk about the major cities in England. Professor Cheng pinned a world map on the blackboard. We pointed to the location of a city on the map while talking about its major features. When I introduced Manchester, an industrial city, I related it to Charles Dickens's novel *Hard Times*, which describes the miserable lives of coal workers in nineteenth-century Manchester. I then asked our Australian friend if I was right. She nodded and smiled.

I was wearing a lemonish silk shirt with two shoulder-length braids tied together. The Australian teacher smiled at me again when I walked back to my seat. When the class was over, she came over to give me a kiss on the cheek. I hesitated, while looking at our political instructor who was still in the classroom. He nodded and I let the Australian lady kiss my cheek.

"May-ping, a foreigner kissed you?" Several male students teased me at lunch time.

"So what? I received permission from our political instructor!" I defended myself.

That was the first group of foreigners to visit our campus. We did not know the rules regarding what we should say and not say, and what we should do and not do with foreigners.

 July 7, 1978, graduation day finally arrived. On this fateful day, our future working units were to be announced. As the government administered our registration book, assignment to a work place was usually for life.

The eve of the fateful day was unusually hot. Unable to sleep, I walked up and down in front of our dorm, where from time to time a tender breeze touched my face. Busy thoughts raced through my ruffled mind. What naive and high hopes I had for university! Crushed to pieces! I once read somewhere that after a devastating rainstorm, the trees were no longer the same, in body and spirit.

Numbly, I walked back to my dorm and took a cold shower. After splashing some cold water on my wooden bed, I put a straw mat on it and tried to sleep. But sleep would not come. I heard my roommates tossing and turning. None voiced a word. Finally soft light crept into our anxiety-ridden room. I glanced at the trees by the window: not one leaf was moving. Another suffocating day!

At eight-thirty, all the graduates of the English Department gathered in a lecture hall where our political instructor was to break the news. We held our breath. I was thrilled to hear that I was going to teach English in Wuhan Second Medical College. But I did not let my feelings show on my face.

Coming out of the hall, I heard whispers, but did not dare to talk to anyone. Any last-minute error in my behaviour could change my work place to a middle school in a mountain area.

Climbing the stairs to the third floor of our dorm, I heard sad, piercing cries of a male student from the second floor, wailing as if his father had died.

"Who is crying?" I asked a male student coming out of the washroom.

"It's Wu-tao." He looked very sympathetic.

Wu-tao was also from Mian Yang County, the same as me. His assigned work place was one of the worst—an isolated mountain village school in Hubei Province where the living conditions were poor and the climate malicious.

For some reason, I had been worried for Wu-tao from the first time I saw his dress and hair style. His leather shoes were usually shining, matched with tight pants. In those days, we did not know those tight pants were called jeans. He grew his hair long, almost two inches longer than that of other male students. Smoking was forbidden among students, but several times he was caught smoking with a female student in our department. Although she was also criticized, she had no worries. Her father was the head of the educational bureau in the city of Jing Zhou.

Wu-tao was tall, slim, and firm, a dashing young man with good grades. Although it was against the rules to have a girlfriend, several girls were attracted to him. When they heard the bad news about his job location, the girls would surely turn their backs on him.

I wanted to sigh, but did not dare to. Running to my room, I put my mosquito net, a straw mat, and a few textbooks into a package. Picking up my purse, which had only eleven yuan in it, I headed for home.

Stepping out of our room, I heard another loud cry. It was my roommate Wang-hong. She said that she deserved to work in a college, not a middle school. I tried to ignore her but she cried more loudly. As I was the only target available, she shouted at me, "May-ping, you listen: you have never been a good Party member. You only paid attention to your studies. Why did you not recommend me to join the Party?"

I told her that I did not have the power to decide who joined the Party. She became even angrier and started to cry more loudly, rolling on the floor. I escaped her madness and headed for the bus station.

I put my hands on my purse while squeezing to the only window to get my ticket, so a thief could not steal my eleven yuan. I paid extra attention to the traffic when I looked for my bus at the station. Whenever I had a piece of good luck, I became very careful.

"Thank God, I never have to deal with the political instructor and that group of mad people again." I felt a huge relief as I sat on the old bus.

I was at my father's working unit in two and a half hours. I had not been able to phone him earlier because the only public phones were in the post office. For an operator to make a long distance call, it often took two to three hours.

Seeing me standing on the stairs of his apartment building, my father did not know what to say. He did not know what to expect— good or bad news. We walked in silence to his room on the second floor.

"Is it bad news?" he asked cautiously.

"No, good news." I tried to contain my excitement. In a calm manner, I told him about my assigned working unit.

Smiling broadly, he poured me a cup of cold tea. Looking at me tenderly, he said, "You must be hungry. Let's go to the dining hall and have your favourite fish dish."

For the first time, his fatherly love really touched my heart!

My father had been the president of Zhang Dang Mouth Hospital for the past three years. The hospital had an outpatient clinic and a three-hundred-bed inpatient clinic. The patients were peasants from nearby villages. Unlike state employees, they did not have universal medical coverage. Instead they were enrolled in a "cooperative medical plan," in which the state subsidized seventy percent of their medical cost. As the hospital was short of nurses, relatives did most of the caretaking for both in- and outpatients.

On my way to the dining hall, I saw patients and their relatives lining up in front of a fruit stand. They were mostly in old clothes and stared at me as I was dressed like someone from town.

There was neither air conditioning nor electric fans in the dining hall. Everyone carried a reed leaf fan. My father fanned my face while I ate.

"Eat more." He turned over the whole fish after I finished one side. When his colleagues passed by our table, he would introduce me: "This is my eldest daughter, May-ping." I could tell that he was proud of me, and I felt wonderful.

After the meal, my father returned to work. I went to his room to rest before leaving for our country home in the evening. I tried to nap, but could not sleep. When I took a new cup to pour some cold tea, I noticed red characters engraved on the side: "Advanced Worker." My father must have worked hard over the last year.

In spite of his devotion to the Party and firm belief in Chairman Mao, my father had been criticized many times at various meetings during the Cultural Revolution. Several times he was made to parade in the street wearing a seven-foot hat made of paper, with both hands bound behind his back, a placard hanging on his chest with large characters: "Down with this capitalist-road-follower Zhao Jian-zhong." His name was written upside down. Anyone who was the head of a working unit was labeled a capitalist-road-follower, since they followed the policies of the State Chairman Lui Shao-qi and Vice-Premier Deng Xiao-ping before the Cultural Revolution.

I heard about this only many years later. He never talked to us about what actually happened to him during the Cultural Revolution. I just knew that his migraine headaches became worse and he coughed constantly, sometimes with blood. He was twice hospitalized for migraine headaches and once for TB.

My father was a self-confident man, but occasionally I saw him confused. A few days after my youngest sister was born, he asked me if we should name her "Little Red." He said that if a person's thoughts were red, everything would be fine with her. I looked at him without a word, suggesting that I disagreed with him. I knew a lot of "red" kids and everything was not fine with them. They were ignorant and thoughtless. I did not want my sister to be like them.

I had just turned fifteen that year. For some reason, my father began to consult me and respected my opinions.

He did not name my youngest sister Little Red. We named her "Jing-ping" which meant "Beijing," the capital of China. She was born the day my uncle's wife returned from a visit to my uncle in Beijing. Since the 1960s, it had been fashionable to name children after our capital as an expression of patriotism.

I poured myself another cup of cold tea and took a pen and some paper out of my father's desk drawer to write a few lines to Su-wen. There among the papers were some handwritten files. Out of curiosity, I took a look. The first one was about a male physician's confession of his affair with a nurse. The man was married, the woman was not. It said, "As Chou's room was close to ours, I sneaked to her room when my wife was asleep during the night. Many times we were together when my wife was working night shifts or visiting her parents." In the end, he said that he would never do it again, for he knew that it was against the rules to have an affair. "I am waiting for the punishment of our Party organization."

I was going to read more when I heard my father at the door. He was carrying a watermelon.

"Ready to go home?" He put the watermelon in a nylon net.

"Yes." I swiftly put the files in the drawer, looking at him innocently.

Taking my things, I followed him out. I sat on the back seat of his bicycle and off we went. It was a splendid evening; the air was beginning to cool and the sun was setting. The cotton fields seemed to be a land of incredible colours, mellow light and lengthening shadows intertwined. My heart fluttered. I felt like a victorious soldier who had just come back from a hard battle. *Yes, I finished university and I am going to make money for the first time in my life*, I said exultantly to myself.

After dinner, my sisters and I sauntered on the moonlit village road. Although younger, they were just as tall as me. The moon was smiling and the stars were dancing as we happily chatted and laughed in the cool country air. They updated me on the latest news in the village.

"Do you still remember Hua-Hua, Ru's wife? She hanged herself after her husband beat her brutally." Nan-ping broke the sad news.

"When? Ai-ya!" Hua-Hua was a gentle creature. I remembered her long dark hair and large dewy eyes. She was shy and soft-spoken.

"About a week ago."

"Ru thought that he could abuse her any way he liked because he paid three thousand yuan for her," Wen-ping narrated indignantly.

Hua-Hua was one of the unfortunates born in Henan province, where cruel climate and poor soil rarely allowed for crops. To find a way to survive, parents sold their teenage daughters to men in other parts of the country as wives.

"What will happen to her baby girl?"

"Nobody knows. Ru doesn't like the girl. He thought Hua-Hua was useless because she didn't bear him a son."

"Auntie Mar said that Ru is planning to throw the baby girl away so he can have a son when he remarries."

As each couple was allowed to have one child only, Ru would not have a chance to have a son in his lifetime as it was. By torturing Hua-Hua to death, throwing the baby girl away and marrying a woman who had never been married before, Ru could hope for a son.

"And he is going to marry a woman from Linjian village next month. Can you believe that?" Nan-ping exclaimed.

I remembered what my mother once said to me after a fight with my father, "Remember, you never commit suicide over a man's beating. You mean nothing to him. He will be remarried in three days."

Our parents were chatting with our neighbours when we got back. They asked if we would like to have more watermelon. We told them that we were more interested in some sleep.

15

SU-WEN VISITED ME A FEW DAYS after I started working at the medical college. It was a hot evening so we decided to take a stroll along the East Lake. Our medical college was situated at the east end of Wuchang District where farmlands and a heavy machinery factory met. A path at the back of the dorms led to the front gate, beyond which was the wide bank of the East Lake.

By this time the dress code was more relaxed. I was in a whitish flower-patterned cotton skirt and white sandals. Being more conservative, Su-wen wore a purple short-sleeved blouse and blue slacks. We walked along a large dam amid the greyish moonbeams. Some way from the lake bank, we felt the cool breezes touching our faces and bare arms. Wuhan was a furnace from June through August.

Sitting down, we raised our faces to catch the breeze.

"Oh, I would be happy to die here, so cool," I proposed.

"Silly, it's unlucky to talk about death."

As we glanced over the vast lake, the darkish water caught Su-wen's attention.

"Why is the water so dark, May-ping?"

I told her that the water had been heavily polluted by the waste from a nearby chemical fertilizer factory.

"Where does the drinking water for your medical college come from?" Su-wen asked in her usual caring tone.

"The East Lake." I sighed and continued, "It's pretty bad, but what can I do about that?"

"Drinking boiled water may help." Su-wen suggested.

"Do you want to know something? Every resident in Wuchang uses the water from the East Lake except our provincial leaders and those in the army headquarters." I had just heard this from people in the college.

She shook her head and said nothing. We walked in silence, the bright moon casting its reflection in the dark lake. Finally, she asked, "Have you heard from Dan?" I knew she had wanted to ask this question for quite some time.

"It's over." Seeing tears in my eyes, Su-wen held my hand.

"Tell me about your boyfriend." I tried to be cheerful.

"I don't have one." Su-wen paused to scratch her ear. "I want a man who is kind and caring." She seemed to be talking from a dream.

"How about his looks?"

"That's not important to me."

"Me neither. A man with good looks is for show, not for real life." I quoted a Chinese saying.

"When did you change your standard, eh? I would like to see you marry an ugly man," she teased.

"Actually my grand-auntie has tried to match me with an ugly medical student for two years. My grand-auntie is my grandpa's sister. She has been very nice to me since I came to Wuhan."

"How ugly is he exactly?" Su-wen could be quite mischievous.

"Well built, about two inches taller than me. He has a flat nose and a flat face." After a pause, I continued, "Actually he is starting work as a surgeon next month. He'll be working in Wuhan Third Hospital, about two miles from me. My grand-auntie told me that he's very kind-hearted, and most of all, hard-working."

"Have you met him?" Su-wen started to take it seriously.

"Once briefly, at my grand-auntie's place in Hankou."

"What was your impression of him?"

"No particular impression."

"Maybe he is the one for you. It's great that both of you work in the same city. You don't want to have someone who is far away. To get permission to move to another place is very difficult, you know. I'm not very happy with my work in the middle school. You were right. The heavy workload makes me very tired. As I have been teaching ABCs, I have forgotten my English vocabulary and grammar rules. I can't even explain an attributive clause now. Can you get me a grammar book? I couldn't find any in the bookstores downtown."

"Sure. I'll give you my grammar book and borrow one from our department for myself," I said cheerfully. "Do you need an *Oxford*

Modern English Dictionary too?" I asked. "Last year, our department had two dictionaries for each class of seventeen students. We had a draw to decide who could buy them. You know what? I got one. Lucky me, eh? Now, I am a faculty member of the medical college. I can borrow dictionaries from the department. If you need one, you can have mine. I am sure I'll be able to buy one later." I patted her on the shoulder.

She looked at me gratefully.

The second day, Su-wen and I decided to tour our old campus. I put her on the back seat of my new bicycle and rode along the East Lake. We were laughing and talking when a guard signalled us to stop.

I slowly stopped the bike and got off gracefully, indicating that I was a skillful rider.

The guard said that we were not allowed to share a bicycle in the area close to the Air Force Army Unit. He said that there were many cars coming in and out of the gate and they did not want an accident. The soldier was in his early twenties and did not look like a sophisticated person.

I smiled at him innocently, "You know we are students from the Normal University right beside your Army Unit. We are neighbours, you know? You do not want to put me in jail, do you? You want to fine me five yuan, right? We don't have the money right now. If you allow me to go to my dorm, I can get some money for you. Is that all right? If you don't believe me, take Su-wen as a hostage. She will stay here until I come back. Is that a good deal?" Both Su-wen and I looked at him without a flicker of an eyelid.

"How come you don't stay here as hostage yourself?" he said to me with a mischievous grin.

"Okay, we'll have a draw to decide," I proposed, taking out a coin.

The young soldier made us promise not to do it again and let us go. Since we could not ride the bike, we had to walk. When the soldier was out of sight, we released our smothered laughter.

I told Su-wen another story. A few months earlier, my uncle invited my cousins from Hankou and me for lunch on May 1, Labour Day. I used to stop by the sentry box at the entrance of the army headquarters and ask the guard's permission to get in. After a few visits, I just walked in as if I were a resident there and nobody asked me any questions.

That day, I walked straight in without looking at the guards. When I arrived, my uncle's wife asked me if I had seen my cousins. I said, "No. I didn't look."

My uncle went to get my cousins who had been stopped at the gate. Civilians were not allowed into the army headquarters unless they knew somebody. When my cousins came in, they asked me, "How did you get in without showing them any identification? We saw you walking in."

I laughed, "Pretend to be a resident here. Walk your steps with confidence and ignore the guards."

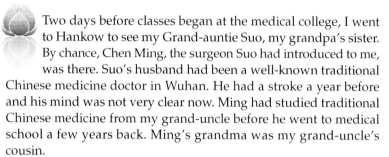 Two days before classes began at the medical college, I went to Hankow to see my Grand-auntie Suo, my grandpa's sister. By chance, Chen Ming, the surgeon Suo had introduced to me, was there. Suo's husband had been a well-known traditional Chinese medicine doctor in Wuhan. He had a stroke a year before and his mind was not very clear now. Ming had studied traditional Chinese medicine from my grand-uncle before he went to medical school a few years back. Ming's grandma was my grand-uncle's cousin.

My grand-uncle had not been treated well by the Communists because his family belonged to the capitalist class. To make things worse, his only son escaped to Taiwan with the Kuomintang troops in 1948, so my grand-uncle's political stand had been in question. Although his son was only eighteen and had joined the Kuomintang troops unwillingly, the fact remained that he had become an enemy of the New Republic. My grand-uncle, his wife, and four daughters were allocated two rooms. One room was fourteen and the other eight square metres. Thirty years had elapsed and my grand-uncle's family were still living in those same two rooms.

All their daughters were married now. His eldest son-in-law, Shi Qi belonged to a capitalist-class family. In 1953, Shi Qi's father was shot and Shi Qi was thrown into prison for having exploited the labouring people. Recently released after twenty-five years in jail, Shi Qi seemed to be a man from another planet. His wife, Jin-hui, was very disappointed with him because he had changed from a young, intelligent man into a derelict. Shi Qi could not find a job and he was not respected by his three grown-up children, who resented him for not doing his share when they grew up in poverty.

To support her children, Jin-hui became a line worker in a factory. No housing was allocated to the wife and children of a prisoner, so Jin-hui moved back to her parents' two-bedroom apartment. Her parents lived in one room, she and her three children, two boys and a girl, lived in the other. There was no bathroom in the suite, only a small kitchen shared with three other families. In the afternoons, a manure cart came by to collect excrement pots from every family.

The couple living across the hall from my grand-uncle were the Wuns, who also belonged to the capitalist class. During the Cultural Revolution, children of capitalist families were sent to the countryside first and returned to town last. When the Wuns' only daughter, Ting-ting, could not find a way back to town after nine years in the countryside, she married a mentally retarded young man, whose parents were in power in Wuhan. They promised to move her back to Wuhan as soon as the wedding took place, but never did.

She asked for a divorce, but it was not granted because her husband did not agree to it. When I saw her in the hallway, I could not believe my eyes: she had changed to a stone! There was no expression on her face. She used to be very attractive and lively: tall, slender with long hair, dark eyes, and a voice as crisp as a silver bell when she laughed.

My grand-auntie whispered to me later that Ting-ting attempted to drown herself in the village pond but was rescued by a passerby. There was another reason Ting-ting wanted to die: she was raped by the Party secretary before she married her husband. When her husband discovered that she was not a virgin, he blamed her and beat her frequently. However, he would not divorce her; he wanted to torture her instead.

My grand-auntie looked at Ming, who was talking to my cousins, and said to me how much she had enjoyed being a relative of Ming's family. Ming's mother was the head nurse in Wuhan Third Hospital and had worked as a nurse in the anti-American war in Korea. For her skill and revolutionary history, she was paid rather well when she returned from the Korean War. Ming's father was an accountant and earned a modest salary. With two good salaries to support three children and a mother-in-law, the Chens were better off than an average family in Wuhan. Furthermore, Ming's mother was generous to her relatives and friends. Whenever she visited my grand-uncle's, she would buy several jin of apples, costing her at least five yuan. As Hubei province was supposed to grow cotton and grain only, apples were not locally produced and were very expensive.

For two years I had heard my grand-auntie saying good things about Ming, and I started to think about the possibility of loving him. I had no objection to his other features, except his nose and face; they seemed out of place.

Later, my grand-auntie found me in the kitchen and said that at least Ming was reliable and had a decent job. When I was about to step out of the kitchen, she held my hand and said, "In Wuhan, many men are bad. They can cheat you. Be careful, May-ping."

I was quite moved by my grand-auntie's sincere concern. She and my grandpa had been quite close since their mother died many years ago. Their brother, Hui Ting, was four years younger than my grandpa, and was murdered by his business partner in the 1940s. I saw his picture every day when I grew up: it was hanging in my grandparents' living room. Unlike her brothers, Suo did not suffer after her mother drowned herself, because Suo's grandparents on her mother's side, who were fairly well off, took her in and raised her as a lady. The wealthy grandparents did not take the two boys because they did not want our Zhao family to prosper.

When Suo was eighteen, she was married. Although not rich, her husband treated her with love and care. In her early sixties, Suo was chubby and neatly dressed. She even smoked cigarettes, which was rare among Chinese women. I heard that smoking helped her to bear the unbearable: not being able to see or write to her only son over the years.

Soon I was summoned to lunch. There were many delicious dishes on the large table and I was to sit next to Ming. As we were starting, a man in his early fifties came in. He was tall and dressed like a merchant.

"Cousin Kuo, come in and join us for lunch," My grand-auntie stood up and greeted Kuo warmly. I had heard my grandma talk about Kuo many times when I grew up. He had left his two-year-old daughter with my grandma for a few months when I was in high school.

Kuo was all smiles and greeted everybody as if they were his old friends, including Ming and me, whom he had never met before.

He talked casually, laughed charmingly, and ate a lot. After lunch, Kuo proposed playing cards for a small amount of money.

"Just for fun," he said smoothly.

While older adults were playing cards, we young people watched. Strange, Kuo won every single game. Collecting money from everybody, he would smile graciously and say, "It will be your turn to win next time. Don't you worry."

I thought of what my grandma had said about Kuo. In the late 1940s, he was a handsome young man from a middle-class family. He was noted for his eloquence and skill with women. One day, he got an invitation from a rich man in the village who wanted to borrow Kuo for a week. This rich man was seventy-five years old. He had three wives still alive and wanted to take a pretty seventeen-year-old girl, Cher, as his concubine. He was afraid that Cher would not agree to it, so he wanted Kuo to represent him for seven days. The rich man offered a good amount of money. Kuo agreed readily since he was short of cash.

Everything went well in the following week—Cher liked Kuo very much. On the seventh night, the old man replaced Kuo while Cher was asleep. When she woke up and saw the old man lying beside her, she understood. She then demanded Kuo's presence every Sunday night and the old man agreed. Kuo and Cher fell in love and could not tear away from each other.

At that time, the Communists came to their village. Kuo and Cher were overjoyed thinking they could live together happily forever since the Communists did not allow anyone to have a concubine. While their wedding was in progress, Kuo was arrested and sentenced to an eight-year jail term. The rich man was so angry with Kuo that he had sued him for seducing and abducting Cher. Kuo was found guilty before he had a chance to explain.

Cher visited Kuo a few times in jail. With tears in his eyes, Kuo asked Cher to find herself a way out, to marry another man who could provide for her. She married a kind carpenter and they had four children. When Kuo got out of jail eight years later, he went to see her. They wept.

Kuo came home only to find that his parents had died a year before and that he was not trusted by the villagers as a released prisoner. He wandered to Wuhan, where he learned to gamble. He did not get very far, however, as the Communists had banned gambling.

Later he married a woman with severe mental illness and she gave him a girl. One day, his wife burned down their house. Luckily their daughter survived. Kuo carried his two-year-old daughter to my grandma and then took his wife to a mental hospital in Wuhan. Two months later, Kuo took his daughter home, and I had not heard about them since.

Looking at his smooth face which was brightened by the winning, I said to myself, *It's amazing what tricks fate can play on a person!*

When I said goodbye to the crowd, Kuo was counting his winnings and smiling.

The sun was setting. Deep red rays leaned over the tall buildings of Liudu Bridge, the busiest commercial centre in Wuhan. Most shops were closed by this time. Residents were cooling off on the bamboo beds in the little yards along either side of the streets. Loud chattering and laughter filled the hot air.

I was about to step onto the trolley bus when I heard Ming's voice, "Hi, May-ping, wait." He jumped on just as the bus started to move. We found seats close to the window and chatted about our university life. His situation had been worse than mine. A few weeks after he started medical school, his political instructor asked him to provide false evidence against a classmate. Ming refused.

"At our Tuesday evening criticism meetings, our political instructor would connect my name with some bad behaviour of other students for no apparent reason, just to make me look bad and feel bad. Thank God, it's over. Luckily, I had the support of a few classmates who had a similar fate to mine. Their friendship meant a great deal. Actually, we are going to have a small gathering in our apartment this evening. Would you like to stop by and join us?" He was smiling and expecting a yes for an answer.

"Why not?" I did not know why I said that.

The trolley bus was crossing the Yangtze Bridge, a few white and yellowish seabirds flew over the surface of the river. I thought of the famous poem by Li Bai, a great Tang Dynasty poet. "The yellow cranes have gone. The white clouds are floating by themselves." Li Bai was exiled by the emperor to this part of the Yangtze where he wrote these beautiful lines. I tried to imagine what it would be like to live in exile. *Wouldn't it be like being away from my water lily pond?*

Though I had lived in Wuhan for several years, I never liked the city. What bothered me most was the flying dust. It got into my hair, my nose, and my collar. Except for the places where government and army officials lived, the residential areas had neither lawns nor trees. Most houses were built before 1949 and they looked shabby and gloomy. I could not help feeling sorry for the people who had lived all their lives in this dusty city.

When it was time to get off the bus, Ming squeezed to the door and jumped off. I followed closely. Otherwise the people coming in would block my exit. Ming walked fast and I could hardly keep up. In about ten minutes, we came to a five-storey apartment building. He told me that his family lived on the top floor. I knew that his mother's status in the hospital was not very high. The top floor was hot in the summer and the first floor was damp in the winter, so they were occupied by people who had lower status. The middle floors were usually allocated to senior leaders of a working unit. The narrow stairway was packed with old furniture, coal, and firewood, which barely allowed a path to climb the stairs. He opened the door while I was still panting. A very old woman greeted Ming.

"This is my grandma. She is eighty-four years old. Still alive, eh?" Ming said half jokingly.

Their apartment was about thirty-five square meters in size, with two tiny bedrooms and a living room. His parents occupied one bedroom and Ming the other. His two teenage sisters and grandma slept in the living room, which also served as their dining room.

Half an hour later, Ming's mother came home with a bag of cooked food. Then two friends of Ming's arrived. We talked about school, graduation, and our political instructors, and congratulated ourselves on being still alive after all.

16

I WAS ASSIGNED TO TEACH ENGLISH to seventy second-year medical students and a group of senior physicians who were going abroad for a visit the following year.

I was twenty-two years old, shy and inexperienced. That morning I was to teach the senior physician class. Most of them were in their forties and fifties. In a slightly nervous tone, I introduced myself and talked about the goal of the course. I then said in English, "Now, I would like you each to tell us something about yourself." I looked around and saw Dr Fong's smiling face.

"Dr Fong, would you mind starting?"

She had a baby face and an energetic expression. But between her sickle-shaped eyebrows and dark eyes, one could trace the black circles of overwork. She was a well-known gynaecologist but not appreciated by her hospital leaders because she was too outspoken.

"Yes," Dr Fong answered.

I smiled and said, "The answer to 'would you mind doing something' is just the opposite to the habit of the Chinese language. If you mean to do it, you say 'no, I don't mind.' If you don't want to do it, you say 'yes.'"

"You mean 'yes' means 'no' and 'no' means 'yes'?" Dr Fong laughed.

"Exactly." I was pleased with her quick understanding.

Besides teaching, I was asked to read the whole English textbook into a tape recorder so the university could play the tape from the loudspeaker for twenty minutes every morning before classes. I often saw students standing under the loudspeakers all over campus reading the text along with my tape. In a few weeks, I became well-known in the medical college.

I was also put in charge of such departmental administrative work as reading newspaper articles at faculty meetings during the Tuesday afternoon political study sessions. I informed Director Yang that I was glad to do things for the department, but I had no political ambition, and I wanted to attend some medical courses.

"That's very good. You should have some medical knowledge if you teach in a medical college. But you are the only Party member in the department besides me. You must help me. I am getting old and I need someone to continue my position."

"I am no material for administrative posts. Please do not put your hopes in me. You will be disappointed." I wished I were not a Party member.

A month later, Director Yang told me that my class had given me a very good evaluation.

"Comrade May-ping, I heard that you are quite experienced and organized the class very well, better than Teacher Bao." I thanked him and escaped to my dorm.

I knew that I would be in trouble if my evaluation was better than Teacher Bao's. She was the woman who taught the other three mornings. In her forties and a graduate from Wuhan University, she had been teaching in the medical college for over fifteen years. She knew the key leaders and had many connections in other departments. The first time I met Bao I knew I needed to be on guard. She made me uncomfortable by smiling at me excessively and praising my looks.

Soon it was mid-term time and Teacher Bao asked me to make up the test. The day before the mid-term, she told me that she was not feeling well and would like me to invigilate the examination. After passing the questions to everyone, I told them to begin. I was sitting in the front and looked at them from time to time. Wong Kai in the back row seemed to be looking at the exam paper of the person sitting next to him—who happened to be his wife. My eyes rested on him for a whole minute to make sure that he knew I knew. He did it three more times, his triangular eyes sheepishly stealing glances in my direction.

I walked toward him. He looked at me and I shook my head at him. He seemed to be embarrassed but continued to look at his wife's answers. While collecting their papers, I said that some points would be taken away from one exam paper because that person referenced the answers of someone else's. Wong Kai looked down.

When I stepped out of the classroom, Teacher Bao stopped me in the hallway and told me not to report Wong Kai to the department. "Do you know who he is? He is the director of the orthopaedic department in the dental hospital. He is a very powerful man. Even President Jong respects him." Bao was smiling and observing my reactions.

"Thanks for telling me this, Teacher Bao. You are very kind." I told her that the answer keys were in the package and left for my room. I always hated cheating in exams. Now I could do nothing about it as a teacher. *What kind of teacher is this?* I was frustrated.

My room was no refuge. I had three roommates and one woman's boyfriend was there all the time, including naptime in the afternoons. He was also there after evening lights out at eleven. Chai was giggling with her boyfriend in her bed with the mosquito net down when I entered. I tried to be polite and asked him to leave since it was naptime. He agreed but did not move. The couple did not have a place of their own and they could not rent one. There was no house for rent anywhere in China. Each working unit was supposed to provide housing for its staff. What we got was what our medical college could afford. Staff members could only get a private room if they had worked for the college for eight years or more. Young married couples were allocated a hut in the back of the college with no bathroom or kitchen. The legal marriage age that year (the policy changed from year to year) was twenty-eight for men and twenty-five for women. Unfortunately, Chai's boyfriend was twenty-seven, and they would have to wait for another year to obtain their marriage certificate. I sympathized with them but I was still annoyed.

The housing situation for single faculty and staff members soon improved. Deng Xiao-ping allocated more money for educational institutes. Our medical college built several new apartments. I was assigned to share a room with Chong-fin in a new second-floor room. Chong-fin was the best roommate I ever had. She was quiet and warm-hearted. She worked as a lab technician in the virology department. Through her I got to know several young women working in the labs and hospitals. We cooked food together and went to movies over the weekends. Sometimes we would go shopping in the department store close to the provincial headquarters, where we could find fashionable clothes and shoes not available in other stores. Chong-fin was also my study mate. Whenever I could not translate a para-graph of medical English properly, I would ask her. She had gradu-ated from our affiliated nursing school and was quite knowledgeable of medical concepts.

One evening in early October, Chong-fin and I were taking our after-dinner walk along the East Lake. It happened to be the mid-August moon festival. As I sentimentally glanced at the full moon, I heard Chong-fin's soft voice. "May-ping, look, the moon has a mes-sage for you." Her black eyes blinked mysteriously at me. She was petite with a freckled round face and pale, baby moon-shaped lips.

"Please, Moon. Do you have a dazzling looking man for Chong-fin?" I lifted my head to the moon, containing my laughter.

"This planet does not produce good men any more. They must be hiding in the moon." Chong-fin's face sparkled.

How I loved to be with Chong-fin! Her heart was pure, not pol-luted by the Cultural Revolution. She seemed carefree, not burdened by social climbing.

She told me that one of my students had asked her if I was married.

"What for?" I laughed.

"Maybe he likes you." Chong-fin smiled.

"I will never fall in love with a student. Are you kidding?"

"He is a little obsessed, I am afraid. But he won't let me reveal his name to you." Chong-fin looked at me amusingly.

"I don't care to know his name anyway." I squeezed Chong-fin hard on her arm until she cried for mercy.

"Several people in the medical college have inquired about you," she said. "Teacher Sheng, my boss, wants to introduce you to a high-ranking provincial official's son. What do you think?" She seemed serious.

"No way. Chong-fin. I don't want to be a servant in a big mansion."

Chong-fin then told me a sad story of a young woman from our medical college who married a high-ranking official's son.

"One nice guy in my group is asking about you too." She was half-joking.

"Really? I know who that guy is. Zhang Yi, right? His head seems not round in some way. Perhaps his mother slept him on one side when he was an infant." We laughed ourselves to tears.

17

FOR A YEAR, MING, THE SURGEON, had been very attentive to me. One time he would ask me to go to a movie, another he would cook some nice dishes and bring them to me. On various festivals, he invited me to have the traditional taro-root rib soup with his family. His mother was very kind. I felt the warmth of a family for the first time since leaving my parents years before.

On a Saturday evening in late September, Chong-fin had gone to Hankou to see her parents. I was alone in the dorm. I heard knocking at the door. It was Ming bringing gifts and some food he had cooked. When I thanked him, he held my hands and told me how much he loved me. He touched my face and kissed me.

"How come your pants are so tight?" I asked him as he walked to the window. He did not answer me. Opening the window, he lit a cigarette. Cool autumn air flowed in. I combed my hair. Finishing the cigarette, he turned to me and smiled. Strange, I did not find his pants so tight this time. They fit well on his strong body and muscular legs.

It was raining hard that evening but we decided to go to an open movie at our campus. The movie had started on the sportsground a few minutes before we arrived. It took a while to find space for our chairs and umbrella in the crowd.

By this time, many movies forbidden during the Cultural Revolution had been released. That evening's movie was *The Family*, based on a novel written in 1931 by Ba Jin. It was a story about three brothers. The eldest brother, Jue-xin, had a tragic personality. He was deeply in love with his cousin Mei, but married another woman arranged by his grandpa. Mei married a man she did not love. A few years later, Mei died and so did Jue-xin's hope. He lived in regret ever after. He was too afraid to say or do anything against the will of his grandpa, who was wealthy and had a teenage girl as his new concubine when he turned seventy. The second brother tried to fight for his fate in a tactful way. The youngest brother walked out of his grandpa's mansion to join the revolution. Besides the main plot, there were a few side stories about romantic love between the brothers and beautiful servant girls. The characters were well developed and the plot intriguing.

On our way back to the dorm, I asked Ming, "Why are the novels and movies made before the 1950s better than the ones made afterwards?" He made up something but did not answer my question. I forgot that he was not a literature major and did not read novels.

After Ming left, I recalled what Dan once said: "Politics is the reason. When Mao says that literature should serve our socialist revolution, a writer's imagination is restrained. Therefore no natural and good writing can be produced."

That night I dreamed of Dan. It was a windy and rainy day. The surroundings looked like a construction site. He was carrying two baskets of broken rocks with a shoulder pole. His steps were slow as if the heavy load was crushing his fragile frame. Oh, how thin he had become! I could not see his face very clearly as he was bending his head to dodge the biting wind and thick rain. His clothes were torn and soaked. His dense dark hair was long and disarrayed. He had no shoes on. "Dan!" As I called out to him, I awoke.

Tears, like the dense rain in my dream, poured down my cheeks. How I missed him! How I longed to see him and talk to him!

"Why am I seeing a man I don't love and not seeing the man I love?" I asked myself. "But he doesn't want you. Go back to sleep. What can't be helped must be endured." My rational voice was trying to convince my emotional self.

To smother my painful thoughts, I borrowed an armful of novels from the library the next day. Although I had read some of these before, I was too young and inexperienced then to understand the depth of the authors. Within two months, I read several prose selections by Ba Jin and several plays by Chao Yu, a great Chinese playwright in the 1900s. How old Chinese literature interested me! I started from Qu Yuan of 340 B.C., then Li Bai and Li Shang-yin of Tang Dynasty, Yang Mo, Xie Bin-xin, and Guo Mo-ruo in the early 1900s.

"Why were people two thousand years ago smarter than us? Their thoughts are sharp and writing style exquisite. I am so ashamed of us modern beings," I exclaimed to Chong-fin one evening. She just smiled. She was not interested in literature either. However, I talked in my room anyway, to myself.

Over the weekends, Ming would bring the ingredients for various dishes and cook them on a small kerosene stove in the corridor. Attracted by the fragrant smell, my dorm mates would come and try out the dishes. Ming loved the compliments. After we finished the meal he would wash the dishes in the large washroom on the first floor. Soon I was generally considered a lucky woman.

Ming had been a professional chef for three years prior to his medical education. When the Cultural Revolution started he was in Grade Five. School stopped. He and his Red Guard comrades took the train to Beijing to be received by their commander-in-chief Chairman Mao.

At fourteen, he escaped death by one inch. One revolutionary day he and his Red Guard comrades stole some rifles from the army headquarters and fought each other for fun. A bullet narrowly missed his head.

In 1967, the second year of the Cultural Revolution, Ming's father was sent to the countryside to raise pigs because he was suspected of treason. Ming's auntie and her husband had gone to the United States in 1946 and had stayed there. That year, the Red Guards ransacked Ming's home and anything suspicious, including letters and postcards from the u.s.a., was confiscated.

When Ming turned sixteen he was sent to Jin Shan County, a poor mountain area two hundred miles from Wuhan, to receive his re-education with the peasants. He was allowed to visit his mother once a year. When he first arrived, he shared accommodation with four other boys and two girls from Wuhan in an old temple. By the third year, Ming was the only one left. All the others had returned to Wuhan because none had relatives in the United States.

He escaped death a second time when he was nineteen.

It was a cold, snowy winter afternoon up on the mountainside. He had chopped a large bundle of firewood. With it on his back, heading home, he fell on a big rock and hurt his knees badly. He could not get up. He shouted for help, but not a soul was around. He shouted and shouted, only to hear his own sad cry echoing in the large mountains. He crawled for some distance. By this time, it was getting dark and he was hungry and exhausted. He thought his end had come, but somehow he managed to crawl home.

During the night, he kept a hatchet by his bedside to protect himself from wolves. His temple was a mile from the village. If a wolf ate him, the villagers would not know until the next day.

To get him back to town, his mother bought expensive gifts for several important directors in her hospital. They finally agreed to offer Ming a job in the hospital kitchen. He was apprenticed to a kind chef who taught him cooking skills. Ming learned to be humble and smile at people, especially hospital leaders. But when he was off work, he lost his temper easily.

On Ming's twentieth birthday, his father slapped him after a heated argument. He struck back, knocking his father down three stairs. Luckily his father was not injured. Ming said that his father had beaten him since he was three, and it was time to teach him a lesson. Sure enough, his father never again dared to lay his hands on him.

I saw Ming yelling at his grandma several times when she fumbled her way to the bathroom and disturbed his afternoon nap. I twice heard his fifteen-year-old sister, Fong-hua, complaining of Ming's violent behaviour. On Sunday mornings, after her violin lesson, she was supposed to practise for two hours. Once, when Fong-hua was resting her hands, Ming broke into her room and kicked her hard on the legs. But Ming assured me that he loved me too much to lose his temper with me. And I believed him.

His mother said that both her husband and son had changed since they came back from the countryside. They seemed to be beyond reason sometimes. "Maybe they will become more reasonable as time goes by." Both she and I hoped.

I wrote to my father and described Ming to him. My father returned my letter immediately and instructed me to wait for another year before I had a boyfriend. He said that the usual time to have a boyfriend was two years after university graduation. Although I was not sure about the relationship with Ming, I disliked my father's rigid number: two years after graduation. Ridiculous! Where did he get this number? For the sake of argument, I asked him, "What if I don't meet anyone I like next year? Do you have someone waiting for me?" I did not like to be controlled any more.

18

UNCLE XIN PHONED ME AT WORK on a cloudy November morning: my big auntie's husband, Wu Guan, was coming to visit me that afternoon. When I grew up, I seldom saw my big auntie Lin, my father's elder sister, who married Wu Guan before I was born. Wu Guan and Lin lived fifteen miles from us. I visited her once when I was twenty years old. As there was no bus to her village, it took my auntie Mei and me a whole day's walk. Twice we got lost and three times we stopped for some food and drink. By the time we reached the village, it was pitch dark.

Lin and her husband were in their early fifties and had six children, five boys and a girl. The girl was sixteen years old and named Second Feng. An elder sister, First Feng, had died young. The boys were at school, but Second Feng stayed home helping her mother take care of her brothers, who shouted at her and ordered her around as if she were their maid.

The villagers liked to play cards whenever they could—mornings, afternoons, and evenings. It was perhaps the only way for them to escape from their poverty-stricken life. Lin was so addicted to cards that she seldom had time to cook, clean the house, or get enough sleep.

Lin was tall, with a wrinkled angular face and red-veined eyes. In spite of this, it was still possible to see traces of the handsome woman she had been. When she talked, she seemed devoid of emotions. Auntie Mei had told me that Lin was the sacrifice of the family. Unlike her younger brothers, Lin received no schooling from her grandfather on her mother's side. Being the eldest and a girl, Lin was needed to help with the caretaking of her younger brothers, my father and Uncle Xin.

Her parents married her to an educated man, Wu Guan, a school-teacher, perhaps as a compensation for Lin's lost education. Being delicate in frame, Wu Guan was not much help in the fields. Being learned, he was above household chores. Being a scholar, he could not love an uneducated woman. Seven years after he married Lin, he had a love affair with an unmarried young woman teacher and they had a baby girl. The Party organization severely criticized Wu Guan and ordered him to pay a quarter of his salary for child support. Wu Guan's lover was moved to another school with her baby girl and lived in disgrace. Although without love, Wu Guan never intended to divorce Lin. With three-quarters of a salary to sustain Lin and their six children, they lived in debt and poverty.

Sometime after my only visit to Auntie Lin, I concluded, "A gentle and educated man can hurt his wife as much as a violent man, only in different ways."

"May-ping, somebody is looking for you." My typist friend, Ling-ling announced. Wu Guan was standing at my office door, smiling. He had made the long trip to Wuhan in order to make a complaint at the newly opened "Visitor's Window" office of the provincial government. I once told my uncle that I had a schoolmate working in that office. This new office was to assess mishandled cases. People who had been mistreated could be compensated in two ways: get their money and/or reputation back.

In the late 1950s, Wu Guan was employed by the state as a school principal. In 1960, when half of China's farmland was flooded, and the Soviet Union demanded that China pay back all its debt at once, Mao called upon government employees to help the state. Some donated money and others volunteered not to receive any salary. Wu Guan offered to be a teacher in his village school, where he was paid one-third of his salary as a state employee.

The provincial headquarters was only about a mile from our campus and we decided to walk. My youthful steps were light because I was excited for Wu Guan and Auntie Lin. *Wouldn't it be great if he gets compensated?*

His steps were weary, as he had learned not to put high hopes on the government.

As we approached the tall buildings and beautiful gardens, Wu Guan sighed deeply. "A big mistake. You help the state; who helps you?" he said helplessly. He was tall, thin with dark-greyish hair. His pale face looked kind and bookish.

I found my friend, Yu-bu, in the Visitor's Window and narrated Wu Guan's case. Yu-bu said that she would have to consult her supervisor for a second opinion. Ten minutes later, Yu-bu came back telling Wu Guan that his case did not belong to the category for compensation.

"We are now correcting errors made to the Rightists in 1957 and to the capitalist roaders during the Cultural Revolution. Your case does not belong to either of the two categories. I am very sympathetic." She looked as if she felt sorry for Wu Guan. In just a year, she had learned how to play the game.

I walked Wu Guan to the bus station. Stepping on the bus, he waved at me. I saw tears in his eyes, which were bulged with red, sad veins.

When I walked back to the medical college, Wu Guan's words kept coming back to me: "A big mistake. You help the state. Who helps you?" Apparently, the government was not encouraging people to respond to its calls. I wouldn't.

Confucius once said that those who win people's trust would gain power, and those who lose people's trust would lose power.

Dan once told me that the famine in the late 1950s and early 1960s was not caused by flood of the farmland or debt payment to the Soviet Union. Mao lied. The famine was the consequence of his unrealistic economic policies. Deeply worried about China's poverty after the war, Mao wanted China to catch up with the West in fifteen years. Thinking that a higher production of steel would raise China's economic status, he mobilized every household to make steel. Furnaces were built in every village; cooking pots were collected and melted down. While the young and able-bodied were making useless steel, grain and cotton rotted in the fields.

I did not tell Wu Guan the truth. I wanted him to live with the heroic spirit that his sacrifice helped his country out of famine caused by natural disasters. I once read somewhere that to be able to believe in something brings peace to the mind.

19

IN EARLY OCTOBER 1979, DIRECTOR YANG announced a piece of exciting news: an American couple was coming to work at our college for five months. The man's name was Arthur and the woman's was Elizabeth, and they were bringing their ten-month-old daughter with them. Elizabeth was to teach us English and Arthur would work in the infectious diseases ward of the Second Affiliated Hospital. Director Yang was always happy to deliver good news and he managed to sound like he had made it happen.

"To be more exact," he said, "Arthur is doing his internship here after medical school and Elizabeth is collecting data for her doctoral dissertation in sociology." We were excited because they were the first Americans to visit our medical college since 1949.

Before 1949, there were many foreigners in Wuhan. They mostly came from Britain, France, Germany, the United States, and most of all, Japan. Some of them were religious missionaries, others were merchants and political envoys who lived in concessions. And some were invaders.

Ordinary Chinese were forbidden to enter these concessions where mansions were located. After 1949, those elegant buildings had been converted to government offices.

During the 1950s and early 1960s, the most popular foreign language offered in middle schools and universities was Russian, as the Russians were our friends. English was not popular because the English-speaking countries were our enemies, and there was no need to learn their language. Some time in the 1960s, the Russians became our enemies, and Russian as a language was no longer popular among the Chinese. Then, in the early 1970s, the Americans and a few other English-speaking countries became our friends.

Most of my fellow English teachers who graduated in the 1950s and early 1960s were Russian language majors. Now it was mandatory that Russian teachers learn and teach English. Although some spoke worse English than their students, they had to manage the class: they could always teach grammar and translation. Now they were very happy to hear that a native speaker was coming to teach them some real English.

On November 15, six representatives from the medical college went to the train station to meet Arthur, Elizabeth, and their baby girl. I was the translator. The other five were Vice-President Cheng of the Second Affiliated Hospital, Professor Chow, director of the Internal Medicine Department, Dr Sheng, director of the Virology Department and two physicians from the infectious diseases ward.

As the train came to a stop, a tall Caucasian man with blue eyes and curly hair got off the train. He was followed by a tall Caucasian woman with straight brown hair, a baby in her arms. Both of them were in their late twenties, well-built and casually dressed. They saw us at once.

"Arthur, Elizabeth!" Dr Sheng hugged them. Dr Sheng had met them when she visited Johns Hopkins University the year before. I stood close to President Cheng, the most important person in the crowd. He was in his fifties with greyish-white hair, a navy blue wool suit, and shiny leather shoes.

"Welcome to Wuhan Second Medical College. My name is Cheng." He shook Arthur's hand and then Elizabeth's.

"Thank you. My name is Elizabeth and this is my husband Arthur and our daughter, Kate. She is asleep right now." Unbelievable! Elizabeth said all this in standard Mandarin.

"You speak good Chinese. Your Mandarin is better than mine," said President Cheng, whose Mandarin had a strong Sichuan accent.

It was Arthur's turn to greet President Cheng. He first commented on their long trip from America to China, then asked for President Cheng's support for his research in the infectious diseases ward in the forthcoming months. I listened very carefully but only understood a few words. As President Cheng did not know any English, I improvised a little.

Observing my awkwardness, Elizabeth came to my help. She smiled and said to me, "Arthur has a strong southern accent. Don't worry. You will get used to him in a few days." Elizabeth's English was easier to understand. I could hear every syllable.

We then sat in the foreign guests' waiting room where tea, orange juice, and cakes were served. President Cheng told Elizabeth and Arthur that their two-bedroom apartment at the college was not quite ready and they would have to stay in the East Lake Hotel for about twenty days.

"We will pay all the expenses since it is our responsibility to make the place ready for you. The East Lake Hotel is only a mile away from the medical college and we can send a car." President Cheng was very generous.

"Thank you, President Cheng. You are very kind. But we have a problem. We don't know how to drive here. We heard that the road signs in China are different from what we have in the United States. A red light means go and green light is stop. Is that right?" Elizabeth was quite a diplomat. We all laughed and admired her knowledge about China.

"Where did you learn your Chinese?" President Cheng asked Elizabeth after a pause.

"In the United States. We had a Chinese teacher from Taiwan. You do not mind me mentioning Taiwan, do you?"

"Not at all. People in Taiwan and Mainland China are one family." President Cheng cited some lines from the *People's Daily*.

By this time, two cars were waiting for us in front of the train station. Before we got in, President Cheng announced that the medical school was going to host a banquet for Elizabeth and Arthur at the East Lake Hotel at seven the following evening and we were all invited.

The banquet room was so grand that I felt uncomfortable when I walked in. I was to sit between President Cheng and Arthur. Elizabeth was chatting with Director Chow in Mandarin.

"Today is a great day for us all. Welcome our distinguished American guests! Let's toast to the friendship between the American and Chinese people!" President Cheng finished his small glass of Mao-tai, the most famous Chinese liquor, in one gulp.

It was Elizabeth and Arthur's turn to make a toast. They said that they were very lucky to visit such a beautiful city and meet such nice people.

"We would like to thank President Cheng for his hospitality. To the health of everyone, bottoms up!"

The first four dishes were cold: roast duck, beef, lily roots, and chicken, all sliced very thin and decorated with flowers cut from white and red carrots. After about twenty minutes, the waiter took the half-finished dishes away and brought four hot dishes: turtle soup in the middle, whole steamed fish, steamed pork, and rabbit. I loved the turtle meat, a rare delicacy. President Cheng put several pieces of rabbit and turtle meat onto Elizabeth and Arthur's plates. It was our custom to offer the best food to distinguished guests.

Arthur looked at the turtle meat and smiled at me. I got his message. I asked Arthur if he needed any help with the turtle meat. Eagerly he said, "Yes, please take it. Thanks." I explained to President Cheng that Arthur had offered me his share since I was busy translating and missed the good food.

"Very nice of him." President Cheng smiled at Arthur and peeled an apple for me. Four plates of fruits had been presented along with delicate fruit knives. It was our habit to peel apples to protect us from the poison in chemical fertilizers.

I was assigned to translate for Elizabeth and Arthur four days a week and teach my classes on the other two days. Since Elizabeth spoke Chinese, I mostly helped Arthur. At 8:00 a.m., Arthur and I did the morning round with other Chinese physicians in the infectious diseases ward that occupied a quarter of the first floor of the main inpatient clinic building. As this was one of the four largest hospitals in Wuhan, it had patients from all over the province.

In the afternoons, we would go over case histories with the chief physician. As there were ever so many charts, we had to work the whole afternoon.

Some days when Arthur did not need my help, Elizabeth would ask me to be with her while she interviewed people in the hospital.

On Sundays, we would shop in Wuchang and Hankou. Wherever we went, children as well as adults would stop to watch Arthur, Elizabeth, and their baby. Kate was the biggest attraction. She had large blue eyes, long eyelashes, and fair skin. Chinese babies had very different features: they had black eyes not half as big as Kate's and short eyelashes.

This was the first foreign baby most people had ever seen. A few could not help touching her hands, which made Elizabeth very uncomfortable. I had to ask the crowd to let Elizabeth and Arthur go.

When I got back to my dorm in the evenings, my friends would ask me a thousand questions about Elizabeth and Arthur. What do they eat for breakfast? Do they change their clothes everyday? Does their baby sleep in the same room with them or in a separate room?

20

ONE THURSDAY EVENING AFTER A QUICK DINNER in our dining hall, I headed for my office to get some marking done. Passing Elizabeth and Arthur's place, I stopped by to see how they were doing. They were eating and talking with Shao-ting, their young chef. Shao-ting was in his early twenties, medium height, slim, and cheerful. He did not speak any English, so he talked with Arthur by gestures. It was very amusing to watch them.

We heard knocking at the door. It was Professor Chow, with a dozen large oranges which were not often available in Wuhan.

"Nice oranges," I said.

"Thank you," Elizabeth and Arthur said to him.

Seeing that his visit was interrupting their dinner, Professor Chow said, "I'd better get going," and headed to the door.

"Goodbye, see you tomorrow. Thanks for the oranges." Elizabeth and Arthur were still eating at their table.

I whispered urgently to them, "Stand up and walk him downstairs!"

When they got back, they said, "Thanks for telling us this, Mayping. Please teach us more in the future. We don't want to be rude to people. They are very nice to us."

"It's our custom to walk a guest to the door or downstairs, especially if he is an elder," I explained.

"Gorgeous oranges! They must be from Yichang, a city near Sichuan province," I said.

"May-ping, in America we don't eat oranges as they are. We extract the juice and throw the rest away," Arthur informed me half seriously.

"Really? Then you are wasting the fibres," I tried to reason with him.

"We don't need the fibres from oranges. We get fibre from cereals."

"What is cereal?" I never heard of it before.

"It's hard to explain. We have thousands of products you don't have here. How can I make you understand? Anyway, America is a rich country," he said proudly.

I did not know what to say.

Elizabeth came to my rescue, "May-ping, he is teasing you. There is poverty in America too."

"Even the poorest people in America have colour televisions and refrigerators. Isn't that true, Elizabeth?" Arthur questioned Elizabeth and then looked at me. "In China, only the richest people have colour TV, am I right?" Arthur laughed, a loud and arrogant laugh.

It was quite awkward to hear somebody making fun of my country. I felt like smashing his big nose. I could feel that my face had turned red. I said nothing. Elizabeth changed the subject. On my way back to my dorm, I imagined what America would be like.

"A country without poverty must be wonderful. People must be very happy there," I said to Arthur the next day when we were heading out from work.

"Eh, that's not true either. Not every American is happy. They are greedy. The more they have, the more they want." This statement seemed to agree with what I had read about America.

"Then what is the use of having all those material possessions if you aren't happy?" I thought of the tragic death of Jay Gatsby and the lonely face of Holden Caulfield, the hero of *The Catcher in the Rye*.

It was Arthur's turn to be speechless. I felt great to have confronted him.

The following Saturday evening, I took Elizabeth and Arthur to a Chinese movie at the auditorium of the medical college. During the movie, I translated the gist of the story for Arthur and left the rest to his imagination.

As we walked out of the auditorium, Arthur said that he missed American movies and newspapers. He told me that he felt like he was living on an island. They were not allowed access to the local newspaper, though Elizabeth could read Chinese. The only way they got news of America was through their short-wave radio, which brought them the latest news of Ronald Reagan's election to the U.S. presidency.

The morning following the movie, Director Yang summoned me to his office. He closed the door and told me that people had seen me last evening with my hair down like Elizabeth's. "I also noticed that you had your hair permed. By the way, when did you buy those high-heeled boots?" He tried to be casual.

"I had my perm done last year and it's almost straight now. I hid my perm in my braids. I washed my hair last evening and didn't braid it because it was not quite dry. As to my high-heeled boots, the heels are not very high, only one inch. I bought them a month ago. If I am not allowed to wear them, I can throw them away." I was angry.

"No, no. I didn't mean to criticize you. Just that you need to be careful about what other people may say about you because you are a Party member. You know I chose you to be the main translator because I want you to have a chance to improve your English." He smiled to show his kindness.

I thanked him and ran to Arthur's office. That afternoon we were scheduled to watch a gynaecology operation using acupuncture anaesthesia in our First Affiliated Hospital. On our way, I told Elizabeth and Arthur that my permed hair and high-heeled boots had got me into trouble. They laughed. Arthur said that I should be living in the United States where I could perm my hair anyway I liked.

"If you grew up in America, you would be smarter too. America is a great country." Arthur's face was lit up.

"That's not true. She is smart enough. May-ping, don't listen to him. There are a lot of bad things in America as well." Elizabeth studied Asian history and seemed to have a more balanced view of the world.

On our way back, Arthur said that he would like to teach me an English idiom and some new vocabulary each day.

"I want to smarten you up, May-ping." Arthur smiled at me.

The first idiom Arthur taught me was "Another day, another dollar." He took out his purse and gave me a one-dollar bill. "Please keep this as a souvenir," he insisted.

I looked around and saw no one watching us. "I am not supposed to take anything from you. It'll get me into trouble, you know." I was quite serious and he took his bill back.

"The second thing I want to teach you is the difference between 'will do something' and 'is going to do something.' Sometimes when you mean that we plan to do something, the right way to ask is 'are you going to' not 'will you.' When we first came, you confused us a lot." He was very sincere and I thanked him.

Elizabeth said that Arthur was very lonely and liked to have an audience. "I hope you don't mind him lecturing you."

"Why should I, Elizabeth? It is a great opportunity for me to practise my English." As time went by, I started to know their ways. Arthur was outspoken and argumentative like me. Elizabeth was more mature and tactful. They were both sharp thinkers and devoted to academia, and they had a great sense of humour. Interacting with them was a good intellectual exercise for me, and I enjoyed every minute of it.

21

On Saturday evening I went to see the black-and-white TV the medical college had bought for Elizabeth and Arthur. As there was only one channel and the program was not very interesting, we started to chat. While pouring me some tea, Elizabeth smiled mysteriously. I was puzzled when she asked if I could tell them the worst swear words in Chinese. They offered to tell me the most frequently used swear words in America. It turned out that in both China and America, it was a person's mother who got cursed most severely.

"Perhaps a mother has the ultimate responsibility to bring up her child right."

"Or cursing the mother hurts the person the most because he or she loves the mother the most." We laughed.

Then they asked if I could tell them how much I made in a month. "Forty-eight yuan." I did not see why it should be a secret though I was not supposed to tell them for fear that they were spies sent by the CIA.

"How much does Professor Chow make, do you know?"

"Probably twice as much as me. Seniority is the sole standard for salary increase. Every few years, everyone gets a raise of seven or eight yuan."

"Good strategy to resolve conflict, eh?" They looked at each other.

"The only thing is that you lose incentive to excel after a while," I added.

"What's the criterion for promotion?"

"Seniority and a good relationship with your director."

"Hmm."

"Or a very bad relationship with your director."

"How so?"

"So your director is afraid that you may make trouble if you don't get promoted."

"Fascinating," Elizabeth made a mental note.

"How much rent do you pay?" Arthur blinked his eyes.

"Seventy-five fin a month," I said as a matter of fact.

"Really? Can't believe it."

"How do you decide who gets an apartment and who doesn't?"

"Seniority."

"Oh."

"But there are exceptions."

"Oh?"

"In our department, Teacher Jin and Teacher Dong are about the same age and both are capable but in poor health. They both live in Hankou and take the bus to work. For twenty years, they have spent two hours on the bus every day to and from work. Recently Dong was allocated a two-bedroom apartment at the medical college but Jin was not. The difference is that Dong is skilled at raising people's sympathy, whereas Jin is not."

"You are a born sociologist, May-ping," Elizabeth encouraged me to go on.

"I concluded sometime ago that getting people's sympathy is an essential skill to have. Teacher Bao uses it to perfection. She is sick almost every day, from a cold to a headache or dizziness. On average three to four times a month she is too sick to teach her class. But surprisingly she has never been too sick for the Tuesday afternoon political studies and departmental meetings. At the end of last year, she became one of the two honoured teachers at our college. I have heard that she is going to be the vice-director of our department next year." After sipping some more tea, I continued, "Bao wears a ready smile for everyone, especially the leaders." It was wonderful to share my analyses with people who would not report me.

With an awkward grin, Arthur said, "Teacher Bao makes us very uncomfortable when she smiles at us excessively." They both laughed.

"That's her way to express friendliness. I have observed that many people smile and nod excessively to foreigners or their superiors to show how agreeable they are. They don't have the skill to interact properly," I explained.

"And she is considered to be very beautiful among the teachers too."

"You're kidding! Anyway, tell us who, according to Chinese standards, is considered beautiful or handsome or good-looking. I would hypothesize that we have very different standards." Elizabeth and Arthur were both interested in this topic.

I nominated a few men and women in our department and then asked them to name a few. Interestingly, the correlation of their votes and mine was very low.

"I know why. The Chinese emphasize the features of the face more than the figure. The shape and size of the eyes and the face are the most important criterion. The simile for a good-looking female face is a flower, often compared to an art object. In the West, the first thing to notice in a girl is her body. What connotation does a body have? Sex, I guess?"

They both laughed, "You're probably right, May-ping."

"In Chinese culture, sex is a taboo word. Platonic love relationships are considered noble and pure. Sex is related to the words hooliganism and decadence."

"So you Chinese have produced a thousand million people in silent sex?"

"Well, reproduction is a duty. You carry out your duty in silence, don't you?"

"True, true."

We all laughed.

"May-ping, how come we have never seen any Chinese kissing or hugging each other anywhere? Do they kiss each other at all? We mean between lovers or husbands and wives?"

"Of course they do, but only behind doors. Kissing in public is considered inappropriate. You know what? Last year I saw a couple of young lovers kissing at Wuchang railway station. A policeman came over and arrested them." I laughed.

"What kind of punishment do you think they would get for kissing in public?" They were very amused.

"A warning, perhaps." I laughed again.

"Is it still taboo for university students to date?" Arthur asked half seriously.

"The rules are not as strict as before. But it's better not to do it if one wants to be assigned a decent working unit upon graduation."

"If a girl doesn't go out with a boy at university, how can she learn? How does she know who suits her and who does not?" Elizabeth was probably talking from her own experience.

"That's a good point. I never thought of that before. Most of the women I know married the first man they were seriously involved with. Maybe that's why there are so many unhappy marriages."

Elizabeth passed me more tea and I continued. "The woman who used to live next door to my room married a teacher at the Embryology Department. Unfortunately she gave birth to a baby girl. Her mother-in-law, who takes care of the baby, is very unhappy. The woman's life is miserable. Her mother-in-law tries to find faults with her, and her husband is always on his mother's side. She has had three abortions in the last two years because her husband wants to torture her. He says that he would like to see a hole in her uterus from constant abortions until she becomes an obedient daughter-in-law."

"How about a divorce? Is it possible to get a divorce?" Elizabeth had infinite interest in social issues.

"If one side does not agree, the other side can't get a divorce. Many people don't even think of divorce as an option. No matter how unhappy they are, they swallow the bitterness and carry on. They think that it is for the good of their children." I thought of my Auntie Mei's sad face.

"That's not true. Constant fighting, especially physical fighting, between parents can have very negative impact on children," Elizabeth said.

"I agree with you, Elizabeth. My Auntie Mei's three children would be better off if my auntie divorced her abusive husband and lived without him. None of the three children does well in school. They fight with other children constantly, a headache to my auntie." I added, "Another barrier in breaking up a relationship is 'people's talk.' The Chinese consider it a social responsibility to interfere with other people's lives. 'People's talk' is more than a person of average courage can bear."

"You know Tong, the woman from the Biochemistry Department?" I asked.

"Yes, she is in my class. Her English is very good," Elizabeth said.

"People at our medical college like to talk about her."

"For what?"

"Because she recently broke up with her boyfriend."

"It is amazing how much everyone knows about everybody else's private life here." Clearly Elizabeth had observed this pattern.

"Of course. We work in the same building, live in the same apartments, eat in the same dining hall and go to movies at the auditorium." I looked at Elizabeth helplessly.

"May-ping, make sure that you don't do anything wrong, people are watching you everywhere." Arthur came into our discussion after taking a look at Kate, who was sleeping in the next room.

"The working unit has enormous power over its members' lives." After a pause, she said, "It seems that Luo is very popular with other teachers at the department." Luo was the other translator and the three of them were about the same age. He was tall, proud, and well-informed about political issues.

"People love to listen to the 'inside news' Luo's father has access to. His father's rank is as high as President Jong's and they live in a beautiful house with wood floors and a servant. They have another apartment in his mother's working unit too, though it is empty most of the time." I sighed.

I thought of what Dan had said about the Communists, "Some people live in slums while others have too much space. They serve themselves, not the people."

Observing my indignation, Arthur said cynically, "This system is rotten. It was all written in a little book, *Animal Farm*, that George Orwell published in 1945."

"Oh? I have never heard of George Orwell."

"Of course, he is forbidden in China. There would be a riot if you Chinese read this book."

"What's it about?"

"Animals. It's a satire. It describes how the animals start out equal; later some become more equal than others. It tells a very simple but relentless truth: Communism does not suit human nature, which is selfish and greedy." He observed my reaction and continued, "Just think: how can human beings be totally unselfish? Serving the people, not themselves? If a person doesn't have a self, he doesn't exist. How can he serve others? Sheer nonsense!" He seemed excited.

"Do you know why China's door has been closed to the West since the 1950s? Because Mao wanted to have absolute control over the thoughts and deeds of every Chinese. I can tell he has been very successful."

"Don't tell a soul what Arthur just said to you. It may get you into trouble." Elizabeth shot me a meaningful glance.

"I have heard about this theory before. Don't worry."

"From whom?"

"An old friend. He is probably in a labour camp now. I have not heard from him for two years."

They looked at each other and said, "Well?"

I got up to leave. It was cold and windy outside. Arthur put on his toque and walked me to my dorm. While we were walking, I signalled him not to talk.

"I know why," he whispered.

"Be quiet."

The reason was simple: I did not want people to talk about me walking with a man in the dark, especially an American man.

22

Arthur was doing a regular morning round in the infectious diseases ward when Dr Zheng, the chief physician, asked him to diagnose a new patient. The patient came in the night before from Dang Yang County where he was a construction worker.

"This is his fifteenth day of high fever. He was first sent to a clinic, then a commune hospital, then a county hospital, and finally our hospital last night. He had no symptoms other than a continuous high fever, and he had been treated for a common cold." Apparently Dr Zheng and other physicians had discussed this case before Arthur arrived and were not sure of a diagnosis.

Arthur asked Dr Zheng a few questions and then went to see the patient. He was twenty years old and his general condition was very poor. He was pale and had been unconscious for three days.

With the case history sheets of this patient, Arthur walked to his office with me. "May-ping, I can't come up with a sure diagnosis either. In America, we rely on technology. We do all kinds of tests first, and the results of the tests help eliminate many possibilities. Then we make our decision. The Chinese physicians eliminate most possibilities first, then decide to do a few tests. They have better skills than American physicians." He was quite frank.

"Well, Chinese physicians don't get sued if they make a mistake either. I heard about the incident of a woman who died in childbirth at Wuhan First Hospital. She had heart disease and the doctors advised her not to get pregnant, but she did anyway. Her heart rate had been normal during her pregnancy. On the day of the birth, her husband brought her to this hospital and waited outside. It was the hospital rule that the husband should not be with his wife during her delivery. She was put on the delivery bed in a room alone and waited for her baby to arrive. It was about eleven in the evening, a time when the nurse from the last shift was leaving and the one from the next shift was arriving. There was a gynaecologist on duty during the night, but she was not informed of the woman in the delivery room. In a hurry, the nurse from the last shift forgot to tell anyone about the woman in the delivery room. The next morning she was found dead. The hospital covered up the accident and lied that the woman had died of heart failure during childbirth. And that is just one of three accidents I heard about last year," I finished in one breath.

At that moment, Dr Zheng came in and said that they had just found several red spots on the patient's back and it looked like haemorrhagic fever. Several cases had recently been diagnosed among construction workers in his area. Haemorrhagic fever is a virus infection transmitted by a species of mouse seen only on construction sites. Unfortunately, there was not much the doctors could do about it. To make things worse, treatment had been delayed for two weeks.

In an attempt to save their only son, the patient's parents asked a fortune teller for help. According to the fortune teller, the young man would be saved if he married immediately. A happy event could cancel an unfortunate incident. The parents begged their future daughter-in-law, who was only sixteen, to save their son's life. A wedding ceremony was held while the groom was lying in the hospital unconscious. Three days later, he died.

One overcast December afternoon during lunch hour, I saw Elizabeth and Arthur sitting on the cement bench in the hospital garden, looking dejected.

"What's new today?" I could not think of anything they should be worried about. They had an experienced nurse taking care of their baby, and a chef cooking for them. They could get a car any time they wanted, and they had two translators.

"May-ping, look me in the eye and tell me whether Vice-President Cheng said that the hospital would pay for our living expenses in the hotel when we first arrived." Arthur looked into my eyes.

"Of course he did," I said without thinking.

"He doesn't admit that he made that promise. Can you believe it?" Elizabeth was quite upset.

"We are students and we don't have much money," Elizabeth continued.

"I'll ask Dr Chow and Dr Sheng, who were also present." I left for Dr Chow's office immediately.

To my surprise, Dr Chow said that he could not remember! I was greatly disappointed with him because I respected him so much. But I did not blame him. I ran out of his office without a word.

Dr Chow belonged to the generation of intelligentsia who were tortured during the Anti-Rightist movement in the late 1950s and the Cultural Revolution between 1966 and 1976. They had learned to be mute and deaf to any controversial issues.

I then phoned Dr Sheng at the Virology Department. She was my roommate Chong-fin's supervisor. I heard that she was a person with integrity.

Dr Sheng said that she remembered Vice-President Cheng's promise to Elizabeth and Arthur.

"Could you please talk to President Jong immediately? Elizabeth and Arthur are very upset." I could not believe Vice-President Cheng's inconsistent behaviour.

The next day, Elizabeth and Arthur told me that President Jong had criticized Vice-President Cheng for making a promise without consulting the president's committee. President Jong agreed to pay the hotel expenses and offered Elizabeth a raise for her good teaching. I was happy for them.

 Winter vacation started on mid-January. I went to visit my parents and sisters in the village. My sister Wen-ping also came back for her winter vacation from her studies in a medical school. I was very pleased to see her still alive.

In the last few years, she had been through a lot. She had worked non-stop in order to enter junior high, then she needed to keep up her grades for senior high, and then university. The first time she took the National University Entrance Examination, her scores were only good enough for a third-rate university. My father expected her to go to a first-rate university, so she studied for another year and took the examination again.

July 7, 8, and 9, the days for the entrance examinations, were the hottest days in southern China that year. Because of constant pressure and lack of sleep, Wen-ping became sick on those three days. My father sent chicken soup to her at the examination site, about five miles from his working place. This time Wen-ping's scores were just good enough for a second-rate university, whereas my Auntie Lin's son achieved higher scores. My father attributed my sister's ordinary scores to her gender, "Girls are useless." He was so disheartened that he decided to give up on his last two daughters altogether. He did not hold any expectations for Nan-ping and Jing-ping, nor did he care about their studies.

When Wen-ping was in senior high, I sent her money via my father. I found out later that she was never told that the money was from me. Once she entered medical school, I mailed the money order directly to her, sometimes with a few extras, a sweater or a pair of fashionable gloves.

On New Year's Day, I wrote to Elizabeth and Arthur about the rituals in rural China on this special occasion. I was invited to have feasts at several neighbours' homes and received dozens of fresh chicken eggs and live chickens as gifts.

When I returned to the medical school, Elizabeth and Arthur thanked me for writing them. They had just received my letter.

"I don't believe it. It took fifteen days for my letter to travel one hundred and fifty miles?"

Elizabeth said that all letters and parcels to and from foreigners were checked, thus delayed. At Christmas time, they were supposed to receive a Christmas party cassette from their friends in America, but instead, they got a substitute music cassette by Mozart.

Arthur had told me several times that he was very homesick. It was his first time away from America, and our cultures were so drastically different. As Arthur did not speak any Chinese, his daily interactions were limited to the handful of people who could understand his English.

In the afternoons, Arthur sometimes worked with Dr Nei to discuss rare-disease case histories of the in-patients at the infectious diseases ward. As Dr Nei's spoken English was poor, they communicated mainly by gestures or writing the words down. Dr Nei was familiar with the indigenous diseases, so he lectured Arthur most of the time, which was more than Arthur's ego could handle, especially since they were about the same age.

One frosty February morning, Arthur asked me to go to the library with him, and off we went. Among the few foreign journals on the shelves, was the *Journal of the American Medical Association*. He took two recent issues and showed me two articles. He was the first author for both publications.

"What makes a first author?"

"The person who contributes the most ideas to a paper becomes the senior author. You see, I am an idea man," he added. I said that I had little doubt about that, and I meant it.

"Do you want me to show the articles to Dr Nei?" I teased him.

"He has already read them." Arthur smiled wryly.

Life was more interesting for Elizabeth since she was studying the culture and the people. She kept a small notebook with her in which she jotted down her daily observations of the patients, physicians, teachers, students, and kindergartners. People found it amusing to see an American speak Chinese and greeted Elizabeth warmly whenever they saw her. Unlike the stereotyped image of an American woman—decadent with expensive clothes and heavy makeup—Elizabeth dressed simply, sometimes with a Chinese-style winter jacket, which made her well accepted.

The English teachers took turns in escorting Elizabeth to our classroom every Tuesday and Thursday afternoons—both to be polite and to practise their English. During one of my escorts, she whispered, "Maybe they suspect us to be spies sent by Taiwan." She was still trying to figure out why the tape was confiscated.

At the same time she seemed to regard this idea as ridiculous. Nevertheless, she became very cautious when she talked about her two-year stay in Taiwan where she taught English and improved her Chinese. She would say to Director Yang that she hated Taiwan, but she told me that the food in Taiwan was wonderful.

Right after our oral English class with Elizabeth that day, Director Yang signalled me to his office. After closing the door behind him, he said gravely, "A number of people have complained to me that you are getting too close to Elizabeth and Arthur. Remember what I told you before they came: always keep your distance and do not talk about our internal affairs." After a slight pause, he continued, "I am thinking that it may be a good idea to let other young teachers practise their English for a while. That is to say, you don't need to be their translator from tomorrow on. Teacher Ren will replace you."

I was angry. "I have heard people say" was a good way to bring anyone down. This weapon had been used by every Chinese leader who wanted to scare and control his subordinates.

"What do you mean by being too close to them? Did I do anything wrong? Please name it." There were tears in my eyes and I could not help it.

"They did not say anything specific. Only that as a translator you are supposed to be a tool for Vice-President Cheng. When he said that he didn't make the promise to pay for the hotel fees for the foreigners, you should have said the same. You are not supposed to be on the side of the foreigners." It did not take long to get the truth out of him.

"When they first came, at the welcome meeting, didn't you say that Elizabeth and Arthur are our friends? I felt that I should not lie to friends," I argued.

"Theoretically, they are our friends. It's quite another matter when there is a conflict between our leader and them," he murmured. I could tell that he was just doing what he was told to do and I saw no point in continuing the conversation. When I was at the door, he added, "By the way, people also say that you look like Dai-yu, not the tough Communist Party member you should look like."

I walked away without a word since there was nothing I could do to change the way I looked.

Dai-yu was the heroine in the Chinese classic *The Dream of the Red Chamber*. A profound thinker and poet, she was proud, sensitive, and sentimental, with a willowy figure—a typical bourgeoise.

During my university days my aloof temperament and fragile physical build were alluded to several times but never explicitly criticized. Now that I had secured an iron rice bowl—a permanent teaching job—I had little fear of such indefinable accusations.

To cheer myself up, I went to a movie. Afterwards I visited Ming who was a cheerful person and could distract me from my battles at work.

The following afternoon, I phoned Ling-ling, the typist at our department and asked her if she had heard anything. Ling-ling served as my ears and eyes when I was not around. She told me that Arthur lost his temper with Vice-President Cheng that morning. He demanded that his trained translator be returned immediately. Arthur also said that he was not here for every English teacher to practise their English with.

Not wanting to harm the newly established friendly relationship with Johns Hopkins University, Vice-President Cheng promised Arthur that he could have me back right away. The problem was that nobody knew where I was.

I laughed loudly over the phone; so did Ling-ling.

On a late February afternoon while Elizabeth was teaching us English, Arthur came to tell her that he had just received a phone call that the U.S. Defence Minister Mr Brown and his advisor Dr Hilton were visiting Wuhan. Dr Hilton was Elizabeth's mentor at Harvard University where she was a PHD candidate.

Elizabeth and Arthur were invited for dinner that evening at a special hotel in the East Lake Park. Around six-thirty, a limousine came to pick them up. As it was pitch dark outside and the limousine window curtains were down they did not know where they went or how they got there. They guessed that it must be the Plum Garden, Mao's luxurious resort on the East Lake.

Elizabeth told me later that she made a direct phone call to her father in the U.S. from the hotel. When her father answered, he did not believe it was Elizabeth. He hung up the first time, thinking that some neighbourhood children were teasing him.

The following morning, Dr Hilton visited the kindergarten at the college and I was the translator. The one hundred and twenty children were divided into four classes and were provided three nutritious meals daily. Each child had a bed for a three-hour daily nap. There were some toys around, but the children seemed just as happy squeezing and chasing each other in the coal-heated rooms.

The nurses for the younger children were mostly older, experienced women. Younger women were in charge of children between the ages of four and six, who were given two classes daily.

"For all these services, the charge for each child is only ten yuan a month," I tried to impress our American visitor.

Dr Hilton spoke excellent Mandarin and had a great sense of humour. From time to time, he would make small errors when asking the nurses questions. I corrected him and he seemed pleased.

He showed me his identification card and a few credit cards.

"In America, everyone has a dozen cards." He asked me if I had any to show him. I told him that I only had one I.D. card, no credit card. He tried to talk me into showing him my card, but I was too embarrassed to do so.

That afternoon, Defence Minister Brown's daughter visited the infectious diseases ward of our Second Affiliated Hospital. She was twenty-four years old and was finishing university that year. Walking about the ward, she suddenly fainted, perhaps due to the strong disinfectant smell on the clean floor. Two physicians carried her to a bed and checked her eyes and heart rate. In a minute, she opened her eyes and smiled. We felt hugely relieved; it was too big a political responsibility for her to fall ill in our hospital.

March came and went. In early April, near the end of Elizabeth and Arthur's stay in China, they were invited to visit Wuhan Medical School in Hankou, and I went with them. We were first led to the president's meeting room to have tea. After tea, a vice-president started his greetings. He talked for fifteen minutes or so, mostly about the weather. I translated four or five sentences and then whispered to Arthur that the rest was "mostly bullshit." Arthur smiled and returned him a few greetings. I translated back to the president and waited for him to go on. He looked puzzled. I explained to him that the English language is a very terse one and that was how much I had to say. "There is nothing I can do about that," I shrugged and smiled innocently. Elizabeth and Arthur smiled at me understandingly. We had discussed a thousand times that the beginning of a presidential talk was very boring.

On our way back Elizabeth and Arthur asked me about Ming, the surgeon. I told them that he had recently visited my parents for the first time. Elizabeth could tell that there was hesitation in my voice when I referred to Ming as my boyfriend.

"You don't have to marry a man you don't love. There are other fish in the sea, May-ping." Elizabeth looked at me with sincere concern.

Nevertheless, I could not see any other fish. Though Ming was not to my standards, I was hopeful. He was cheerful, enthusiastic, energetic, and good with his hands though not with his mind. The latter defect was not his fault, but rather a combination of heredity and circumstances. His father was simple minded and quick tempered, his grandma and mother pampered him, and he lost eight years of grade school education due to the Cultural Revolution. Like the majority of our generation, he was an unfinished product—with a fully grown body but a less developed mind. With persistent efforts, I might be able to refine and reform him.

We were silent for a while. To disperse my melancholy mood, Arthur asked me to recite to him all the idioms he had taught me.

"Another day another dollar. What goes around comes around. If you can't beat them, join them. Play the cards as they lie. At least I've got my health. It ain't over until the fat lady sings. Now you've got everything, see you tomorrow."

"Not if I see you first," he finished the last one for me.

"Very good. Now tell me the long medical words I've taught you." He smiled at me encouragingly.

"Schistosomiasis, haemoglobin, haemorrhagic fever, haemophilia, jaundice hepatitis, meningitis."

"Stop, May-ping, you need a rest. Arthur, let her take a break. May-ping, you can quit working for this capitalist if he makes you overwork," Elizabeth said jokingly. To be honest, I could not remember many days when I felt overworked.

"Tit for tat," Arthur laughed.

"You know what will happen when you see us off at the train station next week?" Arthur asked me jokingly.

"What?" I was puzzled.

"May-ping, he is teasing you. Don't listen to him," Elizabeth smiled.

"You will receive a big kiss on the cheek *in public*." Arthur burst into laughter.

"No. You are not going to do anything like that, are you?" I begged him.

"Don't worry. May-ping. He won't do it. He is just teasing you," Elizabeth assured me.

It was a cloudy April day when we went to the train station to say goodbye to Arthur, Elizabeth, and Kate. A dozen people were present: Kate's nurse, Mrs Kuang, their chef, Shao-ting, Dr Zheng from the infectious diseases ward, Dr Chow, President Cheng, and several teachers from the medical college.

A few minutes before the train left, Elizabeth started her farewells. She first hugged me, then the others. She had tears in her eyes, as did we. Arthur was on the train taking care of Kate and their luggage. I stepped on the train and shook hands with him.

"Am I making progress?" I tried not to let my tears come.

"Yes. You have a firm handshake now." His eyes were moist.

"Write to me, May-ping." He had to shout as it was very noisy.

"I will." I jumped off the train and thought of the time when he told me that it was very important to have a firm handshake. He found that most Chinese had a weak handshake.

"It is graceful to have a weak handshake," I had explained.

"A weak handshake carries the meaning of being insincere in the West. Do what I say. No argument." I liked his sincerity.

The train left. I stood on the empty platform for a long time in a trance before Ling-ling came over to collect me. I felt a great loss. Now I had nobody to discuss social issues with. Most of my Chinese friends were either not interested or did not dare to talk. Although the political grip had been loosened, once bitten twice shy.

23

To COMPENSATE FOR MY LOSS, I dug into the provincial library where I found Balzac and Descartes, more novels by Tolstoy, Chinese and English versions of the complete works of Shakespeare, Sherlock Holmes, and a few novels by Jane Austen. I loved Balzac, for his keen satire and bitter irony regarding the old aristocracy, new wealth, young intellectuals, clerks, and criminals. I rated Balzac very high, as high as Shakespeare, Tolstoy, Mark Twain, and Chao Xie-qing, the Chinese author who wrote the *The Dream of the Red Chamber*. In the summer, we had forty-five days of paid vacation, and I read and read until my eyes were sore. Nothing existed when I read, except the characters, the shell of my brain, and the lightness of my body.

The new semester started on the first day of September. By this time, a graduate degree was preferred for college instructors, especially for those who entered university between 1971 and 1976, the worker-peasant-soldier students who went to university without entrance exams. The fifty or so worker-peasant-soldier graduates at the medical school were now removed from their teaching posts and put to work as lab instructors or administrators. Due to the shortage of English teachers, our department was the only one to allow us to continue to teach.

I asked to take the graduate entrance examination but was denied permission because the medical college needed me that year. "We like your teaching. You will never be removed from your teaching job," Director Yang guaranteed me.

"How do you know what will happen a few years from now? You may be retired. Why do you have to stop me from looking for a way to survive?" I questioned him.

"Our Party organization has decided that you and Luo are not permitted to take part in the graduate entrance examination. We don't want to lose you. But we will let Ren do it because many students don't like his teaching."

It was ironic that Luo and I were punished for being good teachers. "That's not fair. Ren and I came at the same time. If he can do it, I can do it too," I protested.

"If you say so, none of you can go. Ren can do it only if you and Luo write a statement saying that you have no objection to Ren's taking part in the graduate entrance examination." He was firm and clear.

Without permission from one's working unit, one could not take part in the graduate entrance examination. Out of generosity, Luo and I both signed the statement so Ren could pursue his career.

Ren passed and went to graduate school. The girl Ren had been courting for the last two years suddenly became nice to him. We congratulated Ren for his double victory.

On May 1, Labour Day, a colleague of Ming's was getting married and Ming asked me to go with him. I said that I did not feel like going. He begged me, with squeezed tears in his desperate black eyes. He said that the president of his hospital, the director of his department, and many of his colleagues were going, and he would like to introduce me to them all. His director spoke very good English and would like to practise with me, and Ming had already promised.

I understood: I was going to be a showpiece for Ming. Finally I agreed to let Ming satisfy his vanity; I dressed well and talked intelligently to his president and directors.

Ming seemed to care more about the form than the essence of our relationship. He was aware that I did not exactly admire his way of thinking, but he played down my feelings. His simple mind overestimated the power of force and ignored the strength of will and feelings. As long as he could get me to do what he desired me to, he was content.

At the end of that year, Ming suggested that we get married. I wrote to my father and told him our plan to marry during the coming Chinese New Year.

About two weeks before the New Year, I asked Ming if we could travel to Guei-lin, a picturesque mountain resort, for our honeymoon. He said that he did not feel like going.

For our wedding his mother sent him one thousand Chinese yuan, a colour TV and a tape recorder. His mother had found a job in Hong Kong and his youngest sister was attending a university there. As the policies loosened in the early 1980s, those who had close relatives in Hong Kong could easily obtain a passport. Since Ming's grandma on his mother's side was a Hong Kong resident, his mother had permission to live there.

As usual, bus tickets were difficult to get during the Chinese New Year. We bought two tickets but in the rush only Ming squeezed on the bus. I was pushed off by the crowd. He left for my parents' place a day ahead of me. When I arrived, he blamed me for not being able to get on the bus. I did not say anything; I smiled at my mother. I had learned to disguise my misery with a little smile.

I bought gifts for my father, mother, and sisters, and they were all happy for me. The next morning Ming and I went to the county town to visit Auntie Mei. While Ming and my auntie's husband were chatting, I said that I was going to visit a few old friends and would be back soon. I went to see Ai Hui, my high school classmate, then Sun-bin, my first love, who was home for the Chinese New Year.

I had just received a letter from Sun-bin. He had been assigned to work in an airplane factory in the mountains near Xi'an, a heavily polluted city in the western part of China.

In the letter, he said, "As I have matured a great deal during the last eight years, I have come to realize how wrong I was to hurt you so, especially when you were only sixteen years old. No words can express my repentance. If you would give me a chance to apologize in person, I would be very grateful."

I heard from Fang that Sun-bin had been trying to get back to Wuhan. The only way to get permission to move was to find a girlfriend in Wuhan. I had some faint idea that he might want to use me.

I knocked at the door and he opened it.

Our eyes met. In silence, I walked in and stood in the living room. He examined me from head to toe: I had my hair permed and dyed; I was wearing a fashionable watch, an expensive blouse, a long black wool coat, and high-heeled leather boots. I had grown three inches and was much fuller than when he last saw me eight years before.

"I can still recognize you." That was supposed to be a compliment.

He asked me to sit down, but I remained standing. He poured a cup of tea from a teapot and passed it to me. I took his tea; our eyes met again. To break the awkwardness, he smiled and said, "So, I have heard that you graduated with very good marks and now you are a well-known translator at your working unit."

"Not really," I answered as cool as I could.

He told me that just before the vacation, he took part in an English test in his working unit and received the highest mark. He also said that he had been working hard to improve his English with the hope of studying abroad some day.

"Me too," I said, sitting down.

"Will you come back if you get a chance to study abroad?" he asked tentatively.

"No. I won't," I assured him. "I don't want to see the ugly things around me. I know them too well."

"I hope I am not one of those ugly things," he cautiously tested how much I hated him.

"You are not the worst. You are only a product of the swiftly changing times," I said it slowly to make sure that he heard every syllable of my words.

He said that he was very sorry to have hurt me. It seemed that there were tears in his voice. He put one hand on mine but I took my hand back. He then murmured something like, "I still love you, and I am wondering if you would like to consider the possibility of our..."

I cut him off, "Please, the gulf between us is too big, big enough to drown us."

I opened my purse and took out two pictures of me with Ming. We were both smiling sweetly. I used the pictures as my weapon. I asked if he would like to keep one of our pictures and he said yes. I passed him both and asked him to choose one. When he asked about Ming, I changed the subject.

Silence.

For about two minutes, neither of us uttered a word.

I got up and walked to the door. He helped me with my coat and tried to kiss me.

I ran out and let my feverish face cool in the wind until I could walk steadily on the street. I knew he was watching me from the window.

For eight years, I had tried to forget him. But I had not.

How complicated one's feelings are! Yes, I hated him for intruding on my innocent mind with his cheap love, beautifully packaged to deceive my inexperienced eye. He took my heart and tore it to pieces. He never bothered to reflect on his behaviour until someone else hurt him. *Heaven has its way of revenge*: the old saying comforted me.

When I arrived at my auntie's, Ming was about to take the three o'clock bus to my parents' place without me. He asked me why I took so long and where I went. I said that I would tell him later. Picking up our travel cases, we ran to the bus station.

Auntie Mei watched us from her door. I could tell that she was not happy with Ming. She had told me that she did not think much of Ming. I had tried to comfort her, "Maybe he will treat me well."

That evening my father cooked a big carp in three ways: he steamed the tender belly, used the back and tail for sweet and sour sauté, and made soup from the head. After the feast, Ming took out a pack of Eternal cigarettes. He lit one for my father and one for himself. While they were talking about hospitals, physicians, and patients, I told Ming that I was going to visit some friends in Moon Crescent Village. He hardly heard me; he was busy making an impression on my father.

I visited Fang and Rong who had been married for six years now and had three lovely children. It was a chilly February evening. No moon. Only one or two dim stars twinkling in the remote, dark sky. Fang was teaching chess to his two older boys, one about five, the other about four.

"Ha, our distinguished guest from Wuhan city! A swallow made a nest on our roof beam recently, the big one right there. You see, a spring swallow brings happy tidings. Rong, come and see who is here!" Fang was overjoyed to see me.

My eyes searched for Rong. Hearing Fang's calling, she ran out of their bedroom where she was breastfeeding their youngest son. Passing the baby to her mother-in-law, she poured me a glass of hot water from a new thermos, the tin shell painted red.

I broke the news that I was getting married. They reacted quickly and let it pass. Fixing my gaze at Rong, I asked about her brother Dan as casually as I could. She said that Dan had not visited home once in the past three-and-a-half years. His letters were abstract and he never enclosed a return address.

"We have not heard from him for six months," she added.

The only logical conclusion was that Dan was not teaching in a high school. He was working in a labour camp where every incoming and outgoing letter was censored. He did not want to worry his relatives so he gave them no return address. Not wanting to further worry Rong and her parents, I did not tell her what I thought.

To relax the atmosphere, I got up from the wooden bench and walked toward the two boys who were throwing chess pieces at each other.

"You cheated!" the younger one shouted.

"I didn't! I just made a false move. You don't know anything, baby." He stuck out his tongue at the little one.

The bigger boy was like Fang, quick-minded and self-assured; the younger had Rong's delicate features.

"Oh, you are so lucky to have three beautiful boys!" My eyes refused to move away from the younger one; he had a tender complexion, gorgeous dark eyes, and velvet eyelashes.

"It would be nice to have one more! What do you think, my dear?" Fang turned to Rong, who shook her head. I noticed two fine wrinkles around the corners of her black eyes. She looked a little tired.

When I took leave, Rong gave me an embroidered blue satin quilt cover for a wedding gift. We unfolded it on her bed: two happy magpies frolicking at the top of a sunlit willow tree.

"Thank you, Rong. I wish I were a bird!" my eyes still on the magpies. "Happiness like this doesn't perch on the branches of this mortal life," I sighed while helping Rong fold the cover.

They seemed to be surprised and satisfied to hear my sigh. I knew Rong would rather that I married her brother Dan, and Fang still held a grudge against me when I flatly refused him a few years back by the pond.

When Fang walked me home, I told him about my meeting with Sun-bin. After some meditation, he said, "First love leaves the deepest impression on a person. In most cases, what you actually love is your idealized version of the person, not the actual person. But we hold to that image anyway, because it is pleasurable to have it." Fang's philosophical switch was now turned on.

Somewhere a dog barked. My grandma used to say that humans were reincarnated dogs. They seemed to have a resemblance: humans were as fiercely attached to their first love as a dog to its master.

"Come to think of it, you are right," I said. "I actually know nothing about Sun-bin and he knows nothing about me. He has no idea how I think and how I perceive the world. I don't believe he ever had any deep feeling for me. What he loved in me was my pretty face. And that kind of love I can do without."

During my short conversation with Sun-bin, he repeatedly said that he still saw me as I was at sixteen. He showed no interest in learning more about me—he assumed that he knew me well. What a presumptuous man!

"I haven't got over my first love either, you know." Fang gazed at my profile in the dark.

"Please don't think of me. That's unfaithful to Rong." I avoided eye contact with him.

"I am a hundred percent faithful to her. But it doesn't mean that I can't fantasize about other women!" He chuckled self-indulgently.

Men! They are strange creatures. I made a mental note.

"Don't you think of Dan?" The perceptive Fang!

"To be honest, I do. I dream about him a lot."

"Why do you love one and marry another?"

"Me? I have no choice. Marriage is a duty. Even the blind and crippled are not spared. Almost all the young women of my age at the medical college are married. You know the old saying: There are leftover rice and vegetable dishes, but no leftover men and women."

"And Ming is your best choice?"

"Under the circumstances, yes. Better to marry the one who loves you than to wait forever for the one you love."

"Ming loves you but you don't love him?"

"I actually love him in a way. He is cute: simple-minded and quick-tempered. If I can reform him a little, we should be okay."

"I think he has a lot to reform if he is bad tempered." After a pause, he added. "You are awfully naive to expect a man to change for you."

He shook his head and then continued, "Remember the old saying: It's easier to change a dynasty than a person's temperament."

"I know there is a lot of truth in that. But I believe in the power of love. If he truly loves me, he will accommodate." I was confident.

He sighed, disappointed. Apparently he realized that he could not change my mind.

The next morning Ming and I returned to Wuhan. It was cloudy and chilly. When my father and mother saw us off, I felt like crying. My parents were genuinely happy for me. All they wanted for me was a reliable man with a decent job. Love was not a word in their vocabulary. They believed that if two people lived together for long enough time, they would learn to care for each other.

That evening, a simple wedding ceremony and a banquet were held in Ming's apartment, now our new home, with the presence of his hospital directors, and a few of Ming's and my friends. At our wedding, Su-wen met Ming's friend and colleague, De-hua. The next day, De-hua saw Su-wen off and asked for her address.

In the next few days, Ming's colleagues visited us from morning to night. Ming did most of the talking and I served tea, sweets, and cigarettes. From time to time I would sneak out to take a nap in the study. Ming loved the compliments he received about his bride.

My colleagues and friends from the medical college also came to visit. They admired me: a colour TV, a refrigerator, a washing machine, a tape recorder, and a smiling husband. I thanked them and smiled politely.

The second month after we were married, Ming suggested that I give him all my salary and show him my monthly pay slip. He gave me five yuan for pocket money. Once when I lost the payment slip, he said that I must be hiding money from him and nagged me every day for the rest of the month. In order to have some peace, I made sure that I did not lose the pay slip again and handed him every fin. His father was eating one meal with us and he paid Ming some money each month. Once his father gave him five yuan too much by mistake; Ming ran to me, breaking the news and jumping for joy. Looking at him, I thought of the characters in Balzac's *La Comedie Humaine*.

Every now and then his mother would send some money and he would put it in the bank. One evening he received another cheque from his mother. He opened the suitcase where his bankbook was locked and showed me that his savings were up to four thousand yuan, a handsome amount for an ordinary Chinese. He said, "It's ours. You have a key to the suitcase too, eh?"

I congratulated him and returned to my work. I was marking mid-term exam papers for my students.

About ten minutes later, he came in and asked me if I had seen his bankbook. "Strange, I just put it here a moment ago and now I can't find it anywhere." He was panicking.

I got up and looked around but did not find it. I was worried because I was the only suspect. Thank God, he found it a moment later. I then gave him my key to the suitcase to save myself further trouble. I never opened it anyway.

About six months after I was married, Auntie Mei came to see me. I was delighted with this surprise. Ming took two yuan from his purse and passed it to me. "That's not enough. I want to make a good meal for her," I whispered. He put on his jacket and went to work. I tried hard not to let my tears show. When my auntie asked how I was doing, I forced a big smile and said that I was doing just fine.

24

THAT WINTER MY GRANDMA HAD A STROKE and Uncle Xin sent her to the people's hospital in Wuchang District. In a few days, she was improved enough to return home. She said to Uncle Xin that she wished to live in the village for a while, so my father sent a car to take her back. She seemed to be alive again: neighbours came to see her and chat every day.

About a month later, she had another stroke. My father sent her back to the hospital. Unfortunately no modern medicine helped her this time; she was paralyzed from the waist down.

Although her medical expenses were covered under my uncle's medical plan, she could not stay in the hospital once her condition became stable. My uncle and his wife took her in and nursed her in their home. They washed her daily and fed her three times a day. Their two children, Wu-jun and Yian-jun also helped after school. I visited my grandma every Friday afternoon to wash her hair and cut her finger-and toenails. I also took her bed sheets and clothes home to wash in our washing machine as my uncle did not have one.

At first, she could speak softly. By April, she lost her ability to speak but could understand what was said to her. When I visited, I would bring several kinds of her favourite snacks and fruits. Wu-jun, Yian-jun, and I would show one thing to her and ask her if she wanted to try some. If she nodded, we would feed her a few pieces. If she shook her head, we would put the pieces in our mouths which made her smile—those were the last smiles I saw on her face.

One warm morning in early September I bought a few steamed dumplings and hurried to her room so she could eat while they were hot, only to find her breath very slow and faint. I tried to talk to her, but she could no longer hear me—there was no reaction at all. Tears flowed as I held her bony hands and remembered how she had held my hand after I burned myself when I was three.

We had a four-room house then, with a large kitchen where she cooked and I played. One hot summer afternoon, she had stir-fried some vegetables, cooked a large pot of rice porridge, and put them on the large kitchen table to cool off. While she was not looking, I climbed onto a chair from which I could reach anything on the table. After sampling the vegetables, I wanted to try some porridge. I gave a loud cry when my little hand plunged into the hot porridge. My grandma ran to me and put my hand in cool water. I was screaming; the pain from the blisters was unbearable. My father took me to the commune clinic and my grandma stayed overnight with me, since my mother had to take care of my one-year-old brother at home. The doctor put many kinds of "cooling" herbs on my hand to cancel the "heat" which caused the blisters. Sure enough, the burning feeling started to subside after a while. I stopped crying and fell asleep.

My grandma, however, did not sleep at all. She sat by my bedside and held my bandaged hand. Whenever I woke up from the pain, she would hold me up and give me sweet tea. The next day, I was allowed to go home. Putting me on the front seat and my grandma on the back seat of his bicycle, my father took us home. I did not let anyone but my grandma change my bandage in the next few days. Thanks to her care, only a few small scars remain on the back of my left hand.

That September day, I sat beside my grandma until my uncle came home for lunch. I went home and lay down; many vivid pictures of my childhood passed through my mind: she warmed my frozen hands with her cotton coat after I came home from school. She taught me to observe and think before I ever talked and acted. She encouraged me to bear and overcome the worst hardships in order to be successful in life. If, upon returning from school, I could not find my grandma in the house or the yards, I would start to cry, fearing that she might have disappeared. Once after school, I was skipping ropes with my friends when Grandma called me to help her in the kitchen. Reluctant to stop my game, I hid behind a high pile of wheat stalks in the yard so she could not find me. Later she said that if I did that again, she would disappear and never, never return.

Now she was going and would never, never return.

Ming finished lunch and joined me for a nap. I could not sleep so I sat up. Ming asked me to stay in bed for a while because he enjoyed having me lying beside him. I told him I must go to my grandma. She was dying. I jumped out of the bed, put on my jacket and ran to my grandma. She was still breathing faintly but was not aware of my presence.

"I'll stay here. You go to work. I'll phone you if anything happens to her," I said to my uncle.

Toward the middle of the afternoon, my grandma's weak breathing stopped. I called for a neighbour who said, "Yes, she has gone." I tearfully phoned my uncle.

In the evening when my uncle, his wife, Wu-jun, and Yian-jun were sitting around my grandma, I went to the post office to make long distance phone calls to my parents and my aunties. It took two hours for the lines to get through.

My father, aunties, and all the male children of the three families came to mourn my grandma. My mother was not invited to come, nor were any of the female children.

I asked Ming to pay last respects to the remains of my grandma, and he went reluctantly. Her body would be sent to the crematorium the following day and my uncle's wife asked Ming if he could borrow a stretcher from his hospital.

"I probably could, but can't you borrow one from your clinic?" Ming responded distantly.

"I guess I can. It's just that I have a household of guests to take care of." She seemed disappointed.

I heard every word of Ming's conversation with my uncle's wife. *Why should he care about my grandma if he doesn't even care about me?* I reasoned.

In accordance with my grandma's wishes, her ashes were buried in the graveyard near the village where she brought up four children and five grandchildren.

Eight months later, my grandpa joined his wife. He had been a chain-smoker all his life and suffered from severe bronchitis for a year before he died. My mother, father, brother, and sisters fed him and did the washing and cleaning. A few days before he died, I went home to see him. Seeing the many fruits and food I brought him, he smiled.

In the evening, my brother, who had become an electrician in the commune centre, also brought my grandpa food and gifts. It was a hot evening. My brother fed my grandpa pieces of watermelon to keep him cool.

"This is what grandchildren are for: to care for me when I am old and sick." My grandpa's wrinkled face was a thousand lines when he grinned.

Unlike my uncle, who did not care about formalities, my father and Auntie Mei decided to give my grandpa a grand funeral. They rented a big van, put his remains in the centre and decorated the van with many colourful wreaths. Accompanied by the sound of firecrackers, the van travelled through the village to the county town, then back to the village accompanied by his children and grandchildren wearing black bands and white flowers.

"He lived a perfect life." I heard my grandpa's friends say as the van passed the village. My grandpa enjoyed playing cards in the evenings with his many friends. As he could not see very well in the dim kerosene light at the meeting room, he was not often a winner. Several of his friends counted on him for their cigarette money, and my grandpa seemed not to mind. Now they would certainly miss him.

25

In September 1982, it was my turn to take a year off from work to advance my education. I was paid full salary and my bus pass was reimbursed. My alma mater, Wuhan First Normal University, was chosen for my study.

I took four courses and audited three. The first class was at seven-thirty in the morning and I arrived two minutes late. Sitting there, still gasping, I felt unusually light. It was so good to be free of the responsibilities of a teacher! As a student now, I felt fine to be a few minutes late.

Our class had twenty students from every part of China: Xingjiang, Shengyang, Xian, Changcun, Fujian, Hangzhou, and Hainan. We introduced ourselves to each other and the lecture began. It was an English literature class. The text started with Chaucer's *Canterbury Tales*, but Professor Tang began with Francis Bacon, because, he said, quoting Bacon, "Some books are to be tasted, others to be swallowed, and some few to be chewed and digested." Besides reading, we were also going to practise writing. Again he quoted Bacon, "Reading maketh a full man; conference a ready man; and writing an exact man."

He then remarked that our facial expressions indicated that we had some doubts about his choice of authors but that it was okay: "If a man will begin with certainties, he shall end in doubts; but if he will be content to begin with doubts, he shall end in certainties." We all laughed. The professor was in his fifties, tall, well-built with short, greyish hair and scholarly looks.

We marvelled at Professor Tang's ability to make the class vivid and interesting. Bacon was such a wise man! His words were like a spring flowing through my thirsty mind. I felt fresh and inspired.

When the class was over, I was too excited to contain myself. I murmured, "I would like to be a student forever."

"Only if you are getting paid," remarked a thirtyish student sitting next to me.

Devil, how does he know that I am getting paid? I squinted at him and walked out of the classroom. It was sunny and warm outside.

My legs were a little stiff from sitting for so long so I rambled along the gardens where I used to read my beloved novels. The fountain, the flowers, and the sidewalk were the same, but the spirit of the campus had changed a great deal over the past four years. It used to be occupied by simply and formally dressed students; now they were colourfully and casually attired.

At lunchtime, I followed the flow of students to the dining hall. It had not changed much in appearance, but the essence had. Quality service and profit were emphasized, and a variety of dishes was available.

I bought a sweet and sour fish on sautéed cucumber over steamed rice and sat down by a table near a sunny window. In a few minutes, half a dozen students from our class joined me. We introduced ourselves again as we did not remember each other's names from the morning. As we were finishing, Fuji, the man who sat beside me in the English literature class, joined us.

"Were you surprised that I knew that you are getting paid?" he asked, sitting down at the end of my bench. Hearing his cynical remarks, I lifted my eyes from a tiny fish bone to observe him more carefully. Oh! What resemblance to Dan! He had Dan's sun-tanned broad forehead, bright and unfathomable black eyes, sickle-curved lips and muscular shoulders. Even his sarcastic tone of voice reminded me of Dan.

"Don't be. Given my experiences in the countryside and cities, I can usually infer a person's economic and social status after a few minutes' observation." He continued talking but I was not listening; my thoughts were elsewhere.

Someone asked Fuji where he came from and where he had been for his re-education. He replied that he started to work in a mountain village on Hainan Island when he was sixteen. The villagers were very poor. Meat was expensive. Sometimes when the urge to eat meat became unbearable, Fuji and his friends would steal a chicken from the villagers, cook it on a campfire and eat it along with a bottle of homemade rice wine.

"I have experienced everything," he said. "I carried the dead body of my friend wrapped in coconut palm fronds when he was drowned in a flood.

"In the summer of 1969, the water level in Hainan broke records after a month of continuous heavy rain. The Wan Quan River flowing through the island was so full that the big dam was threatened. If the dam broke, half the island would be flooded. Crops would be ruined and many lives would be in danger.

"Every young man was called to save the dam. We tried to stop a leak by making a strong wall with sandbags and our brave bodies. Suddenly, a large wave burst the dykes, washing away the sandbags and the people who were standing behind them. I swam hard to a large tree and managed to climb to the top. Two hours later, the flood ebbed, leaving many dead bodies in the fields and around the houses. I finally found my friend's body, wrapped him with coconut palm fronds and managed to carry him back to our dorm. When I phoned his mother, she fainted.

"Strange, I was right beside him. He was the one chosen by God. I am a religious man, and I believe in God. If God doesn't think you should die, you can live forever."

"What is your religion?" We never heard of any Chinese of our generation being religious, as Chairman Mao banned Buddhism and Christianity in 1949.

"I am a Christian; I was baptized when I was an infant. I was born in February 1949, just before Liberation, you see. My parents studied in Christian schools operated by missionaries from England. The British exported both Christianity and opium to China." He rolled up his shirt sleeves which seemed too long for his arms, or his arms were too short for the sleeves.

"You know why?" he quizzed us.

We shook our heads.

"They have something in common—Christianity and opium." We opened our ears and eyes as wide as we could: Fuji's ideas were very peculiar. "They both put you to sleep—spiritual sleep, so you don't think, you accept without questioning—life is easier if you don't think."

"Why did they do that?" Mei-ling, a vivid, assertive young woman sitting beside me, could not help herself.

"Because it made it easier for them to take our gold bullion away. The Empress Chi-xi in the late Qing dynasty was so addicted to opium that she couldn't stay awake for the morning reports by her ministers. Total chaos and corruption of the Qing dynasty provided the British a golden opportunity to take home half the valuables in Yuan Ming Yuan, our national treasury."

"How come Christianity did not put you to spiritual sleep?" snapped Yao sourly. He had heard Fuji's scholarly discourse and was jealous of Fuji who had, in a matter of minutes, triumphantly captured the attention of everyone, including Mei-ling. Although the class had hardly got acquainted, it was crystal clear that Mei-ling was the most attractive woman in the class. She had large black eyes with thick eyelashes and slender lips slightly raised at the ends like a baby moon. Her lavish dark hair was braided and tied with an elegant silk scarf on her slim shoulders.

"I wish it did, so we wouldn't have to be tortured here," Mei-ling echoed Yao to disguise her apparent liking of Fuji.

"You think listening to me is torture?" Fuji emphasized *me* to imply that his feelings were seriously hurt. But who would believe that?

"What do your parents do?" I liked to study people together with their family backgrounds.

"They are high school teachers. Oh, they are nice, naive people and…"

"They accept everything without questioning," Mei-ling and Yao finished the sentence for him.

"My mother has never had a quarrel with anyone in her whole life. She…" He was still talking when all of us had finished our lunch and were ready to leave. We thanked him for his time and he said that his time was worthless.

"A day's work in the village was worth five fin. Now I am a teacher in Hainan Normal College, I make two yuan a day, not enough to buy a skirt for my daughter," he added jokingly.

To be polite, Mei-ling and I stood beside the table until he finished his speech. He continued after taking a breath, "My wife, my daughter, and I live in a small room with neither a kitchen nor a bathroom. We eat at our parents' place every evening."

"Maybe you want to save money," Mei-ling teased him.

"Could be, could be." Fuji was frank and cynical.

"Well, he is eloquent or what?" I whispered to Mei-ling as we walked to our dorm for a nap.

Later in the week when I was handing in my assignment, Fuji asked me half seriously if he could have a look. Blinking mischievously, I said, "Yes, yes, you may, because you are exceptionally handsome. Therefore we are all at your service." The students burst into a loud laughter.

"Never mind, I only want to get a good mark. As Professor Tang said that your translation was flawless last time, I am eager to learn." He chuckled naughtily.

"So you have doubts about my translation, eh? I didn't copy anyone's work. Remember, it was an in-class test." I made a face at him and ran out of the classroom with Mei-ling.

That afternoon Mei-ling and I were reading in the backyard of the classroom. The still-greenish grass soaked in the autumn sun and a soothing breeze sent dancing shadows from the lemon-green leaves of a poplar.

Fuji sneaked in and surprised us both. We told him that we were studying for a test and asked him to leave, but he refused to go. We ignored him and read Wordsworth's poem together:

> *Though nothing can bring back the hour*
> *Of splendour in the grass, of glory in the flower;*
> *We will grieve not, rather find*
> *Strength in what remains behind ...*
> *In the faith that looks through death,*
> *In years that bring the philosophic mind.*

Fuji said that he did not believe in poems, that he was a realistic man. His university entrance examination scores were high enough to go to a science university but he made a fatal mistake.

"What was your mistake?" We were curious.

"Honesty. I put 'married' in the form, and the university preferred unmarried people." He was indignant.

We giggled.

"But you are a married man, and that is your tragedy. Maybe you have no talent for science anyway."

"That's not true. My wife thinks I am the most talented man on earth." He took out his purse and showed us his wife's picture, then his daughter's.

"The little one is more interesting than the big one actually." He put his school bag on the grass and stared at the fountain in the middle of the garden.

"You are crazy. You'd better leave us alone."

"I am not crazy. I am perfectly normal. Do you want to hear the story of me courting my wife?"

"Sure." We were tempted again.

"She was an attractive woman from the big city, Guangzhou, who went to receive her re-education from the peasants in Hainan. She shared a room with my sister, and that's how I met her. I was an ugly duckling from a small city, Haikow. When I started to be interested in her, people on the farm thought that I was out of my mind. However, I got her attention, then purposely avoided her for two months. It was a hard two months for both of us. By the end, she was asking my sister about me several times a day.

"Then she went to visit her parents in Guangzhou to decide what to do. I wrote her a seven-page love letter which captured her heart. At that time, she was considering a job in Guangzhou and not returning to Hainan. She took my letter to her father and asked his opinion. Her father asked her if she hated me, and she shook her head. Then he asked if she liked me, and she said she didn't know. 'Your decision is made, my dear. Go to the man you love,' her wise father advised her. She returned and I kissed her feet for the first time." He looked proud and content.

"Why feet?" we asked.

"Feet are more sensitive than hands or lips." He looked out of his mind again.

"If you don't leave, we are leaving." We left the madman on the grass dreaming of his wife.

As Mei-ling and I were strolling along the shady path leading to a hill, she told me that her father was also a wise man.

"He is romantic too. He takes my mother for a walk every evening after dinner. God, I admire them: they have been in love with each other ever since they met during their university days."

Mei-ling's parents were well-known physicians working in the Fujian Provincial Hospital. During the Cultural Revolution, Mei-ling's father was locked in a hut for five years because he was a capitalist road follower. Her mother was sent to a mountain area to work in the fields for three years for being born into a landlord family. To keep her mother company, the eight-year-old Mei-ling volunteered to live in the countryside.

"One chilly day in the latter part of November during lunch hour, my mother washed our clothes in a nearby river and put them in a bucket. I offered to help carry the bucket back. When we passed a rice paddy, the shoulder pole slipped off on my end. The bucket fell off and the laundry was all over the muddy fields. My mother slapped me hard on the head, then picked up the laundry and went back to the riverside to wash it again.

"I did not cry. I looked around and picked up a few items my mother had missed. By this time, several children from the village came to help me. We washed the clothes in a nearby brook.

"When I took the clean laundry home, my mother hugged me and burst into tears. 'Why should I hit you? You are my only comfort and support. You are the reason I get up in the morning.' I observed my mother's tearful face: she looked very pale and tired.

"My mother was forty-five years old that year and had never worked in the fields before. Many times she told me that climbing the mountains with a load of fertilizer was killing her. On December 1, my ninth birthday, she gave me a piece of paper with all the information I needed to know in case of an emergency: the address of our apartment in town, the working unit of my father's brother who lived in Zhejian province, and the name of the village where her sister lived in Shangxi province. Then she looked at me and asked, 'If I die here, can you find your way home to town?' Tears pouring down my cheeks, I recite the addresses and names on the piece of paper. She nodded and pulled my tear-stained face to hers. I felt many tears running down my face and didn't know if they were hers or mine.

"She folded the piece of paper and sewed it between the layers of my padded cotton coat together with her bankbook.

"During the night, she couldn't sleep. She was worried about my father and my two sisters. My father was constantly interrogated and beaten by the Red Guards. My two sisters, one twelve and the other six, were living by themselves.

"About a week later, my mother collapsed in the fields and was sent to a county clinic. When her condition got worse, she was transferred to the Fujian Provincial Hospital.

"She had cervical cancer and had an operation. My father was locked up in town, but he was not allowed to see her. After the operation, my mother's leaders allowed her to stay in town and work in the hospital.

"Now our whole family lived together except my father. He was detained for another two years, and my mother was not permitted to see him. My sisters and I were allowed to visit him on Sundays." Mei-ling paused and sighed, "Those were hard days and nights for my parents. Thank God, it's over." A sad smile fleeted through her reminiscent face.

Her elder sister later became an accountant and the younger sister, Lo-ra, went to Shanghai Transportation University.

"Lo-ra's fate has been rather unfortunate since she offended her political instructor during the first year of her university." We sat down on a smooth stone bench under a tall birch tree. "She was seventeen years old and didn't know how to tactfully decline her political instructor's sexual advances. She refused him bluntly. Upon graduation, she was assigned to work in a military vessel manufacturing factory in a remote mountain area in your province, Hubei. The name of the place is ... Yunyang, yes, Yunyang."

"I have heard about that place." I looked at her attentively.

"The working and living conditions in the factory were very poor. Lo-ra's specialty was not used. She was asked to work as a violinist with the singing and dancing team to spread Mao Ze-dong thoughts among the workers."

"Ridiculous!" I exclaimed.

"As the military factory was under direct control of the Ministry of Defence, no one could leave it without big 'back doors.' As my father doesn't know anyone in high places, the only way Lo-ra could leave the factory was to pass the graduate entrance examination. She studied hard every night for a year and passed the exam the following spring.

"Lo-ra has changed. She used to be a vivacious girl full of imagination and ideals. She is now too practical and extremely tactful. She is always ready to bend to please others. She has become a person without a self, the type Mao wanted every Chinese to become." Mei-ling was very insightful.

"You know who she married? Her new political instructor in graduate school." Mei-ling looked at me and shook her head.

"What happened to her old political instructor, the vicious one who made sexual advances to her?"

"Nothing. He moved to another working unit in Shanghai. May God punish him." Mei-ling was indignant.

"Bad people always get away. The world is upside down." I wondered if justice still existed anywhere.

In spite of the hardships, Mei-ling's parents had been loving. Her father never thought that girls were intellectually inferior to boys and he cherished every one of them. Mei-ling could even joke and tease her father, which was hard for me to imagine. I was envious of Mei-ling for having such a democratic father.

One chilly but sunny November day a dozen of us were eating lunch when Yao relayed the news of three deaths by a car accident in the *Yangtze Daily*. We got into a general discussion on the philosophical aspect of death. I said that I was not afraid to die.

"Death is nothing to the dead, but hard on the dear ones left behind," I stated decisively.

"Yes, after you die, you don't feel a thing," several women and men agreed.

"That's the beauty of death, but what if God decides that you don't die? You live with one arm or a massive scar on your face?" Fuji could always make something dramatic out of the ordinary.

"Oh, I would rather have one arm than an ugly scar on my face," exclaimed the vain Mei-ling.

"I would prefer a scar on my face to one arm, for sure," proclaimed the practical Yao.

"I want neither; I would just jump into the Yangtze River. Oh, I love the Yangtze River, the second-longest river on earth! I want my ashes to be spread over it after I die. I should remember to write this in my diary so my parents won't forget," said Jing, a tall young woman in her later twenties. Single and aloof, she had a neck as long as a crane and eyes as fine as a line.

"When you are young, it's easy to talk about death because it's so far away. But when you get into your fifties, you become scared to think and talk about it," a bearded man well into his fifties said, passing us young people his wisdom.

When I was washing my bowl in the long sink of the dining hall Fuji joined me and asked, "You are married and not happy, right?"

"No. I am perfectly happy." I hated men who tried to outsmart me.

"Here is my logic. You may disagree but don't lie or deny it if I am right." He sounded like an experienced conversationist.

"You just said that you were not afraid to die. A young woman with your looks and talent would normally wish to live unless she is unhappily married." He looked me in the eye.

"I said that I don't mind dying, not that I desire to die. The former indicates that I am brave, and the latter means that I have lived enough. Do you see the difference?" He blinked but could not come up with a counter-argument.

"Be courageous and admit your defeat." I laughed loudly; I always enjoyed defeating conceited opponents.

As children, my brother and I would argue for hours and ask my grandma to referee. She would often say, "I think you both have a good point and you have argued logically. The important thing is to form a good argument before you open your mouth."

"If the argument is a formal one, organize your statements well; write down the major points, and choose your wording carefully when you talk." That was my father's teaching.

That day after school, I took a long walk. I needed some quiet time to contemplate Fuji's sharp remarks. I had been deceiving myself and my parents that I was happy. I had hoped to influence my husband, to change him since he said that he loved me. *But why does he yell at me so frequently? Why doesn't he care about my feelings if he loves me? What kind of love is this?* I could not figure it out.

26

ON FRIDAY MORNINGS WE had linguistics classes. From the back row, I heard an almost-smothered sobbing. Looking around, I saw that Gao, over in the corner, was drying her eyes with a handkerchief. After class I asked her if she wanted to talk, and she nodded. We sat on a wooden bench in the backyard. Gao told me that the night before she and her husband had a fight. He was not sensitive to her feelings and lost his temper frequently. Other than that, he was a nice person. Her case sounded similar to mine.

"What are you going to do?" I observed her. Her eyes were red, more tears were coming.

"I am thinking of a divorce."

From her hesitant tone of voice, I could tell that she had not thought about the idea carefully.

"What are you going to do with your baby?"

"I don't know." She shook her head.

"You must think of all the details before you mention a divorce to him. Divorce is a word that you don't say lightly. Think about it for a few days before you make a decision. Okay?"

There were no lawyers and no counselling services in China. Relatives, friends, and working unit leaders were the people we turned to when we had family problems.

A week later, Gao invited me for lunch. She had a one-room apartment on the first floor. The room was crowded with a queen-size bed, a dresser, a table, and four chairs. She had placed the stove in the corridor.

"Here are some ginger eggs Fuji cooked for me last week. He said that it's a tradition in his hometown for new mothers to eat ginger eggs. It took him half a day to cook these." Gao put one egg in my plate.

"I didn't know Fuji could be kind to people," I said, cracking the shell noisily.

"Yes. He is. He helped me carry my furniture last month when I moved to this place," Gao added.

I looked at her baby who was fast asleep.

"He looks like his father." I had met Gao's husband once.

"Isn't it terrible to think that he looks like him, not me? I am the one who bore all the hardships. It's so unfair," Gao complained loudly while gazing at her baby's sweet face with a new mother's tenderness.

"So how are things going with you two?" I looked at her and waited for her reaction.

"I want to wait until my baby is older," she said, at a loss.

"Divorce is not a solution in China. People's gossip is very difficult to deal with. Living by yourself with a baby is more than you can handle. Ignore him and concentrate on the things that matter to you. You don't need to fight with him, either," I advised her like a big sister.

Taking a bite of the egg, I continued, "Professor Xiang, a humorous man in our department, once told us that he didn't know what love was. He has lived with a woman for thirty years and they have three children. According to him, only five percent of all marriages are successful. Love is a luxury few people can find," I sighed, the sigh of Professor Xiang.

"Why didn't you tell me this before?" She looked as if she had discovered a new continent.

A few weeks later, Gao told me that it was hard for her to practise what I advised her to do.

"Sure you can do it if I can," I encouraged her again.

"You must be kidding. Does your husband treat you badly?"

"Very similarly to the way you are treated," I said point-blank.

"You give people the impression that you are the happiest person on earth." She punched me on the right shoulder.

"I am happy most of the time. Nobody can be happy all the time, you know." I tried a smile, the smile of my Auntie Mei.

"Have you noticed any change on my face?" I asked Gao.

She looked carefully and pointed at a new scar on the right side of my face and asked: "Did your husband beat you?"

I nodded.

During the day, I stayed in school as long as possible and went to bed right after dinner. Ming and I hired a girl to help us with cooking and cleaning. Her name was Ze and she was introduced by a friend of my mother's. Her cooking left something to be desired but I cared little. On her first day of work, she broke an expensive dish and lost the valve for our pressure cooker. Ming yelled at her until she started to sob. I felt sorry for her and took her shopping the following Sunday. Ze grew up in a rural family where girls' lives were cheap. Her mother and four brothers treated her like dirt. Her father was a professional thief and had been in and out of jail all his life. I bought her a plum-patterned blouse at the crowded Wuchang Department Store, which cheered her up.

On our bus ride back, she elbowed me and pointed to a dandy-looking young man lifting a wallet from an old woman's purse. I looked without moving my head and realized that we were not the only ones who had noticed the theft. No one said anything nor moved. The young man got off at the next stop and was met by friends. We took a deep breath and looked for our wallets: they were still there.

Anyone who reported a pocket lifter could get into big trouble, which included being robbed, raped, or even killed. Not long ago, a bus conductor was shot to death when she asked one of the passengers not to smoke in the bus. After the passenger was warned a second time, he said, "If you interfere with my freedom to smoke again, I will shoot you." "How dare you?" The conductor could not believe her ears. The passenger blew a mouthful of smoke in the face of the conductor and smirked. He then slowly took out his pistol and shot her in the head.

The young man was a policeman who possessed a pistol. As his father was the vice-mayor of the city of Wuhan, he had always done what he wished and could get away with it. Following the death of the conductor, all the bus drivers and conductors working on the fifteenth route voted for a strike, demanding that the criminal be sentenced to death. Three days later, the man was sentenced to death, but without immediate execution. We all knew that his sentence would be reduced to a lighter term later.

About two months later, Ze's elder brother paid her a visit. He was passing through Wuhan from a trip to Yunnan where he had sold a thousand yuan's worth of herbal drugs to the villagers in remote mountain areas. Yunnan is a province close to Vietnam. I asked him where he got the drugs and he said that they made them in a small factory in his village.

After he left, his sister told me that those drugs were a joke. They were made mostly of dried herbs of any kind and meant to deceive ignorant peasants. Their village factory also brewed rice liquor and sold it to peasants in Anhui, one of the poorest provinces in China. This cheap liquor had been known to poison and kill people.

A few days before the Chinese New Year, my brother came to ask if Ming's hospital needed dried herbs which he had bought at a very low price in rural Anhui. Ming checked the quality of the herbs and arranged to sell them to the drugstore of his hospital. My brother made about three hundred yuan and acknowledged Ming with two cartons of cigarettes.

When I walked my brother to the bus station, I asked him, "Do you think this kind of buying and selling is good for our economy? If productivity doesn't increase, where does the money come from? Some people are getting rich, but from whom? From ignorant peasants who are already in poverty?"

I glanced at his profile. He was thinking hard but did not understand what I was saying.

After a pause, he said, "Many people are doing big business. People whose parents have access to state-planned materials such as steel and wood products buy cheap from the government and sell at five to ten times the buying price to state-owned working units. Premier Zhao Zi-yang's son is doing such business. So do Marshal Ye Jian-ying's daughter and son-in-law."

My brother was trying to tell me that what he was doing was nothing compared to what other people were doing.

"You can do what you are doing, but keep your job. I don't think the economy can afford to have this kind of business for long." I then asked him if he had bought any gifts for his wife and daughter after being away for a month.

"No. They don't need anything," he replied.

My brother was tall and muscular, with good facial features and a feudal peasant's mind. He was one of the millions of Chinese who were lost in our experiment with capitalism.

27

THE SECOND SEMESTER STARTED TEN DAYS after the Chinese New Year. After our first class, Mei-ling ran to me and looked at me from head to toe. "Nice coat!" she said. I was wearing a dark-red checked wool coat my husband's mother had bought for me in Hong Kong. Anything from Hong Kong or a foreign country was considered exotic and superb. When we were alone in the corridor, she confided that I looked thinner and tired. I told her that my husband's sister and a friend had visited us for two weeks. We offered them our queen-size bed and we slept in the study, which faced the north and was cold. As our hired help had gone home for the Chinese New Year, I did all the household chores myself. I did their laundry and cooked three meals a day. My husband adores his sister and wanted me to treat her well. Yet he was too busy to take care of her himself.

"Poor thing." Mei-ling took out some chocolate for me as if I were a child. I wanted to smile but could not. I had a bite of the chocolate and excused myself to the washroom where I allowed my tears to come. Mei-ling's care and warm words were very touching—I had rarely received anything like that from any other human being on earth. My mother thought that my life was heavenly comparing to hers. My sisters were so used to having me looking after them that it never occurred to them that I too might need some attention.

The afternoon class was intensive English. We were required to analyze sentence structures, translate the text back and forth, make sentences with the key phrases, and recite any paragraph the professor happened to be interested in.

Although I was physically with the class, my mind was miles and years away. Mei-ling's comment about my coat reminded me of a small episode years back when I started university life in this same classroom. It was a cold day and I did not have a coat. Lu-wei, a girl from a cadre's family in Wuhan, happened to be wearing a linen coat. "How much was your coat?" I asked her.

"Guess." She smiled with a sniff.

"Twenty yuan?" I tried a number.

"No way! Thirty," she smirked.

I never forgot her proud expression and sarcastic tone. Although she tried to make me feel inferior, I did not let her. I walked away with my head high and seldom talked to her in the next few years.

Professor Tang called onYao, who was sitting next to me. While he was reciting his paragraph I hurriedly memorized the following passage in case I was the next victim. Sure enough, my name was called. I looked at the text once more while slowly standing up. I recited the paragraph without missing one word. "Good memory." Professor Tang said pleasantly. I shrugged and returned to my meditation.

At lunch time, we shared apples from Xian, raisins from Xinjiang, and coconut from Hainan. "Classmates can be loving and caring if they are not trained to hate each other," I reflected.

Everything on the campus reminded me of the trauma of my earlier university days. I had tried to erase those memories but they lingered like a hungry ghost wanting to eat my peace of mind.

Occasionally I ran into my old political instructor. Since our graduation, he had been working in the lab, taking care of the tape recorders, slides, and tapes for the English Department. He seemed to be a nice person now. Maybe he had never meant to be harmful; he just did his job. The day I went back to campus to pick up my luggage shortly after graduation, he offered me a cup of tea and advised me to be careful with men as the outside world was complicated and I was still a naive and inexperienced village girl.

I also ran into old classmates and got the latest news about how everyone was doing.

Wu-tao, the handsome man who cried loudly in his dorm on graduation day, was back in town. As he did not have high-ranking official parents or relatives, the only way for him to get back was to marry someone whose parents were somebody. It happened that a classmate of his was interested in his good looks and talents. Although her grades were poor, she was assigned to teach in a technical school in Wuhan. They married soon after her first letter to him, and he was moved to Wuhan the following year.

Wu-tao had recently gone on a three-week trip to the United States. Before the trip, he asked his wife whether her mother could help to take care of their one-year-old son. His wife growled at him, "Why not your mother? You never ask my mother to help you with trivial things like that. And when you talk, don't compare my mother with yours. You never, never do that. Who is your mother? A nobody." Wu-tao did not know what to say. His mother was a nobody.

For the last three years, Wu-tao had done everything he could to be a husband. He helped his wife prepare lectures and mark papers. She often yelled at him and he had swallowed his pride and anger many times. This time, he chose not to. He pulled the tablecloth so that all the dishes fell off the table.

The following morning he left for the United States. His wife sent their son to Wu-tao's mother, who lived in a small town where medical facilities were poor. One night, the little boy had a high fever. Wu-tao's mother put cold towels on his forehead and decided to take him to the hospital in the morning if he still had the fever. The child died before daybreak; Wu-tao's mother had lived in grief and guilt ever since.

I also heard about our monitor, Zhou-jin. She was always politically correct, wearing only the revolutionary colours, which were usually blue or grey, the ones Mao's wife Jiang Qing preferred. Blue was the colour of the Chinese navy and grey the colour of the Red Army. Flowery patterns were indications of decadent Western style. Upon graduation, Zhou-jin went to work in the provincial library. Soon she got bored and got a transfer to the Municipal Security Bureau, where her father used to be the head. Her job was to guard the two new hotels where foreign VIPs came to visit.

When Zhou-jin married, she had a nice two-bedroom apartment, a colour TV, and a tape recorder imported from Japan. She told us that her father bought them second-hand from the Municipal Security Bureau after they were confiscated from smugglers.

Her chosen husband was Yu-lin, our classmate, a man with no opinion of his own, but he had been the most popular person with our political instructor. His name appeared on the exemplary list every July 1, the Chinese Communist Party's birthday. He was also a "three-good" student: he observed all the rules, got reasonable grades, and was athletic. He was put in charge of our early morning exercises. On Mondays, Wednesdays, and Fridays, we did a twenty-minute exercise. Tuesdays, Thursdays, and Saturdays, we jogged around the campus.

One dark winter morning when we formed our six straight lines, it started to rain.

Somebody said, "It's raining."

"Let's cancel the exercise," a few sleepy voices echoed.

Yu-lin went to check with our political instructor. He soon returned and said, "Our political instructor didn't say that we should cancel the exercise. Therefore, we should still do it." We heard later that our political instructor was still sleeping and annoyed to be awakened by Yu-lin. He did not bother to get up and mumbled something indecipherable. When finished, we were soaked and several students were coughing.

Upon graduation, Yu-lin was chosen to work at our university. Since then, he had climbed several stairs on the social ladder. He was now the director of Foreign Affairs of the university.

I also heard a close-call story about my graduation job assignment. A few days before our graduation, we were asked to fill out a form indicating where we would like to work. I was the only one among all the graduates in our department to write down what I wanted. "I would prefer teaching in a college to a middle school." Everyone else wrote: "Unconditionally obey the call of the Party organization."

"Why college, not middle school?" our political instructor questioned my motive at a job assignment meeting. At that critical moment, Professor Li, a man of integrity, responded, "She was asked to write down her wish, and that is what she wished. I don't see anything wrong with it."

No one said anything. It was a time when professors were beginning to gain respect at universities and Professor Li was a senior lecturer. The associate dean suggested that I be assigned to the medical college since they had asked for two people.

Our political instructor was against the idea. "She is a Party member who hasn't played her role well. She only paid attention to her studies."

The associate dean argued that my English was good as he heard me at the departmental reading contest. About a month prior to graduation, my class had recommended that I enter the contest. Ordinarily I would have declined in fear of raising jealousy and hatred among my classmates. But since it was near graduation, I wanted to make an impression on the dean, associate dean, and other professors who might be involved in the graduation job assignment discussions. Apparently my plan worked. Thus, my fate was decided, largely by chance.

I tried not to think about my old university days. Let time wash away the hurtful memories.

28

THE WEATHER IN FEBRUARY AND MARCH was cold and cloudy, but it started to warm up in April. I had learned to get up an hour earlier and be at the bus station before rush hour. The bus was not crowded at that time and the forty-five-minute ride was pleasant. Seeing the sun slowly rising on the horizon gave me an urge to sing, sing at the top of my voice, an urge I had long forgotten. How I wanted life to be frozen at that moment: the dew on the green trees shining under the morning sun, the air fresh and the road quiet.

But it was soon July, the end of my study. It was a hot evening when I saw Mei-ling and Fuji off at the train station. They left on the same day but in different directions, Mei-ling for Shanghai, then Fujian province and Fuji to Guangzhou, then Hainan province.

Mei-ling's train left an hour earlier than Fuji's. I walked her to the train and we held each other's hands for a long time. She moved her lips and tried to say something, but could not. I looked at her large, moist black eyes for the last time and jumped off the train. Slowly, I walked back to the hall where Fuji was waiting.

Fuji's train was more crowded. He squeezed his luggage in, found a seat, and came out to say goodbye to me. I was in a navy-blue blouse and skirt, with black leather sandals. The platform was dimly lit by a few yellow bulbs; the dusty steel rails were panting with hot breath. Fuji's eyes seemed moist; I tried hard to hold my tears. Neither of us moved or uttered a word. We knew that we might never see each other again. Travel was a luxury few Chinese could afford.

I was still standing there when the train left; I realized that I had forgotten to say goodbye to him.

Nothing can bring back the hour of splendour in the grass, of glory in the flower. Nothing, nothing…

The sunny hour in the garden of our classroom, in the grass, Meiling's laughter, my giggle, Fuji's dazed gaze into the fountain. *Oh, nothing can bring back the hour of splendour, nothing, nothing…*

 I felt like a log the whole night. Lying on the bamboo couch, I fell asleep and dreamed of Fuji in his tropical Hainan Island setting. As he walked to me, his face changed into Dan's. Yet, the voice was Fuji's. Before he reached me, he was greeted by a group of men in labour camp garb. Squatting in the shade of an old palm tree, one of them cracked a coconut with his bare fist and passed the pieces around. I could hear them talking and see them smoking cheap cigarettes but could not make out the content of their conversation. Dan shot quick glances in my direction, but could not come to me as I was a married woman. Sitting on the bulged roots of a coconut palm, I was content and happy. His meaningful glances, like the coconut milk, quenched my thirst for him.

I woke up in a sweat. Stretching, I felt Dan's caresses all over my body. Something stirred in me—something I had never felt for my husband, who repeatedly accused me of being a cold-blooded creature. I sipped some cold tea and went back to my dreamland. How I wished never to wake up from it! *Dan, my love, where are you? If you are dead, please bring me to you!*

29

IN SEPTEMBER I WAS BACK to my teaching job at the medical college. Again I asked Director Yang for his permission to take part in the graduate entrance examination. Again I was denied on the basis that the department needed me. As the Party's needs should be what everyone wanted in life, I had no option but to obey.

I was assigned to teach two identical classes for six hours a week. Since the teaching load was light I spent many spare hours reading foreign novels as well as Chinese stories.

In the early 1980s, there was a renaissance in China: the subjects of love and political persecution during the Cultural Revolution became popular in short stories and novels. I devoured them like a hungry child. However, the best writers began to disappoint me after a while: I smelled political ingredients in their writing. Next, their names appeared in every newspaper as ministers and vice-ministers of the Ministry of Culture. I understood: they had sold themselves. Then they wrote several articles in the *People's Daily* to criticize one of their fellow writers, Bai-yang, for his tendency to seek bourgeois freedom in his writing.

Deng Xiao-ping had reached his limit. Although China was experimenting with vigorous economic reform, political reform was still many years away.

Meanwhile, many foreign novels, in both original and translated versions, became available. There were long lines in front of every bookstore on Sunday mornings: people were looking for spiritual food after being denied for so many years. Although a single novel cost me two days' salary, I bought them all. I usually read the Chinese version first, then the English. I also read them together because the Chinese version lost the flavour of the original while the English version was too difficult for me to understand. Sometimes it took me three to four readings to capture the spirit of the characters.

I read my beloved novels during the evenings and thought about the characters during the day, especially in the crowded and noisy bus to and from work. Talking with the characters became my happiest moments, during which I stopped thinking about the bleak future of my teaching job and my ailing marriage.

In two years, Ren, the lucky one who was allowed to take part in the graduate entrance examination, came back with a master's degree. He was paid one rank higher than both Luo and me, the two people who had generously agreed to stay and let him go. What irony!

I thought of Wu Guan, my big Auntie Lin's husband, who had voluntarily given up his high-salary job in 1960 to help our country in times of difficulty. He never got his job back. History was repeating itself in different forms.

By the end of the fall semester, Director Yang finally decided that Luo and I would be allowed to participate in the graduate entrance examination. By this time, the rules had changed. A new subject was introduced to the exams for English majors: French. As I had never learned French, I marked "D" for every question in the multiple-choice exam, got thirty-one percent, and failed the exam.

The following spring, I participated in another exam held by Beijing Foreign Languages University. This time, there was no French. Participants were asked to write an essay and answer memorization questions. The essay required an argument on the pros and cons of a detective story. Right on! I commented on the story and cited several examples from Sherlock Holmes to support my argument.

A good detective story can not only cultivate the analytical ability of the reader, but also help her to cope with the unbearable hot summer evenings in Wuhan. Reading Sherlock Holmes, I collected every clue, analyzed the dialogues and activities of the characters, reasoned and deduced with the detective for conclusions. The mental exercise was so absorbing that I forgot the suffocating heat and the malicious mosquitoes!

I passed the written exam, but was not eligible for an oral because I was a "worker-peasant-soldier-student" who had entered university during the Mao years. It was true that the majority of those students were not very good, but it was not true that *none* of them was any good. When the dynasty changed hands from Mao to Deng, the policies changed from one extreme to the other. Mao did not want young people to be learned; he preferred them to be followers. Deng said that nobody, regardless of his or her efforts, was any good except those who passed the strict University Entrance Examination. An individual was insignificant in this powerful time machine: she either got a ride to the sky or a hit to the ditch. Millions had perished in body or spirit because of bad luck. Now this gigantic time machine had come to claim me as a victim.

It was a rainy day in June when I got the news. I walked along the East Lake by myself for a whole afternoon, trudging through bushes and over hills where I had never been before: I didn't care whether I got lost or not.

Feeling betrayed, I decided not to take any more graduate entrance examinations.

30

"THE TWO MALE MEMBERS OF THE FAMILY like to control everything. We have no freedom of speech in this house. I don't know how Mother has lived all her life like this."

It was both sad and amusing to read my sister's letters. My second sister, Nan-ping, was only seventeen years old, but she had experienced and thought a lot about life. There was much truth in what she wrote.

One warm afternoon in June, I received a phone call from Wen-ping that Nan-ping had disappeared the day before. Wen-ping had finished medical school the previous year and was now a paediatrician in Mian Yang County hospital.

No one knew where Nan-ping and Ju-ying, a girl of her age from our village, had gone. My mother feared that they had committed suicide in the Yangtze River as Nan-ping had mentioned her chosen spot of death to my mother sometime before.

I phoned all my relatives in Wuhan, but none had seen her. I then phoned the police station asking them to look for the body of a seventeen-year-old girl in the Yangtze.

Around four o'clock, I trudged along the river for quite a distance looking for my sister's body. The sun was hot and the air smothering, the road rough and dusty. The dull sandy water in the Yangtze was swirling and running fast—so fast that my searching eyes could not catch up with it.

"Could Nan-ping be in one of the whirlpools?" This very thought sent chills up my spine.

"My lively, sensitive and sentimental sister, only seventeen, how could you…how could you die?" I refused to believe it, but I still scrutinized every current, every whirlpool.

"What kind of life has she lived?" I asked the rolling river.

Nan-ping had been neglected and abused ever since she was born. My brother's favourite words to her were "you are not wanted in this house," implying that she ought to do anything he demanded in order to justify her existence. She wore old clothes from her elder sisters and ate leftovers from my brother. When she finished junior high, she did not want to go on to senior high because none of her friends were going. My father and brother then arranged for her to take care of my brother's daughter without paying her a fin.

Six months before, Nan-ping wrote me, "Seventeen should be an age to dream of the beautiful things in life, but I have no such dreams. All the messages I receive from Father and Brother are that I am worthless and should obey their orders. I don't see any light in my life and I need your help."

She was quite a writer. Her observations of my father and brother were insightful, her reflections of her existence sad and touching. I decided to rescue her.

Five days later, I took the morning bus home and she was waiting for me. My father and brother were about five hundred yards away weeding the medicinal herb plants in the fields. Nan-ping and I quickly packed her things and ran to the bus station.

Jing-ping wrote me later that Father was angry with me, but I was not afraid of him. I made a plan for Nan-ping and started teaching her English. In about a year, she should be good enough to find a job in any rural primary school because English teachers were in demand. Nan-ping was making good progress with her English lessons. In about two months, she could read simple texts with accuracy. On a Friday morning while I was at work, my brother paid Nan-ping a visit. He threatened that if she did not go home right away, she would be disowned.

"What if you can't find a job in a year? Have you thought about that? If you take care of my daughter now, Father may find you a job in the future." My brother was furious that Nan-ping dared to violate his orders.

When I got home, my brother was gone and Nan-ping was in tears. She had packed her things and was heading home.

I took her boating on the East Lake to give her a chance to calm down and think for herself. It started to drizzle when the rowboat was near the centre of the large lake. On the foggy bluish lake surface, Nan-ping looked rather pretty, a tragic kind of pretty. She had grown tall with fair skin and soft eyes. Neither of us uttered a word during the boat ride.

When we stepped off the boat, she looked back at the enormous lake, and beyond, for a long while, then sighed, tears rolling down her cheeks. "The world is so big but there isn't a tiny spot for me."

With a trembling voice, she said, "I guess I have to do what Father wishes me to do."

I took her to the bus station and offered her fifty yuan which my working unit had given me as bonus. I wanted my sister to have some money of her own for the first time in her life.

 The morning after Nan-ping's disappearance, a man in his fifties knocked at the door of our apartment and said that he was Ju-ying's father.

"Why did your daughter run away, do you have any idea?" I wanted to know if they had any plan beforehand.

"No. Not really. She has been complaining that her brother is in school and she is not. I bought her brother a new bike and didn't buy her one. The usual stuff." He was clearly not aware of his daughter's plan if there was one.

"I'll do the best I can and telephone you as soon as I have any news." I tried to support him.

With a heavy heart I walked him downstairs, and then, I saw my mother, with a little parcel in her arms, looking at the door numbers!

"Ai-yar, Ma! How did you find your way?" As she was illiterate, we never let her travel to Wuhan alone.

"I asked your father to come with me, but he wouldn't. I'm really worried so I just took the bus and came." I looked at her with amazement.

"Oh, come on, don't underestimate me, I remember the way," she uttered confidently.

"Well, how many times did you get lost?" I stared at her.

"You all think I am stupid or what? If I were stupid, how could I have smart children? Oh, Nan-ping, she is the foolish one." Her eyes were red and a little swollen.

"I didn't sleep at all last night. Poor thing, where is she? Any news from her?" she asked anxiously.

Sombrely I shook my head.

After some tea and lunch, my mother asked me to take her to the Buddhist temple in Hanyang.

"The only thing we can do now is ask Buddha to help, to shed light on Nan-ping's blurred mind so she'll come back to me," my mother mumbled, her eyes fixing on a little plant on the windowsill.

"It wasn't easy for me to raise every one of you, not...not...not easy." She choked with sobs. I passed her a warm wet towel and she stopped sobbing. Then we took the bus to the Buddhist temple.

"No matter what, you never commit suicide; things always get better; just keep your faith and be persistent," she murmured as we reached the temple. When I was growing up, I had heard her say that many times. Perhaps those convictions had kept her going through the many hardships in her life.

The magnificent, red-brick temple, built in the 1700s, was located in a quiet neighbourhood with tall trees and green grass. In 1949, the Communists closed it to the public, but allowed monks and nuns to live and practise there. When the Cultural Revolution began in 1966, the temple was completely closed and the monks and nuns were chased away. It was renovated and reopened to the public in 1980 and people, especially older people, visited it from near and far.

My grandma once told me that there used to be Buddhist temples everywhere in China and that most Chinese were Buddhists. But the Communists did not believe in any religion except Maoism, so they used many temples for badly needed government offices. This was the only surviving temple in the city of Wuhan.

"Let's buy some incense over there," my mother pointing at a nearby roadside stand where two peasant women of her age squatted around a few small baskets covered with a red cloth.

We bought two bundles of dark-red incense and followed a crowd to the three-building temple. The building in the middle was the largest, with green and red ancient Chinese flowery patterns carved on the gate. On both sides of the enormous gate were long silk scrolls with famous sayings from Buddha: *I laugh at those who take the world too seriously,* and *I encompass all, human frailties as well as natural disasters.*

Through the gate was a grand hall with one hundred and forty statues sitting or standing in five semicircles, the largest one in the centre. It was so large that we human beings felt like insects in its presence. That was the statue of the great Buddha. He had a round face with an open mouth, laughing at us humans who take things too seriously. He had a huge stomach, inside of which were all the frustrations, blunders, difficulties, and hardships in the world. We, a group of human insignificants, stood solemnly at the giant feet of the broad-minded Buddha seeking enlightenment for our frail souls.

After lighting seventeen incense sticks, my mother knelt down to pray. I murmured, "If only I could take things less seriously, I wouldn't have so many frustrations in life. We humans erect our own barricades to new possibilities. If I had Buddha's broad mind, I would walk with lighter steps and live with fewer burdens. Compared to the flowing currents of the sea of the universe, one human is a tiny drop of water. So why be so hard on yourself and seek to die, Nan-ping? I hope you hear me calling and come back to us."

Walking out of the temple, I felt like a different person: Buddha's teachings had raised my soul and spirit to a height where, for the first time in my life, I saw the universe from high above. I looked stealthily at my mother, who seemed deep in thought. About what? To me, she was almost as great as Buddha: she had swallowed much suffering in life and tolerated all the frailties of my father.

When we passed a peddler with several barely opened packages, my mother whispered something to her and the peddler opened one of the packages. My mother bought a stack of yellowish rough square paper with many hole prints. I recognized those papers: they were the currency dead people used in the *ying* world.

"I am going to burn these on the graves of my parents when I visit them next time. I want them to be better off than when they were alive," my mother muttered, putting the "money" in her parcel.

After some dumplings and cold tea in a small restaurant, my mother announced that she was not going back with me. "I must go home today or your father won't be happy. He is in a bad mood these days." As a wife, she felt responsible for her husband's moods.

I walked her to the bus station.

"Let us know the minute you get any news from Nan-ping," she shouted to me as the bus carried her home.

The following afternoon, Wen-ping phoned to say that my father had received a letter from Nan-ping. She must have posted it before she left. Wen-ping read a paragraph of Nan-ping's letter over the phone:

"I am very sorry to have been born a girl, not the boy you were expecting. You have never treated me well. Except for ordering me around, you never talked to me or looked at me. Now I am gone and may my soul haunt you day and night."

My father was shocked and agonized when he read the letter. Maybe he never realized how much he had hurt Nan-ping's feelings. Wen-ping seemed to sympathize with him but I could not. I was on Nan-ping's side.

Near dinnertime, my uncle's son, Wu-jun, ran to our apartment with good news: Nan-ping had just arrived at their place!

"Oh, God! Thank God," I took a long breath. "Where has she been?" I wanted to know every detail of her journey.

"She said that she had been to Xiang-fang." Wu-jun seemed to think it was fun to travel to a city two hundred miles from Wuhan. He was thirteen years old and had not experienced the dreadful anxieties we adults had during the past few days.

I ran to my uncle's where Nan-ping was having some soup my uncle had made. My uncle was patient and soft-hearted; I wished my father were like him.

"So, you are still alive, eh? You surely scared us to death." I took her cold hands into mine. Tears filled my eyes, and I did not quite know whether they were happy tears or sorrowful ones.

Nan-ping looked detached, her face pale and clothes untidy.

"Now you take a shower and get a good rest," my uncle said gently to her after she finished her soup and a few pieces of tomato.

I rushed home to get a skirt, a pair of sandals, and a few small items of mine for Nan-ping. Afterwards I took her for a walk along the Yangtze River and she blurted out the whole story.

"I wanted to see you for the last time before I died so we, Ju-ying and I, took the evening bus to Wuhan on Sunday night. It was late when we arrived at your apartment. I looked up at your window from the front yard, and the lights were off. I didn't want to wake you as I know you teach early classes on Mondays. We walked to Uncle's place and knocked at the door, but there was no answer. Maybe I didn't knock loud enough. I was afraid that they might discover our intention and talk us out of it. So we spent the night on the long bench in front of Uncle's apartment. The next morning we took the train to Xiang-fang."

Oh, seventeen, innocent and audacious age! I thought, but I said, "Where did you get money to buy the train ticket?"

"I still have eleven yuan left from the money you gave me last time," she confided.

"The train cost me three yuan; I spent two yuan on the train for food, and I had six left when we arrived at the railway station in Xiang-fang.

"While we were looking for a washroom at the station, a sleazy man in his thirties greeted Ju-ying. I really had to go to the washroom so I left while Ju-ying was talking with that man. When I came out of the washroom, I could not find her anywhere at the station.

"I searched and searched in the crowd…I really wanted to die then, alone in a strange place. It felt terrible to die by myself, though.

"Tired and disheartened, I staggered out of the station and saw two trains passing by. I had an idea: I wanted to die like Anna in Tolstoy's novel you read us a few years ago, remember? Anna threw herself under a train, remember? I thought that was a pretty smart idea.

"With that plan, my strength seemed to come back and I walked a distance from the station so people wouldn't pick me up when I lay on the rails waiting for the train to come.

"After choosing my death spot, I waited for the train. Strange, no train came for several minutes. The rails were very hot and I felt hungry and thirsty.

"I figured I might as well die after a good meal. What's the use of having the six yuan after I die anyway? So I walked back to the station and bought myself a good meal at the restaurant. I spent five yuan on the meal, can you believe that?

"Then I thought I might as well use the bathroom before I died; who knows how long I would have to wait for the next train to come to run me over?

"So I stepped to the bathroom and there I saw an old friend who used to study sewing with me. She was very surprised and happy to see me and invited me to her sister's place which was right across the river. While we were on the ferry, I thought of jumping into the river, but did not. Her sister had a nice house and asked me to stay for a couple of days.

"When I talked to her sister, I thought of you: *She would be very sad to see me die.*

"Then I thought you would despise me for being such a coward, wouldn't you?"

I did not answer her as I never thought of despising my vulnerable little sister.

"On the third day, my friend bought me a train ticket and saw me off at the train station. On the train back, I didn't feel like dying any more.

"I guess I should have died. It seems to me that all of you expected me to."

"You don't know what happened to Ju-ying, do you?" I inquired simply.

"No," she said absent-mindedly.

I had mixed feelings about her attitude toward life. "It was a silly idea to think of death when you are only seventeen. Life is not easy, you know. Everyone's life is hard, only in different ways. We should always try our best."

I was exhausted and proposed that we go home to get some sleep.

To have a daughter commit suicide would be considered a disgrace for my father who had always thought that he was a perfect man. A few weeks later, my father found Nan-ping a temporary job and stopped ordering her around in the house. He did not want anything like that to happen again to his good reputation.

31

JING-PING, MY YOUNGEST SISTER, paid me a visit just before the Chinese New Year. As I had written to my parents that I was not going home for the festival, they sent me five big bream fish, my favourite. It was a sunny morning with a cold wind. Jing-ping was helping me prepare lunch in the kitchen.

As the Western wind blew into China through pop music, magazines, and movies, young people picked up fast. Jing-ping was happily singing along with a pop singer from the cassette player of a neighbour, and I hummed along.

"I never knew you could sing!"

There was a sure surprise in her mischievous black eyes.

I smiled sadly. I wanted to tell her that I used to sing songs all day long, even when I was eating. I had changed without my knowing it.

Reviewing my married life, I could not help a heavy sigh. There was one basic way to run a marriage in China: the husband had his way and made the wife accommodate. Ours was no exception. My husband took charge of the household and my life. Indeed he loved me—but only as a piece of furniture.

It took me a few years to come to this realization. At first, I tried to reason with him but he was beyond reason. He believed in control, absolute control through emotional and physical mistreatment. I tried to defend myself; I was only punished more. After a while, I gave in.

Nothing could wound a woman more than an unhappy marriage where she had invested all she had and had high hopes of happy returns. Nothing could insult an intelligent woman more than being owned like a piece of furniture.

Unlike other adventures in life, marriage was supposed to be for life. Only those unfortunate creatures who were stuck in bad marriages understood the true meaning of "for life." To them, it meant a life sentence, imposed by the faithful defenders of our five-thousand-year culture through social norms and values.

A divorce hurt all your near relations as it brought disgrace to them. It also gave everyone who knew you the right to judge and criticize you.

At the age of twenty-eight, I fully understood what my Auntie Mei once said about herself, "Other people live a day, I live a day too."

Near lunchtime, my husband's good friend, De-hua, dropped in. Six months after our wedding, he married Su-wen. As De-hua's brother was director of the Police Bureau in Wuhan, his influence found Su-wen a teaching post in a middle school in Hankou. They had a daughter and lived in a two-bedroom apartment in the same building as De-hua's parents. I saw Su-wen often but avoided De-hua.

I passed him a cup of tea; De-hua asked me to join them. My husband lit cigarettes for De-hua and himself. De-hua looked angry. He said that Su-wen did not care about him any more.

"Oh?"

"She doesn't teach me English any more. She used to teach me every day. She thinks that I have no hope to improve."

He exhaled a mouthful of smoke into the air. "She is a very selfish person." De-hua continued to complain about his wife.

I excused myself to the kitchen. Su-wen had tearfully told me that De-hua had frequently beaten her since their daughter was two weeks old. Before their marriage, De-hua was sweet and loving with her. She became pregnant soon after the wedding and he demanded sex every day even when she was seven months pregnant. Her high hopes for a happy marriage had shattered.

Two weeks after her daughter was born, they quarrelled and he raised his fist at her. Luckily their neighbour stopped him. Although those fierce fists did not hit her body, they hit her heart. She wept all night, grieving for her lost dream of a good marriage as well her fatal mistake of marrying a beast. He did not love her, not at all. This realization was as cruel as it was true.

She learned to speak carefully, making sure not to provoke De-hua. When he lost his temper and yelled at her, she would pretend not to have heard. Eventually, she developed a better strategy: to laugh, and laugh loudly. At first, he was startled. Then he got used to it and believed that she was really laughing, not being sarcastic.

Her neighbours' children would watch her when she started her scary laughter. They thought she was crazy. Maybe she was. She was not sure any more.

De-hua was a devoted surgeon who put his work first. His schedule was always full. In the morning, he practised English pronunciation for half an hour before going to work. Although he practised the same tape for a year, his pronunciation was still dreadful.

She picked up the milk from their neighbourhood distributor, bought breakfast, and prepared her daughter for kindergarten. By the time she was ready to have her breakfast, De-hua had often eaten her share.

"Buy some more when you go to work. It's on the way anyway," he would say. In order to save money, De-hua asked Su-wen to buy several kinds of bread—from the cheapest to the most expensive. The better ones were usually for him.

"Every time he does that to me, I feel like a knife is cutting my heart," she told me.

In the evenings, he needed to read the newspaper and watch TV to relax. House chores were Su-wen's job, although her salary was not a fin less than his.

Since Su-wen's working place was three miles distant from their apartment, she needed to take the crowded bus to and from work. Once when she was near the end of her pregnancy, her movements were so slow that the bus door shut on her right foot. She yelled and the driver stopped the bus and opened the door to let her in. She was not severely injured as drivers in Wuhan closed the doors slowly because last-minute passengers frequently hung on to the door handle. Su-wen was in tears when she got off the bus and limped home. Dinner, however, was waiting for her to cook.

Another way De-hua relaxed was to have sex right before he went to sleep, regardless of Su-wen's wishes. His logic was simple. Su-wen was his wife and it was her duty to provide sex any time he wished. When his wishes were not granted, he would hit his head on the wall to threaten her. Sometimes he would grab her and bang her head against the wall as well.

"I don't want to live any more. Let's die together," he would murmur desperately.

She would go to the living room and lie down on the sofa with a blanket, which he would then take from her, leaving her with no warmth in the unheated apartment. To make sure that she did not get any sleep, he would turn the lights on and off every ten minutes or so. When he thought that was not enough, he would throw shoes at her.

"Sometimes I think an animal is better off than I am. An animal is allowed to sleep, yet I am not." Su-wen talked in a flat tone, as if it was about somebody else's life. She had detached from her feelings, in order to keep going.

During the day De-hua would find faults with Su-wen and shout at her for no apparent reason. As a last resort, she would open the door to the balcony and let the neighbours hear his shouting. That would usually stop him.

In order to get some sleep, Su-wen would sometimes give in and let him have his sex.

"I weep, and he pretends not to see my tears. Very often, I think that there is not much of a difference between being a prostitute for one person and a prostitute for any person. Yet, the former is perceived as a virtuous woman and the latter is called a rotten woman," she said, her facial muscles twisting, her fixed eyes blank.

"Have you two ever talked things over?" I once asked her.

"Yes, many times. What's the use? One minute, he repents, kneeling on the floor and tearfully asking my forgiveness. The next minute, he is roaring like a wild animal."

"Have you ever considered divorce?" I queried.

"Yes. But he does not want a divorce. He would never let me go. He said that if I file for a divorce, he would take my daughter Mulan and never let me see her again. He would also pour acid on my face to make me ugly. I would be insane if it were not for my daughter. She is my only joy in life. When I play with her, I temporarily forget all my troubles."

Su-wen told Mulan the fable of a donkey and a mule. Once upon a time, there were a donkey and a mule. They were good friends and worked for the same master. From time to time, they both carried heavy bags of wheat to the other side of the mountain. One hot summer day, the donkey and the mule were each carrying a large bag of wheat and were struggling up a huge mountain, their master following them in the distance. When they had climbed about half way, the donkey cried, "Ai-yo, Ai-yo! I have a bad stomach ache." He dropped to his knees and then lay on the ground.

The master took the bag and put it on the mule's back. Now the mule carried two bags. A moment later, the donkey started to follow slowly, face distorted with pain. Hours passed, and the donkey still did not carry his share. Suddenly, the mule collapsed and dropped dead from carrying the extra load under the hot sun. The master now put both bags on the donkey's back. Only then did the donkey realize his mistake in playing sick.

Then Su-wen played the role of the mule and Mulan of the donkey. Su-wen crawled on the bed, panting hard from carrying the heavy load while Mulan pretended to have a stomach ache. Su-wen "collapsed" and fell asleep.

"Mama, what happened next?" Mulan wanted to know the end of the story.

"Oh...oh, we will know by tomorrow. Let's go to sleep."

Since Mulan was born, De-hua preferred to sleep in the study because a good sleep was essential for him.

De-hua did not like beef, so they never bought beef. He did not like beer, so she had never had a single beer in the years they were married although she liked to have one occasionally. He liked chicken, so he ate most of it when she cooked one. One afternoon, she cooked a whole chicken and he asked her to eat more.

"I felt strange, so I asked him what was wrong with the chicken," Su-wen told me. "'It's not fresh,' he said without thinking."

"He has never visited my parents once in the six years we have been married. He gives me ten yuan, which is barely enough to buy the tickets when I visit my parents during Chinese New Year.

"My father only visited us once because he was afraid to be slighted by his son-in-law. He bought us fresh fish from the market as a gift. They were quite expensive, you know. I cooked dinner and my husband brought a half bottle of wine to the dinner table. When the bottle was about to be finished, I signalled him to the kitchen.

"Open another bottle in the cabinet," I whispered to him.

"I bought that for your uncle for the Chinese New Year."

"We can buy another for him tomorrow."

"But it's expensive."

"My father bought expensive gifts for you and this is his first visit."

He reluctantly opened a new bottle of wine.

"When I went to visit my parents a week later, my father told me that he had heard every word exchanged in the kitchen. I heard sadness in his voice."

On Sundays, De-hua would ask Su-wen to go shopping with him, and took care of her purse for her. When she wanted to buy something, she needed his permission. Once when she found a skirt she really liked, she looked for him to get some money, but he had disappeared into the crowd.

"Have you ever told your parents about your suffering?"

"No. I don't want to worry them. They cannot do anything anyway." She shook her head sadly.

"Do you have other friends to talk to?" I was very concerned about her mental health. As there was no counselling service in China, I wanted to make sure that she could express her sorrow frequently. I could not visit her much as I wanted to as my husband did not like it.

"Only one colleague at work. I don't want others to know. They would laugh at me."

"How is your daughter coping with the situation?"

"Mulan is scared. Once he started a fight during the middle of the night and woke her up. She tried to push De-hua away and said, 'Go away, go, go.' De-hua was so mad at her that he slapped her very hard on the face and Mulan's nose started to bleed. He can be a brute even to his daughter."

The previous year Su-wen had bought a violin for Mulan with the savings of the bonus money from her working unit. De-hua nagged her for a month. "What a waste of money. Mulan has no talent for the violin. I'm not going to take her to her lessons. You do it."

Su-wen took Mulan to violin classes every Sunday afternoon. The buses were usually crowded. One rainy-sunny Sunday afternoon, after finally squeezing onto a bus, Mulan ran to an empty seat. "Mama, come here, a seat for you."

"After I sat down, Mulan whispered to me secretively: 'Mama, I'm going to bring my stool with me every time we take a bus so you can always have a seat. Isn't that grand?' My little Mulan jumped with joy at her brilliant idea. I was so touched that I decided to live for my daughter. Rain or shine, my daughter has never missed one violin lesson. I want to do all I can to give her a good education, and to give her all the things I didn't have when I was growing up." Her eyes shone with hope, hope for the happiness of her daughter.

Su-wen and her daughter learned and practised violin together. One late afternoon, Mulan was practising the violin when De-hua asked her to stop.

"Dinner is ready!" he shouted.

Mulan wanted to finish the tune so she continued. De-hua grabbed her violin and threw it on the floor.

"Mulan cried for a long time. I had never seen her so sad."

After a pause, she continued, "Sometimes I really want to die. It would be much easier than to live. But who would look after my daughter? What would happen to my parents?"

There were tears in her eyes, but she seemed not to be aware of them. She was beyond sorrow, humiliation, torture, and tears. I wonder how many more women's lives were like Su-wen's: dying but not dead?

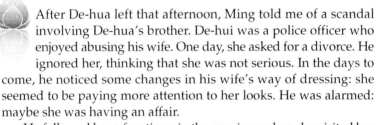 After De-hua left that afternoon, Ming told me of a scandal involving De-hua's brother. De-hui was a police officer who enjoyed abusing his wife. One day, she asked for a divorce. He ignored her, thinking that she was not serious. In the days to come, he noticed some changes in his wife's way of dressing: she seemed to be paying more attention to her looks. He was alarmed: maybe she was having an affair.

He followed her a few times in the evenings when she visited her friends with their three-year-old son, but failed to find anything suspicious. He then started to "check on her" by visiting her at work at odd times. One afternoon, he showed up at the hydroelectric plant where she was a technician. She was not there, and her colleagues told him that she was not feeling well and had left. He then hurried home, but she was not there either. Furious, he was waiting for her at the door when she got home around five-thirty. He put a towel in her mouth, then beat her black and blue. He also hit their three-year-old son because he tried to protect his mother.

The next day, his wife packed her suitcase and left for her mother's with her son. De-hui did not want to let her off so easily, so he continued to spy on her. One evening he saw her walking with a man. He ran to them, punched the man hard on the face, then searched him to find his name and working unit.

A few weeks later, he climbed into the man's apartment through the window at midnight and caught them in bed naked. He tied them up with the rope he had brought with him and put them on a cart. He then woke up the whole building with a loudspeaker and paraded the two naked lovers in the yard. Not satisfied with that, he wheeled the cart to the street to get a bigger audience, but the street was deserted by this late hour.

"Has he agreed to a divorce?" I asked anxiously.

"Yes. But he doesn't want the child."

"Why?"

"With a child, it would be more difficult for her to find somebody to remarry."

"What about her boyfriend?"

"Yes, he is going to marry her."

I felt relieved for her.

As domestic violence was not in the code of law, a husband could abuse his wife in whatever way and as much as he wished.

32

RONG AND FANG, MY OLD FRIENDS IN THE VILLAGE, came to pay me a visit in early March. Rong looked pale so I took her to my room to lie down. She held my hand and told me that she was pregnant again. Although they had three boys, Fang wanted one more son. The problem was that they had not received permission to have another child.

"Not again!" I could not believe my ears. Rong had two abortions the year before. As the facilities in Wuhan were better than the countryside, Fang wanted her to have this one done in my husband's hospital.

My husband said that the hospital required a photo of the pregnant woman before they would operate. That was much more reasonable than asking for a letter from her production team, which had been the policy until that year.

I dug into my photo album and found an old picture of Rong: in it she was carefree and cheerful. I handed her the photo and asked them to stay overnight at our apartment. She nodded.

After lunch, Ming took them to the Gynaecology Department and I hurried to work as we were required to do a general cleaning every Saturday afternoon. The only teacher exempted from the cleaning was Dong, who was handicapped after a fall from a third-floor window while cleaning the windows when she was a university student. That afternoon our task was to pull out all the grass in the yard behind our offices. According to Mao, grass was a breeding bed for mosquitoes and flies. As a result, our campus had no green space, but mosquitoes and flies remained. They seemed more tenacious than the grass.

When I got home, Rong and Fang had left. My husband was not very hospitable to my friends or my family members. I did not say anything, nor was I angry with him. I did not even feel hurt: I had long stopped feeling anything about what he did or said.

But I was very concerned about Rong's health. I could not imagine how, with her frail body, and asthma, she could bear three abortions within thirteen months.

About two weeks after Fang and Rong's visit, I received a letter from Elizabeth and Arthur, saying that Arthur would be attending a conference in Seoul in mid-September. Afterwards he would go to Guangzhou to join Elizabeth, who was going to visit Shanghai Medical School, then Sun Yat-sen Medical School. They asked if I could go to Guangzhou to see them, and I replied immediately that I would be delighted.

In the past few years, we had been writing each other about the latest happenings in our lives. I updated them on the gossip in the medical college and they told me about their academic achievements. Arthur was now associate professor at a teaching hospital. Elizabeth had received her doctorate a year after they returned to America, and was an assistant professor in a medical school.

Several people at the medical college had advised me not to write them because I could be in serious trouble if another Cultural Revolution came. Strangely, I was not afraid. Perhaps I was too naive to fear. Living in the village during the most fierce years of the Cultural Revolution, I was sheltered from the horrors many people experienced in large cities.

I took the evening train and arrived just after nine in the morning. Guangzhou had more trees in the residential areas and was slightly cleaner than Wuhan. It was more open to the influence of Hong Kong but was only an imitation of it. I saw young women wearing heavy makeup and men dressed in bright colours but with no taste. When I asked my way around, most locals spoke only Cantonese, not Mandarin.

The contact person, Professor Hao at Sun Yat-sen Medical School, informed me that Elizabeth and Arthur's plane had been delayed until the evening. I spent the next few hours wandering around shopping and sampling small portions of southern-style food from food stands on the street.

I then sauntered along the Pearl River where I saw two young men sneaking around. They must be selling something illegal. I decided to find out. When I approached, they asked me in awkward Mandarin if I wanted to buy some digital watches.

"Only six yuan each. They work great. Good gifts!" They advertised their products to perfection, and I was tempted. I bought five and paid cash. As I was checking the watches, the sellers disappeared. One watch was not working, and another had only half a strap. So that was "capitalism"!

That evening I waited for Elizabeth and Arthur in The Garden, a magnificent hotel built especially for foreigners. A cup of coffee cost five yuan, ten times the price in an ordinary Chinese restaurant. Nevertheless, many Chinese still went there to have coffee, try the escalator, tour the beautiful garden, and see the fountain.

Elizabeth and Arthur finally arrived. It was an exciting moment for the three of us: we chatted and chatted until we could not keep our eyes open.

The next morning, Arthur received a phone call from his father. His mother, who had been very ill for quite some time, was dying. Arthur took the afternoon plane to Hong Kong, then flew to the United States. Before he left, he told me that the one person in China he most wanted to help was me and he would like to sponsor my study in America.

He then said, "You know what, May-ping, we published a book based upon our experiences living and working at Wuhan Second Medical College." He paused for a moment, and continued, "We feel sorry that we didn't acknowledge you for all the help you gave us because we were afraid to get you into trouble."

I said it was all right.

"You are in the book although we changed your gender," he informed me with a thoughtful expression.

"Really?"

Then he smiled and asked: "How come you don't make as many faces when you talk as you used to?"

"I must be getting old," I said flatly.

"You silly, twenty-eight is not terribly old!" he protested.

He paused and looked at me: "May-ping, cheer up. You have a whole world in front of you."

"I'll try." I tried a cheerful look as if posing for a camera.

That evening at six, Elizabeth was to make a speech in Chinese at the sixtieth-anniversary celebration dinner party held by Sun Yat-sen Medical School. Elizabeth's boss, Mr Brown, would also be present. He was arriving that afternoon after a short visit at Shenyang Medical School in Northern China.

Mr Brown was a tall, heavily built man in his late fifties. While he composed the speech, Elizabeth and I translated the sentences into Chinese. Sometimes when he got stuck, Elizabeth and I would help him out. I then had Elizabeth practise reading the speech in Chinese several times. We were ready ten minutes before the dinner party.

At least three hundred people attended the grand party. Elizabeth's performance was a big hit—foreigners as well as Chinese applauded heartily when she finished. Several people came to her dinner table to congratulate her on her fluent Chinese.

Her blond hair fell lavishly to her shoulders, and her youthful face was beaming. Her tall, slender figure looked gorgeous under the soft light: she was wearing a white silk blouse decorated with a bluish cloisonné enamel necklace and a long navy blue skirt.

Mr Brown was radiantly pleased. Back at the hotel, he offered to have me as a visiting scholar in his department if I had difficulty getting into a master's program elsewhere. I was delighted.

When Elizabeth and I returned to our room, we each had a beer to celebrate our success: me, as the director, and she, as the performer. While I was telling her how proud I was of her Mandarin, she told me an amusing story about her visit to Shanghai.

As it was the first time for her to visit Shanghai Medical School, she gave a brief description of herself to the contact person on the phone, so he could arrange for somebody to meet her at the airport. When she arrived, she looked around, but nobody came to meet her. She sat down on a bench in the luggage section and waited. Soon she was the only passenger left, and still nobody came to her. She got up and was about to call a taxi, when two Chinese girls, dressed like university students, asked if she was Dr Bennet. She said yes. The two girls looked shocked and then giggled.

"We were expecting an elderly lady, seventy-three years old. We looked and looked but could not find one." They laughed to tears.

Only then did Elizabeth realize her blunder. She had said "seventy-three" instead of "thirty-seven."

"Chinese is a tricky language," she sipped her beer.

"Not more tricky than English," I argued.

Observing me, she got up and said, "Arthur said that you have changed, but you have not. Deep down, you are still the May-ping we used to know."

"The hue of the sea is constantly changing but the essence never changes, Dr Bennet." I got up and saluted her.

She nodded, still reflecting.

I opened the window and a breeze came in from the Pearl River. By this time, the noisy city had quieted down, leaving the dim street lights standing lonely against the starless sky.

Elizabeth joined me by the window. She murmured, "I hope it's not too late for Arthur to see his mother before she passes away. Oh, how I wish I could say goodbye to her. She has been very kind to us. Last Christmas, she crocheted a very delicate tablecloth for us; it's pale blue, and I've only used it once for fear of staining it."

Her throat seemed to be choked with emotion and her eyes were moist. I was quite touched by her tenderness.

Westerners have soft feelings too. How little we know them! I thought.

On my train back from Guangzhou, I thought of the story of the ancient Chinese poet and philosopher, Lao Tzu. Disappointed with the corrupt way the emperor was running the country, he decided to live in solitude in the mountains. One sunny spring day, he started his fateful journey. With a small parcel on his back, he walked through plains and mountains where no one ever trod.

To him, the way lay along the no-way. He walked with the rising of dawn and slept with the setting of the sun. On the seventh day, he came to a huge mountain. He saw no path anywhere through the gigantic rocks, steep cliffs, and thorn shrubs. He thought that his journey had come to an end. After drinking his last drop of wine, he lay down to rest.

It started to rain. While enjoying the raindrops beating his wrinkled face and long white beard, he composed a poem, and that poem became the famous Taoist philosophy. He titled the poem *Tao Te Ching*, without the slightest idea that it would become an "ism" and enjoy over thirty translations in English alone.

After writing the lines on a piece of silk, he read it aloud several times with satisfaction. Slowly he folded it into a square and stored it in a small cave nearby. "I have come to the world with no material possession and now I am leaving it empty-handed," contemplated Lao Tzu.

He then fell asleep. When he awoke, the sun was gently touching his face. The air was so exquisitely refreshing that he sprang to his feet. And in wonder, he suddenly saw, among the thorn shrubs, a path hidden behind one of the rocks. He explored further—only to find a large valley full of flowers surrounded by green willow trees!

It appeared that my fate, like the ancient poet's, was going to turn after arriving at a seeming impasse.

33

I HAD WRITTEN ELIZABETH that I wanted to study either psychology or education as these subjects were not available in Chinese universities: all the social science subjects simply disappeared from universities in the early 1960s. Mao labelled many social science professors "rightists" in the late 1950s or "Counter-Revolutionaries" during the Cultural Revolution and sent them to the countryside to "reform through hard labour." Dan once told me that Mao did not like social scientists because they were more likely than hard scientists to see through Mao's revolutionary line.

Elizabeth asked me if a master's program in health education and health behaviour would be suitable. "It sounds good to me," I wrote her. To get into the program, I had to pass the TOEFL (Test of English as a Foreign Language). That was easy. An acceptance score was 550, and I got 608, the highest of any foreign student who ever applied for that program. Second, I had to write an essay on the motives and goals of my application. With the key words "health" and "education," I searched my brain. Suddenly the tired faces of rural women came to me. In the short essay, I enumerated the miserable existence of Chinese rural women who suffered from poor health and hygiene. I then highlighted my goal: to devote myself to educating and helping rural women out of misery.

I mailed a copy of my statement to Elizabeth, and she said that it was moving. But that was still not good enough to be accepted into the program. I needed to prove how my learning was going to contribute to the future of China's health education. It so happened that an official from the Chinese ministry of health was a visiting scholar at the department. She assured the departmental chair that I was going to play a leading role in this field in China, since I would be the first person in the whole country to receive such a degree. Thus, I was officially accepted into the program in mid-March.

The next step was to get permission from my working unit so I could apply for a passport. My immediate leader, Director Yang, "agreed in principle," which meant that he could change his mind if he wished. Vice-Director Bao had alluded to Yang that they definitely needed me in the fall. I was furious and started an argument with Director Yang in the departmental office. I said how he had ruined my future by not letting me participate in the graduate entrance exam a few years back. I also told him that if I was to be sacked from my job in future, I would hold him responsible. We all knew that several recent central government documents indicated that a master's degree would be required of all college teachers in the next few years. Then I asked, "Why do you want to ruin me? Why do you want me to hate you forever when you are going to retire in two years?"

He stumbled and told me to calm down. I knew that my sharp words had hit him. He did not want to be "nailed on the wall of history," that is, to be hated by a younger person.

He then smiled and said that he had no objection to my leaving the department, and that the objection came from Vice-Director Bao. I did not bother to talk to Bao as she was a mean-minded woman.

I went to the office of the president, but he was not in. His secretary, Liang, informed me that President Huang had received invitations to visit several medical schools in the United States, including Elizabeth's medical school. My heart jumped with excitement: Huang would not want to displease Elizabeth by not letting me go. But Liang told me that it was not enough to have President Huang's vote alone, I needed votes from at least two vice-presidents as well. He advised me to talk to two key vice-presidents, and I did.

Finally I got a letter with a red seal of the medical college. I took it to the provincial foreign affairs office and they granted me a passport.

34

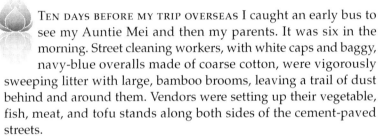

TEN DAYS BEFORE MY TRIP OVERSEAS I caught an early bus to see my Auntie Mei and then my parents. It was six in the morning. Street cleaning workers, with white caps and baggy, navy-blue overalls made of coarse cotton, were vigorously sweeping litter with large, bamboo brooms, leaving a trail of dust behind and around them. Vendors were setting up their vegetable, fish, meat, and tofu stands along both sides of the cement-paved streets.

Half an hour later, the bus was in the countryside, an endless stretch of green fields with dew glistening under the rising rays of the sun. My heart was pounding. I could hardly believe my good luck. I was one of hundreds—in a billion—who were allowed out of China to study for a master's degree. Me? A village girl?

The bus wound along the narrow country road, which was roughly paved with ground stones and pitch, leaving behind tall, dense poplar trees, scattered villages, and meandering streams. Peasants, men and women, old and young, were toiling in the fields, some were harvesting ripened rice ears, others hand-planting new seedlings in the rich soil of rice paddies.

My thoughts roamed as far as the vast land. My friends had not been so lucky. Lan lost her life; Su-wen lost her spirit; Sun-bin lost his soul; Fang lost his dream; and Dan lost his freedom for several years. We were the displaced and lost generation of Red China.

I had just received a letter from Dan, who wrote that he had been released from a labour camp under the new policy of Deng Xiao-ping. He was now assigned a teaching job at Mian Yang Senior High and allocated a one-bedroom apartment a few blocks from my auntie's.

The very thought of Dan made my heart tremble. For the past eight years I had tried to suppress his image, but he nevertheless appeared in my dreams. Since receiving his brief letter three weeks before, I had imagined what he looked like and conjured a dozen beginnings of our meeting.

But my trip overseas stimulated me. Dan had deserted me for his ideals and now it was time for me to show him that I could live without him. I was glad that I was not as helpless as Meggie, the heroine in *The Thorn Birds*, who waited all her life for Ralph to come back to her though he never did.

A jerky stop of the bus pulled me out of my reflections. We had arrived at the station. After a short walk I was in front of my auntie's three-bedroom apartment.

"Auntie! Open the door!" I shouted, knocking loudly.

"Ai-yar, Zhao May-ping! I was just thinking of you!" Auntie Mei unloaded my small travel bag and patted my shoulder. Auntie liked to call me with my family name because she was from our Zhao family. When I gave her the news, she jumped with joy. "Ai-yar-yar! That's great!" Her husband Tie also congratulated me. He said to my auntie, "I am taking the afternoon bus back to Wuhan."

"He has been stationed there this year," Auntie Mei informed me the minute he stepped out of the door.

"Oh." I avoided talking about him as much as I could.

Auntie wanted to make some clothes for me before I left. We shopped for several hours for silk and cotton materials for two traditional Chinese garments, a few blouses, skirts, and two pairs of pyjamas. As usual, we discussed the style and worked out the details together.

While she was sewing, I studied her face: there were more fine wrinkles at the corners of her brown eyes. Besides carrying on with an unhappy marriage, she had been worried about her three children. The two boys did not like school, so they joined the army before finishing senior high school. The younger son, Zhi, was in Heilongjiang, a place close to the border of the Soviet Union. As there was no war, they were sent to build railways which were urgently needed because of the recent economic boom. While transporting logs, a friend of Zhi's was crushed when a log fell from a truck. Zhi was only a few feet away when the accident occurred. This narrow escape had been giving my auntie nightmares.

Her daughter Bee was fifteen, tall, slim, with charming eyes and a beautiful voice. She had been enrolled in a Beijing opera school. Unfortunately, she did not like studying or working hard and had been doing poorly in school, which gave my auntie constant headaches. Fearing her father's scolding, Bee ran away with a boy a few months before, and no one knew where she was.

My auntie's husband blamed her for the misbehaviour of their daughter. No matter how abusive her husband became, my auntie kept silent. She did not bother arguing with him. She had given up on everything except getting up in the morning and going to work like a robot.

While we were cooking together, my auntie said that she would surely miss me as I was her best friend.

"I'll write you often." I looked at her moist eyes.

After dinner, I went to see Dan.

With a shaky hand, I gently knocked at the door.

Dan opened it, carrying an uncertain look on his face. Oh! How he had changed! His dark, dense hair was turning grey and hairline receding. Fine wrinkles had crept around his still shining eyes. He was only thirty-three years old!

"Hi."

"Hi."

That's all we could say to each other.

"Come in."

His apartment was simply furnished, with several posters and framed photos on the yellowish walls.

I sat down gingerly on an old bamboo chair. Dan poured some hot water from a bamboo shell flask to an earthenware cup; put a few green tea leaves in the cup and passed it to me. While he was in motion, I observed him: his hands coarse, his back a little curved, but his face still striking and his shoulders broad.

The changes in him shocked me. I avoided eye contact with him. Holding the teacup, I stared at the floating tea leaves as if to see how long it would take them to sink to the bottom. Dan mumbled something; I hardly heard it. I slurred something back without lifting my eyes from the tea leaves. He poured some tea for himself and sat down.

Observing my awkwardness, he said, "Your auntie has told me that you are soon going abroad. Congratulations!" I could tell he was truly happy for me.

I did not know what to say. I had mixed feelings about my imminent adventure in a foreign land. I had been longing to see the world and meet new challenges, but I was not quite sure if my English was good enough to handle graduate courses at a famous American university. But I had no fear; my grandma had taught me not to fear.

I got up and walked to the tiny balcony. He followed me.

At that moment, we both happened to look up. A bright three-quarter moon was skimming through the wispy clouds like a silver guitar pick.

"We will share the same moon wherever you go." He tried to cheer me up.

"Right, I have something for you." Dan ran to his bedroom-study and returned with a blue satin-covered diary. On the first page stood an embroidered water lily in full blossom. On the second page was a famous Song Dynasty poem "The Spirit of Water Lily," written in neat and small brush, Dan's familiar handwriting.

"I love the disposition of water lily, strong outside, soft inside," I recalled the poetic and philosophical Dan saying that to me on a rainy spring evening during our university days.

When helping polish one of my poems nine years before, he sent me a pen name: Water Lily. He said that water lily described my temperament well.

"What does your husband say about your going to America?" My eyes were still on the water lily flower and my thoughts were years back.

"He is not against it," I answered evasively. Then I added, "He has wanted to obtain an opportunity to study abroad but could never pass the English examination. I am the only means by which he could go to America. You know, he can apply to join me in a year."

"Hmm, I see."

Gazing at my profile, Dan threw out a hard question, "Are you happy?" I looked away and said as coolly as I could, "What a question! One can be happy in a moment and unhappy in another. Happiness is a state of mind, which is transient."

"You don't sound happy." He examined my face more carefully.

"I am fine." I was giving him the message that I did not want to talk about it. I smiled!

"I just want to know whether my sacrifice was worthwhile."

"What sacrifice?"

"The one I made in order to free you; in order that you could be happy."

I pretended not to comprehend him.

"You really don't understand? Do you know how hard it was for me not to write you and see you for eight long years?" I heard tears in his voice but I did not lift my eyes to look at him. A thousand feelings were surging in my chest. I had so much to say to him that I did not know where to start. No words, however comprehensive, could express eight years of longing.

"Say something," he implored.

"How can I be happy if you make a decision about us unilaterally?"

"I am sorry. I couldn't consult you. I know you cared for me and ... " he faltered. "If you had married me, they wouldn't have let you study abroad. I am still on the blacklist." He was grave but gentle.

"If I were happily married, I wouldn't want to go anywhere." Tears rolled down my cheeks.

"Let me show you something." Dan ushered me to his bedroom-study. In one end was a single bed; in the other a small bamboo bookshelf and a small desk.

"Look at this poster." He pointed to a large poster of a young militia woman on the wall in front of his desk.

"Does her face look like yours?" He glanced at my profile.

"You know you have been in my heart all these years. I wouldn't have had the strength to sustain my spirit alone." Emotion choked him. "Cruel you, you didn't even give me a photo," he murmured.

I changed the subject.

"How do you like your job at Mian Yang High?" We walked back to the balcony.

"I like it very much. They have asked me to teach five courses in September because we are short of teachers. I don't mind. I enjoy teaching." He seemed excited.

"Do you want more tea?" his soft voice hardly audible.

I passed him my teacup but he held my hand. *Dong!* The cup fell on the cement floor and broke to pieces. Neither of us uttered a word nor looked; our hands suspended in the air. I felt his breath as if in my dreams.

Cupping my face in his hands, he whispered, "How I have missed you!"

I told him of my many dreams about him, one in particular.

It was a stormy winter night. We sat cold and huddled in threadbare cotton-padded jackets. After years of torturous thought-cleansing, our souls yearned for freedom! The yellow moon struggled through the clouds and shone into our broken window. I could see my beloved water lily pond, and my heart sang, for I knew we would succeed — we would go to America, the land of freedom!

Drying my tears with his handkerchief, Dan whispered, "Yes, one day we will meet in our dream land—America!" He sighed while gazing at my tear-stained face, "You look pale. Sit down here." He moved my chair over but I remained standing. Gently touching his grey hair and wrinkled face, I said, "Oh, how you must have suffered!"

Assuming one of his faraway stares, he said, "Suffering can make us stronger…"

"Only to a certain extent. Beyond that, it can break you."

"No, No. A person's spirit can not be broken unless he agrees to it." Looking into my eyes, he added, "Remember, never let anything or anybody break your spirit."

After a slight pause, he continued, "You have a great deal of hardship ahead, single-handed, in a foreign country."

"I am not going to America, I am staying with you. A divorce is not very difficult nowadays. Ming will make scenes but he can do nothing about it if my mind is made up," I said resolutely, staring at the ceiling, the yellowish lime wash flaking in places.

"No. Dear, I won't let you give up your future for me." He stroked my face with the back of his hand which was softer than his callused palm.

I wanted to argue but could not find the right words. He went on, "This is your only chance of spiritual survival. You have been suffocated for so long."

Caressing my thin shoulders, he said gently, "Poor darling, I can't bear to see your lively nature being distorted. If you don't leave, your spirit will wither and die, like that of your Auntie Mei and millions of others."

"You go to America; divorce Ming from there so he cannot harm you." He sipped some tea then continued, "I may be able to join you in a year or two."

"I don't want to be separated from you again, not ever." I pillowed my forehead on his broad chest.

"You silly, being away, we are together. Our souls are never apart. Being together, we may drift apart. With you being a divorcee and I a released prisoner, our life wouldn't be pleasant here. Constant pressure from our surroundings erodes the closest bond." He passed me a cup of cold tea, then, said, "My soul yearns for freedom! I want to live in a place where I am a free agent, capable of my own thoughts and actions, not fettered by the agenda of the regime." His eyes sparkled, his voice unusually clear.

I refilled my cup from a clay teapot on the tiny kitchen table and observed him. He seemed wrapped in his thought.

"What if your working unit does not give you permission to join me?" I voiced my ultimate worry.

"The Communists' policy is like the shape of the moon—changing constantly. In a year or two, policies may loosen more. China can't be closed and backward forever. In recent years, the market economy has gained a foothold in several coastal cities." He walked up and down just as he had along South Lake eight years before.

"Economic reality dictates people's thinking. As the mode of economy changes from state controlled to market adjusted, people's way of life will change. Our five-thousand-year-old culture will also change. This is the way the wheels of history are turning; no one can hold them back."

Leaning on the cement brim of the balcony and glancing at the lively stars, he could hardly contain his excitement, "A new era has arrived in China! Let's embrace it!"

The exuberant Dan had come back! The fire was still in him—not extinguished by the torturous years in the camp. Tears brimmed in my eyes as I listened to him: *How his young life has been wasted! Eight years! How many eight years of youth does a person have?*

Suddenly, I knew what I should do. I must leave and get Dan out while he still had some fire in him. It would be very difficult for Dan to get out of China—a released prisoner was not entitled a passport. *But we must try! No matter how slim our hope is, a hope is a hope, and it can sustain us both.*

A cool night breeze was rising. The moon poured its silver beams over the contours of earthly objects. "How nice it would be to live in one's childhood forever," I murmured, as the happy moments of our early days flashed back to my mind, one by one.

Dan put his jacket on me. I declined and walked toward the door.

"We will share the same moon no matter where I go," I repeated what he had said. I gave him my hand. He held it with both his hands for a long time.

"Be as happy as a skylark, my skylark." He gazed at my face intensely.

I nodded.

Rambling along the quiet lane sided by grown-up poplars, I kept thinking of the poem and the character of water lily. The author, Zhou Dunyi, was a Song Dynasty poet and mandarin. Greatly disappointed with the corrupt way the emperor ran the country, he resigned from public life and lived in solitude. In this poem, he compared his spirit to that of the water lily, which refused to be corrupted by the muddy water surrounding it.

> *Peony is dazzling with large globular red flower.*
> *Chrysanthemum is charming with alluring blossom.*
> *I love water lily more.*
> *It is pure and clean though it grows out of mud.*
> *It is above the water though in touch with it.*
> *Its petals are pinkish white, soft, yet durable.*
> *Thunderstorms cannot destroy it.*
> *Raindrops only make it fresher and more adorable.*

"I love the character of water lily, strong, upward yet gracious and aloof, unique in that it has seemingly opposing qualities in one." Dan said solemnly, the idealistic and youthful Dan of eight years before.

水陸草木之花可愛者甚蕃晉陶淵明獨愛菊

自李唐來世人甚愛牡丹予獨愛蓮之出淤泥而

不染濯清漣而不妖中通外直不蔓不枝香遠益

清亭亭淨植可遠觀而不可褻玩焉予謂菊花

之隱逸者也牡丹花之富貴者也蓮花之君子

者也噫菊之愛陶後鮮有聞蓮之愛同予者何

人牡丹之愛宜乎眾矣

右錄宋周敦頤文愛蓮說

"Yes, the character of water lily is in my blood and will accompany me to face the unknown in the faraway land," I whispered to myself, and to him.

It was near midnight when I got back to my auntie's. She was still up sewing and waiting for me. After a snack and cold tea, we went to bed. Hard as I tried, I could not sleep. When I got up to get more tea, Auntie asked softly from her room, "Can't sleep?"

We took tea out to the bamboo chairs on the balcony. The moon was shining directly into my face. I told her what Dan and I planned to do.

"Your father won't like the idea of a divorce. But I'll talk to him." She seemed not surprised at all. After sipping some tea, she continued, "A bad marriage never gets better; it only gets worse. Like a cracked teapot, it can't be mended." I knew she was talking from her own experience. Her gaze was far away. Then she suddenly came back to reality and looked at me, "Unhappy marriages run in the family. Do you know your grandpa had an affair with Lu for many years?"

"Oh, I can't believe it!" I had heard of the affair when I was eight years old but had long forgotten it, because I wished to. The confirmation from my auntie was like an explosive.

Lu lived two houses from us and she was about a dozen years younger than my grandma. I could see her round face and alluring eyes. Although in my grandma's generation it was not uncommon for a man to have several wives and concubines, my grandma could never swallow the humiliation of sharing a man.

"I never saw her laugh heartily, not even once when I grew up," I said reminiscently. "Oh, poor Grandma!"

Now come to think of it, my grandparents never shared a bed as long as I could remember. Except one winter when I was about nine. They seemed to be reconciled. My thoughts raced years back.

"Ma didn't tell me this till two years before she died," Auntie's voice hardly audible.

"Anyone else know?

"Your mother knew all along."

"My mother?"

"Your poor mother! She has not had a day of good life since she came to our Zhao family," she said deploringly.

"And you know your great-grandma drowned herself when she was thirty-three?"

I nodded.

"Three generations of unhappy marriages are enough! I want you to get out while you are still young," her voice raised. I had never seen her so resolute.

"Remember what I said tonight. Be strong. I don't know if I will be here for you when you come back." She got up and gazed at the moon, hands resting on the cement rails of the balcony.

"I've been living for my children; now they are grown up. I don't have a purpose or a reason to live any more." She was choked with emotion, tears streaking down her tormented face.

I ran to the washroom and got her a wet towel.

That night neither of us slept a wink.

At noon the next day, we strolled along the open market where hundreds of farm products were for sale at bargain prices.

"Live baby hens, one yuan a jin!" The sweet voice of a girl about thirteen reached my ears. She was thin and dressed in old clothes. We walked to her and bought one hen.

"Vine melon, best for chicken soup!" She opened a basket beside her. My auntie chose three slim melons.

"Moon beans!" A thirtyish woman aggressively pushed her basket in front of us.

"Oh, let's get some," I shouted enthusiastically. But my auntie did not like the rough woman. We walked away and bought moon beans from a white-haired man who looked gentle and kind.

My spirit was up after the delicious chicken soup and moon beans.

Around three-thirty in the afternoon, I took the bus to my parents' place. The village had changed since I left for Wuhan City ten years before. The greatest and saddest change occurred in 1978, when our old village, Riverside, was merged with a neighbouring village. The new village never acquired a proper name; it was simply called Team Two.

Although our new house was larger, I never felt at home when I came back for my summer and winter vacations. The front and back yards were small and had no shady trees. A little brook ran through the front yard, but the water was shallow and muddy. Beyond the brook, tractors and trucks passed by on a new highway. The tranquillity of the old days was gone.

In about twenty minutes I was in front of my parents' house. The front door was open.

"Ma, I am home!"

My two teenage sisters ran out from the kitchen, followed by my mother.

"Are you really going to America?" Jing-ping, the youngest, had the quickest tongue.

I nodded emphatically while taking out their gifts.

"May-ping-ah, I will not be able to see you for two years?" My mother could not believe that I was actually leaving for an alien country across the Pacific Ocean.

Then she was distracted by the nice leather shoes I had bought for her.

"Where is Pa?" I looked around.

"He is fishing," Jing-ping called from the kitchen; she was making tea.

After taking some photos of me with Mother, we went to catch the spirit of my father fishing.

He had changed after the Cultural Revolution: he lost his faith in the Party, his zest for his job, and his trust in other human beings. He talked little and socialized zero. Whenever he was home, he would either go fishing or work in the half mu vegetable patch the collective had allocated to our family under the new policy of Deng Xiao-ping.

When I broke the news to my father that in nine days I was leaving China for the United States, he smiled. He was happy to see his children go far and do well. His life had offered him few chances to exercise his talents.

We looked at his bucket: there was not even one fish. He just enjoyed the peacefulness of sitting by the water in the sunset.

He picked up his fishing rod and walked home with us. Running in front, I took a picture of him walking between the vegetable patches. As I looked through the lens, my heart sank. My father had become an old man! He was only fifty-three years old. He walked with his back slightly hunched, and his legs moved haltingly as if they would run out of strength at any minute. His face was pale, his eyes dazed. The month before, he had written me that he was going to retire in a year or two because of his poor health. I knew the truth: he was tired of the meaningless struggle that his job demanded in the district hospital.

Before we started dinner, he took out a bottle of sorghum wine and poured a glass each for me, my mother, and himself. The wine seemed to open him up. He told me about his plans after early retirement: go fishing, read novels, play with his granddaughters, play chess, and perhaps mah-jong. I suggested that he work in the vegetable patches more and cook more since he never thought my mother's cooking was as good as his.

While Jing-ping and I were making tea in the kitchen after the meal, she smiled sweetly and whispered to me, "Pa must like you the best. I haven't seen him talking this much with anyone for a long time."

She also told me that it was a big event every time my father received a letter from me: he would read it once by himself and then read it aloud to Mother.

In contrast to my father, my mother was full of energy although her hair was turning white and her teeth were falling out. She told me that she did not want me to go anywhere, not to mention a foreign country. She said that no place was better than home. "But you won't listen to me. You only listen to your father." She glanced at my father who was smiling complacently. He enjoyed hearing that his children listened to him.

After tea, the moon had climbed high. I wanted to see Fang and Rong, who lived half a mile away in Moon Crescent village. When I announced my plan to my parents, they frowned and said that it was too late to walk across the fields by myself. I knew the real reason: they wanted me to spend every minute with them during my stay. I patted the eager shoulders of Nan-ping and Jing-ping. They jumped up with enthusiasm and we ran to the road before my parents could react.

The earth road was smooth, wide, cool and lit up by the bright moon. Two deep trenches on each side kept the road dry after rain. The water was drained to the cotton fields to maintain their moisture.

For a moment, all was quiet. We listened now and then to see if my father was running behind to bring us back. All we could hear was the singing of crickets and frogs.

It was early July; the first season of rice had just been harvested. Approaching Fang's village, we saw piles of rice stalks in the front yard of every household.

By this time, Deng Xiao-ping had resumed Lui Shao-qi's policy before the Cultural Revolution: each household had a plot of land, still owned by the state, to till and look after. The people's communes were disbanded. Many households now grew economic crops to sell in town for cash. Others started small businesses of their own, making tofu, fine noodles, and preserved eggs. Watermelon was plentiful in the summer, and the price of peanuts fell to one-fifth that of a few years before.

On rainy days the villagers rested or played mah-jong since the many class struggle meetings were no more.

We reached Fang and Rong's house only to find it dark. We knocked at the front door. No answer. We walked through a lane to the back where the large kitchen was located. There were lights in the kitchen and the door was open. Fang and Rong were delighted to see me. Rong was bathing their youngest child in a large wooden tub. The other two children, now about eight and six, were quietly sitting on a bench by the wall, half-asleep. In the middle of the kitchen was a round table piled with half-finished dishes, unwashed bowls, and chopsticks. They must have just finished eating. Fang cleaned the table and offered us chairs, but none of us took the offer. It seemed that the kitchen was too chaotic to sit in.

After putting the youngest child to bed, Rong lit the lights in the living room, which was lined with bags of grain just harvested from the fields. I could tell that they were prosperous.

"My mother passed away last year and we have nobody to help. Otherwise we would be resting by now." Fang lit up a cigarette.

By this time, Rong had filled two wooden pails with warm water. She woke up the two boys and told them to take a bath and go to bed.

"You have three children?" Nan-ping was surprised, as the "one-child" policy had been around for several years.

"They are boys too." Fang was proud of his achievement.

"How did you get two extra quota?" Jing-ping questioned curiously.

"Naive, naive, you bookish girls. There are always loopholes in every rule," Fang was still the self-confident man he used to be.

Rong made us some tea and sat down beside Fang. She wore her long black hair in two braids at the back with thick bands on her forehead. A few strands of hair were flying over her youthful yet tired face. With the death of her mother-in-law, she was alone taking care of her three young children and husband.

"Do you work in the fields?" I wanted to include her in our conversation.

"Yes. Long hours in the spring and summer, less in autumn and not so much in winter time," she spoke with the soft, sweet, girlish voice I well remembered.

Looking at his lovely wife, Fang continued contentedly, "We were able to have a second child because I am an only son. Then I told them that my second son was mentally troubled when he was five months old, so we were given another quota." He puffed on his cigarette with enormous satisfaction. "I bought an expensive wool coat for the Party secretary too. A little bribery doesn't hurt." Fang was a clever man and he knew that his secret was safe with us.

"My second son is not doing very well in school but he is not troubled at all. He has just inherited his mother's genes." Fang looked teasingly at his wife.

"That's not true," Rong blushed a little.

"Would you like to have another child if you are allowed to?" I asked Rong, looking at her shy, rosy oval face. Around her luminescent black eyes, several fine lines were noticeable.

A sorrowful thought crossed my mind: *It would be a great pity if such a beauty fades in her early thirties.*

Rong shook her head, "I don't want any more. Three is enough, although it would be nice to have a daughter to take care of me and talk to me when I am old."

"I wouldn't mind having another son. The more, the better!" Fang was beaming; it seemed that the very thought of another son thrilled him.

"Oh, 'the more, the better,' it's easy for you to say because you don't have to do the caretaking, cooking, and cleaning," Rong argued mildly. I could tell she worshipped him.

"Ah, you … 'the vision of a woman is as short as a shoe-string,'" Fang cited an old saying and chuckled self-assuredly. Fang had no objection to his beloved wife expressing her little opinions, but in that household he was in charge.

I could not believe my ears. Looking at his messy kitchen and living room, I asked, "Why do you want so many children anyway? You don't have time to take good care of them." I always thought that people who wanted to have more children were insensible and uneducated. I was disappointed with Fang; I did not understand him anymore.

"Okay, let me tell you why. In harvest times, each household can use the large harvester machine of the production brigade for four hours only. As I have no brothers, I have to seek assistance from my brother-in-law who lives across the Han River. I can't ask other villagers because everybody is busy at the same time. I hope the three boys will help each other in future." He sounded so reasonable that I was speechless.

Walking back home in the thin evening mist, I started to lose confidence in my hypothesis regarding the motives to have more children, especially male children. I had started my study on the cost and benefit of male versus female children at the age of ten when the unwelcome baby girl—my second sister Nan-ping—was born. I had noticed the big differences in the way boys and girls were treated in most families.

My brother Nian was a year and three months younger than me. He wore a silver ring on his neck to protect him from ghosts; neither I nor any of my sisters had one. Nian had two fancy fur-collar coats, but none of the girls had one.

Mar had one "precious" son and five "useless" daughters. Her son was sent to school until his grades were too poor to continue; none of her three older daughters went to school. Mar's second youngest daughter had a grade three education, and the youngest barely finished primary school. I often heard Mar loudly scolding her daughters, using abusive words, the worst, to a girl, being "You little rotten whore." Her daughters helped in the fields during the day and did housework in the evenings. When her daughters reached the age of eighteen or nineteen, Mar had a carpenter make them some furniture and married them off.

Chow had five sons and no daughters. From the time their sons were born, the couple began to save money to build five houses. They were the poorest of all the villagers, wearing old clothes with many patches.

Lu had three daughters and no sons. She and her husband never scolded their precious daughters. The two youngest were my good friends: they were healthy, happy, and fun to be with. The Lus lived in a fine house, ate good food, and wore nice clothes.

From these and many similar observations, I had concluded that it was lucrative to have daughters and costly to have sons. Therefore, only those who could not see the truth would want sons. But Fang's strong desire to have more sons cast doubt in my theory. His gleaming eyes and self-satisfied chuckles when talking about his sons brought me to a new realization: when a man has three sons, he can hope that at least one of them will turn out to be successful. The success of his offspring was his statement to the world: *I have not lived my life in vain. I will have left my mark on the world after I'm gone.* For a peasant man, there was no other way to show that his life was a worthwhile endeavour.

The next morning, my mother cooked egg soup with fine noodles. As soon as I finished the soup my father suggested that I pay a visit to all the Zhao clan in the village. "I feel no closer to them than other neighbours," I reasoned.

When my brother Nian and I carried heavy loads of grain home from the fields, the Zhao uncles and aunties helped us no more than other villagers. They were meaner sometimes. From an early age, I learned to distinguish people not by their family names but by their hearts. Some were kind, others were less kind, and some were heartless. The village was an ideal setting to study human nature since we had to compete for limited resources.

My father, however, thought differently. The most important thing he desired from his children was academic success. This brought glory to him and his family name. Sending me to visit his relatives was a way to let them know of my imminent trip to the United States, which, to the villagers, was like going to the moon. They would be envious of my father's successful child-rearing.

"Of course, you will not even visit your parents in a few years now that your wings have grown full," my father remarked half-jokingly. He was alluding to his financial support for me during primary and junior high school. My uncle had supported me through senior high school and the state through university.

I patted Jing-ping on the shoulder. She walked out with me. There was a wonderful tacit understanding among the four girls in our family: when one was in difficulty, others helped. Although the whole society, including my father and brother, discriminated against us girls and tried to put us down, we did not allow them to succeed.

"It's great to have sisters, eh?" I said to her as I passed her a package of sweets and cigarettes my father had prepared. Squeezing her slender shoulder appreciatively, I continued, "Oh, it would be so nice if my little sister could be fourteen forever."

"No, I want to be as tall as you." She pointed her silky fingers at my chin, indicating her humiliating height. Then, "Don't forget me when you are in America," she ordered me squarely, two distinct dimples on her delicate face.

"Is this your worry? Oh, how could I ever forget you? Be real nice to Ma when I am away, okay?"

She nodded, then said, "Mother's eyes are a little red. She must have cried last night," Jing-ping whispered secretively as if I had not noticed those motherly loving eyes. I remembered an old saying my mother liked to quote: *A child travels afar, the Mother worries along.*

"Ah, this is Auntie Yang's new house." Jing-ping elbowed me. I was still meditating on motherly love, the most unselfish and unconditional love on earth.

"Auntie Yang!" Jing-ping shouted at the door.

"Ai-ya, my dears, come in; have some tea." Auntie Yang came out of the kitchen, a dripping dishcloth in hand. She was about forty-five years old, of medium height, and had smooth skin and an oval face. I had always been fond of her. "May-ping is going to study in America and she is here to say goodbye to you." Jing-ping announced, putting some sweets and a pack of Globe cigarettes on the greasy wooden table. A rooster relieved itself under the table; a few chicks were pecking scattered barley on the earth floor of the living room.

"America? Where is it?" Auntie Yang asked loudly.

"It's on the other side of the earth." Jing-ping laughed.

"How do you go through the earth, so thick?"

"You punch a hole and jump with a parachute." Jing-ping giggled.

"Now, don't fool me. Tell me how you get there."

"By plane, it takes twelve hours." I said to Auntie Yang while patting Jing-ping on the shoulder, signalling her to stop giggling.

We left Auntie Yang puzzling.

We reached a new house made of red bricks. Jing-ping told me that it was Sher's home. I remembered Sher: he was a year older than me, tall and muscular. He used to beat all the boys in the village, including my brother. He was nicknamed "red head," meaning that he could make the boys bleed if he wanted to.

At eighteen he joined the army and came back a polite young man. Army veterans usually had the privilege of a job in a local factory. Sher was assigned to work in a large brick factory where he was put in charge of selling bricks. A year before, he was caught forging a five-thousand yuan receipt and sentenced to a four-year jail term.

A few people from the Zhao clan, including my mother, had recently visited him in jail. "He cried like a child and felt genuinely sorry for what he had done. He asked us to help take care of his wife and two young children. His wife also went with us and she was weeping the whole time. Each of us donated some money to her. Very sad," my mother had told me the night before. I wanted to tell her that probably Sher had stolen plenty of money before he went to jail, but I did not want to shatter her illusion that all human beings were innocent and deserved sympathy and assistance.

When my sister told Sher's wife that I was soon going abroad to study, she asked where. She was the first one among the uncles and aunties of the Zhao clan who knew about America.

"For how long?" she asked.

"At least two years," Jing-ping declared, tilting her head.

"Have a seat and I'll make you some tea," Sher's wife offered politely. She seemed to be a very articulate woman with pleasant facial features and fashionable short hair. She was my height and perhaps my age too. But her face was pale.

"It's nice to be by myself for a few days. My two boys are with my mother. I was just sterilized a month ago." She seemed to be a frank woman too.

"Did you have to do it?" I asked with concern. With the poor equipment in the commune clinic, it could be very painful and quite dangerous too.

"They dragged me out of my bed during the middle of the night. What choice did I have?" Her face was expressionless.

My mother had told me that several young women in the village had been forced to have sterilizations in recent years.

"Well, I don't want any more children anyway. I have no energy for them. Two boys are enough. I do not object to the sterilization, but my mother-in-law was against it." I liked her candidness.

"How do you feel now?" I asked.

"Not bad. The doctors say that I'll get better day by day. I feel okay."

She did not look okay to me.

On our way back, Jing-ping told me that she heard Mother say Sher's wife had been bleeding ever since the sterilization.

As we reached Lu's front yard, Jing-ping whispered to me that Lu's second daughter, Qing, had just moved back for good.

"What's happened?"

"Wang-fu returned from the army a few years ago and got a job in our county town as a cargo driver. He sleeps with prostitutes wherever he stops for the night. You know it's quite cheap to get them now, a man can get a young girl for as little as fifty yuan a night." Prostitution was another by-product of our experiment with capitalism. The modern name for prostitutes was *wild chickens*; *home chickens* were wives.

"You know their first child drowned by accident a few years ago?"

"Yes."

What Jing-ping did not know was that the drowned boy was not Qing and Wang-fu's first born. The first boy was born three months after its parents' wedding and died mysteriously nine days after he was born. The villagers suspected that Qing strangled him because she loved her child too much to let him carry a stigma for life. An illegitimate seed—a reminder of Qing's and Wang-fu's *weak willpower and uncontrollable passion, sin of all sins,* as Confucius called.

"They are allowed another child. But they couldn't get a son. They had a daughter. Qing got pregnant again early this year, but a lab test showed a girl so she had an abortion," Jing-ping updated me.

"Isn't it against the rules to have lab tests?"

"Yes, but *money can get a ghost to grind rice for you*," she cited an old saying.

"Do you want to stop by and say goodbye to Qing?"

"No. Not today. Maybe tomorrow." I had had enough sadness for one morning. I saw Qing the year before. Her used-to-be delightful eyes were sunken and surrounded by fine wrinkles. Her round face was pale, shoulders slightly stooped. She was only thirty-three, already a withering flower, beaten by the burden of life.

Approaching our house, we saw a new Flying Tiger bike parked beside my father's old Eternal bike.

Whose bike is that? We both wondered.

I feared that it was Sun-bin, my first love. Dan mentioned that he had talked with Sun-bin on the phone a few days earlier. Sun-bin married a colleague of his a few months after I saw him the day before my wedding. Over the years he had written me once, asking for a TOEFL test bank. He and his wife had recently moved from faraway Xian to Yichang city, about two hundred miles west of Mian Yang.

Before I had a chance to say anything, Sun-bin stood up and greeted me at the door with the same charming, shy expression, "Hello, congratulations! A golden phoenix flying over the Pacific! You are probably the first one in Mian Yang County to study in America." He said that more to please my father than me.

"Thank you. How did you know I was home?" I forged a smile.

"The walls have ears." Observing my reaction, he said, "I missed you by ten minutes at Dan's last night."

"Oh."

"I came to see my father this morning. He is semi-retired now with a little responsibility at the reservoir maintenance office."

I knew the place, about half a mile from our village, by the Han River. The offices are surrounded by high walls. Inside are dozens of tall pear trees and a large gardenia garden. As a child, I used to sneak in with my friends to try to steal a pear or two. But the ferocious dogs would chase us away in no time.

"Now that I have seen you, I'd better get going." Sun-bin nodded to my parents and sisters while walking to his bike. In between, he stole a significant glance at me. I decided to walk him a distance to straighten out the old score. I did not want to have an unsettled account before leaving.

As soon as we were on the road, he winked at me in his boyish naughty way and uttered, "Are you going to write me from America?"

He took out a piece of paper and asked for my address in America.

"I don't have one yet. I will mail it to you when I get there."

"Okay. I get the hint. This is your way of saying no. I don't blame you for not wanting to write me." Folding his paper, he went on, "But, if you see any opportunity for a computer science major, please let me know."

I now understood why he had come to see me. For him, the relationship between humans was mutual utilization.

I decided to be circumspect, "I heard that you have moved to Yichang to be an engineer. How do you like it?"

"I have just obtained a job offer with Wuhan Mechanical University. Yichang is too small a place for further advancement."

"Have you got a job for your wife in Wuhan as well?"

"No. I will try to get her one after I get there." After a pause he added, "Probably it's better for us to be apart for a while. Somehow I cannot love her as wholeheartedly as I wished. I guess my experience with Yang-yang burned me to the core."

Now Sun-bin had chosen to be sincere. I decided to be candid. "Yang-yang has an impact on your love life, and you, on mine, only in a different way."

He seemed taken back.

I went on, "After the little episode with you, I learned to be cautious. In my choice of a husband, I looked for a safe harbour. I did not want another rejection. Unfortunately I aimed too low and found myself in a ditch. I felt it before our wedding but I didn't know it was going to be this bad."

Picking up a withered grass on the roadside, I continued, "In a sense my husband is a victim as well, a victim of this Chinese male syndrome: a violent temper, a presumptuous mind, and a strong belief that everyone in his family should be at his disposal, especially his wife."

I knotted the long grass on my index finger, "The difference between Ming and me is that he dug the hole and went in without any awareness whereas I entered it with my eyes wide open. I dug my own grave by marrying him without being able to accept and love him as he is," I said slowly, to sort out my thoughts. Unwinding the long grass from my finger, I tossed it in the air.

"What are you going to do with him?" He squinted his narrow black eyes at my face.

"Being a surgeon, his career is in China. He won't have any difficulty finding a younger woman to marry."

I added, "Though I would advise him to marry someone who is willing to be a slave." Sun-bin chuckled, but I was in earnest.

"Do you think you can get Dan out of China easily?"

"No. But I will try and try very hard. Otherwise his talent would be wasted."

"I am happy for Dan. He has finally found love and meaning in life."

"Does Dan know what happened between you and me a long time ago?" I asked.

"No. I never told him. Have you?"

"No."

"You know about a year before Dan and you went out at Wuhan First Normal, he told me that I could be interested in any girl but you. I guess he had you in mind then."

"He never told me that." Reviewing Dan's life, I sighed, "Poor Dan, how much he has suffered."

"Yes. But he is not alone. In a way everyone has suffered, only in different ways. I have struggled very hard to get somewhere in my career but I am getting nowhere."

"Do you think it's wise to move to Wuhan without your wife? It may take years for her to find a job there."

"She says the same. A man can't be tied to a woman's apron string; he needs a meaningful career."

"Even at the cost of your marriage?"

"Even at the cost of my marriage."

"Is it because you still can't forget Yang-yang?"

"Probably. Not because I still love her but because I still hate her."

"You couldn't hate her unless you still love her."

"Um, I never thought of that."

"By the way, what you did to her after she broke up with you, the big letter posters at her father's working unit, was a bit too much."

"I was young then."

"No. It was not because you were young. It's because you were brought up to think that if you want something, you should have it."

"You are probably right. My parents spoiled me."

Leaning slightly toward me, he said in a low voice, "I wish I had had a chance to know you when you were sixteen."

"No. You will never get to know me because you assumed and still assume that you know everything about me," I blurted without hesitation. Looking at his half bald top which was shining in the sun, I suppressed a giggle and said calmly, "That's a common defect of bright and talented people. They sometimes assume too much."

"You think I am talented?"

What vanity! I thought but I said, "Yes. Academically you are talented and persistent. But you know very little about people, especially girls and women. How can you not fail with them?"

"I think you are right. I have never wanted to waste my time getting to know them. I have assumed that they are all simple minded and made for the pleasure of men."

"You would rather waste your time suffering from failed relationships?"

"I'm doomed, am I?"

"My grandma used to say that what you sow is what you reap. If you don't sow the seeds of love, your heart will become a desert."

"I am afraid I am incapable of loving any other woman. Yangyang ruined my life."

"It's because you allowed her to."

"Do you think I have any hope?"

"Not as long as you indulge yourself in being a victim."

"Funny, I still see you as sixteen." Squeezing my hand, he exhibited a sly and provocative smile, "Think of the doomed man from time to time when you are in America."

I took my hand back and nodded absent-mindedly. He slid onto his bike and rode away in the warm air of the cotton fields. Unknowingly, we had walked a long way along the bank of the Han River. I stepped to the thickly grassed bank and glanced over the wide surface of the rippling river. My thoughts rolled back to the evening when Sun-bin and I walked here thirteen years before. With an enormous sigh, I thought, *Time flows as fast as the water in the Han River and there is no turning back!*

I sauntered down to the shore to get a close-up of the ever-eastward flow. *Like a tiny drop of water in the river, a person fulfils her destiny no matter where the current carries her!*

I lingered there for a moment, then headed home.

 The following afternoon, I summoned all my courage to pay a visit to my water lily pond, which I had not seen since 1978. I wanted it to be locked in my memory the way it used to be, poetic and dreamlike.

Hatless, I trudged between grown cotton plants and the muddy ridges of rice paddies. Bundles of young seedlings were soaking in a brook waiting to be planted. Shoulder poles and bamboo baskets were lying around.

It was lunchtime. All was quiet, except the chirpings of the crickets.

The spot where the old village had been was now farmland. The trees that had surrounded the old village were gone without a trace.

The water lily pond was still there, alone—without the company of the weeping willows and bamboo bushes. The water in the pond was stagnant and dull. A newly built phosphorus factory mercilessly poured waste into it. No carp or bream swam and jumped in the water: they had been poisoned.

My beloved water lily pond was destroyed. Sadness overcame me. I sat down by the pond and let my tears drop to the ground where I used to lie and sing at the top of my voice.

Minutes later, I got up and glanced over the whole area another time: I saw the reflection of the clear, blue sky in the pond, and it was languid. A few lily pads floated here and there. Among them, I discerned a few pinkish white lily flowers. Blinking to make sure I was not dreaming, I marvelled at the tenacity of the exuberant petals. As I gazed at them and beyond, Dan's favourite poem came to me:

> I admire the spirit of water lily. It keeps its soul, strength, and grace in spite of the conspiracy and persecution of the rainstorms!
> I cherish the water lily pond. It nurtures new life, although hardly escaping death itself.

Numbly, I followed a narrow path to the graves of my grandparents. I wanted to say goodbye to them before I went afar. The afternoon sun was bright and warm, yet I felt chilly. Each time I saw the graves, they had shrunk. The collective had made it so, for they did not have land to waste on the dead. No grass was allowed to grow on the graves as grass harboured insects, a threat to the crops. I gazed at the bare graves for a long time and tried to imagine how they would smile—a granddaughter going to graduate school in a Western country!

As I knelt down and bowed three times to their tombstones, I seemed to hear my grandma's familiar voice: *Great learning comes from diligent study and a bumper harvest from hard work. Think before you speak and plan before you act.*

"I hear you, Grandma," I whispered.

Acknowledgments

I appreciate the comments and encouragement on earlier versions of the manuscript from the following colleagues and friends: Gail Henderson, Megan Terepocki, Jacqueline Baldwin, Marianne Ainley, Judith Lapadat, Gira Batt, Lorne Rosenblood, Ron Hoppe, Alex Michalos, George Deagle, Jane Terepocki, Trudy Johnson, Lorraine Hathaway, Fu Ji-jian, Peter Konkin, Chenoa Ryks, Rosalind Leslie, and Judith Young.

I thank Brian Henderson, director of Wilfrid Laurier University Press, for showing initial interest in publishing this book. I greatly appreciate my managing editor, Carroll L. Klein, whose vision and open-mindedness allowed me to craft the book the way I wanted. I am deeply indebted to my copy editor, Frances Rooney. Her constructive suggestions were invaluable. I thank the two anonymous reviewers for their insightful comments and positive recommendation on my initial submission to WLUP; and Leslie Macredie, for designing a wonderful cover for this book.

Finally I thank Patrick, for believing in me. His severe critique and strong encouragement have made it *this* book.

Life Writing Series

In the **Life Writing Series,** Wilfrid Laurier University Press publishes life writing and new life-writing criticism in order to promote autobiographical accounts, diaries, letters, and testimonials written and/or told by women and men whose political, literary, or philosophical purposes are central to their lives. **Life Writing** features the accounts of ordinary people, written in English, or translated into English from French or the languages of the First Nations or from any of the languages of immigration to Canada. **Life Writing** will also publish original theoretical investigations about life writing, as long as they are not limited to one author or text.

Priority is given to manuscripts that provide access to those voices that have not traditionally had access to the publication process.

Manuscripts of social, cultural, and historical interest that are considered for the series, but are not published, are maintained in the **Life Writing Archive** of Wilfrid Laurier University Library.

Series Editor
Marlene Kadar
Humanities Division, York University

Manuscripts to be sent to
Brian Henderson, Director
Wilfrid Laurier University Press
75 University Avenue West
Waterloo, Ontario, Canada N2L 3C5

Books in the Life Writing Series Published by Wilfrid Laurier University Press